IF YOU'RE
NOT THE
One

## ALSO BY FARAH NAZ RISHI

*I Hope You Get This Message*

*It All Comes Back to You*

# IF YOU'RE NOT THE One

## FARAH NAZ RISHI

Quill Tree Books
An Imprint of HarperCollinsPublishers

Library of Congress Control Number: 2023948814
ISBN 978-0-06-325150-2

Typography by David Curtis
24 25 26 27 28  LBC  5 4 3 2 1
First Edition

*For all the brown girls who feel like
they're juggling two lives, two selves—
May you always see the beauty of both and
surround yourself with others who do, too.*

SATURDAY

**Hey beautiful** 12:28 PM

Hi 🐢 12:28 PM

How's everything? 12:29 PM

**Great!** 12:35 PM

**What about you?** 12:35 PM

I'm doing better now 🐢 12:36 PM

**Haha** 12:39 PM

**Cute** 12:40 PM

**Wanted to let you know about lunch today** 12:40 PM

**I don't think I'll be able to make it** ☹ 12:41 PM

Oh no 12:41 PM

Did something come up with SASA? 12:41 PM

**lol always** 12:44 PM

**Just casually drowning over here** 12:45 PM

**Remind me again why I thought premed AND SASA was a good idea** 12:45 PM

Because you're perfect and can't settle for less. 12:47 PM

Of course, of course 12:55 PM

I'm sorry about lunch, though 12:57 PM

But please don't worry about it 12:57 PM

I'll be fine 12:57 PM

Sorry to keep bailing lately 1:15 PM

I'll make it up to you sometime 1:16 PM

Talk later? 1:16 PM

I really hope so 🫶 1:20 PM

What about trying again for Tuesday? 1:20 PM

SUNDAY 3:12 PM

? 3:12 PM

SUNDAY 9:55 PM

Isaac? 9:55 PM

Delivered

# Chapter 1

## JANUARY 18

Crocs.

That is the first strike against him.

I won't judge a person for their choice of shoe in the privacy of their own home. In fact, I've heard that Crocs and other foam shoes are quite comfortable, and thus make excellent indoor slippers.[1] However. *However.* There is something deeply offensive to me about people, *particularly* boys, who choose to wear such undeniably hideous shoes out in the world. I'm sorry, but no amount of good hygiene will prevent Crocs from wafting the scent of man-childness and rotten cheese.[2]

And these Crocs—in a garish highlighter yellow—aren't even the worst part about the boy who just walked into our Race & Ethnicity classroom. Strike two: he's wearing shorts—*nay, jorts!*—even though it's smack dab in the middle of January and there are still dollops of snow on the ground left by the snowstorm last week. Fashion-wise, he's about twenty seasons too late. And speaking of late, he saunters into the classroom just as poor Professor Friedman is reaching a groove in her "welcome to the course" speech, with some obvious lie about having

---

1    I've also heard they're a popular choice for healthcare workers, and for them I will give a free pass. I'm passionate about fashion, not a monster.

2    Smells that I imagine are quite similar.

been held behind last class to help his professor with something. The sheer audacity of it, on the first day of the new semester.

But it's the third and final strike[3] that really sets me off: The offender in question dares to take the open seat in front of me and repositions it, thereby *completely* blocking my view of the whiteboard with his big, annoying head.

I try to bore holes into it with my eyes. His neck is a deep, dark brown that leads to a kind of burst fade topped with loose black coils, and the tag on his T-shirt is sticking out. I catch other people staring at the boy in Crocs with barely disguised disdain, perhaps equally shocked by his choice of shoes. A guy in a red Halcyon hoodie even smirks darkly before muttering something I can't quite catch.[4]

But oblivious to his classmates' grudges, the offender in Crocs whispers a question to the cute girl in bright cobalt-blue glasses—a first-year, I suspect—sitting beside him. They share a quiet laugh, and for some ungodly reason, the girl *blushes*.

*Ugh.*

I grip my pencil tight. I'm in a bad mood, I'll admit, and I'm taking it out on this stranger. For starters, I overestimated my ability to wake up early and missed the bus at the positively inhumane hour of seven this morning. As a result, I didn't arrive my usual fifteen minutes early, and my preferred front-row seats had been fully pillaged by Halcyon students.[5] Also, I don't really know anyone here, so I'm utterly on my

---

3      Or fifth. I've lost count at this point.

4      I can't read lips, but I bet it was something like, "Jorts? Tim Gunn would weep."

5      Freshmen at Marion College, the all-women's college I'm enrolled in, can take classes at the next-door Halcyon College, a coed school, beginning their second semester. As of right now, I do not recommend it.

own on an unfamiliar campus.

Worst of all, Isaac still hasn't responded to any of my texts.

"I'm passing around the syllabus," Professor Friedman says, pushing her thick glasses back up her nose. "You'll see the grade breakdown for the class. Attendance, twenty-five percent. Final exam, fifty percent. And a group paper due after spring break, which will constitute twenty-five percent of your grade."

The girl next to me passes me a copy of the syllabus with an overeager smile while Professor Friedman explains what we'll be covering this semester. There it is: *Group Paper.* A stain on an otherwise well-organized syllabus.

I grimace. Group papers aren't as offensive as Crocs, but they are up there on my list of Despicable Things.[6] If only Kira, my roommate, had signed up to take this class with me. If she were here, then at least I could take comfort in the knowledge that we'd be partners. Though she seemingly spends hours a day watching videos of her favorite K-Pop group LØVE LIFE, she does take school pretty seriously (something I confirmed with a questionnaire the day we moved in together).[7] Unfortunately, Kira informed me taking a class at Halcyon was, quote, "my worst idea yet."

The only way today can be salvaged now is if class ends a few minutes early so I can catch Isaac coming out of his Multivariable Calc class and confront him. I mean, *two days* without texting back? It's not like him. Something must be wrong. Like maybe he broke all ten of his fingers and hasn't been able to use his phone. Or maybe he hit his head and lost all his important memories. You know, the ones of me.

---

6       Top five on my list of Despicable Things, in no particular order: 1) Tardiness, 2) Crocs, 3) Imperialism, 4) Poor hygiene, 5) Loud noises.

7       Unfortunately, she barely completed one-fourth of the questionnaire before giving up and drawing a doodle of herself wearing sunglasses above a caption that simply read, "*No.*"

"Now I know you're all already worrying about who you'll work with for the paper," continues Professor Friedman, smiling. "But not to worry! I'll be pairing you up."

The classroom erupts in groans.

*No.* Crocs Boy was a *sign.*[8] Taking this class was a mistake, and now I'm going to have to deal with some rando. This is what I get for trying to broaden my horizons. Most of the classes I'll need to take for my English major I can do at Marion, but I *thought* it'd be smart to take advantage of the course offerings at Halcyon. I am a fool.

My arm shoots up; I don't even wait for Professor Friedman to call on me.

"Sorry for interrupting, Professor," I say, "but is there any chance you could reconsider?" I clear my throat when she doesn't respond. "A couple of us commute from Marion, so coordinating with Halcyon students to meet up for the paper could be difficult. Could the Marion students be paired together, or else work independently?"

There are nods and murmurs of agreement all around me. From the corner of my eye, I spot another Marion student whispering to the girl beside her, and their eyes widen in recognition.[9]

Professor Friedman smiles half-heartedly. "What's your name?"

I sit up a little straighter. "Anisa Shirani. You can call me Ani."

I feel probing stares from the other students, but I'm used to it. I do tend to, shall we say, attract the eye. Today, I'm wearing the vintage Dior sweater dress I snagged from a thrift store—most of my closet is

---

8    Updated top five on my list of Despicable Things: 1) Group papers, 2) Tardiness, 3) Crocs, 4) Imperialism, 5) Poor hygiene.

9    Dressing well every day gets you noticed. Fact. Also, I have a fairly popular Instagram (@AniAndEverything) where I occasionally post makeup tips and my outfit of the day.

designer wear I've painstakingly hunted down secondhand—and I've wrangled my long, wavy hair into a neat ponytail. As usual, my makeup is on point, including my new Charlotte Tilbury highlighter that is doing wonders to emphasize my strong, beautiful nose and my Huda Beauty pressed powder that makes the naturally dark circles beneath my eyes hide in shame.[10] My mom taught me the importance of self-presentation at an early age, and it has served me well.

Of course, it's a different story when I get home, but nobody needs to know that right now.

"Mm, Ani. A good thought, but I want you—and this goes for everyone—to treat this as an opportunity. Most of you are first-years or sophomores, so this is likely the first time you're taking a class with students from the other campus. Think of this as a chance to build camaraderie between the two schools and possibly make new friends."

*Yes, but what if I don't care to?* I bite the words back. I see no advantage to making friends with random people I'll probably never see again after this semester. The only reason why I'm here is Isaac, who happens to be a Halcyon student and is also MIA.

Oh, right. Isaac. I should explain. See, Isaac Jamil is my . . . sort-of fiancé, and the definition of a desi parent's dream son-in-law: he's the only son (in fact, the only child), his *very* rich parents own their own cardiology practice, and, importantly (to me), he's gorgeous. Our families met at an Eid dinner party when we were thirteen, and it's basically common knowledge in the tristate Muslim community that we're going to get married. Some might call it old-fashioned.[11] But I think it's

---

10    I haven't been sleeping well lately, so my dark circles are especially rough today. If Isaac doesn't answer my texts soon, I will perish.

11    Which in my experience is code for "anti-Western." Big side-eye.

7

comforting to have my future already planned out—especially when the future looks like Isaac.

Anyway, we were supposed to have our dream college experience together, him at Halcyon and me at Marion, the all-women's college just a ten-minute bus ride away.[12] He's a year ahead, so the plan was for him to help me get acclimated, show me around. It's what got me through my senior year of high school—him calling me in the evenings after his classes to tell me all about college, and all the fun things we could do when I arrived at Marion. But lately, it's seemed that fate is conspiring to keep our schedules as unaligned as humanly possible.

Actually, Isaac was supposed to be in this class with me, but at the last minute he realized he needed to take Multivariable Calc instead, so . . . here we are.

Professor Friedman valiantly returns to discussing the topics we'll be going over in class while I attempt to channel my nervous, frenetic energy into my notebook.

Except I'm distracted by a clicking sound, and my eyes trail back to the offending boy in jorts, who's playing with a ballpoint pen. It could be the lack of sleep talking, but the clicking—a low, dull, quick sound—grows louder with every passing second, and with it, my fury. But then his pen falls to the floor with a clatter, and he doesn't even notice the professor wincing at the sound.

I watch in horror as the pen rolls, seemingly in slow motion, toward my feet.[13]

---

12    I was considering applying to Halcyon too, but Marion has a better English program. And, well, I didn't want to come across as too clingy. I have an image to uphold, you know.

13    Hidden by my very cute, weather-appropriate knee-high brown boots. Not that I don't have nice feet. Not that you need to know. I mean, they're still feet, but

The boy turns around, and his eyes—big and round—meet mine. His mouth breaks into a sheepish, dimpled smile; like everything else about him, it isn't subtle.

I fight the urge to kick the pen away. But there are certain things a decent person does not do. And again, it's not his fault I'm in a bad mood. I lean down, grab the pen from off the floor, and hand it back to its rightful owner.

"Thanks," he whispers.

I make sure to flash him an amiable smile in return. "Of course."

But then the boy's eyes linger on mine as if he's contemplating something, and my smile falters a little under his stare.

*What the hell you lookin' at, Crocs?* I want to ask. But right then, I'm saved by my phone vibrating in my bag; I can feel the rumble by my feet. Discreetly, I slide my hand into the back pocket and peek at my notifications, hopeful, praying—

My heart sinks. It's not Isaac. It's just Mom, texting to ask if I'm coming home for the weekend for the Khalids' dinner party.[14]

She's been texting a lot lately. It's not like her to be *this* clingy. Maybe Zaina, my little sister, is right. Maybe Mom and Dad are fighting even more than usual.

And I don't want to think about what she'd say if she found out Isaac hasn't been texting me lately.

"Okay, I'm going to announce pairs for the group paper—and no, I'm not doing it in order of seating, so don't even *think* about moving now," comes Professor Friedman's voice.

---

like, they're normal. . . . You know what, never mind.

14    Of course the answer is yes. It's *always* yes, and she knows that. I've been home nearly every weekend since coming to Marion.

9

I slide my phone back in my bag. Crocs is facing forward again, and he's back to clicking his pen. I start chewing my lip. Glance at the clock. Forty more minutes of suffering.

Maybe the reason Isaac hasn't texted back is because he got sick. I mean, college campuses are basically giant petri dishes of germs, right? I should be there for him, at his bedside, nursing him back to health with salty soup and coconut water. He'd say, with his husky voice: *"Ani, my love . . . I feel better already with you by my side . . ."*[15]

"Anisa Shirani," I hear Professor Friedman's voice, snapping me out of my beautiful daydream. "Ani—you're with Marlow Greene."

Marlow? I blink. Who—?

The boy sitting in front of me stops clicking his pen and turns around once more. He shoots me another annoying, beaming smile, complete with a thumbs-up.

Oh God. *No.*

I'm paired with the Crocs kid.

What am I being punished for? Is it because I thought not-so-nice-things about Crocs—both the shoe and the person? I don't think it's fair to punish me for thoughts. God is not the thought police. God would be anti-police.

Professor Friedman continues reading out the pairs, but I'm done listening. I enter what I'm pretty sure can be described as a fugue state, because my brain is overloaded and has decided that it is Done. The rest of class trickles by, and the moment Professor Friedman dismisses the class, I stand up so fast that I get dizzy.

It's time to catch Isaac. If I run, I can still make it to the math and

---

15    So I couldn't sleep last night because of my anxiety over Isaac, right? Between us, I had to pass the time by reading a romance novel. Though the title *Lovers' Quarrel* leaves a little to be desired, it's such a swoonworthy book.

science building, Hadley Hall, and—

But Crocs, despite his lamentable choice in footwear, catches up to me.

"Hey," he says, adjusting his backpack strap. "We should exchange numbers. I'll text and we can figure out a time to meet?" Standing up, he's a lot taller than I imagined. I have to look up to meet his gaze.

I blink slowly, trying not to let the annoyance at being stopped show on my face.

"Orrr, you know, you could text when *you* want to meet?" he asks, his voice light, hopeful.

"Sure!" I answer finally, pulling out my phone. "Whatever works for you." *Hurry up!!!* I feel every cell in me screaming.

I tell him my number, fast. A few long seconds later, my phone screen lights up with an invitation to add his number, too, so I do. There it is. Marlow Greene. My—*sigh*—partner.

"Great, got it! Thank—" he starts, but I'm already running, phone still in my hand.

I'm not very familiar with Halcyon's campus, but I know darn well where the math and science building is because it's where Isaac spends most of his time. Unfortunately for me, it's all the way across campus, and even though Halcyon's a small school, it's still far. Too far.

I start to slow down, my heart thumping wildly in my chest.

I won't make it in time.

Then my phone vibrates. Once again, like a fool, I am hopeful: maybe it's Isaac, maybe *he* came to meet *me*—

But it's from none other than Crocs Kid.

> **Looking forward to working with you :D**

I barely stop myself from throwing my phone into a bush.

11

Hi! 😊 11:22 AM

Would love to see you 11:22 AM

If you have some free time? 11:22 AM

Maybe grab lunch or something? 11:23 AM

Or hang out in the library 11:35 AM

Or anything really 11:59 AM

Hope you're doing okay! 2:07 PM

# Chapter 2

"You made it!" I hear my friend Sumra Khalid, an engineering student and veritable angel on this earth, behind me.

It's the weekend, so I'm not sure if Sumra means that literally—that I "made it" to her parents' dinner party—or figuratively, that I survived the week from hell. Either way, she is correct.

As soon as I finished my Friday afternoon class (Medieval Lit), I drove straight home. Normally, this would mean changing into what Zaina calls my True Form: thick-framed glasses with a tiny crack in the corner and my favorite green tracksuit that Dad says makes me look like a Pakistani cricket player. The form only my family knows about. Tonight, though, I change into a shalwar kameez[16] and redo my hair and makeup the way I always do before one of these dinner parties.

The Muslim community in the tristate area is *very* social, which is why tonight the Khalids' sizable house on the Main Line is stuffed to the brim with desi families and life and noise. The polar opposite of the weirdly quiet car ride here—though, in a sense, equally stuffy.[17]

---

16       Tonight's color of choice: a blushing, demure pink.

17       Mom and Dad didn't say a word during the twenty-minute car ride, and then as soon as we arrived, they went to separate parts of the house. I like silence as much as the next person, but not when it's tangibly awkward.

I pour myself some mango juice from the buffet Sumra's parents have set up by the kitchen. "Just because I'm in college doesn't mean I'm going to stop coming to these. Marion's only an hour away."

Nadia Ahmed pokes her head out from behind Sumra and lets out a whistle. "Marion. I still can't believe you got in." Nadia's one of those girls I only ever see at these dinners—she just moved into town, so I don't know her well yet, other than the fact that she's short, studying interior design, and is seeing a cute Bengali guy named Nahid—but I adore all five feet of her and how she always says exactly what she's thinking. "I mean, I *can*, but still. You don't get to be that pretty *and* go to a top school. It's not fair to the rest of us."

I smile graciously. "I got lucky."

That's a lie, of course. I worked my ass off to get into Marion for *years*. My social life in high school was nonexistent; nights were spent studying in my lucky green tracksuit, weekends were spent working or volunteering. I took a full load of AP classes while being editor at the school newspaper *and* VP of the student body. I barely even had time for friends, including Sumra, who was also busy with school.

And being in college now means doing it all over again—but to prepare for law school and become a successful future business lawyer.[18]

It's tiring sometimes, I'll admit. But I can't afford to be average, not for the future I want.

"Let's take a picture?" I suggest, changing the subject before yanking Sumra and Nadia closer for a selfie (they're more than happy to oblige, because frankly *why else does one dress up*?). I'm uploading the picture

---

18     Frankly, I think I'd make a fantastic CEO, but there's something about being in a courtroom—all eyes on me while I deliver the most cutthroat closing argument—that just feels so right.

to my @AniAndEverything Instagram account when Sumra suddenly nudges me in the rib.

"Speaking of lucky, guess who just walked in?" she whispers conspiratorially, pushing her stylish tortoiseshell glasses back up her nose.

I look behind me.

And nearly drop my mango juice.

Isaac's here! I've somehow missed seeing him all week and now he's finally here, standing by the doorway.

I can feel his presence, a tangible thing that pulls me in with its own gravitational force, and I swear there must be a breeze inside because his ebony hair is blowing like he's in a Bollywood movie, or one of my romance book covers. I've known him for so long and practically memorized every detail of his face, but I could never get sick of looking at him. He's got smooth, olive-kissed skin, and his hazel eyes are cradled by eyelashes so thick they make him look like he's wearing eyeliner. His natural beauty would infuriate me if I weren't also madly in love with him. And tonight, he's wearing a deep maroon button-down shirt[19] and black dress pants that accentuate his . . . we'll call it *Isaac-ness*, shaped from his time as captain of his high school lacrosse team.

I tear my eyes away, embarrassed.

"*Have fuuun*," I hear Sumra and Nadia singing behind me, but I barely register it. While Sumra's parents welcome Isaac and his parents inside the house as if they were greeting royalty, I take a deep breath. As tempted as I am to rush to the foyer, desperation isn't becoming. So instead, I set down my juice and take an extra moment to adjust the silky dupatta around my neck before whipping out the pocket mirror I keep

---

19     I curse myself for not wearing maroon today to match him. Not that I could have known. But *still*. Everyone loves a couple who wears coordinated outfits!

in my purse. Lipstick's *flawless*. Good. No food stuck in my teeth. Hair smooth—thank you, coconut oil.[20]

Okay. I'm ready.

Isaac spots me in the crowd and gives me an easy smile that sets off fireworks in my chest. *Breathe*, I remind myself again as I approach.

"Salaam, Aunty Lubna, Uncle Farooq," I say, greeting Isaac's parents first. "It's good to see you."

Aunty Lubna takes me in. She's tall for a desi woman, with arched eyebrows and a strong nose pinched just a tinge too tightly, sculpting her elegant face with a perpetual look of disdain. If she wanted to, she probably could have been a model, which is definitely not intimidating in the slightest bit. Isaac mostly takes after her, except his face is softer. Kinder. For which I am grateful.[21]

"Ani," Aunty Lubna says in her slight British lilt. "You're looking lovely. Your hair's gotten longer."

I puff up under her rare praise. I'd love to try cutting my hair short, but I let it grow out long after I overheard Aunty saying she preferred long hair on girls.

See, Isaac's parents demand things be a certain way. They demand perfection, which makes sense, given who they are: they went from Pakistani immigrants who barely spoke English to owning a ridiculously successful private medical practice. They have several houses to show for it. When you think of the immigrant dream, they are it. I should feel

---

20    My hair is actually ninety-eight percent frizz, but I've concocted an oil mixture that can soften it down without looking too oily. And no, I will not share the full (very secret) recipe. It's proprietary.

21    Can you imagine having the love of your life look exactly like his mother? I would *die*.

16

lucky she's deemed me good enough for her only son,[22] which means that I've managed to meet her three basic requirements: 1) Good looks (self-explanatory), 2) Good education (solidified by my acceptance to Marion and eventually law school), and 3) Good family (that my family has solid social standing, which is just a fancy way of saying no one has dug up any dirt on us).[23]

But sometimes I wonder what Aunty Lubna would say if she discovered what I'm really like at home, green tracksuit and all.

*Perish* the thought. I can't ever let my guard down. Not if I want to *stay* with Isaac.

"Although—" Aunty Lubna's hazel eyes narrow, analyzing, and I find myself shrinking a little. Her thumb suddenly presses against my mouth, and she starts wiping at my lips roughly. "This color's not right for you."

"*Ammi*," Isaac protests beside me. But Aunty ignores him. I blink in a daze as she finishes removing the lipstick I so carefully painted on just an hour ago.

"Much better," she says with a stiff smile when she finishes. She pats my cheek.

"Thank you, Aunty," I say when I finally find my voice. I just bought this lipstick, too—a matte rose pink to match my outfit. I berate myself

---

22    Barely. I think the only reason why she's on board is because I have all the qualifications a good desi family would want in a bride. It's not showing off; it's simply the truth. But I'm not sure Aunty Lubna would consider anyone good enough for her son.

23    Although when I was fifteen, a girl in the community with a crush on Isaac did try to smear my reputation by claiming to have seen me at the movies with not one, but two different boys, which is basically the desi equivalent of saying I ran away to join the circus with my serial killer boyfriend(s). Anyway, it didn't work because I had an alibi (I was actually at a sleepover at Sumra's for her birthday), and six months later, that girl and her family moved to Nevada. I kind of feel sorry for her, but jealousy is unbecoming.

mentally for it—I *knew* this pink was too bold of a choice. But there is nothing to be done. I have failed today's test.

Aunty Lubna nods and walks with Uncle Farooq into the dining room, where most of the guests—including my parents—are congregating for appetizers. That leaves Isaac and I alone, giving us a rare private moment. I should be thrilled; the truth is, even though everyone treats us like we're practically engaged, we're rarely alone together. We share stolen seconds at dinner parties or between classes, exchanging smiles like we've got a secret no one else knows about. We have reputations to uphold, after all. And it's romantic, in its own way. I'm content with moments like these, and the occasional thoughtful text from him.[24]

It'd be nice, though, to have just a few *more* moments.

"You look great, Ani," Isaac says. "As usual, pink looks nice on you."

My cheeks flush. "Thank you." This time I mean it. He's referencing that time he got me a pink cashmere scarf for my birthday—and a kind effort, I think, to sweep away the shroud of awkwardness left behind by his mother.

"You also look nice," I say. "Not that you're wearing pink. I meant, in your maroon shirt. Maroon looks good on you. But I'm sure pink would look good on you, too." *Oh my God, STOP TALKING, ANISA.* "Honestly, anything would look on you. Hunter green, royal blue, plum. Mustard gold . . ."

There's a beat of awkward silence.

As usual, now that I'm face-to-face with Isaac, I've become completely incoherent. I never used to be *this* bad, either. But it's like no matter how

---

24    One such text involved him admitting to daydreaming about running his fingers through my long hair. I don't remember if I responded. I was too busy screaming into my pillow.

hard I try—and God, do I *try*—my brain turns to mush around him.

Thankfully, Isaac laughs a little. "Thanks. You'd be surprised at what neon green does to me, though."

I let out a laugh of my own, grateful for Isaac's geniality.

But then I remember. "By the way, how—how have you been? I texted you earlier this week, but . . . maybe my messages didn't go through?"

"Right, yes, about that"—Isaac runs his hand through his perfect black locks—"I meant to text back, but I've been drowning in studying and club stuff. We got a huge influx of new members."

Despite being only a sophomore, Isaac's the new president of the South Asian Student Association at Halcyon. I knew he'd be busy, but still. Now that we're both in college, I was hoping we'd be able to spend more time together. Hell, even my own parents went on several coffee "dates"[25] before they got engaged. Instead, Isaac and I barely even text anymore.

I put on a smile. "Wow! That's so great."

"It is." He smiles, too. "I know I said we'd hang out more this semester, but I guess I just completely lost track of time. . . ." He takes a step toward me. "Forgive me?"

He says it so earnestly, so sweetly, that I'm swept up in him all over again. That's his power: to take whatever anxieties and worries are thrashing around in my chest and put them to sleep. Of *course* Isaac wasn't ignoring me. He would never. He's even still wearing the bracelet I gave to him about a year and a half ago, before he left for college: a black, braided leather strap strung with onyx beads. The leather looks

---

25    Kira once asked me why I don't know *every little thing* about Isaac if we've been sort-of dating for ages, so I explained that for many Muslims, dating's a bit different; we meet up to get to know each other and our families with the intention of getting married. It's very Jane Austen: lots of pining, maybe some accidental hand-brushing, and the involvement of nosy (though sometimes well-meaning) relatives.

frayed already, like he wears the bracelet often.

"I'll think about it," I say finally, teasing. Isaac's face relaxes. And suddenly it feels like we're floating away on our own little nimbus cloud, far from everyone and everything.

Except I still feel the slightest bit . . . unsatisfied.

"But maybe in the future, you could—I don't know, respond a little sooner?" I ask, keeping my voice light. "I mean, not hearing from you for a whole *week* is a little—"

"God, you two have *no* business looking like you do!" Nadia chimes in out of nowhere. "Just look at everyone's favorite power couple. Don't they look like they just stepped out of a magazine cover?"

Sumra nods vehemently. "Oh, absolutely. They always do! Especially when they're standing together."

Isaac's face goes stiff, and his eyes dart to the floor. Maybe he's feeling shy.

But I swell with pride, my grumpiness evaporating. After all, there's nothing I love more than people confirming what I already know: that Isaac and I look molded for each other. *Of course we do.* First of all, we're both easily tens.[26] We also want similar things in life—enviable careers, a suburban home, a fancy rice cooker. We have the same basic values; I'm proud of my South Asian heritage and culture, and I've always wanted to marry someone who shared it. And we've known each other since we were little kids.[27] People throw around the phrase *meant to be* a lot, but Isaac and I—we're the real deal, like Lucas and Catarina from

---

26      Please, it's not egotistical if it's a *fact.*

27      I remember when we weren't allowed to go to my senior prom, but on the night of, I found flowers by my window, courtesy of Isaac. Jasmine, my favorite. He always used to do sweet little gestures like that. At least, when he wasn't so busy.

*Lovers' Quarrel.* And all the hard work I put into getting into Marion, into shaping how people see me, even dealing with jabs from Isaac's mom . . .

It's worth it to make us happen.

Sumra grins and puts an arm on my shoulder. "So how's everything, Isaac? School treating you all right?"

Isaac slips his hands in his pockets. "It's good. I was just telling Ani I've been really busy, though."

"Aw, that must be rough," Nadia says, pouting. "At least you have the rest of your lives together! You, a future doctor, and Ani, a future lawyer—God, I can't *wait* for your wedding. It's going to be the wedding of the *century*."

A shy laugh escapes me. "Nadia! Please, that won't happen for a while." After I graduate, to be exact. It'll be an outdoor spring wedding, just in time to catch the last of the cherry blossoms. And it'll *definitely* be the wedding of the *century*, with at least five hundred guests. I'll wear a Rahul Mishra lehenga, or maybe an Elie Saab gown. And of course, everyone will be congratulating me not just on the wedding, but on my entrance to Penn Law—to be close to Isaac, obviously, who'll be finishing his first year at Perelman School of Medicine.

Isaac gives me a small smile. "But inshallah, one day," he says softly, and my heart flutters.

The sweet moment is ruined when Zaina, my fourteen-year-old little sister, rushes past us, holding a bowl piled high with dessert. "*There's rasmalai*," I make out before she disappears into the crowd.

Isaac chuckles. He knows rasmalai[28] is my favorite.

---

28    A creamy dessert made of cottage cheese, which tastes a lot better than it sounds, I swear. I just don't know how else to describe it. *Curdled milk balls* sounds even worse.

He gestures toward the dessert table with a nod, not a trace of the dark expression I saw earlier. "Shall we?" he asks, just to me.

"Yeah," I say, beaming.

I follow him toward the buffet setup until some movement in a nearby hallway snags my interest.

It's Mom and Dad, dueling with each other in harsh whispers—presumably continuing the silent fight[29] they were having on the drive here. Mom's arms are folded across her chest, her curly hair bouncing with every animated word, while Dad's face is dappled with sweat, his thick moustache looking a little deflated.

I look around them, panicked, but thankfully it seems no one's caught them. Thank God. They argue all the time, but I can't *believe* they'd risk arguing at a dinner party—especially when Mom's always gone on about the importance of how you present yourself in public. This is *exactly* why I've been telling them to go see a marriage counselor. Clearly, they haven't listened.

I consider saying something to them.

"You coming, Ani?" Isaac asks by the doorway ahead of me. "Is something wrong?"

He starts walking toward me, but I quickly shoot out my arm and block his path. I can't have him see Mom and Dad right now. He can't know about the mess that is their relationship.

I know honesty is technically the best policy in any relationship, but *this*—there are just some things Isaac is better off not knowing.

"Uh, no! No, nothing's wrong!" I clumsily lie. "I just needed a second. To prepare my stomach. Hype it up for the rasmalai. You know how it is."

Isaac blinks.

---

29    Their silent treatment is only marginally better than their arguments.

"Right," he says slowly, "that . . . makes sense. But are you sure there's nothing—"

"Uh-huh! Why would anything be wrong?" I laugh, maybe a little too loudly, and quickly gesture to the kitchen.

"Please, after you, Isaac!"

Isaac stares at me for another moment, looking a little bothered—

But to my relief, he complies.

I let out a breath and trail him into the kitchen before he realizes anything's amiss.

*Everything's fine*, I tell myself.

But I throw my parents a glare that they probably won't even notice.

# Chapter 3

Our house is just outside Philadelphia. A modest stone English Tudor built back in the thirties, but my parents did some extensive renovations over the course of a few years.[30] Mom works as a real estate agent, and Dad works for a medical supply company, so we're not rich by any means—certainly nowhere near Isaac's family—but like me, my parents are good at taking the plain and making it gorgeous. Normally.

"Why does it look like our house threw a temper tantrum?" I ask as I'm coming down the stairs from my bedroom. It's not that far off an exaggeration. Mom and Dad normally keep the place spotless,[31] but tonight it looks like someone's unleashed an army of dirty dishes and takeout containers all over the kitchen counter, and there's a pile of blankets in piles on the floor by the couch, like someone might have slept there.

"Dad was feeling sick last week, so he told the cleaning people not to come," I hear Zaina's voice from an armchair, where she's playing some game on her phone.

Huh. I hadn't heard anything about that. It's also not like Mom not to

---

30      I hand-painted some of the flowers and vines on one of the walls. My mastery of winged eyeliner came in handy.

31      Mostly because they're still hoping an editor at *Main Line* magazine will discover the house and feature it like they did with the Khalids'.

tell me every excruciating detail of their lives.[32] And Dad's *never* sick. Stress must be getting to him.

"Damn. The transformation is so jarring every time."

For a moment I'm confused, until I realize Zaina's referring to me. Finally free of my heavy shalwar kameez and makeup, I'm wearing my glasses (taped down the middle after I sat on them a few weeks ago) and tracksuit, and I've slapped on a couple pimple patches on my cheek as a preemptive strike against my number-one archenemy: zits.

"*You're* jarring," I respond, making a beeline for the fridge. I didn't eat much at the dinner party because my stomach does this fun little thing where it closes in on itself whenever it's around Isaac.[33]

"Plebes like you wouldn't understand," I continue, pulling out a yogurt container. It's full of biryani, a spicy rice dish that immediately awakens my stomach. "It's *exhausting* being me. You know how much effort it takes to look the way I do all the time?" Behind closed doors, if I don't let my hair down occasionally, so to speak, even *I* would break after a while.

"Uh-huh. You know, you could always try being normal. Does Isaac still not have any idea how you really look? Your real *charming* self?"

I slam the fridge door. "No, and I plan to keep it that way, so you better keep your mouth shut."

It's like I said before. There are some things Isaac is better off not knowing.

She snorts. "He's going to find out eventually."

"Don't underestimate my ability. I've kept this up for over ten years

---

32     Example from last week:
Mom: I tried out this new probiotic pill from Whole Foods and it was $28 a bottle!
Mom: Isn't it strange how they can charge so much money for what is essentially naturally occurring bacteria?
Me: Mom, I'm literally in class right now.

33     Maybe I should try the probiotic pills.

now." I've gotten very efficient at dressing up quickly. I practiced the summer before college started. My personal record now is eight minutes, and that includes doing my hair and contouring my face. In the future, I'll just have to make sure I always wake up before Isaac does.

Sleeping next to Isaac. I'm blushing at the thought.

"You're a freak." Zaina puts her phone away. "And speaking of which . . ."

As I'm microwaving a bowl of biryani with the chicken picked out, she rolls off the couch and walks to a closet by the door that leads to the garage. I watch as she pulls out a bag. A gift bag.

I take the bag and peer inside.

"I know your birthday isn't for another month, but I wanted a head start," she says with a small smile. "Mostly for selfish reasons."

I pull out a box.

"A Nintendo Switch?" It's clearly brand-new, and she even picked out these cute pink and green controllers. "How the heck did you afford this? Aren't these expensive?"

Zaina shrugs. "I convinced Mom and Dad to chip in."

"Wow. I love it, but—why a Switch?"

We never had any video game systems growing up, at least not until Zaina got older. It's not like I really had *time* to play. School was everything. But I was always curious to try them, especially when Zaina started talking about how she wanted to get into game design. When I was in high school, sometimes I'd do my homework next to her while she'd play something up on the big screen. We wouldn't really talk, but it was strangely soothing, half watching her play.

"Never too late to get into games." She looks away with an embarrassed expression.[34] "You can look through the Nintendo store library, see what catches your eye. There are a bunch of games we can play together while you're at college."

Is that why she got this for me? To keep in touch?

"Thanks, Zaina." I hug her, feeling deeply moved. "This is really, really sweet."

But the moment's shattered when we hear Mom from upstairs.

"For once in your life, just listen to me. You never listen to me!" she shouts. I can't remember the last time I heard her raise her voice like that.

"I don't have to listen to this," replies Dad. Compared to Mom, he sounds . . . exhausted, like every word takes effort.

I pull away from Zaina. We don't look at each other.

"The only reason we married is because we were young and angry at our parents." Mom's voice wobbles, like she's about to cry. "You never loved me, not really. You just wanted to spite *them*. And look what happened. Look at us."

"Oh, please. As if you didn't use me to get away from your mother."

"See, this is exactly what I'm talking about!" Mom yells. "Our parents were right from the start: we're not good for each other. We argue about everything, all the time. We can't even have a single conversation without arguing!"

"You're being dramatic. If we just talked calmly, like adults, instead of whatever the hell this is—"

"You don't even respect me enough to listen to the words I'm saying! We clearly don't even want the same things! I had to *drag* you to this

---

34      It's so cute how her bangs cover her eyes whenever she looks embarrassed. Ugh, my heart!

party because you never want to go anywhere, and people are starting to notice."

*Crap. Not again.*

I feel my heart collapse into my stomach. Beside me, Zaina has her head down again, practically drilling holes into the floor. I don't even think she blinks.

We've heard it all again and again. You'd think by now we'd be used to it, like background noise. And yet, every time they get into a fight—whether it be about Dad forgetting to unpack the dishwasher for the hundredth time, Mom spending money we don't have, or the two of them talking over each other—Zaina and I shut down.

The wood floor upstairs creaks.

"But Sabina—"

"*Don't*, Sohail."

"Sabina, if you are unhappy, then you need to tell me why. But as soon as you married me, you completely closed off. You changed. Everything changed, and I don't know what I'm supposed to—"

"I *have* told you what's wrong. A *thousand* times. If you still can't be bothered to figure out how to fix it, then we have nothing to talk about."

Footsteps. The slam of a door resounds through the house.

And then it's over.

I swallow hard. The hunger I felt earlier is gone, replaced instead with familiar waves of nausea. The same nausea I always feel whenever Mom and Dad fight.

"You're right. Their fighting does feel worse than ever," I tell Zaina once I can finally speak again. "I even saw them arguing at the party."

"Yeah." She lets out a breath. "But let's be real: Tomorrow? They'll act like nothing happened. Like always."

It's not exactly comforting, but she's right. Mom and Dad arguing—it's just business as usual.

"How are you holding up?" I ask.

Zaina shrugs. "Honestly? Same old. I just go to my room, listen to music. I'm used to it."

I bite my lip. "Yeah. I'm sorry." I know how it goes, obviously. Whenever Mom and Dad would fight, back when I still lived at home, Zaina would slink off to her room, while I'd get lost in a romance novel in my room, hoping it would all stop soon. And it would, eventually.

"Do you ever wonder," says Zaina slowly, "if it would be better if they just divorced?"

"No!" I answer, shaking my head. "God, no. It's like you said. They fight a lot, sure, but then they're fine again for a while. Even if their fighting is getting worse, I'd rather have that than the alternative."

Even *thinking* about them separating feels like a nightmare, for all of us. I'm glad they at least have enough sense not to, especially when they haven't even tried couples counseling.

Zaina's quiet for a moment, then: "At least Nani's coming to visit next weekend, which means they can't fight for the week she's here."

Right. Nani, Mom's mom, lives in Toronto and rarely visits. When she does, though, Mom and Dad usually act like the world's all sunshine and rainbows, because if they don't, Nani will sniff out wrongness and imperfection and stamp it out with her chappal. Sometimes literally.

"Sweet reprieve, I guess." I make a face. "But at what cost?"

"Honestly? I'll take it. My ears need the break."

I look over at my little sister and smile sadly. I've been so stressed out with all the Isaac stuff, I haven't even thought about what all this must be doing to Zaina. At least when I lived at home, we had each other.

Misery loves company and all. Now? She has to deal with our parents' arguing all on her own. It makes me feel guilty. Part of my decision to attend Marion was because of how close I'd still be to home, but I guess it doesn't matter: I get to be free of all this. And Zaina doesn't.

I squeeze her shoulder awkwardly, then wave my Switch. "Hey, so I'm not leaving till Sunday morning. After I finish praying, should we, I don't know, try . . . playing something?"

She gives me a small smile.

"Absolutely."

# Chapter 4
## JANUARY 22

Monday means I'm back on campus, getting ready for my morning Medieval Lit class, but thinking about Chaucer feels even more pointless than usual.[35] It's just a little hard to focus when you're too busy daydreaming about knocking your parents' heads together.

Mom and Dad have never been the most romantic couple. I've never heard them talk about anything that isn't work, community, or house related. I've never seen any affectionate gestures between them: no hands on the small of their backs when passing each other in the kitchen, no sneaky cheek kisses or calling each other *meri dil* or *jaan-e-mann* like Sumra's parents. They don't even sit next to each other on the couch when they're watching TV.

The most mind-boggling thing about it? Theirs was a love marriage, at least in the beginning. Both their parents were against the match, but Mom and Dad went ahead with it anyway. Only, in the end, their love fizzled out. It was as if they'd gotten swept up in the moment—only to realize, years later, that they had nothing in common.

That's exactly why I know Isaac and I will work out; our match is based on actual substantial *criteria*, not just transitory *feelings*.

---

35    Truly a tremendous feat. The way academia loves putting their white Englishmen on a pedestal, I swear.

I just need to make sure my parents' worsening relationship squabbles don't interfere with my future.[36] Like giving Isaac's mom more reason to believe I'm not good enough for her son.

I'm braiding my hair in front of the floor-length mirror by my bed when the scent of Irish Spring signals that Kira is back from the showers.

I scrunch my nose. Unfortunately, Kira notices. "Don't give me that look. Irish Spring smells good and it's cheap."

A few traits I've learned about Kira: she's a comp sci major, she plays badminton, she loves K-Pop, and she's very private. She's also very utilitarian, and what I'd refer to as *the finer things in life*, she'd call a waste of money. Kira and I have learned that agreeing to disagree is the best way to keep the peace.[37] A tip I'll have to share with Mom and Dad.

"By any chance, are you ever going to use that perfume I got you?" I ask politely. Her birthday was back in November, and despite giving her that roommate questionnaire, I still didn't know her well enough to perfectly tailor her gift to her tastes, as I am wont to do. Kayali Vanilla 28, however, is a safe choice for anyone.

"No." She plops onto her bed and begins vigorously towel-drying her hair. "What is up with companies labeling things as 'masculine' or 'feminine' scents, anyway? Why the hell do men get to smell like a pine forest, but *I'm* supposed to smell like flowers, or like I just had a sugary romp with the Pillsbury Doughboy?"

"That perfume was expensive," I mumble.

---

36      It would help, I think, for them to sit down and talk out their issues instead of *screaming* them.

37      For example, Kira believes my side of the room would be brightened up with some LØVE LIFE and other K-Pop band posters. I, unfortunately, disagree.

"And that's why it'll forever live as a beautiful decorative piece on my shelf."

I finish braiding my hair and let out a very loud internal scream at the thought of the perfume collecting dust. My face, of course, remains positively placid in my reflection. Kira's reaction to expensive perfume shouldn't be surprising, though. Usually when people first meet me, they tend to be, we'll say, *overly friendly*. It's all superficial, of course: the reality is, people want pretty people to like them. Not Kira, though. Like my little sister, Zaina, Kira couldn't care less.

Maybe that's why I admire her.[38]

"Hey, are you okay?" Kira asks suddenly.

"Of course I am. Why do you ask?"

"Because you've been braiding your hair for like, ten minutes now."

Ah.

I was going to try to upload a cute photo series on Instagram of my weekly hairstyles, but it looks like that's not happening right now. Clearly, the stress of Mom and Dad is getting to me.

Sighing, I undo my messy attempt at a braid and let my hair out long.

"So while you're feeling so honest and open," says Kira, "you want to tell me what I'm supposed to get you for your birthday? It's coming up, isn't it? February 23?"

"What?" I turn around. "Oh, no, no, you don't have to get me anything."

"You say that, but you are a hundred percent that person who would secretly be upset if I didn't."

I pout. She's not exactly wrong.

"So, what do you want? A new scarf? Earrings?"

---

38    But one of these days, I swear I'll get her a gift that will blow her snarky little brain!

"Mm, I'm afraid earrings are tricky because I'm allergic to nickel," I reply. "Or basically any metal that's not gold."

"You *would* be allergic to cheap metal." Kira gestures to the bag I've neatly tucked behind my bed. "Your sister got you a Switch, right? What about a game? Anything you have your eye on?"

Zaina showed me how to set it all up and download games from the Nintendo library, but we quickly learned that the big fantasy role-playing games that she normally plays might be too hard for a beginner like me. "Not yet," I reply.

"Wait, I think I have the perfect idea. You like smut, right?"

I drop my phone.[39] *"E-excuse me?"*

"Oh, come on, those smutty novels? The ones you read at night when you think I'm sleeping?" And as my smile slips, Kira's grows, thin and curled and fox-like. "Don't tell me you're *ashamed.*"

"No!"

I am, in fact, *mortified.* Yes, it's true that I mostly read my romance novels at night, under cover of darkness.[40] My parents would have a fit if they saw me reading a book like *Lovers' Quarrel,* with its two protagonists embracing on the cover, out in the open.

But reading about other people's relationship dynamics, the slow burn, the inevitable coming together—it's addictive. I get to live vicariously through these women who are ravished and adored, who don't have to care about what other people think. It's just nice to get lost for a few hours in the, uh, steamy problems of others, and know that no matter what happens, everything will be all right.

---

39    Thank *God* for phone cases.

40    And it's not *all* smutty, thank you! And the few that are do it very tastefully. It's an art form that serves the story. Let me live.

"So anyway, there's this thing called otome games," Kira explains. "They're essentially visual novels, like, choose-your-own-adventure books with a focus on romance. You choose which hot character you want to take to Bone Town, and based on the different decisions you make throughout the story, you determine the outcome of your love story. I figured you would like them, since you were probably a love-starved child growing up, but otome games simplify love to a merit-based system, so it makes love feel more attainable and thus you more worthy."

"I'm going to ignore that last part."

"My point is, it's like having your own personal harem of sexy dudes but with no real-world consequences." Kira smirks. "It's *awesome*."

I swallow and try not to show too much interest, but I can already feel my heart thrumming excitedly beneath my chest. Playing otome games wouldn't be a bad idea—I mean, an *interactive* romance novel? It sounds like it would be very educational, to say the least. I almost wish I could give them to Mom and Dad to play, if the idea of them playing any romance game didn't embarrass me to death.

I speak slowly. "So I get to choose who I want to romance? And what, they're guaranteed to love me?"

"Sort of. As long as you don't get the Bad Ending."

Kira starts rummaging through her desk drawer and pulls out her own Switch, covered in LØVE LIFE–themed stickers. "Here, I'll gift you one called *Rose in the Embers*. It's a good first one."

"Um. Sure," I say, laughing weakly. "I suppose I'll give it a shot. Since you're recommending it and all."

"Oh, my prudish little friend. I'm about to change your *life*."

I roll my eyes as I head out the door for class.

# Chapter 5

## JANUARY 23

With everything happening, I almost forgot about Crocs.[41]

Come Tuesday, he walks into class late again. At least this time, he's wearing sneakers—hideous ones, unfortunately—but it doesn't count for much because they're drenched in leftover snow, which of *course* means he's dragged some of that slush into the classroom. And I'm not sure if I misread it, but I think his crumpled yellow T-shirt reads simply, T-SHIRT. Insufferable.

Before he sits down, I can feel him glance over at me, like he wants to say something.

I keep my head bowed, pretending to focus on the timeline of American nationalism from 1815 to World War II that Professor Friedman handed out. I neither have the time nor desire to think about Crocs or our silly paper. As the professor goes off track to discuss culinary nationalism and how school lunches were developed, I think instead about biryani; specifically, the Tupperware of biryani wrapped in a plastic grocery bag that Mom handed me yesterday to share with Isaac. It's a genius move, really: everybody loves homemade food. Giving Isaac food my parents made is a sneaky way of reminding him that he's practically already part of the family. Best of all, it gives me another excuse to see him.

---

41     Again, the person. Not the nightmarish shoe.

Only, I texted him this morning and . . .

Still no response.

It's fine, though. It's only been a few hours. I mean, at least it hasn't been *days*. He's busy, anyway; he said as much when we talked over the weekend at the Khalids'. And honestly, part of me is proud that he's so busy. He wouldn't be the Isaac I know and love if he wasn't.

But he promised to be better about staying in touch. It's bad enough that we haven't been in touch as much as we usually are, and I miss his late-night check-in texts. I miss *him*.

So for the rest of class, I'm taking notes from Professor Friedman's lecture with all the focus and meticulousness of a court stenographer just to silence my brain for the remainder of the hour. Time crawls until finally, finally I hear the magic words from Professor Friedman: "We're ending early today; if I were you, I would take this opportunity to meet with your partner for the class paper and get a head start. That's all."

In seconds, I jump to my feet, grab my bag, and leave the room behind me. This time for sure: I will meet with Isaac after class. No matter what.

*Wait for me, Isaac,* I silently beg, feeling a little like Catarina in *Lovers' Quarrel* when she chased Lucas through the palace gardens in the pivotal final scene.

Outside, the air is crisp and nips at my cheeks. The salt beneath my boots crunches with my every hurried step. I'm alert. Ready. Determined to see Isaac with my own eyes and reassure myself that everything is fine.

That is, until someone starts following me.

"Hey. Anisa, right?"

It's Crocs again. And it looks like there's no shaking him off; for every three steps I take, he takes one long stride. I exhale through my nose, irritated. "Yes."

"I'm Marlow. A sophomore. In case you forgot."

I did.

"I'm pretty bad with names, too," he continues, "which is why I had to double check with yours, even though I have it in my phone now. Honestly, people tell me their names and whoosh"—he makes a dramatic gesture with his hands—"in one ear, out the other."

I stare ahead, but that doesn't seem to deter him.

"Anyway, you, uh, never texted me back. About our paper? I was hoping we could set up a time to meet."

"What? Oh."

I quickly pull out my phone from my bag. He's right; he texted me a couple times over the weekend, asking when we should meet to discuss the paper. I remember seeing it, but with everything happening vis-à-vis Mom and Dad, I completely forgot.

"Right, about that," I reply, putting my phone away. "What if we just did the paper over email?"

Crocs—or Marlow, I guess—scratches his brow. "Hmm, email might be difficult. Personally, I work better face-to-face. Makes things easier to discuss, don't you think?"

The muscles in my face strain against the scowl I feel bubbling to the surface. The nerve of him to be pushy about a class paper while always being late to said class.

He stares back at me expectantly, oblivious.

I can't explain it, but somehow this boy gives off Golden Retriever vibes. I think it's in his eagerness; the way he maintains eye contact like he's waiting for you to throw him a bone.

"Fine," I say with a resigned sigh.

He beams at me, all dimples and unnecessary cheer, the human embodiment of a smile emoji. "Awesome. You know, I haven't had to do any *group* papers since high school. I mean, obviously I've had to write papers to the point where I'm sick of them, but that's all solo, you know? So I'm really looking forward to—" His thick eyebrows furrow. "Oh, sorry. Do you have somewhere you need to be?"

"Yes, unfortunately."

"No worries. We can walk and talk," he says, falling in step with me like it's the most natural thing in the world. As other students pass, I can feel their eyes lingering on us, and I can't blame them: we're complete opposites, Crocs and I, with me in a vintage green tartan coat and cashmere beanie,[42] and him in khakis and his yellow T-SHIRT T-shirt.

I swallow back a groan. At least we're already almost halfway across campus.

"So, what does your week look like?" he asks. Even though we're walking side by side, he's still looking at me. "What if we met here on Friday? Oh, wait, one sec—"

Marlow suddenly breaks off to talk to a nearby girl who's dropped a mountain of papers; she must have been heading back from the library. He quickly helps, and hands her papers back to her with a beaming smile. I can't hear what they're saying, but she smiles back.

*Show-off.*

"Sorry about that," says Marlow back at my side, only slightly out of breath. "She looked stressed. I think she's working on her Art History thesis."

I'm not sure how he gleaned all that in a five-second conversation.

"So anyway," he continues, "what if we meet by the bus stop at Halcyon, maybe around four?"

"At Halcyon?"

---

42       Burberry, obvi. I found it at a thrift store on the Main Line and it had a hole at the bottom, but I patched it up. It's practically *criminal* what people will toss.

Ugh. He expects *me* to get on that God-forsaken bus, just to meet up with him for this paper? A paper that frankly I'd rather do by myself; I mean, I've never gotten less than a ninety-seven percent on a paper. I don't care how almost-*annoyingly* friendly he is. A guy like this would only slow me down (case in point: right now) and waste valuable time that could be used to reconnect with Isaac.

"Yeah," Marlow replies. "I figured since the class we take together is here, it makes sense to meet here. Unless you want to meet somewhere else?"

"Here is fine," I lie. As much as I feel otherwise, in my experience, it's always best to keep the peace—or at least, what little peace I can maintain with someone as *irksome* as Marlow.

"Cool. Friday it is." Another toothy smile. "Damn, that smells really good," he says, eyeing the plastic grocery bag of biryani I'm holding.

I move the bag of food to my other side, away from him.

Marlow feigns indignance, but he still somehow looks . . . *happy* about it. "Wow, okay. I'm not a common bully out to steal your lunch. At least, not until I know what kind of food it is."

"It's biryani," I answer, knowing full well there's a high chance he has no idea what that is.

"All of that, just for you?"

"No, it's for someone else."

"You running some kind of food delivery service? For some black-market biryani? Now tell me, is this an *exclusive* service? Because I would pay *good* money to get in on that."

So maybe he does know what biryani is. I'm pleasantly surprised.

"Huh" is all I say.

Marlow says something in response, but frankly it goes, as he so aptly said, whoosh—in one ear and out the other—because I finally see it: the

Halcyon math and science building, an intimidatingly big, gray-stone fortress with dark windows and metal doors. I check my phone again: it's 2:28, which means Isaac's class should just be letting out. My heart dances behind my ribs. I made it just in time.

I stop walking and put myself by a tree, careful not to trip over the small metal sign by the trunk that reads: Shensi fir, *Abies chensiensis.*

"Hadley Hall?" Marlow blinks, confused. "Is there a reason why we're hiding?"

"Sort of." Now I'm smiling, gripping the bag of biryani close to my chest.

Suddenly, the double doors open, and students begin pouring out of the building. I know I just saw Isaac this weekend but seeing him never gets old. I still get butterflies. Even more so seeing him on campus, because I still can't believe we're here together.

Finally, Isaac appears. Today, he's wearing a dark blue peacoat coupled perfectly with a red wool scarf and brown boots. He's gelled his hair back, so I can see every inch of his glorious face. And that smile of his—so big and dazzling and bright and—

Not at me.

Instead, he's smiling at the person he's opening the door for: a girl I don't recognize, with long auburn hair and freckles that make her look like she's an American Girl doll come to life. She's tall, too, with long legs that keep her at a perfect pace with Isaac. He leans down to say something to her; she giggles and playfully hits his shoulder once. The second time, her hand latches on to his arm, pulling him a little closer. He doesn't push her away. As if—as if they're a couple.

I squeeze my bag of biryani, tight.

Marlow's gaze slides to Isaac and the girl and then back to me.

"Is that guy, uh—?"

"My . . ." I pause. I'm not actually sure of the right word. Boyfriend? Fiancé? Betrothed? To-Be? I suppose we're dating in a sense, but it's more a casual agreement between us and our parents that we're supposed to be married in the future. I've always just considered him mine.

But in this moment, I don't know *what* I could call Isaac. I should be trying to get his attention, but with every passing second, my throat feels more like a vise. Marlow and I watch the two of them—Isaac and the absurdly cute girl—walk away, side by side; a Hallmark greeting card come to life.[43]

He didn't even notice me.

Thankfully, Marlow doesn't press for answers.

"Ah." He scratches the back of his neck, and for a moment, I think I catch his eyes narrowing toward Isaac and the girl. A flicker of anger.

But then it's gone, so fast I'm certain I almost imagined it.

He looks at me again, mouth tugged in a small, tentative smile. "You think he has a group paper, too?"

It's not funny. None of it is.

But for some reason, I let out a broken, involuntary laugh.

---

43      The caption would read something like, "*Wish you were here, sucker.*"

# Chapter 6

In the span of a few hours, I hit each of the five stages of grief. The first stage, denial, meant speed-walking away from Isaac even as Marlow called my name, and taking the bus straight back to Marion, all to pretend that I did not in fact just see the love of my life sharing a spark, a connection—dare I say, *chemistry*—with someone else.

In fact, in all the years I've known him, I don't think I've *ever* seen him smile like that.

But how is that even possible when *we're* the ones who are soulmates? Is God testing me or something? Testing *us*? Or worse: Has he gotten sick of me? But come on now, what is there to get sick of?

I try not to spiral, but my anxiousness starts to swallow me whole. My entire future has been planned around one single immutable fact: that one day, Isaac and I will get married. I thought it was what *he* wanted, too. And together, we would work toward making our own little family, the kind that would be an example to all others—unlike mine. But now I can't stop imagining my perfect future fading into nothingness.

Which is why I decide to flee for home on Friday, and completely forget my meeting with Crocs.

The first thing I notice is that the house smells strongly of some sort of meat curry: like cumin and fried onions and garlic, a smell that makes my mouth water. Nani, who's come to visit, has commandeered the stove and is currently standing over the biggest pot I have ever seen.

Zaina is nowhere to be found; knowing her, she's in her room, playing games. Mom and Dad, however, are camped out in the kitchen; Mom is cleaning dishes and putting away spices, while Dad is sitting at the table reading what appears to be some sort of thick medical journal, probably for work. It's not an unusual scene, my parents doing their own thing while remaining in relative proximity to each other so as not to worry anyone else. They've made a mastery of the art of pretending that they don't argue every other day.

I drop my bag in the corner with a loud splat. Maybe they didn't hear me walk in over the sounds of the exhaust fan and frying onions, but I've been home for minutes now and not a single person has acknowledged my existence.

Annoyance flickers in my chest. It's funny. Most places I go, I can feel people looking at me, taking me in with barely disguised admiration. There are comments on Instagram, too, from people who don't even know me but who seem genuinely interested in my life. But not here. Never here. Unless I'm winning awards or illuminated by a (sometimes literal) spotlight, my parents are too preoccupied to notice me. Everyone's always in their own heads. Normally it doesn't bother me, but today I'm especially annoyed by it.

"*Hi*," I announce myself loudly.

"Salaam, beti," Dad greets me first, peering up from his medical journal. It reads *Cancer Cytopathology*.

This cues Mom to close the pantry and finally look at me. "Oh, Ani!" she exclaims. "I completely forgot you were coming home this weekend."

"Hi, Mom, Dad. Asalaamu alaikum, Nani."

Nani shoves a plate of frozen shami kebabs into the microwave.

"Walaikum Assalam," she replies stiffly. "How is school? Have you started studying for your LSATs?"

No, *How are you?* No, *It's so good to see you after all these months.* As usual, Nani is all business. I suppose it makes sense; she never visits us for pleasure. She's only ever here when something has gone wrong, as a living reminder of the ancestors we risk upsetting with our mishaps.[44]

Which also means I can't relax around Nani. Not just mentally, either: if I were to wear my usual tracksuit and glasses, I wouldn't hear the end of it. And I'd rather not deal with her shame game, especially right now.[45]

"I don't take the LSAT until my junior year, Nani," I explain calmly.

"How's my Isaac, jaanu? I haven't seen that boy in a long time."

I stiffen. Nani should have been a lawyer with her ability to come in with nothing but hard-hitting questions, all with a face incapable of betraying a single emotion.

"Still on campus, I'm sure." At least, I'm assuming; he texted earlier today with a casual *Happy Friday* and we left it at that. In the past, he would have texted to ask if we could catch up, tell each other about our weeks. Not lately, though.

My chest aches.

Oblivious to my anguish, Nani slides a bowl of goat curry with naan in front of me, even though I'm certain I've explained to her a hundred times that I'm a pescatarian. "He can make time for us," she says. "Tell

---

44      Nani reminds me of Isaac's mom. Maybe that's the reason why I don't crumble into dust whenever Isaac's mom not-so-subtly criticizes me. I'm used to it. Relatively speaking.

45      The last time she caught me in my tracksuit, she told me, and I quote, "Only sad people dress like that, beti. And what could you possibly have to be sad about?" Her visiting, for starters. But if I said that out loud, I'm convinced she would beat me with her chappal.

him to come over for dinner."

"That's a nice idea!" Mom claps her hands together, the most enthusiastic I've seen her about anything in a while. "Ani, text him. He's only forty-five minutes away; we'll wait for him to get here."

"Don't pressure her, Sabina," comes Dad's soft voice.

"I'm not *pressuring* her, I'm just saying—"

"It's fine," I say suddenly. "I'll text him and ask."

There's a pause, and I realize it's because they're all waiting expectantly. I swallow a sigh and pull out my phone from my weekend bag. The screen glows with a notification, and once again, my heart soars up my throat, buoyed with *hope*.

Only, it's a text from Crocs.

> **Hey. Been waiting at the bus stop for a while. Are you coming?**

Oh.

*Oh.*

I look at the time; it's already six. Has he really been waiting for *a whole two hours*?

"What's wrong?" asks Mom, but I ignore her.

*Crap.* I need to do damage control. I think this is the first time I've *ever* forgotten about a meeting. I normally keep a calendar, make sure I schedule out my week in advance. But between seeing Isaac with that girl and my newfound love affair with my Switch, it completely slipped my mind. It's unlike me. It's embarrassing. *Infuriating.* I'm supposed to be better than this! I mean, just because Isaac has me turned into a ball of nerves doesn't mean I get to be garbage to other people. Not even to Crocs.

I should apologize, of course; I won't make any excuses. But how do I even *start*—

"Ani," Mom says suddenly, ripping me out of my own head.

"Yes?" I ask, looking up from my phone. "Oh. Uh, Isaac says he can't come," I lie. "He's seriously really busy with the South Asian Students Association and studying."

Mom clicks her tongue. "That boy is always so busy. Tell him to take a break. I'll make him chicken karahi, his favorite. Tell him I insist."

"Karahi chicken? Why?" Dad frowns as he sets down his copy of *Cancer Cytopathology*. "Your mom just made so much food—there's no need to make more. He can eat what we already have."

"It doesn't take any time to make karahi chicken," Mom replies, jaw tight. "He's our future son-in-law. The least I could do is make him a single dish. Or are we so poor we can't even afford that?"

"It's a waste of food. You don't need to bend over backward."

"Who said I'm bending over backward? It's a small gesture and it takes no time. It's what you do when you *care about someone*."

Oh my God. They're arguing again. And in front of Nani!

"It's fine!" I interject. "I don't want to bother Isaac. I'd rather eat as a family anyway. Just us. It'd be a nice change of pace."

"See? She said it's fine," says Dad.

Mom huffs. "Of course you would say that. If we had it your way, we wouldn't even have *anyone* over," she gestures toward Nani, "not even Ammi!"

"Bas karo!" Nani yells, her voice like a sharp knife. "I'm here now, and I did not come all this way to see you two fighting." She looks at me with her steely gaze. "They still fight like this? All the time?"

I quickly nod. I *could* lie, but I'm way more afraid of Nani than my parents.

"Uffo." Nani rubs at her temples. "You are hopeless, both of you. Do you have any idea how worried you're making your family? All this fighting—it's not good for anyone!"

"You're right, Ammi," says Mom quietly. "It isn't."

With that, Mom exits the kitchen, leaving nothing but silence behind. As the seconds stretch by, neither Nani nor I move. The awkwardness is finally broken when Dad finally picks up his copy of *Cancer Cytopathology* again and reads like nothing happened—his face undecipherable, as always.

For some reason, the sight makes my heart ache.

"You should count your blessings, meri jaan," says Nani softly. I'm not sure if Dad can hear. "Despite everything, your future is still laid out in front of you, inshallah. You have Isaac. Your beauty. A set path. Not everyone is so lucky."

And I find myself . . . nodding. Because Nani's absolutely right. Mom and Dad are always talking over each other, but I got lucky: I fell for someone who I've only ever gotten along with. And I bet if I were to talk to Isaac about the weird feeling of distance between us—which, frankly, is a quaint problem to have compared to my parents'—we'd clear things up in no time.

Perhaps I've just been overreacting. After all, besides this one little hiccup, I've never had reason to doubt Isaac. Never doubted *us*.

So there's no reason to start doubting now. After all, if there's one thing I've learned from reading romance novels like *Lovers' Quarrel*, it's that no relationship is free of at least *some* rough waters. It's called character development.

I get to my feet.

"Thanks, Nani," I reply. "I needed the reminder."

# Chapter 7

*I can do this*, I tell myself, smoothing down my skirt. *Of course I can do this.*

*Anisa Shirani doesn't back down.*

This is the mantra I repeat in my head, so many times that the words start feeling funny, before I finally knock on Isaac's dorm room door Sunday afternoon.

After a beat, the door opens, revealing Isaac in his casual weekend wear: this time, a navy-blue V-neck sweater and jeans, with ribbed brown indoor slippers I got him last year when he first left for college (because who wears outdoor shoes in the same place where you sleep). I'm glad I wore the new sweater dress I bought. I even did my eyeliner completely different—I wonder if he'll notice.

Isaac's eyes widen. He seems genuinely surprised—I rarely visit him at his dorm on Halcyon's campus,[46] especially unannounced. I don't want to be an annoyance, after all. Which is why I half consider scurrying away.

"Ani!" He blinks, collecting himself. "Hey . . . ?"

"Hi!" My eyes slide down to my feet. I still have trouble looking

---

46      His dorm building—a giant square brick monstrosity with narrow windows— is on the outskirts of Halcyon's campus, and a general pain to get to. Also, a general pain to look at.

directly at Isaac and his *sunlight-on-dewy-moss*-colored gaze, and I can't let it be a distraction now.[47]

"Sorry to barge in on you like this, but"—I push a Ziploc bag of half-thawed kebabs toward him—"my nani wanted you to have these."

"Oh. You don't have to apologize." He takes the bag with a smile. "Especially when you're giving me kebabs. Tell Nani thanks for me."

"Of course!" I say with all the enthusiasm I can muster, hoping to hide my nervousness.

The thing is, I hadn't thought about what to say beyond giving him the kebabs—my clever excuse to show up at his door. I honestly don't have the faintest clue how to go about bridging this gap. All I did know was, after my talk with Nani, I wanted to see Isaac's face, to sweep away these doubts of mine and start afresh.

And maybe to double-check Isaac's object permanence, just in case.

"You're wearing blue today," I say pathetically, just as the quiet becomes unbearable.

"Yes," replies Isaac. "Yes I am."

"Blue is also one of those colors that looks great on you."

"That is something you've said. Listen, is everything all right? I'm sure you're not here just to compliment my shirt," Isaac asks hesitantly. He leans an arm against the doorway, and my eyes trail to his wrist. He's still wearing a bracelet I gave him—a familiar, comforting sight.

"Yes! Definitely," I lie, then work up to steeling myself. "Definitely. But, um, can I ask you something? It's a weird question, and I know it's completely out of left field, and I—I don't mean to imply anything, obviously, but my thoughts are all over the place and I just have to make sure I'm not—"

---

47    There's a passage in the Quran about averting thy gaze from the opposite sex, and I'm almost a hundred percent sure God meant it for Isaac.

"Slow down, Ani." Isaac chuckles. "You can tell me what's on your mind. Please."

"O-okay. Sorry." I take a deep breath. "It's just, the other day, I saw you coming out of the math building, and there was a girl . . ." *Ugh, why is this so hard?* "You seemed really close. And I was wondering . . . who she was to you."

"Who?" Isaac's perfect brows wrinkle in thought. "Oh, you must be talking about Ellie."

*Oh God, even her name is adorable!!*

"Ellie is just a good friend," he explains, totally composed. "She's doing premed too, so we happen to be in a lot of classes together. Did you think—oh my God, I can't believe you thought that she and I—man, even the *idea* of it . . ." He laughs a little. "Is *that* what you've been worried about?"

"What do you mean?"

"I don't know, you've just seemed a little off recently. Not texting as often. You haven't even updated your Instagram in a few days. I figured something was up."

I tilt my head. Funny, I've had the same thought about him. I guess we both have been feeling the same growing distance between us—though I'm not sure that's a good thing.

"I guess I have been." I laugh. "Sorry. Guess I was just worrying over nothing, huh?"

"Yeah, you should know me better than that." Isaac smiles affectionately and nods. "But I'm glad you said something. You hardly ever tell me how you feel. And I don't want you spiraling over, you know, nothing."

I'm glad I said something, too.[48] It feels good to talk to him and

---

48    Plus, I'm not a fan of the miscommunication trope in romances. Just TALK, you fools! See how quickly things can be cleared up?!

confirm that all my fears are just that: *fears.*

But I'm not a fan of that last little thing he said, about how I never tell him how I feel, or about me spiraling. I should ask him what he meant.

As I'm debating whether it's worth it, the silence is punctured by the ringing of a phone.

"I think that's yours?" I say.

"What? Oh." Isaac's eyes dart behind him for just a moment—to his phone, sitting on the dresser by the doorway and lighting up with a name I can't quite see—and his expression goes stiff, guarded. An expression I've never seen on him before.

He quickly picks up the phone and silences it, before setting it back down, screen-first.

With that wry smile of his quickly plastered back on, Isaac leans against the doorway. "It's just a telemarketer," he explains.

"Ah, how annoying. I've started getting a bunch of spam calls too lately. The other day, someone called to tell me I needed to update my auto insurance, but I don't even have—"

This time, his phone begins to buzz. But Isaac doesn't move, ignoring it.

"Wow, those telemarketers sure are persistent." I say. "You know, my dad says it's better to pick up and tell them to take you off their list."

"Nah, it's fine."

"Are you sure? If it's too much trouble, I can do it for—"

"I said it's *fine!*" Isaac snaps. "God, sometimes you can be so . . ." He trails off.

"So what, Isaac?" I ask softly. My chest is all in knots, and it's hard to breathe. I guess I was blabbering a little, maybe, but he's *never* lost his temper at me like this before.

Isaac sighs, not meeting my eyes. "Never mind. You should go. I just—did you need anything else?"

Everything about this feels wrong. This was supposed to be an opportunity to finally spend a moment, just a moment, together. But right now, I don't want him to see how bothered I really am. How hurt I am. I want to run away.

*What is happening to us?*

"No! No," I say. "Sorry I took so much of your time."

"Sure." Isaac finally looks at me again, a little calmer. "It was—it was good seeing you, Ani," he adds, perhaps to soften the blow.

But for the first time since I've known Isaac, I can't say the same.

I didn't get this far by letting my emotions get the better of me. But now there's a nasty, vise-like ache in my heart that won't go away. It's one thing to have been feeling like there's been a growing distance between me and Isaac, but to see him smiling and flirting with Ellie, to catch him so obviously hiding something and then snap at me like that—

They're subtle, small changes. But together, they point to one horrible, undeniable thing: that our relationship is *cracking*, more than I realized. That I'm at risk of losing the future of my dreams.

And I'm at a complete loss for what to do about it.

So in the safety and confines of my dorm room—and without Kira, who's still visiting family in New Jersey—I decide the only thing I can do now is once again distract myself with something else. I pray Maghrib,[49] then fail to focus on getting some homework done. I even do a Pilates class on YouTube. Then I attempt to record a makeup tutorial for Instagram, but I keep stumbling over my words, so I give up.

---

49      I was worried that praying in college would be tricky or awkward with a roommate, but Kira has been incredibly thoughtful about it, even leaving the room when I pray to give me a few minutes of privacy. Lately, she's been reminding me when I forget. She's like an honorary Muslim.

But then I remember:

*The otome games.*

I already have the one Kira gifted me, *Rose in the Embers*, downloaded on my Switch. Maybe the otome games could give me some direction for what to do next with Isaac. I've seen articles about how romance novels have saved peoples' marriages by reminding the couple of their connection through modeling communication. Maybe otome games could also help me become more . . . emotionally literate.[50]

I quickly strip my face of makeup, change into my tracksuit, and throw on my cracked glasses. Kira, I know for a fact, keeps snacks in her bottom drawer. I grab a bag of Welch's Fruit Snacks,[51] making a mental note to Venmo her back and hook up my Switch to her TV. Finally, I throw myself into the beanbag chair we share and start up *Rose in the Embers*.

The game loads, and an introductory video of sorts begins to play, along with some catchy music that's all violins and gorgeous Japanese vocals, so I increase the volume. I take in the buffet of beautiful boys I get to choose from up on the screen. The story, it seems, is about a girl struggling to live a normal life during wartime in some vaguely East Asian country—and though she's been recently orphaned, she has a group of powerful, magical suitors watching over her. Certainly not the most profound storyline, but I'll take it.

Eventually, I choose the Victor route. Victor is the strong, silent type of character, with thick black hair and dazzling green eyes. He reminds me a little of Isaac, looks-wise, in full HD glory. Except I can talk to

---

50      It's not like my parents have been perfect models for emotional literacy. I should start a support group.

51      I try to avoid foods with saturated fats, processed sugars, or fake dyes for the sake of my skin. But this is an *emergency*. And everyone knows the best way to treat emergencies is with copious amounts of sugar.

him whenever I want, and his only focus is me.[52]

Kira was right. Otome games are amazing, and the story, despite its clichés, is strangely enthralling. These games are like a defibrillator, bringing your cold, dead heart back to life. Or maybe it's more accurate to say they're like a weighted blanket of pure love, smothering away your sadness.

I don't know how much time passes: maybe minutes. Maybe hours. All I know is I'm lost in the world of the *Rose in the Embers*, where cell phones don't exist, where Isaac doesn't exist. Where everything is Victor, and nothing hurt.

But it's not easy getting through the game, I quickly realize. The choices I make end up having horrible consequences that lead me to the aptly called Bad Endings: either my character dies or Victor dies. Somehow, I manage to reach an even *worse* ending where Victor's mind has gotten corrupted by evil, and he keeps my character locked in his own personal prison. At one point, I become so desperate to reach the Good Ending that I call Zaina, who informs me that she's never played otome games, but she's not surprised I suck at them.

"Stop being *rude* and help me pick an answer," I rasp into the phone, feeling—and probably looking—like a sun-starved gremlin.

"Fine, you freak," Zaina replies. "Show me your choice options on FaceTime and give me some context."

I do that, and after some back-and-forth, Zaina decides on Choice B, which gets me through the first big hurdle of the game. I try not to think about the implications that my little sister is infinitely better at otome games than I am—but I suppose that's why I'm playing in the first place.

"Now stop bothering me and use a walkthrough," she says, and hangs up.

---

52    As it should be, dammit.

After much turmoil,[53] finally—FINALLY—Victor is up on the screen, asking me, with distressingly heart-wrenching eyes, if I have feelings for him.

My hands on the controller are damp, and my heart vibrates with nervous energy. I sit up in the beanbag chair as the options for what my character can say next appear on the screen:

1) "..."

2) "I don't know ..."

3) "O-of course not!"

4) "Don't you already know the answer to that?"

Though I'm tempted to select the third option, the story walkthrough I've pulled up on my phone says I have to choose the fourth if I want a happy ending, so I do.[54]

The screen changes. A new image appears on the screen, revealed by a slow camera pan. When the image comes in full focus, I nearly choke on a Fruit Snack as I muffle a squeal.

Victor is kissing me—well, my character, but *still*. V*ictor. Is. Kissing. Me!*

I wanted a distraction from Isaac, but *this*—this is somehow even more intense than a romance novel. I can't breathe. Strangely, I hear a loud thumping. Is that my heart? It must be the rush of blood. Every vein in my body feels like it's on fire, and it almost hurts, but it also feels ... good somehow.

*"I can't stop. Can I ... keep going?"* Victor begs in a deep, sultry voice.

---

53    Which mostly just consists of me searching online for a reliable game walkthrough.

54    Seriously, I cannot believe there are websites dedicated to entire walkthroughs for every otome game out there, just to guide players through every possible ending. Fandoms are *amazing.*

Holy *shit*!!!! My fingers tremble. The thumping noise gets louder; my heart must be rolling around in my ribs like it's lovesick. How the hell are *pixels* supposed to make you feel *this overwhelmed*?!

I swallow hard.

And I slam *Yes*.

The screen goes dark for just a moment. And then I'm rewarded with a new image on my screen, punctuated by the sounds of Victor's heavy breathing.

This time, a shriek escapes me and I fall off my beanbag chair. And just as I do, the door rips open. *My* door.

I'm dragged back into reality. Beams of light cut from the hallway through the darkness of my dorm room. God, I must have wasted *several* hours playing because the sun has long set and I'd even forgotten to turn on the lights. But that's not the problem here.

The problem is who is standing in the doorway.

It's none other than Crocs, who for some abominable reason has let himself into my room, a worried expression on his face. "I'm sorry, I didn't mean to barge in—it's just, I tried knocking a few times, and then I heard a scream and—"

He stops, eyes taking in my mess-of-a-self on the floor, and I watch, in horror, as they glide to the screen in front of me.

Oh God.

Oh *God*!!!!

Crocs—I mean, Marlow—knows what I really look like!

No, worse: Marlow knows what I really look like and *has just walked in on me watching a sex scene in an otome game!*

I want to perish on the spot. Since that's not possible, though, my only other options are to jump out the window or knock him out with Kira's badminton racquet. But wait: maybe he won't recognize me. With my cracked glasses and tracksuit, I look *completely* different. There is no way *anyone* outside my family could tell who I am right now, especially when the room is this dark and—

"Anisa?" Marlow steps toward me. "You're Anisa, right?"

*Oh God!!!!!!!!!!*

Officially panicking now, I jump to my feet. Stand in front of the screen, trying to cover it, to no avail. "Okay, it's not what it looks like," I say, sounding more desperate than I'd like. "It's just a game. My interests are *purely* literary!"

"Not to shame you or anything, but I don't think that makes it any better."

"No, no—see, my friend told me to try it. It's not, um, p-porn or hentai or anything like that, I *swear*. It's a dating sim where you romance these virtual guys and—it just so happened that I *just* got to the sex scene when you walked in, and this is my first time; I don't normally—"

"Again, not sounding any better here."

I run my hands down my face. My eyes are painfully dry, and my cheeks are hot against my palms, and my glasses keep sliding down my nose because again, they're broken, and oh my God I'm so stupid why didn't I make sure the door was *locked*?

"*Please* don't tell anyone about this," I beg. If Isaac and I are already on rough waters, the last thing I need is people finding out about *this*.

Marlow blinks, as if finally absorbing the situation: finding me like *this*, on the floor in front of my screen, paused in the middle of what *definitely* counts as NSFW artwork, with nothing but the painfully corny sax-and-violin music coming from my speakers to fill the silence between us.

Then, slowly, a smile breaks across his face, and there's a glint of something in his eyes that makes my blood run cold. The sudden transformation is unsettling: there's no sign of the guy who followed me around after class, the guy who asked for my biryani. It's like he's gone from being an annoying Golden Retriever . . .

. . . to a cat who's cornered a mouse.

"Or else *what*?" he challenges, tilting his head.

I swallow hard. "Or else . . . nothing. I'm simply asking you. As a classmate."

He folds his arms across his chest. "You haven't exactly been acting like a classmate. Avoiding me, ignoring my emails, my texts, all when we have a paper together."

Right. Of course. I was supposed to apologize for standing him up, but I forgot to respond to his texts. *Again.*

"Not gonna lie," he continues, sighing, "I was pretty bummed about how rude you've been, especially when our grade depends on this paper. I even had to track you down—which, by the way, was not fun because, understandably, people on this campus do *not* take kindly to strange dudes asking where some girl lives. At least, until I had to explain that I was looking for my partner for a class paper *she* doesn't seem to care about, but *I* do."

He leans against the doorway, smug. "On the bright side, you've given me quite the gift here. I get the sense, based on how you act in class, not many people have seen you like this. Maybe even no one. Am I right?"

I clench my fists.

"Look," I respond, "I'm sorry about ignoring you; I really, really am. And I do care about the paper, but I've got a lot on my plate at the moment. It would just be easier to do the paper over email."

"And deal with you ghosting me again? Nuh-uh. Don't you think it's only fair, given the situation, that we work on my terms?"

"I won't ghost you again, I swear."

He snorts. "Given your track record, how am I supposed to believe you?"

I hate to admit it, but Marlow has a point. But I need him to believe me, to forgive me. This boy practically has my life in his hands! It's not like he even needs proof; a rumor this bizarre could be enough to ruin my reputation. If word got out that Anisa Shirani was playing sexy romance games in the dark like some forlorn pervert, and Isaac found out—

Aughhh. How would I even explain myself?

"I don't know! You'll just have to trust me, please. What do you want as assurance? You want to blackmail me? Fine. I'll do your homework for the rest of the semester. I'll act like your personal servant. I'll give you my first-born child! Just please, don't tell anyone about this."

A look of horror crosses Marlow's face. "Jesus, I'm not going to blackmail you. What the hell is wrong with you?"

"I don't know, it's just—it's a trope. People do things like that."

"What *trope*? What are you—*no*. None of that." Marlow rubs at the space between his brows. "Is it really that bad if people know you play these games?"

"Yes."

"Fine. Look." Marlow takes a step toward me. "I won't tell anyone about what I've seen as long as I get an *apology*. And a promise that you act like a nice, decent classmate instead of blatantly ignoring me, so we can get a good grade on this paper."

I purse my lips. I'll admit, I *have* been blatantly ignoring him.

"How do I know you won't just go around telling people anyway?" I ask.

"I don't see how you have much of a choice," Marlow replies, shrugging.

He's right. A fact that suddenly gives me a horrible stomachache.[55]

"Fine. I'm sorry," I mumble. "I won't ignore you anymore. Promise."

---

55     And honestly? I don't think all those fruit snacks are helping.

"Great!" Marlow claps his hands together. "So! We can meet up at the Coffee Ring? Tomorrow, around four?" The Coffee Ring is the campus café at Halcyon. I've never been there, though I know Isaac sometimes holds his SASA meetings there. "Or we could do it at the library, if you'd prefer."

"The library," I mumble again. "I prefer the library."

"The library it is." Marlow turns on his heel, opens the door that leads out into the hallway. "See you tomorrow, *partner*. Oh and . . ." He gestures at the screen, where Victor and my character are tangled together in a fluffy pink bed. "Enjoy your night."

He closes the door behind him.

I wait for the sound of his footsteps to fade. The room goes quiet, save for the frantic slamming of my heart against my rib cage and the sexy saxophone music coming from the TV screen.

I scream into a pillow.

JANUARY 29TH

I'm so sorry to bug you with this 12:28 PM

What's up? 12:28 PM

And this is kind of embarrassing but 12:29 PM

any chance you could . . . 12:35 PM

take care of some laundry for me?
I know that's asking a lot. 12:35 PM

Oh! 12:36 PM

Yes, I can do that 12:39 PM

Thank you. It's for SASA 12:40 PM

We just got these new club shirts in 12:40 PM

I thought it'd be nice to wash
them before handing them out 12:40 PM

I'd do it myself but 12:41 PM

I literally have NO time 12:41 PM

Not a problem 12:41 PM

I can do that tonight? 12:42 PM

Thanks, Ani 🙏 12:42 PM

You're the best 12:42 PM

I try 🙂 12:43 PM

# Chapter 8

## JANUARY 29

Thanks to Marlow walking in on me on yesterday, I have no choice but to keep my promise and face him again,[56] which means hopping on the bus to Halcyon, asking a couple of friendly looking students—who thankfully were all too eager to help me find my way—for directions to the library, and scanning high and low between the stacks to track him down.[57]

I eventually find him at a desk by a window. He has a satisfied expression on his face as he stares at the open textbook in front of him, the light from the window casting a warm glow on his dark brown skin—nary a hint of the jerk who walked in on me last night.

Across from him, there's an empty seat he's saved for me with his backpack.

"Well, well, look who it is," Marlow says cheerfully. "Sans tracksuit, though. What a shame." Even his dimples seem to be mocking me.

I suck in my lips as a response. I guess there's no painting over his memory with my current outfit, a midi-length Coach skirt over tights paired with a cream-colored knit sweater. I even did a deep conditioner

---

56     I made the mistake of telling Kira how Marlow walked in on me playing *Rose in the Embers*—I omitted the part about me looking the way I did—and she laughed harder than I've ever seen her laugh about *anything*.

57     He gave the vaguest of locations, in part, I think, to assert authority. Or piss me off.

mask on my hair this morning for some extra je ne sais quoi.[58] But clearly, even with this get-up, he has no intention of forgetting what I looked like last night.

Of all the people to see me—why Crocs? The nerve of it all, especially when he's wearing an old T-shirt that literally reads *Chin-chillin'*.

I rip his backpack from the chair violently and slide it across the floor toward him. I feel him watching me, seemingly amused as I sit and take out my Race & Ethnicity textbook, colorful tabs sticking out of every corner.[59]

"Whew, you look *exhausted*," observes Marlow. "Up late playing through that, uh, *spicy* scene, huh? How do those games even *work* exactly—"

I slam my hand on the table. *"Shhh!!! What if someone hears you?"*

"Wow. Sorry, my bad," Marlow says, putting his hands up. "Any particular reason why you're so ashamed about your love of romance games?"

"Why does everyone always ask me that? I'm not *ashamed*." Sort of. "I just don't need my personal interests being publicly advertised. In a *library*." Besides, we're on Halcyon territory. What if Isaac got wind of it?

Ugh. My stomach starts hurting all over again.

Marlow smirks. "Well, as long as you're all right, minus the, uh, insomnia."

My eyebrow twitches. I would feel better if he would just completely forget what he saw, but what's done is done. I sigh.

"So, first things first: we need to narrow down a topic."

"Uh-huh," I respond blandly.

---

58    Some people might call it overcompensating. Some might be right.

59    Because despite everything that's happened, I've still been on top of the reading. Even if it's been . . . slow going lately.

65

"How about we write down a bunch of different possible topic ideas and then go through them together? I think I'm going to put down Ethnic Health Care Disparities—I'm definitely interested in that—and then maybe—"

"Actually," I interrupt, "I've already started looking at Siddis in Pakistan and racial intolerance. They're an ethnic African community, and Arab merchants brought many of them over to what is now Pakistan as slaves. But there's some interesting divergence happening within the community regarding dynamics of ethnic identity, not to mention the obvious discrimination they face."

Somewhere along my otome-filled haze, I managed to do a little research for the paper ahead of time. Marlow looks taken aback.

"I was kind of hoping we'd choose a topic together," he says, "but it looks like you've beaten me to it." A beat. "Out of curiosity, are you the kind of person that needs full control all the time?"

I narrow my eyes. "Are you trying to call me a control freak?"

"No! No. Just curious. Aaanyway, I'll let it slide since that's a pretty cool topic. I'm on board."

I feel myself unwind a little. If I'm being perfectly honest, I was expecting Marlow to be more disagreeable. But it seems like he might be surprisingly easy to work with.

It's nice to feel in control of at least one aspect of my life right now.[60]

I clear my throat. "Okay. Great. Let's read through chapter six in the textbook, because I think that'll be a good introduction to the caste and other racial dynamics in South Asia. Then we can start actual research."

I realize I'm being bossy, so I add: "Does that work with you . . . ?"

---

60     As to Marlow's accusation of me being a bit of a control freak . . . maybe he has a point. Not that I'd tell *him* that.

Marlow nods and starts reading the textbook chapter, even highlighting portions with the biggest, most garish orange highlighter I've ever seen.

So I start reading, too. The library feels peaceful for a Monday afternoon. Occasionally, I hear whispers from behind the bookshelves nearby, the flutter of paper, the clicking of a computer mouse. I fight the urge to check my phone, to see if there's anything new from Isaac. . . .

I look up and realize Marlow isn't reading anymore.

He's watching *me*.[61]

My cheeks start to flare. "What are you looking at?" I ask, suspicious.

"I was wondering—you're South Asian, right?" he asks, smiling.

I bristle. "Yes . . . ?"

He laughs. "Sorry, is that a weird question? Maybe it's because of where I'm from, but I figure there's this unspoken rule that we can just get those questions out of the way like it's no big deal. I'm half Indian myself, by the way. Grew up in Jamaica, in Kingston."

I quirk a brow. "Jamaica? But you don't have the accent?"

"Yeah . . ." His voice trails, hesitating. "I never really had a strong accent to begin with, though. So what about you? You said you're South Asian?"

He changed the subject. Well, if he doesn't want to go into details, that's none of my business.

"I'm Pakistani American,"[62] I answer.

"That explains the biryani. Oh right, did you ever get to deliver it?"

---

61    Again, totally used to people staring at me. But not so intently. Not so *shamelessly*.

62    All things considered, I love being a Pakistani American. Being Pakistani means some of the best food (biryani! nihari!), some of the prettiest clothes (lehenga! sherwani!), and some of the best people—except maybe Aunty Lubna.

"I . . . didn't get a chance."

The girl Isaac was with comes to life in my mind again, and unwanted thoughts, thoughts that should be beneath me, invade: how she's taller than I am, bolder than I am, effortlessly prettier than I am. I don't know if I could even blame him if she caught his eye.[63]

"He was busy and I—I didn't want to intrude," I add. Isaac *says* he's been busy, but I can't help but wonder: what if she's the reason? Coupled with how shady he was acting when his phone went off—yeah. I'm . . . worried.

"So the biryani delivery was for the guy, huh? You know, I think I've seen him around before." Marlow looks incredulous as he tilts his head and pauses, deep in thought. "I think I recognize that girl he was with, too—I think they're in my Bio 2 class. Or at least, I'm pretty sure."

I feel an annoying prickle of curiosity. "Is that so?" I wonder if he's seen Isaac and Ellie together in class. If he's seen them sitting next to each other, laughing together.

Marlow leans forward in his seat. "Are they friends of yours?"

"Not . . . exactly."

"But you're clearly friends with the guy, or *something*. If you're going out of your way to bring him *food*." He rubs at his chin thoughtfully. "At least, you *were*, up until you saw him with that girl. . . ."

His gaze snags on mine. I look away and pretend to settle on my notebook, but I can feel him grinning at me.

"Oh, I get it. You have a crush on him, don't you? You got it *bad*."

My jaw clenches. Nosy bastard.

"You should have said something! I could have played wingman—"

---

63    I mean, I *could*, but hell, she even caught *my* eye.

"Isaac and I *are* together," I snap. "Our families have intended for us to be together since we were *kids*. We're practically engaged and have been for a very long time, thank you very much."

"Then why didn't you say hi to him instead of acting like some kind of lovestruck fangirl?" His mouth opens, like he's just realized something. "Ohh. Oh no, I see. Trouble in paradise?"

"Everything is *fine*."

"I didn't say it wasn't. I mean, not exactly, but—"

"You didn't have to," I retort, my voice rising far higher than I intended. "What's your deal? You don't even know him, let alone *me*. And frankly, none of this is your business. You and I are partners for a class paper who've spoken a grand total of maybe three times, so you have no right—*no right*—to say *anything* to me about *my* relationship."

I look away, furious. Marlow can tease me all he wants, but bringing up Isaac is a step too far. Worst of all, hearing someone else voice my own suspicions about Isaac, confirming what it looks like . . . it hurts.

Because if a total stranger can see it, how can I deny it?

I look at him again, expecting to see that infuriatingly smug smile of his. Only, Marlow isn't smiling anymore.

He lets out a long breath.

"You're right. I'm sorry, I shouldn't tease. I don't know you or your situation. It's just, I'm—" Marlow stops and shakes his head. "I hope that changes, though. Getting to know you, I mean. At least for the paper.

"But for whatever it's worth," he adds carefully, "I think any relationship should, I don't know, make you as happy as those games clearly do."

His earnestness catches me so off guard, I don't know how to respond. But somehow, hearing him try to comfort me makes me want to curl up on the ground in self-pity. I'm grateful my hair is covering the sides of my face as I stare down at the unfinished outline in my notebook.

The last thing I hear is Marlow's soft voice, saying something about grabbing us some coffee.

And then he's gone.

# Chapter 9

## FEBRUARY 2

As much as I'm loath to admit it, I'm *ashamed*.[64]

I don't normally lose my cool around people I barely know, but I'm guessing that day with Marlow, between the lack of sleep and a rare bout of self-doubt, I was especially on edge. Vulnerable. Marlow hasn't even asked to meet up for the paper since then; either he's giving me breathing room or he's decided I'm a hot mess and we're better off doing the paper independently after all.

But that expression of his—the way he looked at me at the library, with a pinning stare like he was reading something on my face, something I couldn't see. Was it pity?

My emotions are seriously all over the place. Even the one text I got from Isaac this week, a friendly *Miss you* after I dropped off the laundry didn't quite hit the same way as it normally would.

So when Friday rolls around again and Mom shoots me a text asking me to come home for the weekend, I reluctantly say yes—mostly so I can focus on the Spivak reading I need to do for my Critical Feminist Studies class, and maybe get some extra studying done.

For once, I'm almost looking forward to it.

By the time I half crawl through the back entrance of the house, my

---

64    Which, frankly, isn't something I'm used to feeling.

parents and Zaina are already eating dinner—chicken biryani, from the looks of it, which unfortunately makes me think of Marlow. Nani, however, is standing sentry over a tower of dirty plates by the sink.

"Sweetheart,[65] good, you're home," Mom says, sounding entirely too chipper. Considering the only other time she texted me this week was to ask if she should wear a green or blue blazer for some meeting with a big client, her fake *I'm so happy to see you* voice is especially grating. "Go grab yourself a plate; come, sit. Did you have a good week?"

I head for the medicine cabinet and steal a couple Excedrin Migraine. "Always."

"Figured out what you're doing for your birthday yet?" Zaina asks before wolfing down half the biryani on her plate.

Truthfully, I haven't even thought about my birthday, even though it's in a little over two weeks.

Part of me just assumed that since Isaac and I would be in college together for the first time, he would be the one to plan something for me. I'd hinted as much a few months ago: how nice it would be to have a romantic picnic by the pond at Marion, or a small dinner party with our mutual friends in one of the common rooms. Except I have yet to meet any of his friends, and if he's been planning anything, he certainly hasn't shown any signs.

I wonder if it's safe to take more than two Excedrin.

"Nothing yet," I answer.

Dad speaks up from the dinner table. "You can always come back home and celebrate your birthday with us." His voice is soft. Tired. I wonder if he's getting enough sleep.

"We could even invite Isaac," chimes Mom, smiling. "Unfortunately,

---

65     She NEVER calls me that, so this was an instant red flag.

Nani will have to head back by then."

"You're leaving already?" Normally when Nani visits, she stays for several weeks at a time. "Why so soon?"

Nani goes still at the sink, and at the dinner table, my parents' hands stop moving over their plates.

Mom doesn't meet my stare. "Ani, your dad and I have decided to get a divorce."

I—

*What?*

I feel my heart collapse to my stomach. *Divorce?*

"You can't be serious. Please tell me you're kidding. You can't just— Zaina, did you know?"

Zaina stares at her lap. "They told me yesterday."

Mom clicks her tongue. "Come now, Ani, you're perfectly old enough. You're not a child anymore; this won't affect you in the way you're probably thinking."

My voice comes out strangled. "Of course it'll affect me! It'll affect all of us! You're telling me we're not going to have a family anymore!" Maybe I was being naive not to think all their fighting would eventually lead to a choice. Naive to not expect divorce as a strong possibility someday. But I can't accept it. I don't *want* to accept it. Even if they fight sometimes, at least we'd still be *together.*

A divorce, though—that's the end of the road.

What would happen to us? Where would Zaina live? What happens during the holidays, during Eid—how will we celebrate together? What about my future wedding? Won't Mom and Dad be so lonely? I know divorce is the best option for some couples, but Mom and Dad don't have people they can talk to, no personal therapists who'd help them sort through the emotional aftermath—how would they recover from this?

And worst of all: What does this mean for me and Isaac? Will our love be doomed to fail, too?

I've seen the stats, the studies: daughters of divorced parents have a sixty-percent higher divorce rate in marriages than children of non-divorced parents. It doesn't even matter how accurate the study is; divorce is still very much taboo in brown communities. Some parents, like Aunty Lubna, will look at that and assume it's definitive that I'll be a crap wife, that despite all my accomplishments, I won't be good enough for their son.

I can hear the gossip now: *Anisa comes from a broken family. What if she takes after her parents? What if she brings a broken home wherever she goes?*

Aunty Lubna's disapproving face flashes through my mind, and my vision warps.

No. I can't let this happen. Things between Isaac and I are already precarious as it is; if news of my parents' divorce gets out, it could be the final straw.

Why is everything falling apart?

"Anisa," Mom says slowly, like she's trying to calm a petulant child, "I need you to understand and respect our decision. Don't be selfish. It's like I said to Nani: you need to think about what's best for us, not just you."

"I *am* thinking about what's best for us!" I snap. "Divorce is permanent, for one thing. If you do this, there is no going back. You've been married for over twenty years. Why divorce *now*? It'll ruin our reputation in the community."

"You think I don't know that?" Mom replies. The rims of her eyes look red. "This isn't something we take lightly. We know, better than anyone, how this could affect our reputation. You think we're happy about how people will talk badly about us? You think if we had a choice, we'd go through with this?"

"I don't know! Because you *do* have a choice, Mom. You two could have gone to couples counseling, but you didn't. Zaina and I are the ones who don't have a choice. Okay? You mapped out our entire lives for us, and we've met every expectation you've placed on us." Mom raises a hand to interrupt, but all my anger's flooding out of my mouth and I can't stop. "Every expectation! Straight As all throughout high school, making valedictorian, getting into a top college, no social life to speak of—whatever you wanted! So the—"

"Anisa!" Mom yells. I nearly jump at the sharpness of her voice.

The silence settles down between us like a concrete wall.

Calling my parents selfish was definitely a step too far—not to mention I never raise my voice at my parents, especially not when Nani's here. But I'm hurt and I'm broken and I'm confused. I don't know what else to say. Getting a divorce when they haven't done a thing to repair their relationship, when they haven't even tried counseling, feels like a total cop-out. Am I supposed to just smile and nod in this situation?

"Dad, please. You can still fix this," I whisper. "Please reconsider. Or at least hold off. *Please.*"

Dad's normally stoic, unchanging face falters for a moment: his moustache twitches, like he's trying to find the words to say. He looks strangely pale.

Finally, he sighs. "We've already made our decision. I know you're worried about the future, but things happen for a reason. I'm sorry, beti."

My last hope. Shattered.

"Yes, well." I swallow bitterly. "Me too."

I pick up my overnight bag. "I'm going to my room," I announce, already making my way up the staircase.

No one says anything. No one even tries to stop me.

And suddenly, I feel more alone than I've ever felt in my entire life.

# Chapter 10

"How do people live not knowing the future?" I ask Kira Monday morning. After Mom and Dad dropped the bomb of their divorce on me, I spent the rest of the weekend giving in to my insomnia and finishing the Victor route in *Rose in the Embers.*

In many ways, Victor has become my 2D emotional support boy, for which I am grateful. But now it's time to move on to a different route, and this time I choose Collin, a youthful, angelic-looking blond man with a dark past. Unlike my real life, the otome game, at least, is going smoothly.

Meanwhile, Kira is sitting on her bed, relaxing after early-morning badminton practice. She's changed into her PJs—pastel blue shorts and a black T-shirt with Ha-ru's (her favorite LØVE LIFE member) face plastered on it—and she's scrolling through her phone. Probably reading another webtoon.[66]

"So you're asking me," Kira says slowly, "how everyday, normal, mortal humans live?"

"Yes."

"I don't know what kind of existential crisis you're having, but I can tell you it's probably not that deep. Not knowing exactly what the future

---

[66]    She tried to introduce me to webtoons the other day, but after she introduced me to otome games, I am fearful of her recommendations. They're too powerful.

holds has its own perks. Think of it this way: every day is an *adventure*."

"Um. Why did you say it like that?"

"Like what?"

"Like you're in pain . . . ?"

"It's called being human." Kira's eyebrows crinkle in annoyance as she stares at her phone screen again. "Unlike XOLOVE47823 who is *clearly* a bot!"

"What?"

"I'm trying to win this damn auction," she explains. "LØVE LIFE's management is auctioning off a signed LØVE LIFE EP for charity, and somehow I keep getting outbid by some user named XOLOVE47823 who's currently number one on my shit list. I swear I'm losing hair over this."

"Oh, I have a fantastic rosemary oil serum for hair—"

"No thank you."

While Kira goes back to fighting bots on an auction site, I set down my Switch, contemplating if I should post photos of the new Kulfi Beauty cream eye shadow palette I bought. But I know I'm just stalling. What I *should* be doing is texting Isaac, asking him out to lunch or something. Anything. I should be in full disaster-control mode. For all I know, his mom has already found out about the divorce and is cackling in a dark tower somewhere, making plans to marry Isaac off to someone else. Someone who isn't *me*.

I grab my phone and shoot him a message, inviting him over to grab something together at the Halcyon dining hall, and get a response almost a minute later.

Except it's Marlow.

> **Want to meet later today to wage more war on our paper?** ⚔️

We left things on an awkward note last time, but I suppose I don't have a choice; time's ticking for the paper, due in a month and a half now. Not to mention there's no telling what Marlow will do if I ignore him again. But I'm kind of glad he reached out first. Especially with a message that's so . . . casually normal.

I send off a response to Marlow:

> **The wise warrior avoids the battle. But sure. See you later.**

"Prince Charming?"[67] Kira asks, not looking up from her screen.

"No," I reply, trying my best not to sound so forlorn about it.

"He's been MIA recently, huh?"

Last semester, during the first couple months of school, Isaac would take me out to nearby restaurants for dinner—to "get away from cafeteria food," he'd said. Kira even met him once, when he came to pick me up from our dorm. She's been calling him Prince Charming ever since, though as usual, I can't really tell if she's being sarcastic or not.

I guess it was a matter of time before even she noticed his absence lately.

"It's a lot of work, juggling all his premed classes and being president of the SASA. You know there's like, thirty members this year, and they have four different events they're hosting this semester?" I turn in my chair and start organizing the top of my desk, even though I'm pretty sure I organized it a few days ago. "He's busy. He's always busy these days. Poor guy barely has any time for himself, much less me."

Even I can tell it sounds like I'm making excuses.

"Mm-hmm. Definitely." Kira sets down her phone. "You know, I was VP of the K-Pop Club back in high school. I was swamped all the time."

---

67     You know when people give you a nickname but you're not sure if it's a compliment or an insult? That's how I feel about this one.

"Really?" I can't imagine Kira willingly being a leader of any club. She's the kind of person who'd rather rule from the shadows. Or at least watch the chaos unfold with a bag of popcorn.

"Yeah, trying to convince teachers we were actually doing legitimate work was a pain in the ass. But I even managed to get them to believe we organized a day-long field trip to Koreatown in New York, for educational purposes. We didn't even go. We all just used it as a skip day. Personally, I slept in, went to a boba place, and then played video games till two in the morning. It was a good day."

"How on earth did you pull that off?"

"Nearly didn't. One of our clubmates turned traitor and almost told on us. But I got him to see reason." Kira leans back against her headrest, a smug queen on her throne.

I don't want to know how she managed that.

"This is all to say," she continues, "if Isaac is neglecting you, and you're bummed about it, then there's no shame in fighting for what you want, by any and all means."

She turns back to the webtoon on her phone. "Otherwise, bring him to me. I'm *very* good at scaring people."

"One iced coffee for you, one iced coffee for me," Marlow says, setting down two clear plastic cups in front of us, condensation dripping onto the table.

I move my notebook out of the way, narrowly avoiding the mini pool of water taking form, and hope the annoyance isn't too obvious on my face.

We're back in the library, at the same spot as last time. I only have two morning classes on Monday—a Writing Seminar and my Arabic class—so Marlow and I agreed to meet in the late afternoon to beat the evening rush of students hogging all the good spots. We need to hash out this paper fast if we have any hope of finishing by the end of spring break. And that means getting my head on straight.

Marlow tosses a few packs of sugar and wooden stirrers on the table and takes the seat across from me. "You do drink coffee, right?" he asks, like it's the most obvious question in the world. "I mean, who doesn't?"

Isaac doesn't, but I decide not to tell him that. It's also quite the choice to have iced coffee in February when it's about thirty degrees outside, but I'm running on fumes and won't complain about any form caffeine takes.

"Yes, thank you." I take my cup, start dumping in two packets of sugar and half debating whether to add a third. "Oh right, how much do I owe you?"

Marlow smiles. "Nothing."

The sleep deprivation must be really getting to me because I'm almost touched. It's been a long time since someone's treated me to something for no reason.

I swallow a sigh.

"So how do we want to split up the paper? Section by section?" asks Marlow. "Or you could write the first ten pages, and I write the last ten? I'm pretty good at finishing, if I do say so myself." He pauses. "That was supposed to be a joke, though judging by your expression, not a good one. Anyway, what if we just focus on finishing the outline for the paper and—"

I watch him talk: his big, expressive eyes, his dimples and unfading grin, his openness.

I don't know anything about Marlow, I realize. Well, I guess I know he has horrible fashion sense; today, his rumpled T-shirt reads *Will Run for Food* with the image—for some ungodly reason—of a sprinting hot dog beneath it,[68] but the text is so faded from overwashing it's almost

---

68    Is this supposed to be funny? Why a hot dog? Why is it running? What is it running from? I'm so confused.

impossible to tell for sure. He's also in Bio 2 with Isaac, which means he's likely a science major. But that's where the similarities with Isaac end.

Truthfully, I don't understand him at all.

"Anyone home in there?"

I'm yanked out of my head by the sound of his voice, embarrassed he's caught me off guard. Seems it's becoming a habit.

"Sorry," I reply sheepishly. "You were saying?"

"I was saying I wanted to apologize again for the other day." Marlow's smile is rueful. "I was being an ass, and I don't want my behavior to get in the way of us working together."

I'm taken aback by the sincerity in his voice. "Oh. Thanks. I . . . I appreciate that," I say, and I genuinely mean it. I guess last time we talked was really bothering him, too.

"Anyway, like I said before, I don't know the whole situation," Marlow says carefully, "but I'm sure whatever is happening, it'll be okay."

"I . . ." I open my mouth. Close it again. "I don't know. Maybe it will be; maybe I'm mistaken about the whole thing. But it's obvious there's still *something* wrong."

Marlow's face falls a little. But he waits, patiently, for me to continue. And strangely, I do.

"I think I mentioned this, but Isaac and I are intended to be married. Like an arranged marriage, sort of. It's not uncommon for Muslims to have arranged or semi-arranged marriages—"

"I'm aware," Marlow interrupts. When I stare in surprise, he continues: "I took an Islamic Studies class last semester. I like learning about different religions."

I have so many questions, but I decide to leave that for another time. "Well, anyway, it's what we've always talked about. We both want it. Our parents obviously want it. Except lately, Isaac's completely distanced himself from me, and when I tried asking him about it, he said it was because his schedule's swamped. He's been acting a little . . . weird, and it feels like he's hiding something. I don't know what to think."

I suddenly remember the text I got from Isaac yesterday, after I'd asked if he wanted to catch up over the phone:

**I'm so sorry but I'm drowning in work for Orgo right now. Barely have time to eat ☹ Rain check soon?**

These days, it's the same old story. Every time.

"That doesn't mean anything. He really could just be busy," offers Marlow, shaking his head.

"He could be . . ." I trail off. God, I must be *desperate* if I'm talking to a random classmate about this. But Marlow letting me unload on him—it doesn't feel as bad as I thought it would. Maybe it's because for once, I don't feel like I have anything to prove.

Before I know it, the words are practically falling out of me.

"When I saw him the other day with that girl," I go on, "seeing him smiling like that with someone else—it made me feel like I'm on the verge of losing him. I'm not the kind of person to get totally insecure seeing him talk to other people, but the timing of it—it worries me. Between him suddenly pulling away from me and all these other anxieties that've been piling up, it's like this perfect future with him I've been working so hard toward, for *so* many years, is on the verge of breaking. Plus, I have no idea how to be honest with him about my feelings, or even talk to him properly, and it's only gotten worse over the years. And now I'm having trouble focusing on school or anything and—I don't know what to do to fix it. Any of it."

All I do know is, if I want our relationship to survive my parents' divorce, and Aunty Lubna's inevitable concerns, we need to be *bulletproof.*

But . . .

"Honestly? I think I need help."

I swallow hard, but it feels like something's lodged itself deep in my vocal cords. Admitting that there's something I can't do hurts. That at the heart of all my fears, the biggest one is that Isaac might not feel the same way I do anymore.

Apparently, playing games about romance is one thing, but living one, *fixing* one, is another.[69]

Marlow stares at me, blinking back what I imagine are a hundred thoughts, probably none of them good.

"Anyway, it's fine," I say, backtracking, suddenly desperate to change the subject. The laugh that comes out of my mouth feels strained. "I'm being stupid. I'm only telling you all this because I feel like I owe you an explanation for why I was ignoring all your texts earlier. I had a lot on my mind, and the paper kept slipping out of it. So I'm sorry."

A slightly awkward silence settles between us, so my eyes fall back to my notebook, unsure of what else to say. Desperate for something to do, I pick up my pencil, gripping it tightly.

"I'm really sorry you're going through that," Marlow finally speaks, his brows knitted together. "Dealing with all this alone—it's not easy. I'm sure it hurts, trying to get through to him but feeling like you're getting nowhere. In a way, it might be easier to move on. To give up."

"Giving up isn't an option," I interrupt. "I won't. Not on him. Not on us."

"Right . . ." Marlow hesitates, and briefly I swear I see a flicker of something unbearably sad in his eyes. "Right. I guess the bright side is, it sounds like you still trust him. And as long as there's still trust,

---

69    It's just not fair. The otome games were supposed to help me get better at this! I'd write a strongly worded letter to the video game company, but Zaina would probably stop me.

then maybe nothing is broken beyond repair. So knowing that . . ." He swallows before continuing.

"What would you be willing to do to fix things between the two of you? Just how far would you be willing to go?"

My pencil stops. I look up, and Marlow's warm brown gaze collides with mine.

"What do you mean?" I ask, my throat tight.

"I'm asking if you'd do anything to fix your relationship—not because your families expect you to be together, or anything else, but because he is the one you want to be with. Full stop, no reservations whatsoever. No regrets."

"Of course," I answer immediately. "I'd do *anything*. No matter the cost or effort or the doubts I have right now. Without Isaac . . . I can't imagine a future without him."

It's the first time I've said it out loud. But as pathetic as it sounds, it's the truth.

"All right. If you're certain." Marlow's smile is surprisingly gentle. "In that case, the answer's simple."

I look at him, confused, so he goes on. "It sounds like you two have just hit some hard times. If you feel like there's distance between the two of you, then I think the only way to fix that is to find a way to reconnect. That's where I'd start, if I were you."

"Yeah, but you forgot an important detail. He's too busy for me. How am I supposed to reconnect if I rarely see him?"

Marlow shrugs. "It's not like you're on opposite sides of the planet. He's still close by. What's stopping you from seeing him whenever you want?"

"I . . ." I remember how Isaac looked talking to Ellie. His relaxed smile. "I don't want to be a bother, I guess."

He leans forward. "And that's the problem. If your heart is really set on this, you'll need to change your mindset. Someone who really loves you will never see you as a bother. I mean, what, any time he's busy, you're just going to *back away*?"

I'm taken aback. I don't know what I was expecting from the guy who wears meme T-shirts and Crocs in the snow, but it certainly wasn't this level of thoughtfulness. Kira had even said something similar: *If Isaac is neglecting you, and you're bummed about it, then there's no shame in fighting for what you want.*

I clear my throat.

"All right, fine," I concede. "I see your point. But that doesn't change the fact that I have no idea what to do differently."

"Well, let's start with the basics. What is it that you like doing together? When he *actually* has the time."

"Um." I blink. "We ate lunch at the cafeteria. That was nice." Of course, that was nearly two months ago, before Isaac started growing distant.

"Okay," Marlow says slowly, "but I meant more hobbies or fun activities. Things you both love to do together, to get to know each other."

I frown. "I know him well enough."

"That doesn't sound convincing."

"It's not like we need to know *everything* about each other before we get married! We text. And we hang out occasionally. Isn't that good enough?"

"In some cases, sure, that's valid. But just because you know you're going to get married later doesn't mean you shouldn't, I don't know, spend *some* time together now, even if it's just to talk. How else are you supposed to close the distance?"

"I . . ."

I bite my lip. The frustrating thing about all this is that Marlow's right. I know Isaac—I know Isaac's favorite book (*The Road* by Cormac

McCarthy), his favorite food (chicken karahi), his biggest dream (to take over his parents' cardiology practice). But are those superficial kinds of details, these bits of biodata, a good basis for a future together? For some people, they certainly are. For Isaac and I, though, there's something else, something deeper, in our way.

Marlow chuckles. "Wow, you *do* need help."

I look down, my stomach wringing itself. "I know." As if dealing with my parents wasn't enough. At this rate, I'll lose Isaac, too.

It's like life is throwing me a Bad Ending in an otome game, and there's nothing I can do about it.

Marlow says carefully, "What if—and hear me out before you say anything—what if I acted as your love coach?"

"I'm sorry, *what*?"

"You know. Someone you get relationship advice from. *Real* relationship advice, not something you'd get from an otome game. I do have real-world experience; unlike you, I've dated before. Plus, I'm pretty good at this stuff, if I do say so myself."

"Uh-huh."[70]

Except—the more I think about it, the more I *could* believe it. I've *seen* the way he goes out of his way to help others, the way he brings out smiles in other people with his own disarming smile. He seems unsettlingly good at breaking down walls. He may not be my type exactly—that's reserved only for Isaac—but I suppose I could see how others would find him . . . charming.

"No, seriously," Marlow insists, his hand tapping the table. "Based on what you've told me, I think the biggest issue here is that you two have

---

70      I'm reticent to trust a guy who says he's good at romance, the same way I wouldn't trust a guy who says, "I'm good with women."

been bound to each other since you were kids, right? Maybe that's made you both a little complacent."

"I am anything but complacent, thank you very much. This"—I gesture at all of me—"takes *work*, and I have studied my ass off my whole life to ensure I'm always running at Isaac's pace and then some."

"Sorry, maybe complacent isn't the word, but you know what I mean. It sounds like you haven't really bonded on any deeper level, nor even had the opportunity to learn how. Don't get me wrong; good relationships usually flow naturally, but cultivating good relationships is still a *skill*." He sat up straight again, all business. "So, I can be your sounding board, if you want. We can brainstorm ways to improve your relationship. Plus, he's a guy, I'm a guy; there might be things I pick up on that you don't."

My shoulders slump. All good points. "It's not . . . a bad idea. . . ."

The truth is, I don't know if I have any other options; I've hit a dead end, and it's not like I'm getting any less awkward around Isaac. It's gotten so bad that I've even considered asking Kira for relationship help. But knowing her, she'd just tell me to run Isaac over with a car or something.

Working with Marlow on this, though—even if he can't help me completely fix things with Isaac, Marlow simplifies things. It's almost like he helps me think a little clearer. Most important, despite everything he's seen and heard about me so far, he doesn't appear to judge.

And it'd be nice to have someone in my corner, someone who I can finally talk to about all this in a completely unfiltered way.

But maybe that's all I need right now.

"So does Isaac know about you?" asks Marlow suddenly, as if reading my mind.

I bristle. "Know *what* about me?"

"You know, your *true* form. The *undressed* version."

"Why do you have to say it like that?"

"Because you get flustered like that."

"To answer your question, no," I retort, trying to keep my expression neutral. "And for the record, Isaac can *never* know. You've seen him. He's perfect. And if *I'm* not perfect, too, then—" A sigh escapes me. "Let's just say I look this way for a good reason and that's my business."

"All right, suit yourself," Marlow says, grabbing his Race & Ethnicity textbook off the table and flipping through the pages. "If you don't want him to see that version of yourself, that's your prerogative, but I think eventually you're going to have to find some way to be fully honest with him and let down your walls." He winks. "Then again, I don't mind keeping another a secret."

I feel like I'm in a daze. This is ridiculous. Not only have I trusted this menace with my personal sob story, I'm agreeing to Crocs being my *love coach*. Ugh.

"So we're really doing this," I mutter.

"Yep. We're going to come up with a plan, get you and your fiancé—"

"Intended fiancé."

"—*intended* fiancé or whatever out of this rut and get you your Good Ending."

I release a long exhale. And then I ask him the most burning question of all, the one that's been nagging at the back of my head this whole time.

"But *why*? Why would you want to help me? You barely even know me."

Marlow looks past me for a moment, the pensive look of someone searching for the right words. "Because I know what it feels like to be alone in situations like this," he says after a while. "I know how hard it is, and I wish someone had been there for me."

The way he says it—it makes something in my chest grow soft. I wonder what his situation was. But something tells me he wouldn't say even if I asked.

"Oh, but I should also add, in the spirit of transparency," he says, "I think I like you."

I blink hard. I'm 100 percent certain I've misheard.

"I'm sorry, *what*?"

"I just think you're an interesting person and it'd be cool to get to know you, I guess. That's all there is to it. Call it a little crush or whatever. And if that makes you uncomfortable, we can drop this whole thing right now and forget it happened. But I just want you to know that I respect your feelings and your relationship with your intended fiancé."

He can't possibly be serious, so I wait for him to say he's joking. But he doesn't.

A crush. Crocs has a crush on me? *Why*?[71] I haven't exactly been nice to him—unless he's a masochist? Or just plain delusional? Maybe I should feel a little sorry for the guy.

I tap a finger on the desk, deep in thought. I've gotten a confession or two from other boys, back in high school,[72] but I never took them seriously. I had Isaac, after all, and after a short while, the other boys gave up. Crushes, passion—it's all fleeting.[73] Marlow will be no different. As long as he doesn't let it interfere with this whole love coaching deal, I can put up with mildly uncomfortable feelings for now.

More than that, I find that I believe Marlow when he says he respects my feelings about Isaac.

---

71      I mean, from a logical standpoint I get why, but *still*.

72      Dan Vargas did a whole promposal for me back in junior year, which I had to turn down. He and the strawberry cupcake he got me (which read PROM? in pink icing) were very sweet. I did have to ask him what bakery he got the cupcake from, though, because seriously, that cupcake was DIVINE.

73      Just look at my mom and dad, for example.

Finally, I clear my throat. "It's okay. I'm sure you'll get over it, anyway."

Marlow laughs softly. "Wow, that just feels insulting."

But all this does bring up an important question, one that I decide to ask. "If you really did like me, though . . . wouldn't it make more sense for you to hope things *don't* work out with me and Isaac?"

Marlow makes a bewildered expression. "It's *because* I like you that I hope it does. What kind of sicko doesn't want the person they like to be happy?"

When I stare back in stunned silence, he shrugs. "Anyway, that's why I want to help, simple as that," he says. "Whatever happens, moving forward, it'll be okay, and if your feelings change about this in the future and you no longer feel comfortable, we can just pull the plug and go our separate ways once the semester ends, right?"

Before I can formulate any response, he's pulling out a bunch of printouts for the slideshow and shoving them toward me.

"And speaking of which: Should we get back to work?"

## MARLOW + ANISA

**Howdy partner** 12:28 PM

**Ugh** 12:28 PM

**What?** 12:29 PM

**Just wanted to thank you for taking care of the Works Cited page** 12:35 PM

**I owe you my life** 12:36 PM

**It's nothing** 12:39 PM

**Don't be dramatic** 12:39 PM

**You don't understand** 12:40 PM

**Organizing all that makes my brain numb** 12:40 PM

**Tell me if I can do something in return** 12:41 PM

**You may keep treating me to coffee** 12:42 PM

**Preferably not iced, though** 12:42 PM

**Roger that** 12:42 PM

**By the way, where did you learn to put PowerPoints together?** 12:43 PM

**This is looking really good so far** 12:43 PM

**Weird hobby I guess?** 12:43 PM

**Does making slideshows really count as a hobby?** 12:44 PM

**Nerd.** 12:44 PM

**I don't want to hear that from you** 12:45 PM

**Do you even have a hobby?** 12:45 PM

**Besides drooling over what is basically anime porn** 12:46 PM

**Jfksdjfd** 12:46 PM

**Hjkdfhsdkfdsf** 12:46 PM

**Kfjdsklfjdskf** 12:46 PM

**Dsfkdsjkfhsdfjkhdjkfsd** 12:46 PM

**sdfjjdkfjdksfjksdjfkdsfjksdfjkdjf** 12:46 PM

**Are you ok** 12:47 PM

**Don't PUT THAT ON MY PHONE YOU MONSTER** 12:47 PM

**I'm trying to push the chat down in case someone looks over my screen.** 12:47 PM

**Why are you so ashamed??** 12:48 PM

**It's perfectly natural** 12:48 PM

**Maybe add meditation to your hobby list** 12:48 PM

**Deep breathing exercises** 12:49 PM

**Lol can you imagine someone calling themselves a "deep breathing enthusiast"?** 12:49 PM

**I'm going back to work now** 12:50 PM

**You're no fun.** 12:50 PM

**Btw, just emailed you a list of rom-coms to watch** 12:51 PM

**Make sure you study them** 12:51 PM

**Pray tell, how does one study a rom-com?** 12:52 PM

**Just observe the relationship development, I guess?** 12:52 PM

**Take it all in** 12:53 PM

**There's a study that claims watching rom-coms helps marriages, etc etc** 12:53 PM

**The study is a little suspect imo** 12:54 PM

**Obviously couples that watch rom-coms together would likely have a better relationship to start with** 12:54 PM

**But I figure it can't hurt to try.** 12:54 PM

**Oh. Wow** 12:55 PM

Ok—thank you. 12:55 PM

I'll start watching tonight. 12:55 PM

Sweet 12:56 PM

I'll stop bothering you now 12:56 PM

It's prayer time too, right 12:57 PM

Um . . . yeah, actually. 12:57 PM

Thanks. 12:57 PM

Good, you can apologize to God
for your sinful hobby 12:58 PM

I dislike you very much. 12:58 PM

# Chapter 11

Thursday evening, I find myself standing in front of the door to a tiny restaurant called Taco Time.

The restaurant was Marlow's choice; I let him pick since I still don't know what's good in the area, and it'd be hard to feel sad, he claimed, in a taco joint. Most important, the restaurant is almost exactly in between our campuses.

I pause, my hand hovering over the door handle and my breath emerging in pillowy clouds. All I have to do is open it. But even though it's freezing outside and the warmth of the restaurant is beckoning me, I'm hesitating.

"If you're comfortable with it, I think we need to start with you giving me more information about you and Isaac," Marlow told me one evening in the library, wresting his eyes from his laptop. "Every relationship is different, so it'd help me formulate a better plan if I knew more about what makes you two tick. Maybe we can eat off campus sometime. I need a break from cafeteria food, anyway."

Now I glance at my phone. Five minutes until our meeting time. I'm half considering fleeing back to my dorm room when I hear footsteps behind me.

"Having second thoughts?" comes Marlow's voice.

I spin on my heel to face him, ready to completely deny such an accusation, but for a moment, I don't even recognize him because—

"Oh my God." My mouth falls open. "You're wearing decent shoes."

Today, Marlow's opted for simple white trainers—still not exactly winter shoes, but close enough. He's even wearing a weather-appropriate crewneck sweater, fitted under a dark green wool coat, and brown corduroy slacks. A perfectly normal, dare I say, decent seasonal outfit.

"I know." He grins. "I kept noticing you making a face every time you saw my Crocs."

I'm completely taken aback by the gesture. It's not like I made it obvious I disliked his choice of shoeware; being the elder daughter in a desi family means I'm a pro at hiding my dislike of things.

"I just don't think Crocs are appropriate winter attire," I mutter.

"Hey, don't dis Crocs. You know you can eat them? I'm just being eco-friendly."

"In that case, maybe we can forget the tacos and I can watch you eat your Crocs."

"No thanks, I want tacos," Marlow retorts. "Shall we?" He opens the door to the restaurant, and I notice a laugh playing on Marlow's mouth.

*"What?"*

"Why do you look so nervous?" he whispers.

"I'm not nervous! Why would *I* be nervous?"

"Uh-huh. That is the quintessential nervous person response. You also keep looking around the restaurant like you're looking for an escape route."

Actually, I'm looking to see if I recognize anyone here—if some aunty or uncle sees me out with some guy that isn't Isaac, I'm doomed—but close enough. I guess this is the downside to Marlow's ability to read people: he can read *me*, a little too well.

We slide across from each other in a booth, and I practically snatch the menu from the waiter's hand, desperate for something to distract myself with, to hide myself behind.

"So . . ." Marlow says, steepling his fingers, "first of all, how's life?"

"Weird," I reply. And getting weirder by the minute. Meeting at a restaurant—this almost feels like a date. I can't even remember the last time Isaac and I went out for dinner. Of course, this *isn't* a date, and the only reason I'm here is to discuss Isaac, but still; I haven't really thought about what this whole *love coaching* thing would entail.[74] And having someone I still barely know act as my love coach seems risky. What if Isaac found out? What if anyone found out?

I stand. "On second thought, this is a stupid idea. I don't know why I thought—"

"No, no, wait." Marlow's fingers are hot as they lightly clasp my wrist. "Just five minutes. Give me five minutes. I mean, you can leave if you want to, but"—slowly he pulls his hand away—"you've already come out here. Just give it a chance."

He has this annoyingly earnest expression on his face that stops me in my tracks.

I sigh.

"Fine," I say after a while, heaving myself back into my seat and opening the menu. "May as well."

"Good. Otherwise, you'd just go back to playing your otome game and then where would we be?"

I bristle because he's right, not that he needs to know. "*Shush.* On that note, we should establish some ground rules if you're going to be my love coach."

"This I gotta hear."

---

74     Namely, it entails talking and being told what to do, some of my least favorite activities.

I lean forward, my hair draping across the table.[75] "You *have* to keep this a secret. *No one* can know that I'm meeting with you for"—I make a face—"*advice*."

"Hmm, fair enough. In that case, I also propose a rule."

I brace myself.

"You have to trust me. That means being fully up front and honest, because that's the only way this is going to work. If I don't know what you're really thinking or feeling, I can't help you." Marlow reaches a hand toward me. "Deal?"

Unfortunately, his rule makes sense. And the truth is, I think a part of me has already decided to trust him: because unlike me, Marlow seems to notice things—people, I mean, and what makes them tick.[76] Which is probably how, despite barely knowing Isaac and me, he's somehow able to get a read on our situation. To make me feel like there's hope.

He may not be fairy godmother material exactly, but I think if anyone could help, it's probably him.

I close my eyes and imagine the future I'm working for: Isaac's and my color-coordinated wedding rings and our degrees hanging behind us on a wall in our modest but tasteful house on the Main Line.

I reach for Marlow's hand and give a gentle squeeze. "Deal."

"Good." He smirks. "That reminds me. I saw your Instagram account."

*Ugh.* "If you're trying to get me to stay, revealing that you've been stalking my socials is a surefire way to get me to run."

"It was necessary. I was doing research."

"On?"

"You."

---

75      Reasons to be annoyed with long hair, #204.

76      If I'm being honest, people like this scare me. They notice too much.

I pick up my menu to hide my embarrassment. "And? What did you learn?"

"I don't know," Marlow answers, frowning. "I feel like there's a bit of a disconnect between the person sitting right in front of me and the person I saw on Instagram."

"Social media is only the tip of the iceberg for most people," I say, shrugging. "It's not like you'd know a person just by looking."

"Rock, paper, scissors," Marlow says suddenly.

"What?" Confused, I throw out rock just as Marlow throws out paper. I've lost.

He grins. "Knew it."

"How did you—?"

"Rock tends to be the standard starting play for rookies. Your hand was already clenched to begin with, too. You're right that social media isn't a good indicator of the full picture, but frankly, you're easy to read."

For a moment, I frown, indignant. But then I start to wonder if maybe that's the point.

"Should we play again?"

"No, thanks," I reply, pouting.

"I did like the quote in one of your captions though, the one about how *'for some, makeup is a sword; for others, a shield. For me, it's self-expression.'* I've never thought about it like that before. I always thought of it as a mask, but maybe that's misogyny." Marlow pauses. "I don't know if you noticed, but I know jack shit about makeup. But part of me was wondering why you insist on this whole other look of yours. It feels like a lot of work."

Marlow actually sat there and read the captions for my recent posts? And his questions are thoughtful. He's taking this whole love coach role . . . surprisingly seriously.

"It kind of started off that way for me," I say slowly. "I probably did use makeup as a mask at first. In all honesty, I think I used to wear it because I wanted Isaac to think I was beautiful. After these girls called me ugly back in fourth grade, I became hyperaware of my looks. That was around the time I met Isaac. I'd convinced myself that if I stood a chance of him noticing me, I had to be pretty. Otherwise, how could I dare to even consider being with him? His mom would laugh me out the door."

It was in high school when I started getting really good with makeup—when conversations between my parents and Isaac's parents started getting serious about our future. I worked day and night to get the perfect grades, but still. There were times I never felt good enough. That's when I'd put makeup on, and suddenly, I'd feel *powerful*. Worthy of anything, and anyone.

"The day-to-day reasons change, but now, no guy has any sway over why I wear makeup anymore. Mostly, I just wear it to feel confident, because I love the artistry of it. I'm still learning how to navigate Euro-centric beauty standards as a brown girl, but I think makeup has made me appreciate my South Asian features more."

"Makes sense," he replies. "But all of this is to say, you obviously don't need some dramatic, Cinderella-style makeover. You're already . . ."

"Already what?"

He shrugs. "Well, beautiful."

I'm startled by his matter-of-fact tone. Though I guess he's only flattering me because of his silly little crush.

"And that's *good*," he quickly adds, "because, I don't know if you noticed, but fashion isn't exactly my forte either. What you need is a, a *heart makeover*, so to speak."

I almost gag. "Excuse me?"

"I'm sorry. That was inexcusable. The point is, you need to learn how to emotionally connect to people, how to be vulnerable with people. Which, based on everything I've seen, *isn't* your forte. Which is why I think *this*"—he gestures between us—"is important. We talk and then I can best figure out a way to help you."

"That's not—"

*True*, is what I want to say. Instead, I look away.

I want to argue, but if I really think about it, maybe Marlow's right. I do tend to keep my cards a little close. Maybe I am a little afraid of saying everything that's on my mind to other people, of showing Isaac everything about me. I think of what Zaina had said the other day: *Does Isaac have any idea how you really look? Or, you know, your real charming self?*

No. Isaac doesn't. And sometimes lately I've even gotten the sense that Isaac suspects I'm hiding something. I tell myself it's better this way, that it's my choice to live like this and it's fine—and it all very well could be. But what if Isaac's been misinterpreting the whole time? What if because I seem closed off, he's been closed off with me, too?

I don't know. I could be overthinking it.

Either way, I just hope it's not too late.

After the waiter takes our orders, I take a deep breath. "So? Where do we start?"

"Like I said before, I think it would help to brainstorm ways to get you more involved in Isaac's life." Marlow rests a finger against his bottom lip, deep in thought. "You said he's always busy with South Asian Students Association meetings, right? What if we went to one?"

"Why?"

"I'm glad you asked, young grasshopper." Marlow grins. "I did some reading on love psychology and there are whole *treatises* people have written on ways to help, we'll say, *encourage feelings* of love. From what I've gleaned, it basically comes down to three main things: 1) showing interest in each other's interests, 2) fulfilling unmet needs, usually through acts of kindness, and 3) finding opportunities to have new experiences together.

"Going to a SASA meeting is you showing interest in his interests. If Isaac can't step away from his SASA obligations, then you could help him out while simultaneously spending more time with him, and hopefully share your interests with him as well."

Truth be told, when I first started classes at Marion, it did cross my mind to attend SASA meetings at Halcyon just to see Isaac, but since he never asked me to come, I figured he didn't want me there. It's his club, after all. Granted, Marion students do attend Halcyon SASA meetings—Marion's SASA is so small, it hardly ever meets—I thought maybe Isaac would feel embarrassed having his future betrothed randomly show up to a meeting. Maybe that was why he never invited me to one.

"Pretty sure I've seen the posters for it all over campus—their meetings are open to new members, so it's not totally weird to just show up. I think their next meeting is on Tuesday? Plus, it's a joint SASA and ISA meeting, and I'm technically an international student, being raised in Jamaica and all."

"Have you ever gone to any ISA meetings before?"

Thinking about it now, I don't really know what Marlow does in his spare time, when he's not helping me. I find myself growing increasingly curious about his day-to-day.

For a moment, Marlow looks taken aback. "Nah, being part of the ISA would just feel like more work, honestly; they put on way too many events throughout the year. My old roommate Charlie did convince me to go to a couple Black Students' Association League meetings last semester, but I stopped going after a while."

"Why?"

He lets out a little sigh. "It's complicated; I was going through a lot at the time. It was hard just leaving my room those days. I'm still friendly with some of the people I met there, though. They're probably some of the only ones that still . . ."

Marlow trails off, and a faraway look replaces his usual sunshiny one. But before I can push for more details, he's already moved on.

"So? Everything make sense?" he asks suddenly.

There's a little pinch in my stomach—a weird feeling of somehow being pushed away—but I ignore it and clear my throat. I have no business prying, anyway. "So I get the part where we go to this SASA meeting of course, but then what . . . ?"

"What do you mean, *then what*?" Marlow looks exasperated. "You establish yourself as his number one. Stake your claim on him or whatever!"

"I have no idea what any of that means."

"Okay, humor me for a sec. Pretend I'm Isaac."

"That's literally impossible."

"You want my help or not?"

*"Fine."*

*"Pretend* I'm Isaac," Marlow continues, "and we're out at dinner. It's the first time you've seen me in a while, one-on-one." He looks at me expectantly. "What do you do?"[77]

"Uh. I ask how you are, and if you're taking care of yourself?"

"Don't tell me. Do it, ask me."

I grit my teeth. "How are you, *Isaac*?"

Marlow leans forward. "I'm okay, all things considered." His voice has gone down an octave. "What about you?"

"I'm sorry, are you *trying* to act like Isaac? Your facial expressions

---

77    Cry internally, usually.

are all wrong—he's way cooler; he has this natural suaveness. You look like a pick-up artist."

"I've only heard him talk a couple times in class! *Work with me here.*"

"That's great, *Isaac*," I say, my teeth clenched. "I'm happy to hear you are okay. I am okay, too."

"It's been a while since we've sat down and talked, just the two of us," Marlow (a.k.a. Imposter Isaac) says. "I'm really glad you're here."

"I'm . . . glad . . . too?"[78]

Marlow runs his hands down his face. "Okay, if anyone saw you and Isaac acting like that, there is no way anyone would think you're together. You are *way* too stiff." He huffs. "You need to make an effort to continue the conversation. If you just answer the question and leave it at that, then you've killed it. This conversation is dead and now things are awkward because we have this dead thing on the table. You get what I'm saying?"

"*How?* I have to rehearse what I say. I can't just open my mouth and say whatever's on my mind. What if I say the wrong thing?" This is why I love otome games. I never have to think about my words; I can just *choose* them from a short list of options.

"You've known Isaac forever, right? There's got to be more you can talk about together—and no, *not* just school-related stuff."

"You're not the boss of me," I mumble.

"Technically, I am. I am your love coach. And you know why? It's because you don't actually have any inner confidence. You freeze up around him and you don't know how to be yourself. Just look what happened when you saw him outside Hadley."

I swallow. It hurts, but I have to remind myself I need to hear this.

"Anyway, since we've just established communication isn't your strong

---

78    This whole interaction has confirmed to me that I'd have zero chance at being any good at role-play.

suit and you're, some might say, *romantically stunted*—"

"*Hey!*"

"—we're going to have to focus on things you can actually *do*."

Marlow pulls out a notebook I recognize as the one he uses for our Race & Ethnicity class—though to my horror, he's barely written anything in it—and starts furiously writing. "I think we should focus on more substantial ways to show you care. So: we'll start with you showing up to the SASA meeting. Care packages, maybe, especially since you said he's busy. We can also have you write handwritten letters and you can just drop those off at his student mailbox. Everyone loves handwritten letters."

"Did you just whip those ideas up?" I fold my arms across my chest. "How do you know so much about relationships, anyway?"

Marlow's pen stops moving, and I catch a brief flicker of melancholy in his gaze just before he pastes on a casual smile. "Just a natural gift, I guess." He goes back to writing, only there's something about his jaw that looks more . . . tense than usual.

"A natural gift, huh,"[79] I say, rolling my eyes.

"Doubt all you want. *I'm* not the one with fiancé troubles."

I click my tongue. "*Rude.*"

Message received, though. There's definitely something more to his answer, but I don't know him well enough to press anything, and I certainly don't know him well enough to read him. For all I know, I could be wrong. I misjudged Marlow when I first met him, after all.

Clearly, lately I've been wrong about a lot.

The conversation effortlessly flows for the next hour as we stuff our faces with tacos. It's strange, but I think I'm having fun. I've never had the time to go to a restaurant for dinner with a college friend before

---

79    I don't *love* admitting it, but it does actually feel that way. Marlow's insightful. More than I am, at least.

(though Kira and I ordered takeout and watched *Moulin Rouge* once, and never spoke of it again) and talking to Marlow like this, completely unguarded—it feels so normal. I don't feel tense and afraid of saying the wrong thing, the way I usually do with my parents or Isaac's mom or even Isaac at times, because even if I do, here, it can only help. And if none of this works—if the worst-case scenario happens and Marlow can't help me bridge the distance between me and Isaac—Marlow and I can simply go our separate ways and never speak of this again. I can't lose.

I suddenly feel even more determined. "Let's try this again," I tell Marlow. "Act like Isaac, but make it believable this time."

Marlow coughs dramatically and speaks, his voice deeper once more: "So, Anisa, what is your favorite—"

"He never calls me Anisa," I interrupt. "He always says Ani."

"Wait, what? Any particular reason why?" says Marlow, breaking character.

"I don't know. It's just what he's always called me. It's what most people call me." I've honestly never questioned it before.

"Anisa," he says again. But he doesn't say it like he's tasting an unfamiliar, foreign word on his tongue and is unsure of the flavor. He says it the way it *should* be said. Like it's the most natural word in the world. "Is that okay?"

"Yeah," I say softly. "I think I prefer it."

"Good." Marlow's expression softens. "For what it's worth, I do, too."

## THE "GET YOUR MAN" PLAN

- Get more involved in Isaac's interests
- Attend an SASA meeting?
- Research what else Isaac enjoys ~~(besides being the human embodiment of a Ken Doll)~~ and do that
- Random acts of kindness
- Care packages
- Spotify playlist
- Handwritten letters
- Show Isaac you care (and also that life sucks without you)
- Create opportunities for fun new experiences together
- ~~Play otome games together~~ *NO!!*
- ???

**Favorite color, go.** 3:18 PM

**What?** 3:19 PM

**What brought that up?** 3:19 PM

**Don't question it,
just answer it.** 3:20 PM

**Is this because I said I was
bad at small talk?** 3:20 PM

**PICK A COLOR.** 3:21 PM

**Fine.** 3:21 PM

**At the moment, it's burgundy.** 3:22 PM

**Or any jewel tones, really.** 3:22 PM

**They look best on me.** 3:22 PM

**That is the most you answer** 3:23 PM

**BURGUNDY???** 3:23 PM

**Jesus** 3:23 PM

**Ok now ask me mine** 3:24 PM

**Is this really necessary?** 3:24 PM

**Yes.** 3:24 PM

**OK Marlow, what is your favorite color?** 3:25 PM

**Blue, I think. Or maybe green.** 3:25 PM

**That tells me nothing.** 3:26 PM

**?? what do you mean** 3:26 PM

**What SHADE?** 3:26 PM

**Shade?** 3:27 PM

**I'm not an artist, leave me alone** 3:27 PM

**Dear God.** 3:28 PM

**You are hopeless.** 3:28 PM

**I'M hopeless?** 3:29 PM

**Somehow you are turning my attempt at small talk into** 3:29 PM

**Well, literal and figurative SHADE** 3:29 PM

**I—** 3:30 PM

**It's your fault for asking me such a childish question** 3:30 PM

**Why would I randomly ask Isaac what his favorite color is?** 3:31 PM

Because that's the thing about
small talk with people you care about 3:31 PM

You say and ask whatever's
on your mind, no pressure 3:32 PM

And the conversation just starts to flow 3:32 PM

So even though you're talking
about seemingly nothing 3:33 PM

you're still somehow learning new things about
each other you wouldn't have otherwise learned 3:33 PM

Now ask me a question 3:34 PM

Remember, it can be anything 3:34 PM

Umm . . . 3:35 PM

You can do it! 3:35 PM

Don't mock me!! 3:36 PM

Sorry, sorry 3:36 PM

All right 3:37 PM

Why do you know so much about
rom-coms and romance? 3:37 PM

You want the real answer? 3:38 PM

Obviously. 3:38 PM

Truthfully . . . . . 3:40 PM

I'm ... 3:40 PM

A hopeless romantic  3:41 PM

Ah, so you are hopeless 3:42 PM

😨😨😨 3:42 PM

# Chapter 12

**FEBRUARY 10**

After our brainstorming session, Marlow gave me a list of famous romance movies to watch,[80] telling me I need to take notes and write my favorite romantic lines to help generate ideas. *It'll put you in a romance state of mind,* Marlow said. *Treat it as free counseling.*

But mostly, I end up spending my afternoons and evenings, class notwithstanding, in the library, digging through musty tomes of South Asian history books printed in the eighties, while Marlow remains glued to his laptop, looking through databases.

It's my fault we're so behind on our paper. The truth is, I've been uncharacteristically behind on *all* my schoolwork.[81] Thankfully, Marlow doesn't remind me it's my fault we're playing catch-up—whether it's out of sheer pragmatism or kindness, I don't know. And working in the library with him feels . . . kind of nice.

I hate it to admit it, but I think the reason why I can focus on work

---

80    Some notable entries on the list: *Sleepless in Seattle, Notting Hill, 13 Going on 30, When Harry Met Sally, Much Ado About Nothing, How Stella Got Her Groove Back,* and *You've Got Mail.* I also watched *It Happened One Night* on his recommendation, and so far, it's my favorite. Also, how many movies has this guy even watched??

81    The last time I was late turning in homework was in seventh grade, when I had a bad case of the flu. When I eventually did turn in my homework, I cried so hard that Mr. Velasquez decided not to mark down my grade.

again is Marlow's offer to help me with my relationship issues.

Which is also why I decide to go home for the weekend and check on my parents and Zaina—although from the looks of it, Zaina is taking the news of their divorce surprisingly well.

"Think of it this way," she'd told me over the phone, "this means they're not going to be fighting anymore. Imagine. A quiet house, with no yelling. With no having to lock ourselves in our rooms just to hear ourselves think."

"I guess . . ." For Zaina, who still lives at home, that is a *big* benefit. "But what about holidays?" I ask, half whining. "It's going to be awful when we're on school break and our parents are living separately. What if they get remarried?"

"Then they get remarried. I'm not going to stress about the what-ifs. It'd suck, yeah, but you and I are still family. So who cares."

Before I got too weepy, Zaina made some excuse about having to meet up with some friends on her online game and hung up. I just hope Mom and Dad haven't told anyone about the divorce yet. Because if they did, it's only a matter of time before the news reaches Isaac. Or worse: his mom.

I'm texting Marlow[82] to let him know I just arrived home for the weekend and that I'll be working on our shared Google Drive when the door leading to the house suddenly swings open. It's Mom, who takes a beat before realizing I'm leaning against the car, phone in hand. "What are you doing just standing around in the garage?"

"Nothing. Sorry." I shove my phone in my back pocket. "I was texting Kira." The lie comes out faster than I can figure out *why* I need to lie.

---

82    I considered telling him about Mom and Dad's impending divorce but decided against it. Marlow knows enough about my personal life; he doesn't need to know about the situation with my parents, too.

Mom's face contorts with suspicion, but then she huffs, exasperated. "Come in, come on," she waves me in before disappearing into the house.

I grab some heavy grocery bags from the trunk and follow her inside. Mom had asked me to stop by the grocery store and texted me a long list of ingredients just before I left campus. She doesn't offer to help me carry them, though.[83]

"Good. You got everything?" Mom asks, gesturing toward my hands.

I shuffle toward the fridge, my arms screaming for relief. "I think so. So you wanted me to take care of dinner tonight?"

Not that I mind. I'm a *very* good cook. And if there's one thing to know about desi people, it's that nothing brings them together more than good food.[84]

"Yes. And how is your makeup?" She inspects my face, then nods, satisfied. "And brought enough food to feed five? Nani left, but she'll be back in a few weeks."

"Really?" Why did she even bother leaving, then, if she's just going to come straight back? And more important: "Wait, then who's the fifth—"

Before I can finish my thought, a familiar figure waves at me from the couch. I drop the bags with a loud thud, narrowly missing my feet.

"Isaac." I blink. "You're . . . here."

Seeing someone when you've been talking about them is rattling, like maybe you manifested them somehow by saying their name. It's a power I'd normally love to have, especially with Isaac. But it's awkward

---

83    Maybe she's still mad at me for how I reacted to the news of their divorce.

84    Except maybe music. Or weddings, but even then, sometimes those can be absolute messes and tear families apart. So yeah, really, food's your best bet.

seeing him here in my house, when he was acting so cagey about his phone the last time I saw him.

Not to mention I've just agreed to have Marlow be my love coach.[85]

Isaac meekly smiles as he stands. He looks a little tired but glorious; the light from the setting sun behind him makes him look like he has a halo.

"It's been a while since I've seen you, so I thought I'd surprise you," he says.

"I thought you'd be happy to see him," Mom says, eyes narrowed. "Isn't it sweet that he wanted to surprise you?"

"I mean, I *am* happy, obviously—but, you know, it really is a surprise!" I laugh nervously. "Not that I'm upset about it, by any means, just—this is kind of out of the blue."

I'm conflicted. My plan was to make a nice dinner, get Mom, Dad, and Zaina at the table so we could all talk, play some board games, or—or *something*. Like a *normal* family. Isaac is the wrench in that plan. It means I can't talk about the divorce.

Mom squints at me, like my audacity personally insults her. "Do we have to have a *reason* to have dinner with my future son-in-law?"

Behind her, Isaac's mouth briefly twists in some semblance of a smile, but it doesn't reach his eyes. A fake, plastic smile. Like he's uncomfortable being here, too.

"Of course you don't need a reason," I reply, mustering some cheer. "Good thing I got extra ingredients. I'll get started on the food." I look over Mom's shoulder. "Isaac, feel free to relax."

"Thanks, Ani. I'll do that."

---

85    These are dark, dark times.

Mom sits with Isaac in the living room, partly to keep him company, but mostly so she can chatter away to a polite prisoner who can't say no. It's like all that talk about her and Dad divorcing is a faraway dream. She's acting like it never happened, that nothing's changed. I almost admire her ability to pretend. From the corner of my eye, I watch Isaac, now smiling attentively at Mom, nodding at all the right places. *His* ability to pretend everything's all right, on the other hand, terrifies me.

I can't take it anymore. I dump a ton of water into a giant pot and turn on the stove to boil, then nearly trip over my feet sprinting to the hallway bathroom, phone in tow.

Before I even fully understand what I'm doing, I call Marlow.

"Hello . . . ?" His voice sounds rusty, like he's just woken from a nap.

I put my hand around my mouth, muffling the sound. "Hi. So fun fact. Isaac's here at my house, and—I'm kind of panicking and I'm not sure what to make of him just *randomly* showing up and I don't know what to do—"

I hear a sharp intake of breath on the other line.

"Hello? Marlow?" I sigh. "Sorry. I didn't mean to call out of the blue. I can text—"

"No, no," says Marlow finally. "It's just, I didn't expect you to call." There's rustling on the other line. "You know, you sound a *lot* nicer on the phone."

"One of my many talents, I guess?"

Marlow chuckles. He must have his mouth pressed up close to the phone because I can almost feel the warm vibration of sound waves brushing against my ear. "So, what? Isaac's at your house? Is that why we're panicking?"

"Yes. We left things on a really weird note the last time we saw each other, and now he just showed up at my house for dinner. I had no idea he was coming."

"That's what she said."[86]

"*Stop.* Seriously, what do I do? You're supposed to be my love coach. So coach me."

"First of all, take a deep breath. He's not an intruder; he's the guy you're in love with." I hear the crackle of plastic, the familiar sound of our dorm mattresses. "Anyway, I can't just improvise a step-by-step plan out of thin air, over the phone, which, by the way, I can't even *remember* the last time I've talked on the phone—"

"Okay, how is this helpful?" I barely manage to wrangle my voice from raising.

"Sorry, sorry, just—" He groans. "Okay, the only thing you should do is enjoy the rare moment you have together. Your family's there, right?"

"Right."

"So remind him he's part of your family. Who wouldn't love that, you know?" He pauses. "Unless, you know, your family's awful."

"Uh."

"In any case, this is a good thing. He showed up. At your family's house. Maybe that's his way of trying to close the gap, too. Try to have fun. Don't overthink it."

Easier said than done. But Marlow's right—all this worrying about the future has me forgetting just to breathe. Maybe I should take Isaac being here now as a good sign.

"Yeah, okay." I feel my body deflate a little. "I'll try."

"Good enough. Any fun plans? More important, what's on the dinner menu?"

---

86    These jokes need to be made illegal. I've had it.

"Um, baingan bharta, karahi chicken, and chawal.[87] I'm cooking it all."

"All by yourself? Isaac's not helping?"

"No?"

"Ugh, men," chides Marlow without a hint of irony. "Get him to cook with you. And while you're at it, make plans to see him again. Bat your lashes and guilt him into spending more time with you if you have to. No shame in that."

"Right." I need to be assertive. I can't keep letting Isaac slip through my fingers anymore. Not if I want our relationship to stop fading.

"Good luck. I'm going back to sleep, and you don't want to waste your evening talking to little old me."

"True," I reply, cracking the smallest of smiles.

The call ends. I set down my phone, roll up my sleeves, and head to the kitchen, a little calmer.


The house fills with the smell of cumin and caramelized onion and basmati rice, and even though my forehead's lightly dappled with sweat, I feel weirdly rejuvenated. Isaac and I share a victory high five. He's not much of a cook, but getting him involved was a good idea. Isaac even seemed to enjoy cutting up tomatoes, watching me throw them into the giant pot.[88]

I'll have to thank Marlow later.

I call my mom over; the smell from the kitchen was enough to summon Zaina from upstairs, who unlike me is in her lazy weekend sweats, complete with a cowlick and bleary eyes behind her glasses.

---

87    Translation: Eggplant curry, chicken curry, and basmati rice, a.k.a. some of the best foods known to humankind.

88    He's terrible with a knife, but seeing him try? So cute.

"Hi, Zaina. Been a little while, huh, kiddo?" says Isaac, wiping his hands with a paper towel.

Zaina takes her seat at the table with a grunt, not looking at Isaac.

I get the feeling that Zaina has never really liked Isaac all that much. It probably doesn't help that Mom keeps joking that she wishes she had a son like Isaac instead of *two* daughters, usually when Zaina is in earshot. I've told Mom to knock it off, but she only laughs and says Zaina and I are taking her joke too seriously.

There's an awkward silence as we realize one member of the family's still missing.

"Sohail!" Mom yells for Dad. "Dinner's ready."

After a while, Dad finally arrives. His face is a little pale and clammy, and he's wearing a thick sweater vest over another sweater like we don't already have the heater on higher than we should.

"Asalaamu alaikum, Uncle." Isaac is the picture of politeness, as always.

"*Honey*," Mom's forced term of endearment for Dad brings out a cringe from Zaina and a deep inner-cringe from me. "We have a *guest*. Don't you want to change into something nicer?"

Dad doesn't answer either of them. Instead, he stares at the spread on the table, looking like he's trying not to throw up. I can't even be insulted because he genuinely doesn't look good.

"Dad?" I ask, worried.

He looks up at me, startled. "I'm sorry, beti. I'm not feeling well again. Can you bring me some chawal and yogurt, and maybe some tea upstairs?"

I feel weirdly guilty. I've been so caught up in things lately, I haven't been spending any time with him.

"Of course," I tell him.

Dad gives me a grateful look before trudging back upstairs, his slippers making tiny scratching noises against the floor.

"Well," Mom claps her hands together once he's gone, signaling for us all to sit down at the table. "I guess it'll just be the four of us."

"What's wrong with Dad?" I ask.

I remember what Zaina said before, about Dad feeling off a few weeks ago. Is it the same sickness? Is it the stress from the impending divorce? If there's one thing I've learned these past few weeks, stress can definitely mess with your head *and* your body.[89]

"It's nothing to worry about," Mom answers quickly as she pours a ladle of chicken karahi onto Isaac's plate. "It's a stubborn cold that won't go away. Now let's eat. I'm *famished*. Come, Isaac, have some roti."

After we eat and I bring out some tea, Zaina leaves to play video games, and Mom finally leaves under the guise of checking on Dad.

"You look distracted," Isaac says, now that it's just the two of us. "Something on your mind?"

"No, nothing. Just happy you're here." I grab at a strand of my hair, nervously winding it around my finger. A cute, elegant gesture, if it weren't for the fact that even my finger is sweaty, so strands of hair keep getting caught, but I try to play it off. "My mom forced you to come, huh? Let me guess. She called and went on about how lonely she is not seeing you and guilt-tripped you?"

Isaac laughs softly. "Yeah, but it's fine. I wanted to see you anyway, especially since last time. . . ."

He twiddles his thumbs. I guess he's been thinking about the whole phone spat we had, too.

"I see how it is," I reply, making a show of pouting. "So you'll come when my mom forces you, but not when *I* ask?"

"Your mom is a little less forgiving than you are," he whispers.

---

89    Which only stresses a person out more, so I ask God again: Why? WHY?

"Sad but true."

I'm stalling. I just need to ask him out again, like Marlow suggested, to make plans with him like any normal couple. But I'm nervous.

"Rock, paper, scissors," I blurt instead.

Isaac furrows his brow but throws out scissors just as I throw out paper.

"Ha. I lost," I mutter. Isaac looks at me questioningly, so I explain. "Did you know there's a whole psychology behind what people choose for rock, paper, scissors? Apparently rock is the most common move, because beginners panic and take it for the strongest choice. There's actually a thirty-five-percent chance someone will choose rock. Paper is considered the subtle option but—"

"What's all this about?" Isaac interrupts, chuckling. "Are there actual studies on this? Peer-reviewed studies?"

I tuck an unruly stand of hair behind my ear. "Um, I don't know about that—it's just something I read about." At least, it's what I remember Marlow telling me.

"You can't really put much stock into things you read online, Ani."

"Yeah. No, you're right." But something about his tone of voice—something almost dismissive and prickly—hurts a little.

I try not to let it deter me from what I need to do.

I take a deep breath.

"Anyway, I was wondering—when are you going to take me up on that rain check? For dinner sometime soon?"

"Right, of course." Isaac looks away. Like he's . . . thinking.

"What about this week?" I press. "How does Tuesday evening work for you? Or any day, really?"

"Tuesday, Tuesday . . ." Isaac rubs the back of his neck. "Ah, right. I have a meeting every Tuesday evening. The South Asian Students Association's working with the International Students Association to do something for Holi in March, so this whole week is swamped with planning." He looks at me with a sorrowful frown. "I'm so sorry."

"Oh. Right." My voice sounds strained. I can only push so much, and him being busy is nothing unexpected—and that SASA meeting is the one Marlow and I had planned on crashing, anyway.

But just because he has that meeting doesn't mean his *entire* Tuesday is shot, right? Why even bother coming here to my house to have dinner with my *family* when Isaac's just going to shove me away again while we're on campus?

"Well, it can't be helped," I say evenly. "Maybe later, then."

Relief flashes across Isaac's face. He puts his hand on my arm, such a brief gesture of affection I'm almost convinced I imagined it.

"Also, I meant to say this earlier, but you look beautiful, by the way."

My smile widens. It's such a sweet, out-of-the-blue compliment, normally, I'd be swooning.

But I'm not sure I even feel the usual butterflies anymore.


That night, I dream.

It's a memory of a year and a half ago, when Isaac was first leaving for college. It was the middle of the night, and he'd tossed pebbles against my window to get my attention. My parents were fast asleep, and I'd been in bed, drifting in and out of some romance novel.

I open the window to find Isaac standing just below me, beaming up at me as if I were the moon itself.

"What are you doing here?" I whisper-yell. Internally, I'm freaking out for myriad reasons. But if my parents found out about Isaac sneaking over to our house in the middle of the night, they'd probably be furious—even though I'm pretty sure secretly Mom would be happy about it.

"I wanted to see you."

The smile I've been fighting breaks across my face. "And what will the rabble say if they catch you out here, just outside my bedchambers, under cover of night?"

"I would tell them, 'Avert thine eyes, for your beauty is mine to enjoy,'" he says with a straight face.

I laugh. "Astaghfirullah. You're horrible," I say, even though part of me wants to jump out the window into his arms. "Aren't you leaving for college tomorrow?"

Isaac's eyelids fall a little. "All the more reason why I wanted to be here."

It wasn't like him to risk being seen with me late at night. No, there was another reason he was here. I could *feel* it. Because I knew Isaac, perhaps better than I knew myself.

"Are you nervous?" I ask softly. It's a silly question. I've never known Isaac to be nervous about anything. But it's not like him to act like this, so . . . vulnerable.

"How could I not be?" He gently kicks at a tuft of grass. "I don't know why, but I can't shake off this feeling. . . ."

"This feeling?"

"This feeling that things are going to change forever. That this is a whole new chapter, and I might not see you as often." He gives me a sad smile. "I don't know, I just—I just wanted to see your face and remind myself everything's going to be fine."

I find myself at a loss for words. I've thought about the same thing, over and over, felt that same unexplainable shift in the air. Agonized over it. The idea of not seeing him as much *burns*.

But knowing he's been worrying about the same thing is comforting somehow. Yes, maybe things will change. But as long as we're still on the same wavelength, nothing else matters.

Right?

"Oh. Well . . ." I swallow hard. "I'll always be right here," I say. A promise, to him and myself. "Nothing will change."

"Yeah," Isaac responds sadly.

We don't say goodbye. In the past, it's because we never liked saying goodbye—it always felt too final, like we'll never see each other again. So for us, there's never been a need to say it.

But this time, it feels different.

This time, it feels like we already have.

I watch Isaac from my window as he hops back into his car and drives off, headlights disappearing into the midnight dark.

Why are you almost always late for class? 12:28 PM

I'm not late 12:28 PM

Ok, maybe by like one minute 12:29 PM

But that hardly counts 12:35 PM

Late is late. 12:35 PM

What are you even doing before class? 12:36 PM

Isn't your dorm close by? 12:39 PM

Well, this time I was late because
I was watching football 12:40 PM

And not your stupid American crap 12:40 PM

Real football ⚽ 12:41 PM

Huh. 12:41 PM

I never took you for a sports fan. 12:42 PM

Excuse me, I contain multitudes 12:43 PM

Anyway why do you ask 12:43 PM

Are you . . . interested in my life? 12:43 PM

Get the hell away from me 12:44 PM

I'm not even near you rn!!!! 12:44 PM

You texted me FIRST!!!! 🙄 12:45 PM

Lies and slander. 12:45 PM

So? Is that something you're interested in? 12:46 PM

I mean yeah, but it's not like I'm looking to make a career out of it 12:46 PM

What do you want to do? 12:46 PM

You know, when you grow up (if that ever happens) 12:46 PM

Ha ha. 12:47 PM

Honestly, I think I like the idea of going into therapy 12:47 PM

One of my dad's close friends is a crisis counselor, and his work inspired me to look more into mental health, especially for marginalized communities 12:48 PM

I like the idea of being someone who can give hope to those who feel hopeless 12:48 PM

Or maybe it's just an excuse to be nosy 12:48 PM

Suddenly everything about you makes sense 12:49 PM

What can I say, I like finding solutions to problems ☺ 12:49 PM

**What about you?** 12:50 PM

**Lawyer.** 12:50 PM

**Business law** 12:50 PM

**Whatever pays me the most** 12:50 PM

**Why's that?** 12:50 PM

**What do you mean, why?** 12:51 PM

**My options were doctor, lawyer, or engineer** 12:51 PM

**I chose lawyer because I like tailored suits** 12:51 PM

**Ok but why were those your only options??** 12:51 PM

**Oh, it's just the understanding I have with my parents** 12:53 PM

**Maybe I'll be a corporate finance attorney** 12:53 PM

**You scare me sometimes . . .** 12:54 PM

**???** 12:54 PM

**Thanks for reminding me, I should do more research** 12:54 PM

**Jesus** 12:54 PM

# Chapter 13

I show up on Halcyon just in time and find Marlow waiting for me by the bus stop.

On his suggestion, I stopped by at a local bakery to pick up muffins for the meeting—mostly for my sake, so it would feel like I actually had a purpose to my randomly showing up at an SASA meeting I've otherwise never shown interest in attending. I even organized the muffins in a cute little basket and looked up videos on YouTube on how to tie professional-looking bows with ribbon on the handle.[90] Bringing treats unprompted, as Marlow puts it, is the "perfect *house-spouse* move."

The sun is just starting to set, casting the campus in a pale gold hue. From the little bus stop shelter, Marlow greets me with a wave. "Wow, you were almost late. What's next? Is the world ending?"

"Sure feels like it," I say, my teeth chattering. Another cold day in February, and there aren't enough coats in the world to warm me up right now.

We walk across campus in tandem, feet crunching through snow. We're headed to Brighton Center, a small building used mostly by the

---

90    Apparently YouTube has an abundance of channels dedicated solely to wrapping things nicely. Who would have thought. . . . And yes, I spent entirely too long watching them.

anthropology department and for club activities.

Marlow breaks the silence with a nod of approval. "You look great, by the way."

"Thanks, I know," I reply, waving a hand dismissively. I'm wearing a beret, for God's sake. *Everyone* looks cute in a beret. "More important, are we sure this is a good idea? What if it comes across as too clingy or, I don't know, stalkerish?"

"Didn't Isaac just surprise you at your house the other day?"

"Yes?"

"And both your parents actually intend for you two to get married? You're definitely not making it up?"

"Yes? I mean, no, I'm not making it up—"

"So do you really think it's *clingy* to reciprocate and show up at his school club?" He points at the basket I'm holding. "With free *muffins*?"

My shoulders slump. "No. It's just . . ." I trail off.

"Anisa," says Marlow in a soft warning.

Right. I did agree to ground rule number two: Be honest. And Anisa Shirani does *not* shirk agreements. Marlow waits expectantly, which somehow only makes this harder.

I stare at my shoes. "Lately," I begin slowly, "sometimes, I feel like Isaac only wants to spend the bare minimum time with me to keep me off his back. Like, to him, I'm a clingy annoyance he wants to be rid of, and that he only deals with me because it's expected of us by our families. Like I'm just his ball and chain."

And that I'm the only one who's in love here. "So, I guess I'm just nervous, is all."[91]

"The ol' ball and chain." Marlow scrunches his nose. "I never understood

---

91    Panicking is perhaps the correct word.

that phrase. Why even be in a relationship with someone if you view them as your *ball and chain,* a cage that keeps you tied against your will? If anything, I'd want us to both be each other's balls, you know?"

I stare at him.

"Wait. That metaphor just went somewhere horrible."

This time, I laugh.

"No, but you get it, right?" Marlow says, uncharacteristically embarrassed. "I'm just saying, a relationship should feel like an equal commitment—a willing and equally beneficial bond that connects you—"

"Yes, I get it." I sputter, still laughing. "Don't worry."

Marlow smiles. The kind of endearing smile that makes me feel like my face is being cupped in warm, gentle hands. "What I'm *trying* to say is, you don't have anything to worry about. Unless Isaac's said as much—that you're somehow an annoyance—you can't assume that's how he feels. You shouldn't assume how anyone feels. You can only focus on you, and doing your best to bridge the gap. Which, I think it's safe to say, is what you're doing right now."

I nod, clutching the basket of muffins tightly. I'm still nervous, but . . . I feel a little more reassured.

*For my picture-perfect future.*

"Right." I take a deep, chilled breath. "Ready?"

Marlow nods. "Whenever you are," he answers as he opens the door for me. "But I'm claiming two of those blueberry muffins as payment. Just so you know."

And with that, I walk through the doorway.

I spot Isaac at the front of the meeting room, wearing a dark blue knitted sweater. He runs a hand through his effortlessly mussy hair as he talks to someone balancing a laptop on their arm, typing notes as he talks to them. I'm surprised by how big the club feels—way bigger than our tiny SASA at Marion—filled with at least thirty or forty students. It's no wonder Isaac is so busy all the time. They already have chairs neatly lined up throughout the room, a whiteboard at the front where someone's written: HOLI: 3/25, and a table off to the side, where there's already an array of juices, coffee, and cookie trays covering every inch. I'm not sure my basket of muffins will even fit.

For now, I take a seat in the second row and Marlow settles down just behind me, already slouching in his chair. As usual, Marlow looks comfortable wherever he goes—unlike me, literally sitting on the edge of my seat, my basket of muffins balancing on my lap.

Except I feel people stare frigidly in our direction and begin whispering. For a moment, I'm self-conscious—their unfriendly staring isn't the kind I'm used to—but then I realize their looks are directed at *Marlow*. One of the guys in a red Halcyon hoodie, maybe a sophomore or junior, I recognize from our Race & Ethnicity class. He doesn't seem happy to see Marlow there, either.

But Marlow doesn't seem to notice. Maybe he's pretending not to.

*Or maybe I'm just imagining it.*

I adjust my beret and take a fortifying breath.

Isaac hasn't noticed me yet, and part of me is grateful because I feel completely out of place, and to top it off, an army of butterflies has decided seemingly to wage war in my bowels. But Marlow said if nothing else, I should use this as an opportunity to get to know Isaac better, to see him in his element.

Everyone takes their seat, save for Isaac, who finally starts the meeting.

"Thank you all for braving the cold to come to our joint South Asian Students Association and International Students Association meeting," he says. There's a smattering of applause throughout the room, and Isaac gives a cordial smile. "As you know, both groups have committed to raise money for Save the Children through our upcoming spring Holi event, which had a huge turnout last year."

Holi is the celebration of the arrival of spring, the end of winter, the—ironically—the blossoming of new love. It's a Hindu event, but it's fairly common to find Muslims joining in;[92] at the end of the day, it's a festival for everyone, with people throwing colorful powders at each other, filling the air with a joyful rainbow haze.

Doing something like that with Isaac would be incredible. The exact kind of college experience I wanted to have with him. I imagine the coming of spring; Isaac in a white kurta, me in a white dress, laughing and tossing handfuls of powder, dousing each other in our colors. We'd take pictures that would go into our wedding slideshow. It would be the kind of formative, core memory that we'd look upon fondly, years later, together.

It'd be *perfect*.

Isaac continues, and throughout the meeting, it's clear he has full control of the room. People listen to him; his fellow club members quiet down as soon as he opens his mouth. His voice has this calming quality you can't help but *want* to hear, like warm fingers running down your neck after a long, hard day.

"So here's the thing," says Isaac. "We're hoping to double the attendance and donation this year, so we need to brainstorm ways to make it bigger and better than ever—and *no*, Kasim, once again this does *not* mean you can bring paintball guns to Holi; I'm pretty sure that'd break

---

92      My theory is that Pakistani Muslims will look for an excuse to celebrate most things. I've heard Pakistanis back in the motherland will even celebrate Thanksgiving. Thanksgiving! Who are they even giving thanks for?!

132

a *hundred* different campus regulations."

A beefy boy in the back—Kasim, presumably—lets out a disappointed groan.

Isaac rolls his eyes. "Yeah, yeah. If you have any complaints, I suggest you bring them to the president of the ISA." He points to the back of the room. "I'm sure she'd love the opportunity to boss you around."

From somewhere in the room, laughter rings like the chime of a bell, the twinkle of freshly fallen snow. "Don't tell them that!"

I turn around to find the source, and I feel all the blood drain from my face.

It's her. Ellie. Why is she *here*?

"Too late," Isaac replies, grinning from the front of the room. "What are you doing back there? Come up here. You're supposed to help me run this thing."

Ellie laughs again and hops out of her seat. With the grace and lightness of a fairy, she bounds toward the front and stands next to Isaac, and—o*h no. She's cute!* She has her long red locks tied in a gorgeous braid that runs halfway down her back, and she's wearing a floral corduroy dress that fits her like a glove. I don't even think she's wearing any makeup; her cheeks just naturally have the pink flush of a goddamn milkmaid.[93] Like God, as God does His chosen ones, had blessed her with a permanent beauty filter.

Seeing them standing side by side, I can't deny Isaac and Ellie look good together. And *close*. Like they belong on the cover of some fairy

---

93     FYI: I love my strong nose, my captivatingly dark, earthen eyes, the silky olive-brown of my skin. Being good with makeup means being familiar with my face and my features, and learning how to bring out the best in them. But everything about Ellie just screams . . . effortless. She's a different kind of beautiful. One that I really admire.

romance novel. One I would happily read.

Isaac and I have never had the opportunity to work on anything together, and I wish . . .

I wish it could be me up there.

Ugh. Jealousy, I've decided, is the most pathetic excuse for a feeling *ever*. It should be beneath me. But her being here has completely thrown me off.

"She's president of the ISA?" Marlow muses softly behind me, but I'm only vaguely aware of the room around me and it sounds like he's underwater. Like he's drifting somewhere far away. Or maybe I'm the one drifting.

I close my eyes.

Okay. This is fine. This changes nothing. All this does is confirm that Isaac and Ellie spend a ton of time together. Planning charity events together, on top of taking a lot of classes together. Which, the more I think about it, is comforting me less and less.

But it doesn't definitively mean he's not still in love with me.

It doesn't mean I've somehow come up short. That I've bored him.

That I'm a thorn in Isaac's side.

I clutch the basket of muffins in my lap tightly. I'm starting to wish I hadn't come here. But in this case, would ignorance really have been bliss? I remember Nani telling me about my choti nani—her younger sister—and how she raised her kids all by herself, knowing full well that her husband had tons of affairs. Everyone knew she was trapped in a loveless relationship, but she couldn't admit it to herself.

Is Ellie the reason why Isaac is pulling away so much lately? Is it my fault? Am I being paranoid? Or am I in denial, like Choti Nani?

The meeting continues with Isaac and Ellie expertly tag-teaming the brainstorming session until it feels like they've written down dozens of fun ways to make Holi better this year. Even I almost find myself getting swept up in the excitement of all the possibilities.

Isaac rolls up his sleeves, and I see it: the bracelet I gave him, in its usual place on his wrist. "All right, before we start wrapping up this meeting, the folks over at Save the Children wanted us to go through this presentation about where all our money goes." He starts fiddling with a laptop setup and frowns. "If I can just get this PowerPoint up on the screen . . ."

I jump from my seat. Maybe he and Ellie look cute next to each other, but he's my fiancé. We're partners. And now I have a rare opportunity to help him.

"Let me try!" I say loudly. I suddenly feel the weight of forty pairs of eyes landing on me and instantly regret opening my mouth.

But I rarely get an opportunity this good. Not only could I help Isaac during one of his own SASA meetings—i.e., integrating myself into one of his interests—but this would definitely count as an act of kindness that Marlow was talking about, right?

Isaac blinks. "Ani," he says, a puzzled expression on his face. "I—I didn't know you were here."

"Hi!" I give an awkward wave. "Sorry to drop in without saying anything. But I've always wanted to come to one of the SASA meetings and see what it's all about!"

"Uh, this is Ani, everyone," says Isaac, by way of explanation. He doesn't expound any further.

My smile fades a little. I hate to admit it, but it feels like the mood in the room has shifted to something uncomfortable.

"Are new members not welcome . . . ?" I ask. "Because I can leave—"

"No! No, it's fine," Isaac says. "You said you could get this Power-Point to work?"

"Yeah, I can try! I've helped with my dad's work PowerPoints a bunch of times."

Maybe a little too enthusiastically, I walk over to Isaac and take a seat by the laptop in the front of the room. The room, by the way, has gone completely quiet. Waiting.

My sweaty finger slides against the laptop's touchpad and I click around on PowerPoint hoping to find some miracle that will get the slideshow up on the projector. When that doesn't work, I tap the settings.

Someone sniffs loudly.

"I, uh, did that already," Isaac whispers over my shoulder.

I feel every hair on my neck stand, mostly from his proximity. And also because I have no idea what I'm doing.[94]

I glance at our audience, frantic, and catch Marlow's stare; his eyes are darting around the room, like he's trying to communicate something to me, but I can't tell what.

"Oh, I found the problem!" says Ellie, bent over on the floor by an outlet. "The projector's not plugged in."

"Wow." Isaac chuckles. "I guess it was inevitable I made that mistake one of these days." There's a loud booing. "Damn it, Kasim. Go easy on me, man."

Ellie laughs and pats his shoulder comfortingly. "It happens to the best of us."

My fists clench. I failed.

From the corner of my eye, I see Marlow again, his head in his hands. I get it now: he'd been trying to tell me about the plug.

"Okay, now that that's sorted—everyone, feel free to talk amongst yourselves while we figure out this PowerPoint?"

---

94    Love feeling totally useless in front of Isaac. Absolutely love it.

On cue, the room erupts into conversation. I stand to give Isaac his seat back at the laptop, feeling utterly defeated.

I start heading back to my seat when Ellie stops me. "By the way, what's that thing you brought?"

She's pointing to the basket sitting in my chair.

*Right!* I grab the basket, and the baby blue ribbon on the handle flutters as I unveil its contents.

"I brought these," I answer proudly. "I thought you all might want some snacks." My eyes trail to the already full snack table. "But I didn't realize . . ."

"Oh, yeah, we always try to have food available since these meetings run late. . . ." Ellie's eyes widen. "Wait, are those muffins from La Luna Bakery? I love that place!"

"Yes, actually!" Her genuine happiness is infectious. "I love it, too."

"That was sweet of you," Isaac adds, and I feel my heart soaring.

Yes! Redemption!

"Should I—?" I ask, gesturing to the table, and Ellie nods vigorously. From across the room, Marlow gives me a thumbs-up. Basket in tow, I cross the room toward the table.

Yes, being here is awkward, but I've accomplished the most important thing: showing Isaac that I want to be more involved in his life. I still have a long way to go, I know, but I'm hoping he's gotten the hint. Which means progress, for the first time in weeks.

Except my boots are a little wet from the snow outside, and so is the linoleum, so before I know what's happening, I'm falling forward.

"Ani!" I think I hear Isaac shout. It's like everything's in slow motion: I grab at the snack table, desperate for something to stop my fall, but I only manage to grab the plastic tablecloth, yanking the juices and cookies clean off the surface all at once.[95] I land, thanks to the cushioning of a hundred cookies and cupcakes and muffins, with an actual, literal *splat* noise.

Marlow is at my side in seconds.

"Hey." His hand's on my shoulder. *"Hey."*

The room spirals. I'm winded and dizzy. My cheeks feel hot.

But more than anything, I'm embarrassed. *Humiliated.* I can't believe I fell. In front of everyone. God has punished me for my hubris. Why today, of all days, did the universe decide I was going to make an utter clumsy fool of myself?

I slowly lift my head. "Hey," I mutter.

"Did it hurt?" he asks softly.

"What . . . ?"

"When you fell from heaven?"

I groan. "So annoying."

Marlow looks relieved. "If you can insult me, then you're all right." He helps me sit upright and starts gently wiping what appears to be muffin crumbs off my hair.

"God, are you okay, Ani?" Isaac kneels beside us, breathless. "You didn't break anything, did you?"

Behind him is a literal pile of mess. *I've* made a mess. "Oh no," I whimper. "The table, it's—"

"He meant any *bones*, Anisa," Marlow interrupts.

"Oh. No. I think I'm okay." I run my fingers down an icing-and-crumb-coated strand of hair. "Except I ruined your meeting. I'm so sorry, Isaac."

"It's *fine*. I'm just glad you're—" Isaac notices Marlow, and his eyes

---

95    I've always admired magicians who can yank tablecloths without spilling anything. I wish, especially now, that I could pull that off. Literally and figuratively.

narrow. "You. I think I've seen you before. You're Rosie's boyfriend."

"Ex, actually," Marlow corrects.

*Ex?*

*Marlow had a girlfriend? Someone at Halcyon?*

"Anyway, I'm going to take this one to the Health Center." Marlow puts his shoulder under my arm and carefully lifts me to my feet.

"Really?" Isaac looks at me. I can see the questions on his face, but he doesn't ask. "I should take her. I just need to wrap up the meeting, and then . . ."

I shake my head. "Don't worry about it." Plus, I want to get away from here as soon as humanly possible.

I lean on Marlow and let him lead me back out the door.

For a while, he doesn't say anything. There's just the quiet, and so many panicked thoughts in my brain, whirling at such a high speed that they've all mushed into one indiscernible color. All I know is, if this were a test, I would have completely flunked. Of course I would. How presumptuous was it to think that I could just show up to one of Isaac's club meetings on a whim and suddenly be helpful?

Finally, Marlow looks at me, his expression somber. "You know, I'll have to charge you at *least* three muffins for this," he says.

It's not even funny. Nothing about this is.

But I laugh so hard, I snort.


After I'm all checked out at the Health Center, I decide to go home for the day. Home-home, not my dorm-home.

And no, it's not because I'm a coward—that I'm so embarrassed by what happened that I can't even bear to show my face around campus. It's because, conveniently, I have approximately fifty pounds of laundry I

139

need to do, including several pieces that require my dad's steamer. Some of those pieces belong to Isaac, which he'd asked me to wash for him.

Also . . . doing laundry clears my head.[96]

It's also a good opportunity for me to catch up on homework and catch up on Marlow's list of rom-coms. I can't exactly watch them all in my dorm without Kira saying something about it.[97]

So, yes. I go home.

When I walk through the door from the garage, carrying two very full laundry baskets, I find Dad in his usual spot at the kitchen table, a mug of chai at hand.

He looks up at me, startled. "Asalaamu alaikum, Ani. I didn't know you were coming today."

The naturally dark circles beneath his eyes feel even more sunken in than usual, and I can start to see flecks of gray sprouting along his hairline. I wonder if work has gotten stressful. He started his own medical supply company from scratch, but it also means he has trouble not taking everything on by himself.[98]

"It's a clothing emergency," I tell him, dragging the baskets behind me toward the laundry room.

"Ah."

I bounce to the mirror Mom hung in the tiny hall that connects the

---

96    It's hard to feel bad about anything when the fresh scent of lavender fills your nose. It's just *science*.

97    Last time I tried, she asked if Isaac and I broke up. When I indignantly informed her that no, that was not the case, she proceeded to try watching them with me. Only, she decided she hated almost all the love interests and proclaimed that none of them was good enough. It was not a good study environment.

98    At least, the co-owner of the company and Dad's friend, Rashid, has complained as much. At length. At dinner. At least until his wife, Tara Aunty, told him to hush.

laundry room to the kitchen and rip out a couple cotton pads and makeup remover from my overnight bag. As soon as the layer of foundation leaves my face, I let out a happy sigh.

Dad chuckles, amused. But he doesn't say anything. Unlike Mom or Zaina, he's the only one that hasn't said anything about my double life. I remember the first time I started wearing makeup, he just shrugged it off, acted like it was no different than me trying on a new T-shirt.

I think that's why even though Dad and I aren't exactly close, we've always gotten along. I know he just wants the best for me, no matter what.

I tie my hair in a bun and start prepping the washing machine with fabric softener. "Where's Mom and Zaina?"

Dad takes a slow sip of his chai. "Your mom is finishing up a paper at work. Zaina is still at school."

"What about you?" In goes the laundry detergent. I start to feel better already. "What are you up to?"

"Resting." Another long sip.

Good. Thinking about it now, I don't think I've ever seen my dad just sit around, doing nothing. Same goes for Mom. It's probably why I also have trouble sitting still.

I start shoving armfuls of laundry into the washing machine, willing my mind to empty. But that only seems to trigger a cruel replay in my head of my epic face-plant at the meeting. Then over and over again.

Muffins flying. Crumbs in my hair. Bruised elbows. Isaac and Ellie, staring back at me in concern. Like a two-headed monster.[99]

I let out a groan and start violently shoving more piles of laundry into the wash. But then I feel movement behind me.

It's Dad, staring somberly. He looks strangely lost, and I swear I can see

---

99     But painfully cute. Damn it.

the start of a dozen sentences behind his mouth, none of which he voices.

Worry gnaws at my insides. "Dad? What's wrong?"

"Nothing, nothing. I just wanted to tell you something."

I set down the laundry detergent. "What is it . . . ?"

"Your mom and I . . ." His gaze slides to the floor. "We're thinking of postponing the divorce."

"Really?" My mouth falls open. "That's—that's great! What happened? What changed?"

"We've just been doing some more talking, and we've decided that maybe now is . . . not a good time."

Just like that?!

Dad says it so casually, I almost can't believe it. Does this mean Mom and Dad are actually *talking things through*? This is *huge* for our family! Honestly, I never thought I'd see the day my parents would talk through a problem and come to a mutual decision. I'm dazed, like I've been suddenly transported to a parallel world of warm rainbows and good news—both rare and wonderful things. "Wow. That's, I just—*wow*. So what's the plan, then? Do you think you'll finally try couples counseling?"

"Maybe."

It's not a no. That's *progress*. And if they've decided that now isn't a good time to divorce, maybe with a little more time and therapy, divorce will never be an option again.

I smile.

And then Dad wraps his arms around me and pulls me into an awkward hug.

For a moment, I go limp. My dad has *never* hugged me. Maybe he did when I was a child, but certainly not in the past ten years. He's never been one for affection, and frankly, our family's never been touchy-feely. His way of affection is through money: making sure Zaina and I have enough in the bank to help with our education. That's it.

It feels nice, getting a hug from Dad. But it's so out of character that I find myself confused.

"Dad . . . ?" I croak.

"I love you."

I blink.

"O-okay," I reply. "I love you, too?"

He squeezes one last time before finally letting me go.

"Where is this coming from?" I turn to face him. Is he that relieved about the divorce postponement? Maybe he's been worried about how it would affect me and Zaina. Maybe like me, in his own way, he's been worried about the future. Alone.

He shakes his head. "Nothing. I just want you to be happy."

"I *am* happy." Granted, I'm still anxious about Isaac, and I wish things with him were better. Especially after I just totally humiliated myself at the SASA meeting. And I wish this whole thing with Mom and Dad was resolved once and for all. If all of that was fixed, then life would pretty much be perfect; I'd be coasting through Aunty Lubna's three requirements to marry her son, knocking down the door to my happily ever after.

But lately . . . I feel like I'm finding more moments to relax a little, too. And hanging out with Marlow, making plans to win Isaac back—it's almost, well, *fun*.

So why would Dad say that?

Dad gives me a sad expression. "I know" is all he says before walking back to the kitchen table.

I frown and close the washing machine.

**Hey** 6:19 PM

Hey yourself. What's up? 6:20 PM

**So . . .** 6:20 PM

**You heard about Mom and Dad postponing the divorce.** 6:20 PM

Yeah 6:21 PM

Dad told me 6:21 PM

I mean, I'm thrilled but it almost feels too good to be true? 6:22 PM

**Ha, yeah** 6:22 PM

**But maybe now you don't have to stress so much about it** 6:22 PM

**Knowing you, you're losing hair about it lol** 6:23 PM

Don't even JOKE about that!!! 6:23 PM

Are they still fighting though? 6:25 PM

**Not really, surprisingly** 6:25 PM

Well if they decide they hate each other again 6:26 PM

You're always welcome to come here 6:26 PM

You can sleep in the common room in my dorm 6:26 PM

No one will bother you 6:26 PM

I'm not THAT desperate 6:27 PM

But thanks. 6:28 PM

**MARLOW + ANISA**

MAYDAY, MAYDAY 2:12 PM

?? 2:12 PM

What's wrong? 2:12 PM

My mom's birthday is coming up, too 2:13 PM

What kind of gift do I get 2:13 PM

Oh, that's easy 2:14 PM

I would recommend a cashmere scarf: it's appropriate for the season, classy, sophisticated. 2:15 PM

Alternatively, try a perfume. 2:15 PM

Hmmm 2:16 PM

Wait wtf 2:18 PM

Why is perfume so expensive 2:18 PM

Why would I pay 300 dollars for smells? 2:19 PM

Hell no 2:19 PM

I'd rather go with something personal, something with heart 2:19 PM

Excuse me!! 2:20 PM

**Perfume makes a fabulous gift, trust me.** 2:20 PM

**I got one for my roommate's birthday** 2:20 PM

**Ok but does she use it** 2:21 PM

**. . .** 2:21 PM

**Not exactly . . .** 2:21 PM

**Yeah no shit** 2:22 PM

**The best gifts are tailor-made with the person in mind** 2:22 PM

**You can't just shove something expensive and expect them to love it** 2:23 PM

**Ok, smartass, what would you have gotten her?** 2:23 PM

**No idea** 2:23 PM

**Gotta get to know her first, figure out what SHE likes** 2:24 PM

**Not just what I like** 2:24 PM

**And go from there** 2:24 PM

**All right, I'm getting her two boxes of chocolate oranges and her favorite tea** 2:25 PM

**If she likes tea, get her a box of cinnamon and ginger tea—I forgot the brand but I'll look it up** 2:26 PM

**Perfect** 2:26 PM

Look at you, being thoughtful and using your imagination 2:26 PM

Never mind, I'm not telling you the brand anymore 2:27 PM

I'm sorry I'm sorry JUST KIDDING 2:27 PM

# Chapter 14
## FEBRUARY 20

All throughout my Race & Ethnicity class, I keep feeling Marlow glancing over at me. *Concerned.*

Maybe he's right to be: the last time he saw me, I embarrassed the crap out of myself at the SASA meeting. Not to mention I quite uncharacteristically fumbled the answer when Professor Friedman asked me about the reading on Frantz Fanon, even though I'd actually done it last night. If Marlow's sad-puppy face was distracting, it wasn't nearly as distracting as the news about Mom and Dad.

Obviously I'm relieved to hear they've decided against divorcing for now, enough that it almost made me forget how I'd face-planted in front of Isaac. Temporarily, at least. But something about the way Dad dropped the news feels . . . *too* anticlimactic. And the way he hugged me—it almost felt like there was something else he wasn't telling me.

I'd texted Zaina to ask if she knew anything about it, but she'd only responded with:

**Just try to be happy about it.**
**You do know how to be happy, right?**

I leave class in a daze, but Marlow stops me on my way back to the bus stop.

"Want to grab a late lunch? To debrief?" he asks, stepping in tune to my slower walking pace. The crunch of salt crystals and the slushy remains of snow resound beneath us. With the foot of snow we got last night, even Marlow is wearing a jacket.[100]

My phone starts vibrating in my hand. It's Mom. Guess she finally decided to call me back, but as usual, she has awful timing. I wanted to hear more about why she and Dad decided to postpone the divorce, but she never picked up this morning.

I text her with a quick *I'll call you later.*

"I don't know," I tell Marlow, slipping my phone into my pocket. "I'm pretty tired. I think I might head back to my dorm, get some sleep." Just because I overslept doesn't mean the sleep was restful.

"Something quick, then? Getting food in your stomach might help."

We're nearing the stop, and it's cold outside, and all I can think about is curling up beneath my bedcovers.

"I'm not hungry. And haven't you seen the state of my hair? It's *monstrous.*"

He blocks me off, stopping me in my tracks. I almost bump into his chest.

"Come on," he murmurs. "I insist. Also, I'm sorry you feel that way about your hair, but for what it's worth, it looks nice."

I make the mistake of looking up at him. His large, liquid-brown eyes are imploring. Like despite seeing me as a total fool who's very likely fighting a losing battle, he's genuinely worried about me.

I look away.[101]

---

100      A somewhat ill-fitting green bomber jacket, but still, at least he tried.

101      Feeling bummed is the worst when you're trying to pretend you're not bummed to will the bumness away but people keep insisting that you are in fact bummed, which only makes you more bummed.

"Fine. Sure." It's a weird thing to insist on, but I'm too tired to argue, anyway.

"Great." Marlow smiles, victorious. "Cafeteria, then? My treat."

"The food's already paid for. It's part of the meal plan."[102]

"Hey, it's the thought that counts," he points out, and we walk, side by side, back through the snow.

If only that were true.

In a daze, I pile various salad toppings onto my plate until I have a sufficient heap—I get the feeling me not eating properly is only going to make Marlow more annoying—and trudge toward our table. It's mostly empty in the cafeteria, seeing as it's almost 3:00 p.m., and the only sounds are the clattering of serving trays and the spray of water on steel pans from the kitchens.

Out of habit, I scan the cafeteria for Isaac anyway. But all I see are a few exhausted student workers and dozens of posters plastered on the walls for the upcoming Halcyon Winter Dance.

"Thinking about asking Isaac?" asks Marlow, peering at me as I take my seat across from him.

"To the dance? I'd like to. . . ."

"You should, if you want." He takes a sip of water from his cup. "I think that would be a good way to work on the whole 'creating opportunities for new experiences together' step."

"Oh. Yeah. Then maybe I will."

An awkward pause settles between us, neither of us knowing what to say next. But surprisingly, it's not unbearable. Maybe it's because between the two of us, there's no pressure to fill the silence.

---

102    An expensive one, at that. Criminal.

I stab at my salad with a fork.

"So . . ." he starts.

"So." I shove a forkful of tomato in my mouth.[103]

"Oh!" Marlow's eyes suddenly go wide, like he's suddenly remembered something. "I got you a birthday present. A little birdy told me it's this Friday?"

"Didn't *I* tell you about it? Last time we met up for the paper?"

"Shhh." He digs through his backpack on the floor.

Despite myself, a corner of my mouth hikes up. I hadn't expected him to remember, much less get me anything. In fact, between everything that's been happening lately, I almost forgot myself. And there's still been no sign of Isaac remembering, either.

Eventually, Marlow pulls something out from his bag. "Here."

It's a brand-new notebook, the fancy kind that you can only get at Japanese stationery stores, with creamy-smooth paper and a crackly spine. He even slapped on a tiny ribbon at the front edge.

I smile. "Thank you. This is . . . really nice, actually."

"Anytime."

On the chair beside me, I notice my phone's vibrating again. The word *Mom* flashes across the screen. Patience has never been her forte. Why won't she just *text*?

"How"—Marlow rakes a hand through his curly hair—"how are you, uh, holding up? I know that SASA meeting was . . . a lot."

"Tired. But perfectly fine. Really." I smile weakly. "At least now I have a new notebook, so things are looking up."

His mouth twists like something I said pains him.

---

103    I dislike tomatoes. But I do it for the antioxidants. And because if I don't eat them, I can practically hear Nani in my head, scolding me.

"Look," he begins, "I know it can't feel great, trying to do something nice for someone and having it blow up in your face. That probably wasn't your finest hour. Yes, you may have royally embarrassed yourself. And yes, you did it in front of Isaac and Ellie and all of their friends—"

"Okay, I get the point."

"But I think it actually worked out. Isaac has now seen you trying, hard, for him. It's probably the first time you've ever been vulnerable. You actually looked human for once."

"I can't tell whether that's a compliment or an insult."

"It's *endearing*. It was a clumsy attempt, literally, but you showed up. That's progress." Marlow leans across the table, resting his chin against his interlocked hands. "So what do you want to do now?"

I spear a baby tomato and bring it to my lips. "What do you mean?"

"Do you want to keep going with the plan?"

I stop chewing. Swallow. My salad's starting to feel more like sand going down my throat.

Of *course* I want to keep going. Giving up isn't an option. And I refuse to call it quits after one measly attempt, especially when Marlow's worked so hard on this whole plan for me.

But yesterday presented the possibility of a much bigger problem.

I poke at another tomato on my plate. "Did you see the way he and Ellie were at the meeting? The vibes they gave off?" I take another bite. "I don't know, but the whole time I saw them, I just kept thinking—they seemed so close. So great together. The way he smiled with her, it's just—I wish he would smile like that for me, I guess."

Ugh.[104]

"Their relationship might seem different," Marlow says thoughtfully,

---

104    Uggghhhh.

"but it doesn't mean anything. That closeness just comes with time and opening yourself. You can still get that, too. With him." He sets down his glass of water.

"Out of curiosity, though—is there a reason you want that with him so badly?"

"Sorry?"

His expression softens, but his voice sounds more gravelly than usual. "It's not any of my business, I know, but I'm just curious, especially given all these doubts, the way you can't even be yourself around him, the way you're clearly stressed by it all—why exactly does it have to be him?"

I blink. Look away.

It takes a few seconds for the question to sink in. It certainly wasn't one I was anticipating. But it should be easy. It's *obvious*. It's because it's Isaac. Because it *always* has been him. Because he's the ideal. And who wouldn't want him? Plus, everyone who's watched us grow up knows we are meant to be together. The ultimate power couple, as Nadia said.

Of course Marlow comes in with the hard-hitting questions. I wonder if this comes from his experience.

Right. Experience. Isaac had mentioned at the SASA meeting that Marlow had an ex-girlfriend; Rosie, I think her name was. I wonder what happened.

As for Isaac—do I even need an answer? Love doesn't have to make sense, right? But the more I churn my answer in my head, the more the answer doesn't feel right. Like it feels more like I'm trying to justify it.

Why *does* it have to be Isaac?

Why am I having trouble answering this right now?

"That's . . ." I falter as Marlow peers at me, waiting patiently.

We're interrupted by a familiar voice. "There you are."

I look up.

It's Mom.

I nearly jump out of my chair, my heart rate spiking. What horrible, god-awful timing. "What are you doing here?" Despite all efforts to sound calm, my voice is shrill.

"I've been calling and calling, but you didn't pick up." Mom adjusts the heavy canvas bag around her shoulder. The strong smell of desi food wafts throughout half the cafeteria which would normally make my mouth water, but right now I'm too busy panicking. "Thank God for your roommate, Keera.[105] I swear, she's the only one who is respectful to me these days."

"Okay . . ." My laugh is strained. "But that doesn't answer my question. And it's *Kira*, by the way."

She ignores me. "I was in the area visiting Ayesha Aunty—she wants you to come visit her, Ani, she hasn't seen you in forever—and she wanted me to give you some leftovers and cake. Talha's birthday was a few days ago, but Rashid Uncle's prediabetic and can't have sugar around the house."

Her sharp eyes land on Marlow. "Who is this?"

Oh no.

My bleary, sleep-deprived brain has finally caught up to the enormity of the situation: Mom has just caught me alone with a boy who isn't Isaac.[106]

"He's my partner for a paper," I explain quickly, trying not to trip over my words. "For my Race & Ethnicity class. We're in class together."

Mom's mouth tightens. "I don't see any paperwork here."

---

105    In Urdu, this means bug. But no matter how much I correct Mom, she keeps forgetting. It has to be willful at this point, right?

106    For my parents, fraternizing with the opposite sex, beyond work necessities, is Not Good. It's partially why they pushed me to go to Marion instead of a coed school. But honestly, I don't mind; I've seen Halcyon, and the idea of sharing a bathroom with boys makes me want to dig a hole and jump into it.

Marlow stands, taking that as his cue, and puts out a hand. "It's nice to meet you. I'm Marlow. We were just grabbing lunch to celebrate a hard day of class." I shouldn't be surprised that even in the face of Mom's terrifying glower, looking very much like she's seconds away from unhinging her jaw and eating him whole, his carefree smile doesn't waver. If he had a tail, it'd be wagging. Hard to tell if he's brave or just clueless.

"What is there to celebrate?" Mom asks, head tilting. "Do you always celebrate after doing mandatory classes?"

*"Mom."*

"Where is Isaac? I'm sure he'd love to be a part of the *celebration*, too." Her eyes shoot back to Marlow with undisguised distaste. Eyes that say *get away from my daughter, interloper, for she is claimed by another.* "You know how supportive Isaac is."

I don't like the implication. That I purposefully didn't tell Isaac about lunch, that I'm trying to hide it from him. Like I'm the one who just got caught cheating or something.

And with Marlow, of all people! Marlow, who's just a classmate, a friend—

Huh. I hadn't really thought about it before, but yeah. A friend.

"Excuse us," I tell Marlow before scurrying off, half dragging Mom by the arm out of earshot to the cafeteria entryway.

When it's relatively safe, I round on her. "Isaac's not here," I force between gritted teeth. *More important, how should I know where Isaac is? Am I supposed to know his location every damn second? I thought I was his soulmate, not his handler.*

"I can see that," Mom says, her voice low, yet somehow booming in my ears at the same time. "And does he know you're here with another boy?"

"I don't see how that matters. Again, it's for *school*. We're in the school cafeteria, for God's sake. I—" I try to steady myself, but today my brain's on overdrive and my emotions are a seething mess. "I don't understand why you're treating me like a criminal." Especially when I've been spending the past few weeks agonizing over trying to make things between Isaac and me better. It's literally the reason I'm with Marlow now.

Mom folds her arms across her chest. "There's no need for attitude. Isaac adores you. His whole family adores you. What do you think they would do if they saw you flirting with someone else? There are other desi kids at this campus who know Isaac's family; what if someone says something? Do you want to ruin your reputation? Branded as a, as a—"

A burning sensation creeps up my neck. *Slut.* She doesn't have to say it. I know what she's thinking. Apparently, the conversation we had about slut-shaming didn't take.[107]

Mom closes her eyes and recollects herself. "I know you think I'm being unfair, but I'm just trying to *protect* you, Ani. People can be cruel. If you want to be with Isaac, then you can't be doing things like this."

I still don't understand this reaction. Mom's always been protective over Isaac, almost obsessive about our relationship, but this is *ridiculous*. I've had the suspicion that Mom is living vicariously through me; that in terms of Isaac, she just wants me in a stable, happy relationship. Something that maybe Mom feels like she doesn't have.

But surely she gets how unreasonable she's being right now? I mean, even for Mom, this level of . . . desperation, or paranoia, feels far beyond the ordinary. Sure, normally, I don't really go out of my way to talk to other guys—in part because I don't care to, but also, again, no social life here—but now Mom's acting like if some other guy were seen even *breathing* in my general direction, it could sabotage my future with Isaac.

---

107    Or it did, but it doesn't change the reality that internalized misogyny still rampages on. It, in a word, sucks.

"Did you really just come here to deliver some cake?" I ask. "Why are you being so pushy about this?"

Mom's head falls a little. "I wanted to check on my daughter. Spend time with her, especially with her birthday in a few days. I can see now you don't feel the same way."

I exhale through my nose. Mom's flare for drama and guilt-induction is on point—that hasn't changed.

"Mom," I say calmly. "Is it about you and Dad?"

Mom stiffens. "Did Zaina tell you something?"

"It was Dad, actually. Because I deserve to know whether my parents are getting divorced or not."

"Right, yes . . . the divorce. Then you already know: for now, we're putting the divorce aside." Before I can ask why, she continues: "But that's not important right now. I need you to wrap up whatever"—she gestures toward Marlow—"*this* is. I don't want to be getting a phone call from Aunty Lubna asking why you're being seen out with some other boy. She'll start thinking you're fighting, that you did something to her son."

I clench my fists, barely containing the wildfire spreading through my chest. "How come you're assuming that if something's wrong between us, it's *my* fault?"

"Because that's how it works in the world."

"You're right," I answer, and manage a small, good-natured smile. "I'm sorry."

She puts her hand on her cheek. "Make sure you fix your makeup. Your eyeliner is smudged. You don't want Isaac seeing you look sloppy."

"I will."

Since Mom has said her piece and she's in a rush to beat traffic, she hands me the canvas bag full of leftovers and heads home.

I heave myself back into the chair across from Marlow, who's already done eating, and now seems intent on swirling the remaining ice cubes of his drink into oblivion.

"Hey," he asks when he sees me, perking up. "Everything okay?"

"Yeah," I answer with a smile. But then I feel myself deflating.

"No, actually." I feel frustrated. Angry. Sad. And strangely guilty. I'm not even sure why.

Marlow looks at me sympathetically.

But he doesn't press.

**Happy birthday!** 12:28 PM

Hey you remembered 🐿️ 12:28 PM

Thank you! 12:29 PM

**Of course** 12:35 PM

**What kind of guy would I be if I forgot?** 12:35 PM

Not you, that's for sure. 12:36 PM

**Think I can stop by tomorrow and drop something off?** 12:39 PM

No way, is it a gift? 👀 12:40 PM

**Maaaybe.** 12:43 PM

**Wish I could take you out to celebrate though** ☹️ 12:44 PM

**Hope this'll make up for it** 12:44 PM

I'm sure it will. 12:44 PM

It just means a lot that you remembered, 12:44 PM

especially with everything going on 12:45 PM

 12:58 PM

**Thank you for always being so understanding** 12:58 PM

**Of course!** 12:58 PM

**What kind of girl would I be if I wasn't?** 12:59: PM

**Not you.** 1:18 PM

 1:18 PM

# Chapter 15

## FEBRUARY 23

Friday comes with the forced enthusiasm of a person who despises showing up anywhere, and for the first time in a while, Kira and I both have decided to stay on campus for the weekend.

So far, I've spent half the day at the library, and I managed to drag myself through enough work to stave off the shame of how unproductive I've been lately, until I'm one Olde English stanza away from dying of exhaustion.

I despise the fact that I've been having trouble focusing. And now, I'm back in my dorm, killing time by trying on different outfits in front of the mirror, planning out my wardrobe and using the new notebook Marlow gave me: a futile effort to find calm in the mundane.

Happy birthday to me.

"My stomach's been hurting all the time," I announce, standing in front of the floor-length mirror hanging off our door to my dorm room, and smoothing down my silk Kate Spade blouse.[108] "Do you think I look jaundiced?"

"No, you're just Asian," Kira answers. "Welcome to the club."

I spin to face her, hair whipping around me. "I'm serious!"

---

108     Sixty dollars off at a secondhand online shop. I know. My ability to sniff out a good deal is unmatched.

Kira's reflection stares back at me from her bed, where she's been flipping through her *Foundations of Computer Science* textbook, her decal-coated laptop beside her.

"You look *fine*, Birthday Queen. Don't worry."[109]

I smooth down my shirt again. If only it were that easy. The truth is, it feels like the world's been playing with the color wheel of my emotions lately. I suppose Mom's surprise visit is affecting me more than I'd like to admit. Not to mention the other thousand and one thoughts currently plaguing my brain.

Marlow's ex, for starters. He still hasn't said anything about her, and at this point, I'm not sure I can ask.[110] There's still the issue of Mom and Dad's sudden divorce postponement. And then Mom's pushiness earlier this week was a lot, even for her.

"First, the store is out of my favorite lavender bodywash," I mutter, "and now all *this*. You know the only bodywash they had was an *herb-and-shea-butter*-scented one? What am I, a turkey to be *basted*?"

"You can use my Irish Spring—"

"No, thank you."

Outside our dorm room, the hallway is loud with a group of girls who've decided to celebrate the coming weekend by playing drunk Twister. Sounds of laughter, of normalcy. Something about it makes me feel . . . lonely. In a parallel universe, another version of me is spending her birthday with Isaac. Damn her.

I'm attempting a new hairstyle involving a mermaid braid and a silk

---

109     I think one of Kira's new favorite hobbies is making fun of me in ways I can't really tell, at least not straightaway.

110     Plus, whenever I think about her, I get a weird prickly feeling in my chest. Not sure what that's about.

ribbon, thanks to a YouTube tutorial, when there's a knock at our door. I look over at Kira, but she only shrugs—apparently she wasn't expecting anyone, either.

I open the door, eyebrows furrowed.

It's Isaac.

"Hi," he says sheepishly. He's wearing a cream-colored fisherman's sweater that brings out the hazel in his eyes, and most important, he's holding a white box, which he thrusts toward me.

Oh my God. He's actually here for my birthday. With an actual birthday gift. The texts from him earlier weren't a sad little daydream!

"Isaac," I reply, dazed. From behind me, Kira gives him a casual wave. "Yo" is all she says before getting back to her textbook.

"I know I texted earlier, but I wanted to say happy birthday in person." Isaac smiles. "This is for you; it doesn't quite make up for the fact that I'm too swamped with classes and SASA stuff to take you anywhere tonight. But it's a Black Forest cake. I got it from the same bakery where you got the muffins, actually."

The muffins he didn't even get to try at the SASA meeting, but he kindly leaves that part out.

"Wow."

Okay, yes, showing up last minute with a cake feels a little . . . lack-luster, as far as birthday celebrations go. For my birthday three years ago, for example, he climbed up to my window at midnight to give me a pink cashmere scarf he'd wrapped in sparkly silver paper himself.[111]

But at least he actually came to see me in person! With a cake from

---

111     I of course responded the year after by gifting him a Tom Ford Oud Wood cologne that I knew would suit him perfectly (which I could afford only after babysitting Ayesha Aunty's kids throughout the summer).

a bakery I like! Maybe Marlow was right—maybe showing up at the SASA meeting worked! Hahahaha!

"Ani . . . ?"

"Yes! Hi!"

"How are you? How are things at home?"

*Pretend I'm Isaac*, Marlow's voice echoes from my memory. Right. Normal small talk. I can do that.

"Everything's been great!" *You have to say something that leaves room to continue the conversation.* I set down the cake on my bed. "Mom's been acting a little clingier than usual, but you know how she is."

"Is she now?" His lip twitches, like he has something more to say, but then he takes notice of my hair, my outfit. "Are you going somewhere? You're . . . pretty dressed up."

I stare back, confused, before I remember. "Oh! No! No plans." Actually, this hairstyle was one I was hoping to master before Isaac and I went out somewhere. A cute café, maybe. Or—

Right. This is my chance. I can ask Isaac to the Winter Dance. It's my birthday; he can't say no, right?

"I—I, um . . . actually, I had a question for you."

Isaac lets out an exasperated laugh. "You don't have to go in with a whole preamble. Just ask."

"Right. Yes, okay." I discreetly wipe a palm on my cardigan. "So what would you think," I say slowly, "about going to the Winter Dance tomorrow night? I've seen the posters around—it looks like it'll be fun. We don't even have to dance! I don't really care to, anyway. We could just go in, take in the ambiance, the music—I've never actually been to one, so—"

"Oh, sorry," Isaac answered, eyes darting away from mine. "You know I'd love to, but my study group's going to be holed up in the library to study for a Bio test. I'm so sorry, Ani. I feel like I'm saying no a lot these days, but even ripping myself from my desk to come here—I barely had the time." He sees my expression and immediately pedals back. "I don't mean it like—you *know* I'm happy to see you, it's just—"

"It's fine," I respond, shaking my head emphatically. "I get what you're saying, and I totally understand. Maybe next time." Of course, I expected as much. But I have to admit, I'm starting to reach my limit.

I ball my hands into fists. *No.* Even if it feels like the world's trying to pull us apart, I can't give up now.

"Definitely." Isaac gives me a sad smile. "Well, I should get going now. Hope you enjoy the cake."

"I will! Thank you for bringing it."

We say our goodbyes, and I gently close the door.

After the sound of his footsteps have faded, I lean my back against the frame, but I can feel Kira staring at me.

"What?"

"Nothing." Kira presses her lips together. "Hey, what's 127 divided by 4, off the top of your head?"

"About . . . 32?"

"Thirty-two pages of reading a day before my next Writing Sem class. Yeah, that's doable." Kira stands up and stretches. "Are you sure you don't want to play Twister? Could be fun. Or at least funny."

"Pass. My stomach's been playing enough Twister as it is." I'm starting to understand what they mean when they say stress is a killer.

"Somehow only slightly less horrible than the real thing." Kira heads for the door, throws it open to the sound of drunken cackling and music blasting from someone's phone. "Now go have fun or something. It's your birthday, for God's sake."

I wave my outfit planner at her, which I've now begun color-coding. "I *am* having fun."[112]

"You're sick."

"Hey, but—when you get back," I ask faintly, "can you help me eat this cake?"

Kira does something she rarely does: she smiles.

"Gladly."

And with that, she closes the door behind her.

Since I've finished my yearly birthday tradition of cleaning, I decide to change into something more casual and go to Marlow's to, as he put it, *debrief*. Specifically, he wants to go over the "vigorous notetaking" that I "surely had the common sense to do" while watching the rom-coms he assigned as part of my training.

It's not how I thought I'd spend my evening, but here we are.

Marlow throws open the door leading to his dorm, breathless.

"Wow. You actually came," he says.

I shrug, then look him over. "Nice Henley."

He tugs at his collar. "Huh. Is that what this shirt's called?"

*Hopeless.*

I roll my eyes and follow Marlow to his room.

I brace myself as I peer inside, but everything looks . . . normal. Marlow's room is about as big as Kira's and my room, but it lacks our older, Gothic room vibes: instead of a creaky hardwood floor, he has a faded blue, thin carpet, and where our walls are a clean plaster, his are cement blocks painted in thick coats of white. His bed has been pushed

---

112    Listen, having the time to organize is a privilege. One that I fully appreciate.

up against the one large window, with dark blue bedsheets and a single red, lumpy pillow. But that large window—it lets in so much light, casting his room in a warm orange glow, while giving an amazing view of the central campus quad. Otherwise, the room is a little threadbare. Pleasantly tidy, though, with the faint smell of lemon; a cleaning spray, I'd venture. Good on him.

But I'd be lying if I said I wasn't a little nervous about being alone in a guy's room, even though I know Marlow wouldn't try anything.[113]

Still, I stand awkwardly in the doorway.

"Come in, you creep," says Marlow. With my feet feeling like lead, I walk in and close the door behind me.

I notice more about his room now. Above his bed, he's hung a couple decorations: artwork from some space video game and a bright green-and-yellow poster that reads "Jamaica Football." And on a small set of drawers, which Marlow's using as a side table for his bed, I see a family photo in a wooden frame: with a slightly younger-looking Marlow, front and center, in red graduation robes, and two friendly looking people on either side of him. His mom and dad, I assume, have their arms wrapped around his shoulders. Marlow's dad is a tall Black man with close-cropped curls speckled with gray; in the photo, he's wearing an elegant gold chain around his neck. Marlow's mom is a short woman with dark brown skin and beautiful, bright eyes; Marlow, I realize, got his dimples from her.

"They look so proud of you," I say, pointing to the photo.

Marlow laughs. "Yeah. My parents are the type to get excited over every little thing. You should have seen them when I first rode a bike."

"That's really cute. Sounds like you and your parents are close." I

---

113     I've never gone into Isaac's room either, of course. . . . I may have daydreamed about it, though.

didn't go to my own high school graduation; Mom had said she didn't feel like sitting for hours for something I was expected to do, and that was that. "I envy you."

"Yeah, we are pretty close. It was hard being away when I first came here for college. But I make it a point to call them a lot. I swear it's why I'm late for so many of my classes; I call them when Mom and Dad are on their afternoon walks, or I'll call my best friend, Winston, who's still back in Kingston—I've known him since primary school—and completely lose track of time."

Marlow flops onto his bed, which sinks a little beneath his weight, and frowns. "Wait, why do you look like that?"

"Like what?" I ask, suddenly even more self-conscious.

"Like you just got told Christmas is—wait, no, like Eid is canceled."

*Damn him and his ability to read me.*

"I"—I sigh softly—"asked Isaac to come with me to the Winter Dance earlier today."

Marlow gives me a sympathetic look. "Ah."

"Yeah." I stare at my feet. "Too busy. He did stop by my dorm room to drop off some cake, though."

"Hey, that counts for something."

"Sure. I guess." I try to put on a smile, but lately it's been difficult to pretend.

"Hey, none of that pessimistic crap, not on your birthday. You did good. Maybe today didn't get you what you want, but there's always next time." Marlow waves me over. "Okay, show me what you've got. We're only focusing on nice things for the rest of the day."

I sigh again. But feeling more comfortable now, I toss him my notebook, the one Marlow gifted me that I now use for all my romance research. Marlow flips through it, eyebrows furrowed.

"I'm sorry, does this say you didn't like *10 Things I Hate About You*?" He stares down at the page. "It says you didn't '*get it*'? What kind of notes are these?"

"Excuse me, I also took notes on the wardrobe choices. Whoever did Julia Stiles's hair needs to be charged for war crimes. So unflattering."

"And?"

"*And* it felt a little toxic to me. Outdated. Kat had a lot of internalized misogyny. I mean, who doesn't, but still. I kind of liked Bianca more."

"All right, but what about Heath Ledger?"

"What about him?"

"*What about him?*" he repeats.

I shrug. "Isaac's handsomer."

Marlow pinches the bridge of his nose. "You know what, this is my fault. I don't know what else I was expecting." He looks up at me. "Okay, we're going to rewatch *10 Things I Hate About You*, right now. And while we watch, I want you to think about three things." He puts up a finger. "1) How do they treat each other?" Another finger. "2) What is communicated, good and bad, verbally and physically?" And another. "3) What do you think could be done differently? And after we've got all that, we can start brainstorming that care package idea you had for your fiancé, who, I'm sorry to say, is not quite up to Heath Ledger's level."

"Agree to disagree." I fold my arms across my chest. "But *fine*. Geez. Why have you watched so many rom-coms, anyway?"

"Honestly? For my own education. I've also had a lot of time on my hands." I get the sense he's just giving me a throwaway answer. "You know, for someone who plays a lot of those romance games, you really don't know *squat* about rom-coms."

"I wasn't allowed to watch much TV growing up. And the otome games are a *recent* development. I did read a lot of romance books, though."

"Amazing. And yet you still know nothing." He crosses his room and starts tinkering with a small TV setup that I'm pretty sure is just an oversized computer monitor. "You want a drink, by the way?"

"Oh, I don't drink."

"Not booze. I don't drink, either."

"Wow, a rare Marlow fact. Any particular reason?" I ask.[114]

"Nah, just, uh, not into it," he answers, avoiding my eyes. "Haven't had a drink since my first-year and don't really have the desire to drink again. I've got some bottles of Ting, though—it's like grapefruit soda, I guess. I don't have much by way of snacks, sorry. I do have these gizzadas my mom mailed me."

"I don't know what that is."

"They're like Jamaican coconut pastries." Marlow gestures under his bed. "Should be in a box under there. One night, when we were kids, my friend Winston and I ate like, six, and we felt sick for days, so maybe just don't eat that many."

I bend down by his bed to find, lo and behold, a small cardboard box, already opened. Someone's written MARLOW GREENE in big Sharpie letters on the side of the box, and there's even a tiny heart drawn next to it. I feel a small smile creep across my face. Somehow, I shouldn't be surprised Marlow would have a loving mom.

I move a few bags of plantain chips and green bottles of Ting out of the way, and grab a small, plastic-wrapped gizzada. As I carefully unwrap it, the coconut scent hits me in a wave, and the maraschino cherry on top glitters like a jewel. "That reminds me," I say, "have you tried biryani before?" I remember the way he'd eyed the plastic bag of biryani meant

---

114     Then again, I'm pretty sure Kira said she doesn't drink, either. Something about alcohol making her too powerful.

171

for Isaac right away, back when we'd first started talking.

Marlow's plugging his laptop to the monitor. "Oh yeah, my aunty Shiv—that's my mom's sister—makes *really* good veggie biryani. But that was rare. I grew up mostly eating goat and chicken curries. Oxtail."

I take a bite of the gizzada. It's delicious.[115] "I've never tried oxtail."

"*You've never tried oxtail?*" Marlow looks at me in mock indignation. "You barbarian. You *heathen*."

"I'm pescatarian, first of all. And second, *heathen*?! Those are some choice words, Mr. *Joseph Conrad*. Mr. *Rudyard Kipling*."

"You take that back."

My response is the kind of hideous face I'd only make with Zaina.

Unfortunately, Marlow is undaunted. "Wait, can you hold that pose for just a little—" he says, not-so-stealthily pulling out his phone.

"No! You already have enough blackmail material on me. God, *now* who's the heathen?"

"Both of us, according to Rudyard Kipling."

"True. Screw that guy."

Marlow nods in agreement. "Screw that guy. Truce?"

"Truce. We should focus on the true enemy: white British men."

"Of which, I'm happy to report, none exist in the world of *10 Things I Hate About You*. That I know of, at least."

An ugly snorting sound escapes me. It's only been a few minutes, but I already feel so much more relaxed.

Marlow walks over to me and hands me back my notebook. I open it to a clean, new page and dig for a pencil from my purse.

He smiles. "You've been using the notebook I gave you?"

"Yeah," I answer simply as I scribble *10 Things: Redux* on the first

---

115    I will never say no to a sugary coconut dessert.

line. I don't mention the part about the notebook he gave me being one of my favorites. It's a good-quality mechanical notebook, and I'm a *stickler* for good paper.

He sits on his bed beside me, a comfortable distance away.

"Happy birthday, Anisa," Marlow says as the movie starts, his voice warm and malted.

This isn't exactly how I'd envisioned what my perfect birthday would look like: not here, in a Halcyon dorm room, with my partner for my class paper. But this is surprisingly comfortable. Nice, even.

I stare down at my lap.

"Thanks, Marlow."

And for the rest of the evening, I focus on the movie.

# Chapter 16

## FEBRUARY 24

The next day, I'm putting the finishing touches on the care package for Isaac when I get a notification on my phone.

It's Marlow. His texts come in a flurry.

> You busy? We should work on the paper later

> No wait let me guess

> You have a hot date

> With some guy in your visual novel

I frown at my screen. Wow, way to hit me where it hurts.

*Shut up*, I reply. Although he's not wrong; I have four more routes to complete in *Rose in the Embers*, and I am nothing if not thorough. That will have to wait until later, though.

> Oh right, did you get the goods?

> Yes.

> Operation Care Package is a go.

> GOOD(S). I'll meet you at the bus stop.

I gotta 👀 inspect 👀.

You can't take anything from the care package.

It's not for you

J'ACCUSE

But yes you caught me

I smirk. I wouldn't blame him for trying, though. I grabbed, some might say, an unnecessarily huge assortment of snacks from the Coffee Ring (including bags of fruit snacks), some vitamin C powder, and even some ThermaCare heating pads for sore necks I found tucked in the corner of the school store. It is the perfect care package for a hard study session.

After you drop off the care package
at the library, wanna camp out somewhere?

Race & Ethnicity paper's due in a month

My fingers hover over my phone. It's a good idea; I could use some time outside my dorm room.

But I can practically feel Mom shaking my shoulders, telling me to be careful. That even though Marlow's a friend, even though Marlow's been the only person I can open up to about Isaac, I shouldn't be seeing him any more than I must.

I ignore her.[116]

Thirty minutes later, I hop off the bus, wearing a long, sensible camel-colored sweater dress beneath my elegant black double-breasted coat, and step onto Halcyon's campus. It's dark, and cold enough that the air

---

116    Which I wouldn't dare do in real life, mind you.

stings my neck and cheeks. My limbs feel heavy despite the weekend liveliness in the atmosphere; Halcyon's campus is bustling with groups of kids walking to and fro across the quad, the central open space on campus just in front of the hall, stitching uneven trails of footprints into days-old snow.

I stand under a lamppost by the bus stop. I bundle my coat closer around my body while clusters of Marion and Halcyon students move narrowly past me, a stubborn rock in the middle of a river.

It's not long before I hear a familiar voice. "Boo." Marlow pops out from behind me. Unfortunately for him, his attempt at surprise utterly fails.

"May I?" he asks, and I nod robotically before I understand what he's asking—which is a big mistake, because the next thing I know, his warm fingers gently grasp my chin, tugging my face toward his.

"Wha—?" is the sound that comes out of my mouth, but it chokes in my throat when I realize just how close his face is to mine.

"Huh." Marlow's dark eyes focus on my lips, and he seems oblivious to the fact that my cheeks are ablaze. I know my makeup is especially on point tonight—I made sure of it, since I'd be seeing Isaac—but this level of closeness is not *right*. I can practically taste the toothpaste on his breath—and there's something else I smell, something sweet and familiar, but I can't quite place it. All I know is I—

Wait. What is happening.

*What is happening?*

My brain feels like it's short-circuiting as his finger grazes my chin a final time. I hold my breath until finally, he lets go.

"Sorry to be the bearer of bad news," he says sheepishly, "but uh, I think you missed a hair or two there."

The warm, tingling heat I felt in my chest evaporates in an instant.[117]

"*What?*" I shriek. The urge to slap him is strong. The freaking *nerve*. I can't believe for a second I thought—

Thought *what* exactly?

Oh no. No, no, no, no. I've been playing too many otome games. Why would I even—there's no way he would—

I raise a hand.

"No violence!" he says, putting up his arms defensively. "I'm just trying to make sure you look and feel your best, I swear!"

Maybe that's partially true, but he's also definitely making fun of me. Also, how he even notices these tiny details is beyond me. I turn away from him, and rummage through my purse for my compact mirror and the extra pair of tweezers I carry with me, thank God.

"I'm sure there's a nicer way to inform someone," I mutter.

"How?" Marlow snorts behind me. "Should I have just not said anything and yanked it out? Should I have asked you straight up if you shaved this morning?"

"I don't *know!*" I stare at my chin in the mirror. It's not obvious, but he's right: there is in fact a single thick black hair just under my chin. I violently yank at the wayward hair with my tweezers. "God. This is *unforgivable.*"

"Can't all be perfect, huh?"

I slap my compact closed and throw him a glare. His grin only widens.

"I feel like I learn something new about you every day. It's only natural, though. Nothing to be ashamed about."

"Shut up."

---

117    Remember when I said I didn't like people who were too observant? This is precisely why. They see too much! Too much!

"Is that it?" Marlow suddenly gestures at the cardboard shoebox in my hands. It's the care package for Isaac, which I've painted a pastel blue and added some sparkly star stickers for a much-needed makeover.

"Yes. And I think I've outdone myself, if I may say so." I put away my compact mirror and tap the box with a finger. "Thank you, by the way," I add. "For the lovely idea."

Marlow nods. "He'll love it."

"Oh, and"—I dig through my pocket—"it's not the muffins I still owe you, but I did get you this. Even though you don't deserve it for making fun of me."

I hand him an extra heating pad.

Marlow takes it, stunned.

"Is this really for me?" He turns it around, reads the back of the packaging. "Oh *hell* yeah, I'm using this bad boy tonight. My neck's been killing me." He smiles. "*Thank you*, Anisa."

My mouth twitches. "It's—it's nothing." In truth, the guy at the school store gave it to me for free when I bought the first one for Isaac's care package. I've never seen someone look so happy over something so small.

"Clearly my lessons are working," Marlow adds, winking. "I'd give you an A-plus."

My mouth goes dry for reasons I can't quite grasp. Maybe it's because I hadn't even thought about practicing for Isaac when I decided to give Marlow the heating pad. I just wanted to give it to him. To thank him.

I suppose it doesn't make a difference.

I shrug. "I have a decent enough teacher," is all I say, and start walking.

Together, we cross the quad, Marlow asking me a bunch of questions about my day. (What did you eat for breakfast? How do you choose your outfit? What was the worst part about the homework you did today?)

After a blistering five-minute walk, we finally reach the library. I clutch the care package close to my chest as my heartbeat quickens.

I hope he'll like it.

"Okay, so we just have to find him, and then we can . . ." I trail off and scan the familiar expanse of the entryway. The library is so quiet, I can hear my own breathing like a howling squall. I mean, the library is *always* quiet, but this is different. Like there's a long undisturbed stillness in the air. It is the night of a big dance, so the emptiness shouldn't be too surprising. But there's no sign of *anyone*.

Marlow and I split up and search every corner, but we can't find him anywhere. Eventually, I track down a librarian, giving her a (arguably long-winded) description of Isaac in case she's seen him around. She shakes her head.

It's almost like . . .

He's not here.

"Maybe he's studying somewhere else," I say weakly when Marlow's found me near the reference desk. "Or maybe he stepped away for a sec?"

I'm not sure who I'm trying to convince. I've already looked at all the tables; usually if people have to get up, they'll leave their stuff behind to ensure their table doesn't get stolen. But all the tables are clear.

"Yeah . . ." Marlow glances at me. "That's always a possibility. Just double-checking, you're sure he said he'd be at the library? *This* library?"

"Yes."

The room's spinning, and horrible, panicked thoughts whirl around my brain. Isaac's not where he said he'd be. On the same night there happens to be a big dance. The same dance he said he couldn't go to with me.

I have to admit, it doesn't look good. "Hey—" I hear Marlow, but I'm yanking out my phone from my coat pocket to text Isaac. Maybe I'm worrying over nothing, but I need to know. I need to confirm, just for my peace of mind.

*Hey! How's studying going?* I type with numb fingers. I hit send, imagine the signals bouncing all throughout Halcyon, then wait.

A minute passes.

Two. Three.

I grip my phone, tight. Pace the nearby library stacks nervously. Marlow leans against one of the empty desks, waiting too.

A full ten minutes go by, and still no word.

"You know, a couple years ago, my dad disappeared," Marlow says softly. "And my mom freaked out. She looked everywhere, couldn't find him. She thought the worst. Turns out, he was just hanging out in the backyard, gardening for three hours." He looks at me, really looks at me.

"Point is, don't think the worst just yet. Let's be patient. We can always come back later."

I bite my lip, feeling utterly pathetic.

*You know I'd love to, but my study group's going to be holed up in the library to study for a Bio test.*

Being too busy for me is one thing, and I can forgive that. In a way, it inspires me, pushes me, too. But lying to me—

No. Like Marlow said, I won't think the worst just yet. There *has* to be some sort of explanation. If I'm being honest, though, I'm getting tired of always relying on faith. No matter what happens, I just want to know what's going on. And maybe if I were the Anisa of two months ago, if I were alone right now, it'd be a different story. But with Marlow here, I . . .

I'm less afraid of the possibilities.

"Marlow," I say, steeling myself. "Would you like to go to the dance with me?"

# Chapter 17

**FEBRUARY 24**

To call Keystone Hall just a *hall*, where the Halcyon Winter Dance is held, would be an understatement. Contrary to the relatively modest, unadorned tan stone exterior,[118] the inside of the main hall is more like the ballroom from *Anastasia*: floor-to-ceiling rounded windows fit for a cathedral or castle, a polished black-and-white-checkered floor with a sheen so fresh it almost looks wet. Arched ceilings and intricate 1800s crown molding that spans several inches along both ends of the walls. My parents would swoon over the design, if, you know, it wasn't mostly covered by sweaty college students.

It's packed in here. Even with some of the windows open, the air is thick with oppressive heat. There must be hundreds of students, limbs in the air undulating to the pulse like the rhythmic crests of ocean waves, cast in dozens of different colors from the shifting spotlights. The DJ is playing a song with a strong tabla beat that makes my skin buzz; the music thumps in my chest, carried by the cavernous expanse; so loud, I swear I can feel the sound waves bouncing between my bones.

Marlow says something to me, but I can't hear him over the din. I can't even hear my own thoughts.

"What?" I scream back.

---

118    Halcyon has Quaker origins, which I guess informs the simple, oops-all-squares! architecture.

He leans down, his face approaching mine. I freeze; he's so close, I can smell the sweet mint toothpaste again on his breath[119]—but then I realize he's only bringing his mouth closer to my ear.

"Have you ever been to a dance before?" he repeats.

I run my fingers down a strand of my hair, suddenly needing to do something with my hands. "Um, no. Never."

I didn't even go to my senior prom. It's not like I ever had the time, and my parents wouldn't have let me, anyway. *What would people say if you went to dances*, Mom would warn. To be fair, I'm not sure I ever cared to; I'd have no reason to go, unless Isaac invited me. Which he never did, of course: mostly for propriety reasons. He'd be too busy, anyway.

I take a deep breath, but now that I'm actually here, my earlier rush of courage has been smushed. Now I'm afraid. Afraid of what we'll find. Afraid of what we won't. And if my parents found out I was at a dance—and with Marlow, after everything that Mom said—there is at least an eighty-percent chance they'd murder me.

But the music—it's *infectious*. Everything is so big and loud and colorful and alive. And yes, I feel completely out of my element, but . . . it looks so fun. I can see the appeal. You could get lost in this crowd and completely let go. It's stepping into an alternate reality where no one really cares what you look like, what you're doing. Everyone is focused on simply feeling. I watch, mesmerized, as a girl with short hair and a nose ring dances by herself nearby, her body moving in such perfect unison to the music it's almost like it's coming out of her, like she's controlling it.

She looks so *free*.

Unfortunately, my focus on her means I don't notice the hulk-of-a-guy next to me dancing a little too enthusiastically; just before he almost rams

---

119    I approve. Sweet mint is better than spearmint.

into me, Marlow quickly puts out an arm to protect me.

The guy scowls at Marlow. Like he recognizes him.

But Marlow ignores him.

"You good?" he asks, voice raised so I can hear him over the din.

"Yeah. Sorry. Thanks."

The corner of Marlow's mouth quirks up. "You look tense."

"How can I not be?" I'm not exactly here for a good time. My love life could be on the line. What am I supposed to do if Isaac's here?[120]

Briefly, he puts a hand on my shoulder. "Whatever happens, it's going to be fine. Promise."

"You can't actually believe that."

He shrugs. "No, not always. But since you can't control what life throws at you, you might as well try to have fun while you can."

I open my mouth to argue when Marlow grabs my hand and spins me so suddenly—once, twice—that the care package nearly goes flying from my grip. No one's ever twirled me before, so the sensation of my hair umbrellaing around me is new and not terrible.

I stumble and catch myself, disoriented.

"There. Feel a little better?" he asks.

"*No.*" Although now my nervousness has been replaced by dizziness.

Marlow laughs. I'm not sure what's so funny, but seeing him laugh at my expense doesn't even annoy me the way it should.

I squeeze the care package closer to my chest. "Are Jamaicans always this chill?"

"Are Pakistanis always so uptight?"

"*Ha.*"

Marlow smiles before going back to searching, his eyes darting back

---

120    Besides spontaneously combust?

and forth around the room. But Keystone Hall is so crowded, it's hard to see anything beyond a foot from us.

Right. I need to focus.

"Any sign?" I ask.

He shakes his head. "Could be that he's not here after all."

My heart flickers a little with hope. I try to add a few inches to my height by getting on my tiptoes and look around, too. I don't recognize anyone here. In this huge crowd, the only person I know is my class partner who has somehow managed to shove himself into my personal affairs.

"Come on," Marlow says suddenly, grabbing my hand. "Let's go in deeper."

I don't respond, too surprised by how normal and comfortable it feels having him hold my hand. I let him lead me, clear people out of the way so I don't have to. He brings me to one of the open bay windows, where there's a ledge, and effortlessly pulls himself onto it. With the few added feet of height, he scans the crowd.

"Anything?" I ask again. I'm standing by his long legs dangling off the side of the ledge and take this brief pause to wipe at my forehead, damp with heat.

The song changes to some other dance song with a bone-tingling bassline, which causes the hall to erupt in happy screams.[121]

"Nah," Marlow answers, eyes squinting ahead. "Maybe if we try the other side. . . ."

He hops down next to me, and I move to follow him back into the throngs of people—

---

121    I don't recognize the song; I swear, most of the music I've been listening to has been courtesy of Kira, which means most of it is K-Pop. Not that I'm complaining, though. I mean, I did at first. But damn, does it grow on you. Just don't tell her I said that. I'll never hear the end of it.

Until he's stopped by a girl.

Marlow takes a step back, and I nearly crash into him.

I can't see his face, but his back has gone stiff. Whatever he's seeing, it's put him in straight up fight-or-flight mode, and either way, I am nervous. I peek my head out from behind him and catch a glimpse of his face; his eyebrows have sunk low, his expression uncharacteristically stiff.

"Hi, Marlow," says the girl in front of him. She's pale, with straight dark hair and ice-blue eyes and a thin, upturned nose. Almost elegant, despite the glean of sweat on her neck from the heat. But there's something barbed about her that makes me uneasy.[122]

Based on Marlow's face right now, she must be Rosie.

Marlow's ex.

She smiles. "I thought that was you by the window. Kyle told me you guys are in Race & Ethnicity together. Long time no see."

*"Rosie."* He returns the smile, but his fists clench at his side. "I don't know; they do say time is pretty subjective. It hasn't felt nearly long enough to me."

"Funny as always." Rosie's gaze shifts to me. "I'm sorry, you are—?"

"I'm a friend of Marlow's," I yell over the music. "We were doing work in the library but decided to stop by for a little break since I've never been, and Marlow didn't want me to miss out. You know him: Nice Guy Marlow." I laugh weakly.

She quirks a brow. "Yes, *Nice Guy Marlow.*"

Marlow blinks, at a loss for words. I've never seen him look like this, so uncomfortable and unsure. I might not understand the situation

---

122     And it's not just her overplucked eyebrows, which devastate me. Regardless of my immediate dislike of her, I would punch anyone who committed such a crime against her brows.

between them, but I can see the way he's shutting down.

Finally, he seems to regain himself. "Well, I'd say it was nice seeing you," he says, already turning on his heel, "but I've been told I'm *brutally* honest."

"Hey, can you *wait*—" I call after him, but he's already gone, leaving me alone with Rosie.

I have a thousand questions bubbling on the tip of my tongue. I wonder how long they were together. I wonder how Isaac knew about Marlow and Rosie once dating. I wonder what happened between them to make them feel like . . . this. Does it all have something to do with why Marlow's trying to help me now?

And is he okay?

Rosie's stare remains glued on Marlow, even as he's swallowed by the crowd. The music changes again, this time to something a little softer, and intimate—a welcome change, because my head's throbbing.

"Thanks for—meeting you—" I manage to say to Rosie, my brain short-circuiting, before fleeing after Marlow.

I fight my way against the crowd until I finally catch up to him and tug at his sleeve. "Hey, *wait*. Are you all right?"

Marlow doesn't stop. "We should hurry. Who knows when the dance will wrap up. If you want to catch Isaac, it's probably now or never." I look up at Marlow, gratitude fluttering in my chest. Marlow's always so straightforward, but right now, for the life of me, I can't tell what he's thinking. Even in the midst of all this awkwardness, he's still focused on helping me find Isaac.

"Right." I narrowly avoid shoulder checking a girl shorter than me, dancing with her girlfriend. "But it's pretty obvious you're shaken up. We could step out and talk about it, if you want—"

"Rosie's . . . just a bad ghost." For once, Marlow doesn't appear to be in a talkative mood. But the fact that Marlow has a past—a romantic one, even—I'm curious to know more. What was it that Chaucer said? *Forbid us something, and that thing we desire.*

"Isaac knows her," I keep going. "Knows about you two dating. Was the breakup . . . recent?"

"Kind of." Marlow whips around to face me. "Can we just—drop it? Please?"

I flinch. "Yeah . . ." My gaze lowers. I've crossed a line I shouldn't have. As if any of this is my business. "I'm sorry."

He opens his mouth as if to say something else but seems to reconsider. His mouth twists into a bitter smile, and he keeps walking ahead. But then he stops.

"You know what?" He suddenly looks back at me. "Maybe we should head back to the library. Looking for Isaac—maybe it's a bad idea."

"What are you saying?" But I see it in his face. Marlow's hiding something.

I weave past him, even as Marlow tries to stop me. And then I see it, too.

It's Isaac, leaning against a wall, not far from the DJ. He's with a couple other people I don't recognize—two guys, two girls. And Ellie, her cheeks a sweet peony pink.

She's standing beside Isaac, her arm wrapped around his. It's obvious they've been dancing: hair sticks to their foreheads, and sweat glistens off their skin, bathed in color. He leans down and says something into her ear. She smiles. Radiant.

Isaac is here after all. Which means . . .

He . . . lied.

*Why?*

I know part of me obviously suspected he'd be here, but to actually confirm it, to actually catch him in a lie—it's just not computing.

Plus, he took such a risk coming here; if my parents would murder me for being at a college dance, his parents would murder him, bring him back to life, and murder him again. But the strangest part about it all is that seeing him here, with Ellie—I've never seen Isaac look so relaxed, so comfortable. It's an Isaac I've never seen before. The flashing lights on his skin make him glow as they bounce off the droplets of sweat on his forehead, his cheeks. He looks beautiful. They look beautiful.

It's not fair. Nothing about this is fair.

I watch, feet rooted to the ground, as Isaac slowly lifts his head, and for a moment, I think his familiar hazel eyes collide with mine. But there's no flicker of recognition, no sign that he knows who I am. Maybe it's because I'm the last person he expects to see here. Maybe he's purposefully ignoring me. Either way, he gives me nothing more than a casual glance before turning his attention back to his friends. To Ellie.

I thought I'd feel a smoldering rage at catching Isaac in a lie. Or the kind of choking sadness that leaves you breathless for days.

Right now, I don't know if I feel anything.

"Anisa." Marlow's voice is right by my ear, but it's taken a serious tone. "What do you want to do?"

I don't answer. My mouth is too dry. And my eyes are doing a funny thing where everything looks glazed over, like I'm looking at the world from underwater. All I can think about is how Mom said I wasn't trying enough.[123]

So much for that.

The crowd, the music—everything fades. The care package falls from my grip and I make a beeline for the exit, fighting my way through the crowd.

---

123    There's something . . . especially painful about your own parents saying that.

"Anisa!" I think I hear Marlow behind me.

I shove myself into the giant double doors and plunge into the cold night air outside. I don't even know where I'm going. All I know is I want to get myself far, far away from here. Are the buses still running? I can always walk—

"Hey!"

Marlow holds my wrist to stop me.

I sniffle. It's cold.

Slowly, I turn to face him. My lips settle into a practiced smile.

"I'm fine," I say, with as much certainty as I can muster. "I'm sure you're feeling all over the place, too. After seeing Rosie. Are you sure you don't want to talk about it?"

He lets go of my wrist. "There's nothing to talk about."

"But—"

"And it's not important right now," Marlow adds softly. "I'm far more worried about you."

I appreciate the sentiment. But I wish he'd talk about Rosie, if only to give me something different to think about. I guess he doesn't feel comfortable enough with me yet. It kind of hurts.

"Really. Don't worry about me. I just need a breather."

Marlow doesn't look convinced, so I keep walking until I spot a familiar pond off the path. My legs come to a halt. The water is mostly frozen; cattails and other long grasses at the pond's edge gently sway in the breeze. Moonlight hits the water at its icy center, casting a serene, almost ethereal glow on the whole scene.

I bite my lip.

Marlow notices and stops walking. "Anisa?"

"You know, I've seen the pond before, in passing," I say, my voice carrying soft on the wind, "but I've never really *looked* at it."

Marlow's expression is sad. "Guess you don't really get a chance to see everything on campus, right? I'll show you around sometime, if you want. Make it easier for you to find classes in the future."

My eyes prickle.

"Isaac was supposed to do that for me," I whisper. It's an admission more than anything.

Marlow stands at my side. He doesn't respond.

"Oh." I realize it then: "I dropped the care package." What a waste. My first care package and I didn't even get to deliver it.

I attempt to clear my throat of the lump that's formed, but clearly my body's not cooperating because now it feels like my throat is squeezing in on itself.

Before I know what's happening, his arms wrap around me. They're bare; he isn't wearing his coat. In his rush to chase me, he must have forgotten it back at the hall.

Stranger still, I don't stop him.

Over his shoulder, I catch a glimpse of a group of upper-division students heading back to their dorms from the dance. As they pass, it almost feels like a few of them frown when they spot Marlow.

"People can see us," I mumble.

"Is that really something to care about right now?" Marlow says.

I say nothing. Only dig my fingers a little tighter into the fabric of his shirt.

"It's okay." His voice is soft. Comforting. So much so, that for a moment, maybe I don't have to care about anything else.

"It's okay," he says again.

And with that, the dam in me breaks, and I cry into his chest.

## TEXTS FROM ZAINA

**Visiting you tomorrow** 11:54 PM

**Hope you don't have any plans** 11:54 PM

**you probably don't tho lol** 11:54 PM

## TEXTS FROM MARLOW

**Hey you** 9:03 AM

**Text me when you wake up** 9:03 AM

**Just so I know you're ok?** 9:03 AM

# Chapter 18
### FEBRUARY 25

"There's nothing in this world that would make me happier than knowing you returned my feelings," Collin says, his deep, honeyed-voice oozing through my headphones.

*Yes, Collin. God, yes, I do.* I slouch deeper into my bed, letting out a dreamy sigh.

I've decided to spend my Sunday reaching the end of the Collin route in *Rose in the Embers.* Collin has revealed himself to have a curse that turns him into a monster when he is hit by moonlight. Initially, I didn't think I'd like his story route—I'm suspicious of characters who pretend to be happy all the time—but his hidden depth has won over my heart. Sorry to Victor.

"Having fun?" Kira is watching me from her desk with an amused expression.

I yank out my headphones. Crap. I forgot I wasn't alone. And I feel like this keeps happening lately. My daily routine remains the same, of course—I still wake up before Kira to apply my makeup so she won't see my real face—but during the day, I'm finding that I'm letting my guard fall. Just a little.

I'm not quite sure what's changed. Maybe I'm getting too relaxed in my dorm. Maybe I'm getting tired of keeping up the charade all the time. Or maybe it's Marlow's fault for making me wonder why I need to keep it up all the time.

I clear my throat. "A little."

She looks smug. "I knew you'd enjoy it."

I look away and pout. Annoying smugness aside, she is right. Wait, actually, she's *wrong*, because I don't just enjoy it. I *love* it. In fact, I'd say this otome game is the only thing keeping me afloat right now, the only thing that's stopping me from thinking about—

Isaac. My ribs knit together.

*No. Don't think about it.*

"So?" Kira asks softly. "Are we going to talk about what happened last night?"

My grip on my Switch tightens. "What do you mean?"

"I don't know," she shrugs. "Which is part of the problem. What I *do* know is, you were dropped off here late last night by some guy I've *never* seen before and you both looked like someone died." Her eyes narrow. "Did Prince Charming do something?"

Last night, after I finished the ugliest sob session in the history of humankind,[124] Marlow insisted on seeing me back to my dorm. Neither of us said anything, instead opting for a gloomy silence befitting two people who had just committed some unspeakable crime. So I get why Kira's worried. And I suppose I shouldn't be surprised that she figured it all had something to do with Isaac.

"Sort of," I answer eventually.

"Do you want to talk about it?"

Right. Because any normal, healthy person *should* want to talk about what happened last night. Because no amount of otome games will erase

---

124    And spewing possibly half a gallon of snot onto Marlow's shirt.

the fact that I saw Isaac at the very dance he told me he would be too busy to attend with me. And the problem with catching someone in a lie is that it makes everything they've ever said suspect. For example, did Isaac really mean it when he said he loved my parents' karahi? Is his name even Isaac? Is Ellie really just a friend?

Or worse: Does he actually love me?

I don't know. I'm not sure I'll ever know anymore.

"I don't think there's anything to talk about."

Kira doesn't look convinced. "Fine. But if he did something to you . . ." She starts mumbling something that sounds an awful lot like *I will drop-kick his ass.*

"Mumbling isn't polite, you know."

"Neither is you stealing my fruit snacks, but that doesn't stop you."

I laugh softly. I think I like her.

"Speaking of impoliteness"—I point to the huge pile of laundry taking up real estate on Kira's bed, desperate to change the subject—"do you need help with that *lovely* little situation you've got going on?"

"It's part of the process." She turns back to her laptop. "Now stop distracting me; I lost the last auction, but LØVE LIFE's management is auctioning off another signed EP, and of course it's between me and that damned XOLOVE47823 bot. But I refuse to lose again. I am in the middle of the *Machine War* here."

"Uh-huh."

There's a knock at our door then, giving me a horrible sense of déjà vu.

"Are you expecting someone?" I ask.

Kira shakes her head.

Oh God. If it's Isaac, I think I'll die. What if he saw me at the dance after all? What if he's here to tell me . . .

I can see it now: him, arm in arm with Ellie. *I've decided I'm marrying her instead.*

"You get it," I say, panicking.

"Did I not just say I'm fighting a literal bot right now?"[125]

I whimper. Take a deep breath. Slowly, I make my way across the room, nearly tripping on a stray T-shirt, and throw open the door.

But it's not Isaac.

*"Zaina?"*

It's my little sister, swallowed by a heavy coat and carrying a small overnight duffel bag. Her messy black bangs have been swept off her forehead from the wind outside, and her cute aquiline nose—like mine—is a cheerful pink.

"Hi," Zaina says with a wave before letting herself in.

I stare, dumbfounded. "What—what are you *doing* here?"

"I texted you last night." She sets down her bag by my bed, takes off her coat, her shoes. She spots Kira and gives her a little wave. "Hey."

"Hey, Z," Kira replies, a faint smile on her face. She doesn't seem remotely surprised, but then again, with Kira, I think Godzilla could walk in here to borrow some sugar and she'd just shrug and say sure.

I set down my Switch and take out my phone, scroll through my texts until—

There it is. A single text from her at 11:24 p.m. last night: *Visiting you tomorrow. Hope you don't have any plans.*

I frown. "Pretty sure Emily Post would say you need to await confirmation before inviting yourself over."

---

125    As much as this inconveniences me at the moment, let it be known I am all for the fight against bots and AI and the like. Especially if it is annoying Kira.

"Emily who?"

God help me.[126] "Anyway, it's not like you to just show up. What's the occasion?"

"Nothing. Just wanted to get out of the house."

My face falls. "Oh no. What did Mom and Dad do now?"

"Nothing, it's just—"

"Ugh, I *knew* it was too good to be true. Let me guess: divorce is back on the table?" I pinch at the skin between my brows. "I swear, all this back-and-forth is toxic at this point, it's like they don't even care about—"

"No, no. I promise it's not that. Surprisingly." Zaina tugs at her bangs. "I just wanted a change of scenery is all. Haven't seen you in weeks, either. Our school has Monday off for parent-teacher conferences, too."

My panic comes to a standstill. "Oh."

I guess I'm just so used to expecting the worst that I didn't even consider that Zaina could visit for no real reason. Like a good little sister. I quickly pivot; I'll have to postpone my study plans until tonight, but for once, I'm actually fine with that. After all, I've been looking for a distraction, and I can only spend so many hours staring at a screen, thirsting over Collin. And with all this Isaac stuff, I haven't had a chance to spend time with Zaina much. I missed her.

"Zaina . . ." My eyes burn.

She glowers, disgusted. "Ew, *don't.* You're hideous when you cry."

I hear Kira snort from her desk.

"Zaina!" I wrap her up in a hug. "You're too sweeeet!"

---

126    I should have honestly known better than to expect Zaina to have any familiarity with Emily Post. But then again, why is some American white lady considered the world expert on etiquette?

As Zaina yells at me to let go, resulting in me squeezing even harder, Kira gets up to open the door again. For a moment, I think Kira's leaving—maybe she wants to give my sister and I some one-on-one bonding time—but then I hear her say in her usual deadpan voice: "Oh. It's you again."

A familiar head of black curls appears over her shoulder. Now it's Marlow standing at the doorway, carrying a plastic bag.

"Why—?" I yank myself from Zaina, eyes wide. "*What* is happening?"

White-hot embarrassment about last night floods my body. I haven't quite figured out how to face Marlow. Holding me until I stopped crying—that's a perfectly normal friend thing to do. I think. But it was so kind and unexpected, especially since I've never cried like that in front of anyone before. And I can't get his expression out of my head. Like he was genuinely hurt by seeing me that way. I've never had anyone feel so strongly on my behalf.

Marlow lifts his arm, letting the bag dangle in the air. "I brought juice! Mango and peach. Also brought Gatorade."

I blink. "Is someone *sick*?"

"I just thought—I don't know, in case you weren't feeling well." He looks away, sheepish. "Stress is bad for you, you know."

"You're sick?" Zaina asks from behind me.

"No, it's—" Well, technically, you could say yes. You could probably call it lovesickness. Or heartbreak.

I shake my head. "No, I'm fine."

Marlow glances at Zaina. "Wait. Who is that?" he asks.

"Oh, this is Zaina. My little sister."

Marlow's eyes light up. "You have a little sister? Wow, you even look alike!"

"No we don't," Zaina says immediately. "Ani, do you know this guy or should I throw something at him? And what the hell's up with that shirt he's wearing?"

Today, Marlow's sporting a shirt that says *Neon Genesis Evangelion*, but for some reason, there's an image of Garfield the cat next to it.

"He's a friend. His name's Marlow. Don't say anything about his shirts; it'll only encourage him."

"You have *friends*?" Zaina mouths.

I glare back at her.

"There are too many chaotic characters in this room, and it's feeling crowded," Kira announces.

"What are you talking about?" I raise a brow. "But she's right. Our room's too small. Let's go somewhere else."

Zaina stands, her hair even messier than before.[127] "Should we go to the common room? Do they still have that ancient GameCube setup?"

"Those still exist?" Marlow is practically glowing. "I'm in! If they have Mario Kart, it's over for all of you."

"Those are fighting words, stranger. Also, who even invited you?"

"Agreed." Kira chimes in, getting up from her chair. "But if you're playing, I'm destroying both of you."

"I've got nothing but time." Marlow looks at me and smiles. The light from the window hits his eyes, and for a moment, I'm mesmerized by how they look like glistening pools of amber. My chest does a weird little somersault.

Marlow, nosy, nosy Marlow, always just going with the flow. Acting like last night didn't happen. I'm almost a little jealous.

But I'm also a little grateful.

---

127    I swear, it must be a family trait. Our hair gets messy for literally no reason.

And that's how the four of us—me, Marlow, Zaina, and Kira—end up spending the rest of the day playing video games together.

The sun has fallen, and Marlow has ordered us two pizzas, so now we're taking a break and stuffing our faces in the common room.

Zaina emerges from the hallway bathroom, wiping her hands on her jeans.

"You guys are doing a Holi festival?"

I nearly choke on my mango juice. "What brought that up?"

She gestures behind her. "Saw some posters up in the bathroom."

"Oh. Yeah. Well, Halcyon is." I'd gone hours without thinking about Isaac, and honestly, for once, it was a welcome reprieve. Now it feels like long fingernails are raking down the insides of my stomach all over again. I wonder what Isaac is doing now. It's Sunday, so maybe he's studying in the library somewhere. Maybe he's working on SASA stuff. Maybe he's with her.

I pull my knees to my chest, trying to ignore the accompanying ooze of self-loathing down my back.

"Looks fun. You do know what that is, right? Fun?" Zaina looks at Marlow. "Does she know what that is?"[128]

Marlow mouths an enthusiastic *No*.

I roll my eyes. "Har har."

This is the first time I've seen Zaina talk so much to other people. Apparently, in the past few hours, Zaina and Marlow have bonded. I chalk this up to two things: their newfound video game rivalry, and their mutual love of trolling me. Seeing them get along so well—it feels strange. She never acted like this with Isaac.

---

128    No one roasts harder than a younger sibling.

"You know, all throughout high school," Zaina says, sitting next to Marlow, "she would lock herself in her room after school until, like, eleven at night. I'd have to bring her dinner up to her room."

Kira swipes another slice of pizza, nodding. "I believe it."

I throw Zaina a warning look to stop, but she's not deterred. "Then on weekends, she'd run ten miles to build mental and physical endurance. She's not right."

I feel my cheeks grow hot. I stand by the fact that my quest for perfection is a noble one, but this is embarrassing. Not to mention Zaina's getting dangerously close to telling Kira the truth of how I really am. "Can you please stop?"

"No, this is *fascinating*." Marlow flaunts a grin. "I had absolutely *no idea* you were like this."

My cheeks redden even more. I don't like this. I don't like this at *all*.

"I'm going to get some tea!" I announce, standing.

Before anyone can respond, I flee.

I'm in the kitchen, waiting for my black tea to finish steeping, when Marlow sneaks up behind me. He leans against the doorway, watching. There's no sign of his earlier teasing mood now, which means he's followed me in here for only one other reason.

I brace myself.

"So. Last night."

I bounce the tea bag in the hot water, willing it to steep faster. "Last night? What happened last night?"

"Anisa."

"I don't want to talk about it. I don't even want to think about it."

He looks at me sadly. "You're going to have to eventually."

"I know." I look down at my cup, watching thin white foam swirl into dizzying spirals.

I can't ignore what I saw last night at the dance. But what is there to talk about right now?

No, the only thing I should do, once I'm ready, is properly confront Isaac. In fact, I should storm up to his dorm room, bang on the door, and demand answers. I deserve answers! This isn't something small and forgettable in the grand scheme of things, like him not being able to spend proper time with me on my birthday or being too busy to have lunch every now and then. He gave me reason to *distrust* him.[129]

And listen, I'm not afraid of confrontation, if I must. I've stood up for myself before. For example, an aunty very publicly told me off at the masjid for wearing nail polish, and I whipped out an *Well actually, Aunty*, and politely schooled her on the existence of press-on nails until she huffed and fled, embarrassed. So I can confront Isaac, too.[130]

It's just that this feels . . . so much harder. Because even if I *do* confront Isaac, what then? What if I risk losing him forever? This is the problem with shaping out my entire future based on us being together. Living without Isaac would be like . . . drowning in some fathomless ocean.

"Last night sucked," says Marlow. "And I hate that he made you feel like this. But for now, I think it's totally fair to take a couple days to process."

"Then what?" I mutter. "What am I supposed to do?"

---

129    I don't even think my parents, for all their faults, have ever lied to each other. They are *very* honest and open with how they feel about each other. . . . It just so happens those feelings aren't good.

130    I can! I swear! Don't look at me like that.

"At the end of the day, Isaac deserves a chance to explain himself. Everyone deserves that chance, even when things look bad—and in *his* case . . ." Marlow sighs, shakes his head. "But if we don't like his answer, I will personally hold him down for you to slap all you want."

He gives me a soft smile. "Okay?"

I feel my sore eyes start to burn again, this time with relief. It's not fair. How does he know exactly what to say? And with such comforting assurance. It almost makes no sense, why he's so nice to me.

In any case, what kind of explanation could erase the fact that Isaac lied about where he'd be?

But I guess that's the point of faith. You just have to hold on, even if you don't have any good reason to.

Marlow reaches forward.

"Atta girl," he says, patting me on the head. "We'll figure this out. Who knows—maybe this will be a moment of bonding for you two. Going through hardship together and all that." His voice is calm. It makes me feel like a child. "It's not over till it's over."

It feels like a cloud's been lifted from my mind and I can suddenly see a little clearer. It could be the emphasis on the *we*—the reminder that I'm not alone in this—or maybe it's just Marlow's straightforward logic. But things with Isaac don't feel as dire as they did only minutes before.

"All I know is, I just . . . don't want to doubt Isaac. Not yet." I don't want to give up on us. I'm not sure I even know *how.*

He nods. "Okay. Then we won't. Not yet."

It's funny. These days, it feels like having faith in Isaac has been getting harder and harder. Faith in Marlow, though . . . despite everything, it's almost becoming second nature. I wonder if that's the power of friendship. Real friendship.

I sigh. Smile weakly. "I hate that you keep seeing me at my worst.

Feels a little unfair, don't you think?"

"You've seen me at my less-than-best, too," Marlow replies.

My heart rate quickens. "You mean with Rosie?" I've been wanting to ask about her again, but even I can tell how uncomfortable the topic makes Marlow. Not to mention I've been feeling a little . . . bothered after seeing Marlow and Rosie at the dance. Like it was a reminder that there's a part of Marlow I don't know, that I haven't been let in on yet.[131]

"Are you—" I swallow. "Are you going to tell me about her?"

A sad smile tugs at his mouth. "I don't think I'm ready to just yet. But I've decided maybe—maybe one day, it could be okay. Because it's you."

His gaze tangles with mine, and his expression turns uncharacteristically serious, making heat rise palpably up my neck. I'm so thrown by the sudden change in the air, by his sudden earnestness, that any coherent reply simply dies in my throat. "And the thing is, I want to see you at your worst," he goes on. "The same way I also want to see you at your best. I want to see you all the time. . . ."

He edges closer.

"Every day . . ."

I'm backed against the counter, and despite myself, my heart is throwing itself against my rib cage with all the force of a jackhammer: made worse when I remember what he'd said about having a crush on me. Could it be? Is he actually trying to make a move?

"In every state."

Marlow reaches a hand behind me, and for a moment I think he's going to hold me again. His face is close—close enough for me to observe the perfect Cupid's bow on his full, dark upper lip, the light stubble on his

---

131     I've never thought of Marlow as *mysterious*, but I guess lately he's been showing me all sorts of sides.

impressively chiseled chin, the deep divots of the dimples on his cheeks that appear whenever he smiles. I tremble as heat spreads across my own face like a bad skin rash and my head feels white hot, every thought going up in flame.

But instead of holding me, Marlow reaches for the kettle behind me. With a tap of his finger, he flips the on button.

. . . What?

. . . . . . . . . . . . *What?*

Seeing my expression, Marlow grins and pulls back.

"Ma'am, why are you blushing? Could it be—oh, did you think I was going to try something?" He tuts. "Clearly my love coaching is working if it's putting you in *that* frame of mind."[132]

"I wasn't thinking *anything*." I swallow, attempt to regain myself.

"Uh-huh."

"I *wasn't!*"

"Interesting." His eyes crinkle in amusement. "I think you're more flustered now than when I caught you playing that otome game."

"Leave me alone." I purse my lips as I silently demand the frantic thump in my chest to slow the hell down. "You *always*—ugh, I'm just entertainment for you, aren't I?"

"Got it in one," he says.

A strange, unfamiliar sensation alights on my spine. I fold my arms across my chest. By now, I should be used to his teasing. Him and his cheesy, throwaway flirty lines, how he makes fun of me for, well, everything. Now I'm annoyed. No, deeply unsettled. And I'm not even sure why.

I clear my throat again. "Must be fun for you, huh? Knowing that you could tell everyone, ruin my reputation on a whim."

---

132     It could be the love coaching. It could also be the otome games.

Marlow pours himself some green tea in a mug. "I would never do that to someone. Honestly, I don't even see how that would be *any* fun."

"What do you mean?"

"I mean, there is nothing you could do that would make me want to go around telling people I caught you playing otome games while looking like Gollum." He smirks and takes a sip of his tea. "I prefer feeling like I've been let in on a secret just the two of us know. Why would I want to share that with anyone else?"

I don't respond, so Marlow leaves me with my thoughts.

I stand alone in the kitchen, and for a long time—I'm not even sure if time exists after that—I'm in a daze, feeling a maelstrom of emotions I can't quite sort out.

But by the time I'm back in my head again, my tea has gone cold.

You ready to finally finish our
RACE & ETHNICITY paper??? 8:08 PM

Mentally, yes 8:10 PM

Physically . . . 8:10 PM

Can we just work over
Google Docs tonight? 8:10 PM

Oh dang 8:11 PM

Everything ok? 8:11 PM

Do you need some space
after . . . you know . . . 8:11 PM

No, this isn't about Isaac 8:12 PM

I can head to the library in a day or two 8:12 PM

But not tonight 8:12 PM

WHY SO CRYPTIC??? 8:13 PM

Holy shit, now I'm nervous 8:13 PM

Oh my God. 8:14 PM

FINE, if you MUST know 8:14 PM

It's because I'm currently bleeding my guts out. 8:14 PM

Are you hurt?? 8:14 PM

. . . Oh 8:15 PM

Wait 8:15 PM

I get it now 8:16 PM

Haha 8:16 PM

Yeah. 8:16 PM

Good thing I have an extra heating pad 8:16 PM

What? 8:16 PM

Brb coming over 8:18 PM

Hope you like chocolate 8:18 PM

Wait what??? 8:18 PM

MARLOW 8:18 PM

You get home ok? 10:01 PM

Yeah 10:04 PM

Thanks for letting me crash 10:04 PM

Ew don't be polite 10:05 PM

It's weird 10:05 PM

Haha my bad 10:05 PM

Meant to say you suck and I can't wait
to kick your ass in Mario Kart again 10:06 PM

There we go. 10:06 PM

Anyway, you sure
everything's ok at home? 10:07 PM

Yeah 10:07 PM

We'll see 10:07 PM

You know Mom and Dad lol 10:07 PM

Don't I. 10:08 PM

# Chapter 19

Before class on Monday morning,[133] I knock on Isaac's door with all the enthusiasm of a debt collector. I've even put on a thrifted Vivienne Westwood black top and a long, edgy plaid skirt paired with a black beret. An outfit meant only for the toughest of tough.

So when he finally opens the door, my voice is surprisingly steady.

"Can we talk?"

Isaac stands in the doorway wearing a bewildered expression. "Anisa? What's wrong? Why are you here? Is everything—"

"I saw you at the dance." *Talk to him, don't beat around the bush; be clear why you're upset.*

I straighten my shoulders, stare back at his hypnotic, amber-flecked gaze. "I kept telling myself there was no way, that I was just being paranoid, but—I saw you there when you said you wouldn't be, and it makes me feel . . ."

*You can do this.* "It makes me feel like you lied . . . ?"

Silence. My chest is heaving. But I did it. I said my piece.

Isaac flutters his eyes, like he's taking the time to absorb my words. Finally, he waves me inside his dorm room. "Um, just—come in."

---

133    And once my cramps have died down, thanks to a heating pad.

I'm startled. He's never invited me in before.[134] I take a deep, nervous breath and walk past him. The door closes behind us, making me jump.

I take in the space. Unsurprisingly, it's clean by any standard: his maroon bedsheets are freshly washed (I can smell the fabric softener wafting off them), his shoes tucked in a neat row by the door, his books stacked neatly by size on his desk. I get the sense that his parents demanded he always have a clean room, and now he maintains it by sheer habit.

Like everything else about Isaac, the room is perfect.

Isaac runs his hand through his thick black waves. *So it was you,* I think I hear him mutter beneath his breath.

Before I can ask what he means, he turns to face me. "Look. I'm sorry you saw that, and I know it looks bad, me being there when I said I couldn't go with you. But if you saw me at the dance, you also saw I was with a group of my friends, right?" I nod. "We were in the library before that, and we needed a break. So Ellie suggested we go to blow off some steam. It was totally unplanned, I *swear*. And we headed back to the library right after."

I've never heard Isaac have to explain himself. It's weird. Unlike most people in his situation, he's so relaxed. And not how I'd like. If anything, there's no emotion whatsoever in his explanation. Wouldn't most people be at least a little frazzled, if not devastated, being accused of lying by the person they love? In Collin's route in *Rose in the Embers*, for example, the protagonist finds him alone with his ex after he's confessed. When I chose the option to confront him, he practically begged the protagonist to believe him. Which I did, and it turned out the ex in question was trying

---

134    Normally, I wouldn't dare be alone with him in private, for fear we could succumb to temptation and lose ourselves in the fiery throes of passion, heaven forbid. At least, that's how my daydreams go. But this is different. Very different.

to murder the protagonist—but that's beside the point.

Is that why I feel so unsatisfied with Isaac's answer? Because he sounds so . . . distanced from it all?

At least it makes *sense*. It's not out of the realm of possibility that it was all just a spur-of-the-moment thing and that seeing him at the dance is all just a matter of bad timing. And I don't think he's making it up. But . . .

"That's . . . not all I saw, though." My feet shift beneath me. "I saw Ellie and you—" I swallow. "You were holding her. She was holding your arm. Do you get how that'd make me feel?"

"Then if you *kept* looking, you would have seen me push her away," he answers, his voice level. "I told you: Ellie is just a friend. And I told you I was studying at the library, which I was."

I say nothing. Again, he's saying nothing wrong. Nothing that feels suspicious. Only something else feels wrong, and I can't put my finger on it.

After a while, he sighs. "Take some time to think about it, okay?" He says softly. "Cool down, look at it with fresh eyes. We can talk about it again later. I've got class soon, so . . ."

There it is. He's doing it again. Putting that space between us.

Wait. *Wait.*

I take a step forward. "You're pushing me away—and *don't* say it's because you're busy. We're in college; *everyone's* busy. But that doesn't mean you stop making time to see each other."

"I'm sorry." His expression looks pained. "You're right. I'll work on it. Will that make you feel better?"

*No.* That's not what I want to hear. I . . . I'm so tired of hearing him say he's sorry.

"I honestly don't know anymore. It just feels like you make time for your friends." *For Ellie.* "So why not me, too? I don't expect to always be a priority, obviously, but—don't you think we should spend more time together? Especially since we're supposed to get married?"

I feel so pathetic. Like I'm the Collin in this situation, begging to be heard. But I don't know what else to do. I don't understand why it feels so hard to get through to him.

Isaac's face changes, warps into something cold and unrecognizable.

"What about that other guy you're always hanging around with now? Marlow?" His laugh is hollow. "Don't you think it's a little hypocritical to imply anything when you're doing the same thing?"

My pulse spikes.

"What—what are you talking about?" My head becomes a frantic slideshow, recollecting every memory I can with Marlow to figure out what Isaac's implying. I come up blank. I mean, how are we even comparable? It makes no sense.

"You really don't know?"

"The only reason I'm with him all the time is because—" *Because he's helping me win you back. Because he's the only one who listens. Because he is my love coach,* I want to scream. The irony of it all! Is that why he's been pulling away even more from me?

I clamp down my teeth, hard.

"Forget it." Isaac's shoulders slump, his face now one of tired indifference. "I'm sorry. That was uncalled for. I'll try to be better. About making time for us. About not giving you reason to worry."

He puts his hand on my shoulder and gives me a weak smile. "Okay?"

After a while, I shake my head. "Okay," I reply.

Then I lift my gaze to meet his.

"Me too."

* * *

The next day, I'm trudging my way back from class to my dorm[135] when out of the corner of my eye, I spy Ellie—her red hair a beacon against the snow.

I have to do a double take. Not just because I'm confused why I'd see her here, on my campus, but because my first thought is whether it means Isaac's here, too. Which means my brain has already associated them together as a pair.

If my mood was already edging in the direction of foul, it is now fully yeeting itself off the edge.

And it's immature, I admit. But after making a fool of myself in front of her, in what can only be called the Muffin Incident, and then seeing her with Isaac at the Winter Dance, I don't want to see her. Preferably ever again. So I adjust my bag on my shoulder and start walking in the opposite direction.

The universe, as usual, seems to have other plans.

"Ani?" I hear her call behind me.

*Damn it.*

I take a deep breath. Relax my face. This is just a test. This is just a *test.*[136]

I turn to face her with a smile. "Ellie! Hi!"

She jogs up to me, beaming. Once again, her face is bare of makeup,

---

135    Which is a shame because I'm wearing white boots and the only way to walk in white boots is to confidently strut, but my mental health clearly hasn't gotten the memo.

136    The Prophet Muhammad (PBUH) once said, "The people who face the most difficult tests are the prophets, then the righteous, then those following them in degree." It's kind of like that saying about how God tests his strongest soldiers. But please, I'm tired of *tests*! I've got midterms coming up, damn it!

and I marvel at how perfect her skin is, how her pores are so tiny. Like her. Like she's the protagonist of an otome game.

"I'm so glad I bumped into you!" She catches her breath. "How are you?"

"Oh, you know." My mouth feels tight around my teeth. "What are you doing here?"

"I tutor French, so I'm here sometimes. Being French Canadian has its benefits."

"Ah." Of course she tutors French, on top of being president of the ISA.[137] I guess anyone who hangs around Isaac would have to be a top-tier student, too.

*She's just a friend*, Isaac's voice echoes.

*If you kept looking, you would have seen me push her away.*

Would I, though? I mean, why would he push her away? When she's so pretty and perfect and—

No! Ew! Jealousy is unbecoming.

"It was so good finally meeting you the other day at the Holi planning meetup with SASA." Ellie's face falls. "Was everything okay after? You didn't get hurt, did you?" She looks genuinely concerned.

"No, no. I got checked out after—nothing broken." Except my pride.

She walks in step with me. "Shame about the muffins you brought. You inspired me, though—I went to the bakery the next day and bought three just for me." She giggles. "Ended up eating all of them on the way back."

I don't know what to say, so I keep walking until I feel her staring at me. "What?"

"How do you do your makeup so well? I kind of, um, stalked you

---

137     To be fair, I am fluent in Urdu and Arabic, and I was a Latin tutor in high school. Unfortunately, I forgot most of my Latin. *Est quod est.*

a little. And I found your Instagram. Sorry, I know that's weird. But I really wanted to message you and ask you if you were okay, but then I was worried that would be even weirder and I lost the nerve—anyway, I love it. I got this lip gloss you recommended because of it."

So honest. Like she says whatever's on her mind. Like Marlow.

I feel a smile tug at my lip. "Thank you. It's just a lot of practice."

I don't know what to do in this situation. She's into Isaac, that's for certain, and to no fault of her own. But it doesn't exactly foster feelings of friendship. How am I supposed to be friendly with the person who could very well take Isaac away from me?

"But yeah, Isaac was really worried about you. After you left the meeting. Have you known each other for long?"

"Yes. Since we were thirteen," I answer stiffly.

"Wow. You practically grew up together. Makes sense. You seem close. I'm a little jealous."

I stare down at my feet. *She's* jealous? Why? *How*?

"Your friend was worried, too. Marlow, right? He's in a class with me. I've never seen someone move that fast. Boy straight-up pulled an Edward Cullen."

I almost laugh. Almost.

"What about you?" I venture carefully. "How long have you been friends with Isaac?"

"Mmm, since last semester." Ellie curls a strand of her long red hair with a finger. "So not long. But we're in so many classes together, it feels like I've known him for longer, ya know?" She shrugged. "It's weird. He seemed so cold and unapproachable at first. Like, weirdly unflappable. I'm sure you know."

I nod. "Definitely. He's always been like that. It's like anything he touches turns to gold." And he's the full package: handsome, rich, a perfect student at school. The crown jewel of the desi community.

It's what's made Isaac feel so far away.

"Yeah, but . . ." Ellie smiles softly. "Then I started seeing the *real* him. He's generous, and surprisingly funny, and even vulnerable at times. I think he also feels a lot more than he lets on. He expects so much of himself, too, but never of others. He takes you as you are." Ellie smiles, her big, round eyes shining. "He's actually *relaxing* to be around."

I mull over her words, confused. That doesn't sound like Isaac at all. Not to me, at least. Of course, I know he's wonderful minus his recent less-than-wonderful behavior. That he's kind and hard on himself. But I can't exactly say I've ever felt *relaxed* around him. I mean, how can I, when he's so intimidatingly perfect? And isn't it normal to feel nervous around the person you love?

But it feels like Ellie is describing a total stranger. Like she knows sides to Isaac that I don't.

I bite my lip. I guess this means Isaac really does act differently with Ellie. Ellie managed to get past Isaac's barriers, something I still can't seem to do.

And her expression just talking about him, it's like . . .

Someone in love.

I wonder if Isaac knows about Ellie's feelings. Why would you hang around someone you know is in love with you when you're already taken?

Never mind. I don't want that answer.

A cyclist rushes from behind her like a gust of wind. But Ellie doesn't see.

"Watch out!" I grab her arm and yank her out of the way just in time, and the cyclist zooms past us without slowing down. Ellie stumbles, but

216

grab her shoulders to steady her.

"Jackass! You think you own the road with your stupid little bike?!" yell as the cyclist flees, the coward.

I spin to face her, breathing hard. "Geez. Are you all right?"

"I'm—I'm fine." Ellie laughs, breathless. "Oh my God, it's like—sorry, it's like you transformed into a different person just now." She dissolves into a full-on giggling fit now, holding her stomach.

I freeze. Damn. I must be losing my mind, screaming the way I do when Zaina's eaten the last of the biryani.

"Sorry, it's just"—I look away, embarrassed—"that jerk nearly ran you over. He deserves to be *flogged*."

"Please don't be sorry. That was *hilarious*." She wipes at her eyes. "Thank you. I seriously have to treat you to coffee sometime for saving me."

She clings to my arm. "Actually, are you free now? I have a couple hours open. I will treat you to anything from the menu. Trade you for some of your makeup secrets?"

In another life, that could be really fun. And maybe if I were a bigger, better person, I could do it. But . . .

Gently, I pull away. "I can't. Sorry."

For a moment, her big eyes waver.

"Oh. Okay. Maybe next time?"

I smile sadly. "Yeah. Next time."

# Chapter 20

Marlow grins at me from across the table once we've hit a good place to take a break. "I like your roommate, by the way. Kira. She's funny."

Marlow and I have been hunkered down in the library for the past few hours, working on the finishing touches for our Race & Ethnicity paper. With midterms coming up soon, too, the library is packed with students, which means the library is warm—almost too warm—and vibrating with the anxieties of a thousand panicked minds. You could cut the stress in here with a knife. Or a katana, I'm sure Marlow would say.

I snort. "Don't tell her. She hates it when people like her." Though I'm pretty sure she felt comfortable around Marlow, too. Not that she'd ever admit it. But after a couple matches in Mario Kart, resulting in her wiping the floor with him—losses which Marlow graciously accepted, acknowledging her prowess—she started to get talkative, relatively speaking, especially after Marlow asked her what kind of music she liked. And Kira, as you can imagine, hardly cares to talk to anyone.

That's the effect he has on people, I guess.

"Meeting your little sister was awesome, too," Marlow adds. "Think she'll come visit again soon?"

"Probably. I can tell her to. Maybe for spring break? If you'll be on campus." I'm sure Mom will try to convince me to come home for break, but after our last fight, I'd rather not. I doubt Isaac will go home, either.

"Nice. Hell yeah. It's a hassle to fly back to Jamaica just for a week, so I'll be here." His face turns serious. "Is everything okay with Zaina, by the way?"

"Hmm?"

"She kept checking her phone." He frowns. "I think your mom was texting a lot. Saw 'Mom' pop up on the screen a couple times. Unless she has a friend named Mom. Which would be weird."

My fists tighten. I wonder if pushing Mom away forced her to annoy Zaina instead. "Hard to say. Mom gets anxious whenever Zaina's away, so maybe that's why. But . . ."

Mom was acting so strange the last time I saw her. Like there was something about the decision to postpone their divorce that they're just not telling me. And then for Zaina visiting out of the blue—I'm not convinced everything's fine like she said.

I hesitate. I wonder what Marlow would think, what he'd say if I vented about my parents. These days, I'm finding that I'm curious to hear his advice, or even just have him listen. To tell me it's going to be okay, like he always does.

"So?" Marlow asks carefully. "What did Isaac say? About the dance?"

"What? Oh." I stare down at my notebook. It's been a couple days now since my talk with Isaac, and I've had time to gather my thoughts. "You were right—it was all a misunderstanding. Isaac *was* part of a study group, and they *were* in the library, like he'd said he would be. But they decided to check out the dance, spur of the moment. It was just bad luck I saw him."

"And you're . . . satisfied with that answer?"

I tilt my head, confused by the question.

Ultimately, I decided not to doubt Isaac. To take this all as the test on the road to our happily ever after. After all, what great romance doesn't have a good test or two? One cannot get a diamond without pressure and all that.

But truth be told, I'm still bothered by what Isaac insinuated about Marlow. He basically accused me of spending too much time with him, of two-timing Isaac. As if. If Isaac and I make the picture-perfect couple, Marlow and I are—well, we wouldn't even be on the romance scale. We're fire and water. A cat and a dog. Chloé Boots and Crocs. Total opposites.

And when would Isaac have seen us alone together, anyway? The only time he saw us was at the SASA meeting, so where would he even get such an idea?

It's absurd.

Anyway.

"Isaac apologized and had a good reason. Why wouldn't I be satisfied?"

Marlow's brows flick together. Like something I said bothers him.

"Are you sure?"

"What do you mean?"

"I don't know. I've just been thinking." He sucks in his lips thoughtfully. "Is this really what you want?"

"You mean *Isaac*?"

He nods. "I know my job is to help you no matter what, and I plan to do that, but . . ." Marlow looks at me, unusually serious. "Does it really make sense to keep trying to be with someone who's only making you miserable?"

*Miserable?* "He doesn't make me miserable, not exactly. It's just our situation. Things are just . . . a little rocky right now. That doesn't mean I stop *trying,* right?"

"But what happens if you keep trying and he keeps doing things that hurt you? I think maybe we should consider—"

I feel my eyebrow twitch. "I'm *not* giving up. I can't. What happened to *it's not over till it's over*?"

"That was before he gave you a shitty excuse for what we saw at the dance." Marlow breathes. "Tell me exactly what he said."

"I already told you. That him being at the dance was totally unplanned and that they headed back to the library right afterward. And that what we saw with Ellie—he pushed her away right after. They're just friends." I can feel my voice sound weaker with every word.

"Uh-huh." Marlow leans back in his chair, forehead furrowed. "And you don't see how *convenient* that is?"

I look away. "I—I mean, maybe, but—"

"I know it's hard, and I'm sorry. But I just think you deserve better. Better than someone who, I strongly suspect, is lying to you. You deserve someone who undeniably wants to be with you."

I feel my chest puff. Sometimes, I hate how it feels like Marlow gives voice to the thoughts I try so hard to smother in the back of my head.

"He still could! Why else would he wear the bracelet I gave him two years ago? If he didn't want to be with me, he'd at least do the honorable thing and *tell* me, right . . . ?" Marlow's right on some level, I *know* he is; Isaac's excuses about being at the dance, about how it looked with Ellie, are flimsy at best. But I can't accept us being over. I'm not going to roll over on our relationship like my parents, not without trying as hard as I possibly can.

Worst of all, as pathetic as this might sound, if I give up now, a part of me will wonder if somehow I really wasn't good enough for Isaac.

I couldn't take the humiliation.

Marlow gives me a pitying look that somehow only pisses me off even more. "It's not always that simple," he says softly.

"*Noted.*" My fist clenches. "Then here's something simple: either you help me or you don't."

I know it probably makes no sense to keep pushing on like this, but I wish Marlow would respect my choice—the same way I've respected his discomfort when it comes to talking about Rosie.

We lapse into an uncomfortable silence. I glance at Marlow's T-shirt. Today, he's gone with one that reads *Live Good, Die Great*.

He closes his eyes for a beat, then opens them again, like he's made a decision.

"Fine. Forget I said anything." His voice lacks its usual sunshine. "So you want to continue? Trying to repair things with Isaac?"

I give him a prickly look. "Yes. Obviously."

"*Fine.*" He yanks out a piece of paper from his backpack and shoves it in front of me. It's a flyer. "Here. There's a ski trip coming up. The Bi-Campus Ski and Snowboard Club is hosting their annual ski trip to the Poconos in about a week. Anyone is welcome to join. It's the perfect opportunity to build a 'memorable experience' with him." I don't miss the tinge of sarcasm.

I pick up the flyer and read, my head spinning. At least this actually seems like a good idea. This could be perfect, the kind of event that could change *everything*. This ski trip could be the equivalent to the New Year's party in *When Harry Met Sally*, the school carnival in *Love, Simon*, the dinner date in *You've Got Mail*. It could be the spark Isaac and I need.

Besides, I've never been on any sort of trip with Isaac before, unless you count that one time our Sunday school class went to Six Flags for Muslim Family Day. And I've been skiing once before with my family;

I still have the white and iridescent pink ski jacket I bought off Depop somewhere in my closet. It's very cute. I will look *irresistible*.

"Okay. I'm in."

"I'll sign you up." Marlow sighs. "Anyway, now you just have to invite Isaac. You think he'd be down?"

"Hard to say, given his schedule." I fold the flyer and pocket it. "But I'll ask."

I'm actually looking forward to it.

I'm debating whether to say anything when annoyance flashes in Marlow's eyes. Someone clears their throat by our table.

I turn around.

"Isaac." My chest jolts.

Isaac is standing behind us, wearing a black peacoat and mustard-gold sweater, and his cheeks are slightly flushed, like he's just come in from the cold.

*What is he doing here?*

"Hey," he says, a little out of breath. "Glad I found you."

Isaac's eyes land on Marlow.

"Oh. It's you again."

He smiles politely. But I can tell it's stiff. Fake.

I stand, fast. "Yes! We're here, working on a paper together. Because we were paired together," I blurt.

"Ah." Isaac glances at the surface of our small table, covered in notebooks and our laptops, as well as our Race & Ethnicity textbooks. "I see. . . ."

He strides past me, making a beeline straight to Marlow, and I feel my body go tense.

That fake smile of his deepens. "I think I've seen you around in class before and we kind of briefly met at the SASA meeting, but—I'm Isaac. Ani's partner, basically." He looks at me before reaching out a hand to Marlow. The black bracelet on his wrist glints beneath the light. "It's nice to formally meet you."

Partner.

*Did he say partner?!?*

I throw Marlow a triumphant look: *See? Would someone who doesn't* undeniably *want to be with me call me his partner?* Marlow rolls his eyes, but I notice how the corner of his mouth curls up slightly.

I'm floating. I'm dreaming, right? I have passed away. I would have been elated if he'd said boyfriend, but *partner*? That's even better. That implies *long term*. That implies *big leagues*. He might as well have said fiancé and made it official right here and now!

Marlow grabs Isaac's hand. "Likewise." He smiles. "Anisa's told me *so much* about you."

Maybe I'm drunk with happiness right now, but something about Marlow's tone feels different than usual. Their handshake lasts a moment longer, and when they finally separate, Isaac's hand seems a little redder than before.

"What brings you here?" I ask Isaac, trying to hide my elation.

He pockets his hands and looks at me, eyes softening. "Actually, I was hoping I could take you to lunch."

Oh my God. Is today my birthday? No, wait, that was last week. So he's just randomly taking me out? On a *date*?

This is exactly what I've always dreamed of. Which means Isaac really meant what he said.

Did I finally get through to him?

"That's great," says Marlow, looking at me. "You should go."

There it was, that usual gentle, encouraging tone, not a sign of our earlier disagreement to be found.

Which is why I'm confused when it stings, fractures something deep in my chest.

I try to shake it off. I should be happy. Isaac is finally making an effort, finally meeting me halfway! As much as it feels wrong to just ditch Marlow, this is a chance I can't miss.

Marlow deserves it, anyway, for implying I should give up. *Suck it, Crocs! You were wrong!*

"Ani?" comes Isaac's voice at my side.

"Sorry!" I smile cheerfully. "Let's go!"

Isaac nods, and I grab my things, feeling strangely frazzled.

*Have fun*, Marlow mouths at me before Isaac leads me away.

But I can feel his eyes, the warm weight of them, on my back. Like a familiar hand. Pushing me forward or pulling me back, I can't tell.

It takes all my willpower not to turn around.


Isaac has picked a halal Mediterranean spot a short walk from campus.

It's warm inside, intimate. Quiet.

We're ushered into a couple of window seats, and Isaac even takes my coat for me, places it on the back of my chair before carefully pushing me closer to the table.

It actually feels like a date.

Isaac sits across from me. The dim lighting makes his square jaw look even more chiseled than usual. "I've ordered takeout from here before. It's good," he says.

I blink, still in a daze. "That's wonderful."

He smiles politely and opens a menu.

Silence. I open a menu, too, racking my brain trying to remember everything Marlow told me when we went on that practice date. But my head's gone blank. My body's also painfully tense, and I'm suddenly hyperaware of every vibrating cell in my body. I'm grateful for the vaguely Arab music in the background, filling what I can't.

At what point do I start feeling comfortable around him? I want to tell him what I've been up to—make jokes with him and laugh and not be afraid of what he'll say. I want it to feel easy.

But I guess . . . the distance is still there.

"Ani?" Isaac's gentle voice shakes me out of my head. He's frowning, concerned. "Are you feeling all right?"

"Yes. Perfect," I answer a little too quickly. I will my muscles to relax, but they refuse. Ugh. It's *obvious* I'm nervous. It's just that I've been waiting so long for a chance like this and now that it's here—

I'm honestly not sure what to do. I was too busy focusing on the dream of him asking me out that I never considered the *during* and *after.*

Eventually we order and our food arrives; I'm grateful when Isaac finally starts to talk: about SASA activities and preparations they've been making for the upcoming Holi festival. He tells me about MCAT study programs he's been considering enrolling in, how his classes are going. It's a little more of a one-sided conversation than I'd like, but slowly I find my limbs unclenching, if only a little.

"I miss relaxing," Isaac says eventually, smiling. "It's been a while since I've gone out to eat."

I nod. "With midterms coming up, I hear you." Then I remember: "Oh yeah, Zaina came over to visit the other day. It finally gave me an excuse to take the rest of the day off and play some video games." I chuckle, remembering how heated things got between Zaina and Marlow and Kira. "It was fun."

Isaac raises a brow. "Since when do you play video games?"

"Oh, it's"—I feel heat rising to my cheeks—"it's a new hobby, I guess you could say."

"Mom never let me play growing up. Now that I live on campus I play sometimes, though. When I have time."

Which is probably never. My heart aches for him. My parents are strict, but his are even worse. "I can't imagine Lubna Aunty letting you play much of anything."

Isaac chuckles bitterly. "Right, you'd get it. You and I basically grew up under our parents' thumbs. No childhood to speak of. No freedom. Every decision in your life already made for you . . ."

He trails off to stare out the window, at some faraway thing in the blue depths of the afternoon sky. I can see his pained expression reflected back at me. "And God forbid you don't follow the path they've set for you. Or else they yank the financial rug right out from under you. Or worse."

I swallow, my throat dry. The truth is, I think I know *exactly* what he's talking about. It's nice having parents who can cover tuition—a privilege, really. It does, however, come with the downside of parents being able to hold that against you for the rest of your life, to use it as a bargaining chip to control and shape your future.

Not that I could ever admit that, of course. If it ever got out that I felt even a little bitter toward my parents, I'd be cast off as ungrateful. It certainly wouldn't look good to Aunty Lubna. As much as my parents make me want to pull out my hair, especially lately, I have to play the role of a good daughter. I can't disparage them, not even to Isaac.

Especially not to Isaac.

It's funny. It feels easier to talk to Marlow somehow. Maybe it's because he's on the outside, but for some reason, there's less pressure with him. No need to impress or wear a mask. I don't have to worry about the three marriage requirements, I can just be myself. All my selves.

If I married Isaac, I wonder, would things change? Could I talk to Isaac the same way?

*No, stop that. It doesn't matter right now. I need to focus on the present.*

"Anyway, sorry. That took a gloomy turn, huh?" A sheepish half smile flits across Isaac's face. "I don't mean to complain. I shouldn't. They're the ones covering my tuition, after all, so it's only fair."

I don't know what to say, so I throw back a weak smile. I can't agree with him. I can't comfort him. I can't really say anything at all.

So I change the subject. "What's your favorite color?" I ask brightly.

Isaac's head cocks to the side. "Why?"

"Just wondering. Don't worry, I won't awkwardly start listing every color in the rainbow."

He thinks for a moment.

"Probably dark blue," he answers. "Honestly, I think I like it because it looks good on me."

"Right! Yes, that's what *I* said! That's totally a valid reason! And truly, you do look good in navy blue." *Suck it, Marlow. Isaac even gave a proper shade.*

I feel Isaac watching me, and I clear my throat, embarrassed.

Right. Don't think about Marlow. We're here for a reason.

I wait for Isaac to ask me my favorite color and when he doesn't, I don't let that deter me. I take the opportunity to pull out the flyer Marlow handed me earlier from my bag. "Before I forget, there's a ski trip coming up." I slide the flyer across the table. "I know you're busy and all, but do you think you'd want to go? Treat yourself to a little more relaxation time?"

Isaac reads the flyer, considering. "Yeah. I could use the break." He pushes the flyer back in my direction. "I'll invite some of my friends. Feel free to invite whoever you want, too."

My stomach falls. I was hoping it would just be the two of us. But if he brings his friends . . .

"Right. Sure. That sounds great." I force a smile. "I'll ask Kira. I think Marlow's coming, too," I add. It might be good to give Isaac a heads-up now so he's not confused when he sees Marlow there. "Actually, they all met the other day. When Zaina was over. We all ended up playing Mario Kart. Maybe you could join us some—"

At the mention of Marlow, Isaac's mouth has pressed in a thin, tight line. "Having him hang around Zaina . . . I don't know, Ani."

"Huh?"

Isaac takes a long sip of water while I wait at the edge of my seat.

"I don't think you should hang around him anymore," he says finally.

Something about his tone rubs me the wrong way. It reminds me of Mom. "Why?"

"Has he told you about what happened last year?"

I feel a ball in my throat bounce as I swallow. Part me feels like this is wrong, talking about Marlow behind his back. It's clear something happened to Marlow—the way he'd clam up whenever Rosie came up, the way he hardly ever talks about himself. But every time I'd ask about it . . .

My curiosity gets the better of me. "No," I answer, shaking my head. "He didn't."

"Figures." He sighs. "Then allow me to tell you the secret history of

229

your supposed friend," he begins, leaning his arms on the table.

"Last year, he was dating this girl, Rosie," he begins. "I'm not sure how long their relationship lasted. What I do know is, their relationship was supposedly . . . turbulent. *Toxic*. I heard one of them even threw a glass bottle at the wall in a rage during one of their arguments; someone in their dorm had to call campus police on them. They were pretty sure it was Marlow who did it."

My stomach tightens. Is this really the same Marlow we're talking about? Tame, golden retriever Marlow who sits in his dorm and watches rom-coms?

"There has to be a misunderstanding," I say. "I'm not going to make assumptions based on hearsay, especially when we don't even know the details."[138]

"I'm just telling you what I've heard from someone who lived at the dorm. Anyway, long story short, they broke up eventually, and Marlow spiraled hard after that."

"What do you mean?"

"We were in the same Bio class together, and he just stopped showing up to any of his classes. Most of us thought he'd drop out, honestly. And whenever I'd pass him in the common room, he didn't look"—Isaac shakes his head—"well, like he was in a good place. Definitely not stable. It made me feel kinda bad for the guy."

My fists curl beneath the table. "Who'd feel stable after a situation like that?"

It's no wonder Marlow reacted the way he did when we bumped into

---

138    I'll always believe women first, but let's be real: Marlow is mixed, half-Black, and the fact that Isaac would jump to assume that it was Marlow who threw the bottle, without *any* proof? I'm a little disappointed.

Rosie at the dance. The way he fled. Both Halcyon's and Marion's campuses are small. The rumors must have traveled like wildfire. Even the thought of breaking up with someone you once loved, and then having everyone know while horrible rumors follow you around—

I wonder if he felt ashamed. Lonely.

"As far as I know, this all happened last semester," Isaac says, gently rubbing his chin. "I doubt he's fully over it yet. Which is why I don't like that he's hanging around you."

Last semester?

That's not long ago at all.

"Why wouldn't he tell me . . . ?" I ask softly, a question mostly directed at myself. I'm surprised by how sad I feel. How much I wish I'd known. This whole time, I'd been so wrapped up in trying to win Isaac back, never having a clue that Marlow had a past like this.

"I think *that's* the question of the hour," Isaac says. "Why *wouldn't* he tell you?"

I remember Marlow's pitiful expression after we'd met Rosie at the dance. "Maybe he simply wasn't ready," I reason. A more depressing thought: maybe he thought *I* wasn't ready.

"Or maybe he didn't want you to know about his past because he thought you'd run away," says Isaac. "I mean, it doesn't exactly look good that he was in a possible altercation with his ex."

"Again, we don't know what actually happened."

"*Something* must have happened. And he obviously didn't tell you because he's in love with you."

"*What?*" I laugh loudly. To be fair, Marlow did tell me he had a crush on me from the very beginning, not that I took it seriously. But he hasn't even mentioned it since. Probably because that crush has long faded.

"Come on. Marlow is my partner for class, my friend. He doesn't *love* me; that's ridiculous. And"—I clear my throat—"he knows about *you*."

Isaac lets out a dismissive snort. "Don't be naive. You really don't think that matters? You can't trust guys so easily, especially when they're a little too eager to be your friend."[139]

"The only reason we're friends is because he's coaching me—" I stop myself. *Coaching me to better connect with you.*

"Er, he's just coaching me to be better at communication," I finish weakly.

"Communication?" Isaac scoffs. "I'm sure he'll try to coach you right into bed with him."

My spine prickles. *"Stop."*

"Have you ever considered he's just using that as an excuse?" Isaac continues. "You think he's just helping out of the goodness of his heart? He thinks he's in love, and he'll follow you around like a lovesick puppy because he's *waiting*, hoping you'll fall for him. *That's* the only reason."

"Marlow isn't like that," I retort, annoyed. "Regardless of what you might have heard, I know Marlow better than that, and I'm going to trust *my* judgment."

I can't deny that the rumors don't paint Marlow in a good light; and I may not know the details of his past, sure. But I'm going to believe what I've seen. And I've seen that Marlow's a good person. A romantic. That he likes movies and video games. That he loves gizzada and biryani. That for some reason, he enjoys making fun of me—but never too much.

More important, I care about Marlow. Maybe he can be *vexing* at

---

139     Ouch. Is the thought that someone genuinely just wants to be my friend so hard to believe?

times, but he's also calming and thoughtful and sincere. He helps those who need help. He listens when no one else will, keeps my secrets when he has no real reason to. He sees me, and despite it all he accepts me. That can't be faked. Ipso facto, I *refuse* to believe the rumors. Even if they come from Isaac.

"Why are you even bringing this up, Isaac?" I ask. "Is there something else about Marlow you're not telling me, or is this all just based on rumors?" I ask. His concern would normally make me a little happy, but there's something about this situation, about the timing of it, that feels off.

"Look, I'm just trying to say you should keep your distance," says Isaac. "His reputation around campus is garbage. I'm sure he's been nice to you, but the reality is, if there's even a one-percent chance he wants you, it's going to put you in a difficult position. And frankly, if Marlow didn't trust you enough to tell you *his* past, I'm not sure you should trust him and his motives, either."

His words make my stomach take a nosedive.

On one hand, I'm sad that Marlow has been keeping me in the dark about his past, especially when Marlow knows *my* biggest secret. I've definitely noticed how whenever the topic of Rosie gets brought up, Marlow deftly sidesteps. I should be patient, I know, but I wish he felt comfortable enough to open up more, the way I have.

On the other hand, maybe Marlow's life isn't any of my business. I'm not even sure I have the right to feel this way.

To not trust Marlow, though? I don't know if it's possible anymore.

Isaac's hand reaches for mine, and he gently clasps it.

"I'm sorry. It's just, if there's even a small chance he threw a bottle in a fight with his girlfriend, it means he's dangerous. I'm just looking out for you."

Eventually, I look up and meet his eyes, even as a storm of mixed emotions rages in the pit of my gut.

"I know," I say simply, even though I'm not sure I do.

## ZAINA + ANISA

Are you on campus right now? 2:17 PM

Huh? 2:19 PM

No, why? 2:19 PM

I'm on a ski trip for two days 2:20 PM

Does Mom know? 2:20 PM

No, I didn't tell her . . . 2:21 PM

Why? 2:21 PM

Nothing 2:21 PM

Was just wondering 2:22 PM

??? 2:22 PM

It finally happened 8:46 PM

I suppose it was inevitable 8:46 PM

But I did it 8:46 PM

I broke my bed 8:46 PM

Wow, Marlow. Wow. 8:47 PM

I know what you're thinking 8:48 PM

And it would be a fair assumption 8:48 PM

But literally I just jumped on my bed too hard and it BROKE 8:48 PM

Now I'm just in the hallway waiting for maintenance to show up 8:49 PM

And either judge the shit out of me OR give me a look of, how should we say, appreciation 8:49 PM

. . . 8:49 PM

I've made you speechless 8:50 PM

Aniiiisaaaaa 8:50 PM

Pay attention to me dammit 8:50 PM

😐 8:52 PM

**Anisaaaaaaa** 8:53 PM

# Chapter 21

## MARCH 2

"It should be illegal to have to wake up this early," Kira groans.

We're standing by the bus stop at Halcyon, where the Ski Club has us all waiting for a shuttle to take us to a lodge in the Poconos. But the air is particularly nippy, even for early March; the sun hasn't even risen yet, and frost crunches under Kira's feet as she bounces on her heels to stay warm.

"It's not *that* bad." At least, it shouldn't be. I should be used to waking up early to get ready before Kira and catch my morning prayers. Sometimes I'll even fit in a quick yoga sesh from YouTube. This body doesn't maintain itself. This morning though, my body was being less than cooperative. The cold certainly doesn't help—and as cute as they are, my white ski jacket and Stuart Weitzman platform boots[140] can only do so much.

I glance over at Isaac, who's standing in the nearby parking lot with his friends. I recognize a few of them: Kasim, from the SASA meeting, along with a few others. And Ellie. Earlier this morning, Isaac told me they'd decided to pile into his car and drive to the lodge. He invited me, of course, but I politely declined.

I'm glad Kira agreed to come with me, even if it took a little convincing;

---

140    Once again, my skill at finding secondhand designer products proves itself beyond measure. You may bow.

she's *determined* to win that auction for the rare, signed LØVE LIFE EP. But if she hadn't been here, I'd feel especially alone right now.

Isaac catches my stare and gives me a little wave.

I wave back. But my smile feels stiff, and I don't think it's just because of the cold.

Is it possible to suffer an emotional hangover? Because after what Isaac said about Marlow, my limbs have felt like lead, and I could hardly sleep because my imagination kept running wild.[141] Isaac acted prickly during our walk back from the Mediterranean restaurant, too. I wonder if he thought I was too defensive of Marlow. But how could I just take rumors at face value?

And as if I didn't have enough to worry about, when I drove back home to pick up my ski suit, the house was strangely quiet. I texted Zaina to ask where they'd all gone, but her answer was cryptic: All she said was that Mom and Dad had stepped out somewhere and she was at a friend's house.

I let out a muffled yawn, and just as I do, I can feel a familiar presence even before I see him approaching. I hate that for the past couple weeks, I've become hyperaware of a certain someone. Maybe Isaac is right to be worried. Maybe I've gotten too reliant on someone I barely know.

"Surprise," says Marlow, handing Kira and me two steaming Styrofoam cups.

"What's this?" Kira asks, taking one with narrowed eyes.

"Coffee." He grins.

Kira makes a sound that can only be described as an impossible combination of a squeal and a grunt, and starts gulping hers down without a word.

---

141    It probably doesn't help that Kira's recently been having me watch K-dramas with her.

Marlow stares back in horror. *"How is your tongue not burning off?"*

When Kira's finished chugging, she looks up and wipes at her mouth, breathing hard. "Thanks to the cold, I feel nothing."

"Isn't that just you all the time?" I ask.

"Correct. Feelings are for lesser mortals."

I snort.

"Thanks." I take my cup from Marlow, grateful.

But I avoid meeting his gaze.

I've been . . . sad since that talk with Isaac,[142] and I wish he hadn't said anything. Even though I've decided not to believe the rumors on their face, it's like Pandora's Box has been opened. Like something between us has *changed*, and now we can never go back.

I've known Marlow for a little over six weeks, but I thought we'd grown relatively close in that time.[143] So what's the real reason he didn't tell me about Rosie? There has to be something I'm missing.

I throw back some coffee, eager for the warmth in my stomach. I have to talk to him about it. Plus, it's like Marlow said: everyone deserves that chance to explain themselves, even when things look bad.

Except I thought confronting Isaac was hard. But Marlow? What if—what if I talk to him, and Isaac was right all along?

*You have to trust me. That means being fully up front and honest, because that's the only way this is going to work.*

I take a deep breath. I want to trust Marlow. He's never given me any reason not to. But there's this horrible, gnawing little piece of doubt,

---

142     Truly a rare occurrence, though becoming a little too frequent for my liking.

143     Not that I have anything to compare it to; it's not like I had time to hang out with friends outside of school or community events. Besides Kira, Marlow is the first real friend I've made.

planted by Isaac. What if I'm wrong? It certainly wouldn't be the first time I've been wrong about someone.

I'm still lost in the slipstream of my thoughts when I feel Marlow mouthing something at me.

*Your lipstick's smudged.* He discreetly points at his own lips.

My cheeks bloom. Of course he'd notice. He always does.

I quickly turn around and dig for my mirror in my bag before carefully wiping away the excess lipstick.

When I finish, Marlow's mouth tugs in an affectionate smile. *Much better.*

My heart does a strange little dance, and I look away again.

No. Marlow isn't the kind to act with ulterior motives.

"I think it's going to snow tonight," says Marlow thoughtfully, looking up at the sky.

Kira's lip curls. "God, I hope not."

"Really?" I smile faintly. "I love snow."

I know people consider spring the season of rebirth, but there's something about snow that brings me hope. To me, it feels like *change.* It's cold, yes, and it's bitter. But it gives the earth pause: time to heal and take in the nutrients it needs to come back with a vengeance.[144]

It's inspiring, really.

Just then, with a squeal of tires and rattle of metal announcing its arrival, the small blue shuttle pulls into the bus stop. Kira lets out a loud, relieved sigh. "Finally!" The other twenty or so Halcyon and Marion students begin picking up their bags off the ground, eager to board.

But for some reason, I feel nervous. It could be because it's my very

---

144    *Snow,* baby. She is the moment. Summer could NEVER.

first overnight trip, but I am suddenly nauseated. And no, I still haven't told my parents. The guilt's not great, even if it's also the teensiest bit exhilarating. Mostly, though, it's that void-in-your-stomach feeling of dread. Like something bad's about to happen.

"Heating! Blessed heating!" Kira grabs me by the arm. "Come on. You too," she adds to Marlow, who seems strangely happy about it. He shoves his hands in his pockets and follows us while Kira leads me toward the bus.

But it's not until I glance at my periphery that I notice Isaac standing by his car, watching us.

After a three-hour drive, we arrive at the lodge, and as soon as I get off the shuttle, I'm hit with the sharpness of fresh, mountain air. The sun has risen, illuminating the snow in eye-aching brightness. The lodge itself is just one building of many on the ski resort: a multitiered building with steep red roofs and log-paneled walls. A plume of smoke snakes its way from somewhere behind the roof with the promise of a cozy fireplace somewhere within.

Kira and I are barely settled in our room when I start to feel antsy.

"I don't know about you, but I'm diving headfirst into the nearest jacuzzi, skull-damage be damned," says Kira, digging through her small weekender bag. How she manages to pack so little astounds me.[145] "What about you?"

"Skiing!" I respond, a little too enthusiastically. "I'm here to have fun and ski."

She arches a brow. "You sure? You don't want to settle down first or—"

---

145     Though I deserve an award. I managed to pack only one giant suitcase. And a duffel bag. And a purse.

"No!" I stretch out my arms, my legs. "I could really use the exercise."

I refuse to sit around and mope. If I have time to be sad and confused, then I have time to conquer these mountains, show 'em who's boss.

Determined, I shoot Isaac a text:

> **Going to try out the blue square slope. Want to join?**

A minute later, I get his response:

> **We're heading to the lobby to find some lunch first. You're more than welcome to come with us.**

My fingers hover over the screen. This is progress, sort of. He's actually inviting me to hang out with him and his friends. Normally, I'd jump at the opportunity. Only, I was hoping it'd just be the two of us—I was hoping to talk to him again, to ask him more questions about Marlow. I'll have to find another chance.

*I'll catch up with you later*, I eventually respond. Some one-on-one time with me might do me some good, anyhow. I'll take photos. FaceTime my sister. Sort out my head.

I pack up my things, including my ski boots, sunscreen, and an extra hat, and head out the door, chin high—

Only to, quite literally, bump into the last person I want to see right now.

"Oof." I bounce back from the impact, nearly dropping my ski boots.

"Hi," says Marlow, holding me steady, an amused glint in his eye.

He's wearing a black crewneck sweater that reads *Cringe But Free*. It's funny; his shirts used to annoy me to no end, but now, I almost find them comforting.

At least, I would, in slightly different circumstances.

"I was just looking for you." He scratches at the back of his neck. "Want to tell me why you're ignoring me all over again?"

*Because my betrothed doesn't trust you and thinks the only reason you're my friend is to seduce me, and even though I don't believe him, a tiny part of me still wonders why you've been so nice to me, especially when it seems you don't trust me enough with your own secrets!!*

"What?" I summon a smile. "No. No, I'm not." I adjust my full arms, rebalancing my things, and continue to walk as if nothing is out of the ordinary. Silently though, I'm repeating every curse word I know and directing it at the entire universe.

"Uh-huh. This feels familiar." He falls into step with me. "And here I thought we were making good progress. Talk to me?"

"Why should I?" I mutter, barely audible. "It's not like you talk to me."

As soon as the words fall from my mouth, I feel a little . . . annoyed with myself. "I just need some time alone, is all," I quickly amend. "Sorry."

What is *wrong* with me? I can't expect Marlow to tell me about his previous relationship, about his traumatic past. It's not like I expect *Kira* to tell me her deepest darkest secrets of her childhood in Delaware.[146]

Except . . . except it hurts. He's been giving me all this relationship advice while keeping what happened with his last relationship a secret. Teaching me how to trust him, to be more honest and open with my feelings, when *he's* been locked up tight. And what hurts the most is realizing I've been too self-centered to even notice how this friendship has felt lopsided since the start.

Maybe the right question here is, were we ever really friends? That question scares me most of all.

---

146    Though I am very, very curious.

"I saw Isaac in the lobby downstairs, by the way," says Marlow. "By the fireplace. In case you didn't know." He smiles weakly. "Just wanted to give you a heads-up."

"Okay." Unable to hold his gaze, I decide instead to look at my shoes. "Thanks."

Marlow hesitates, like he's debating something internally. I can practically see the tiny storm cloud above his head.

"Seriously, what's wrong?" he pleads softly. "You've been acting off all day." There's the lightest touch on my shoulder. "Did something happen with Isaac? Or is it because of what I said last time about giving up . . . ?"

Why is it so hard to tell him how I feel, to get an answer? Marlow is always poking and prodding for my feelings; it should be easy, at this point, to spill.

I take a deep breath. I have to ask. I have to know the truth.

"Remember when we talked about our two ground rules?"

Marlow's eyebrows furrow. "Yeah, of course. Me not telling anyone about your secret, and"—the lines on his forehead deepen—"you have to trust me, as your love coach, and be honest."

I nod. Bite my lip.

"Does that trust go both ways?"

Slowly, Marlow nods. "I think by necessity, trust *has* to go both ways."

I look up at him. "Then why won't you tell me what happened with Rosie?"

"Rosie?" His eyebrows furrow. "Where is this coming from? It's like I said before; we dated and then we broke up. What does that have to do with any—"

My heart starts to hammer in my chest. "Because I think it's weird that you don't want to talk about her." I swallow. "With me."

For a few seconds, Marlow says nothing. Then realization dawns across his face, which slowly gives way to something that looks like irritation. I haven't seen him look like that in a while. The last time I saw his expression darken like this was the first time we saw Isaac and Ellie outside the math and science building.

"Did Isaac say something?"

My jaw tenses. "And if he did?"

"Nothing, just—" He runs a hand down his face. "So what, are you worried hanging out with me will hurt your reputation?"

*"No."* I'm surprised by how much I really mean that. How that didn't even cross my mind. "No. That's not it at all. First of all, I've been painfully oblivious about your reputation, and apparently most things about you, until now. But really, I guess I've just been wanting to know what really happened. Why you didn't tell me."

"I've already told you. I really don't like talking about it."

There's that wall again.

I blow out air through my nose. "Don't you think you should disclose what happened if you're going to be my love coach and help me with my own relationship problems? You can't just tell me you're going to help me and then forget to mention—"

"Mention what?"

"That your own relationship fell apart."

Marlow flinches, and I immediately regret it.

I look away, ashamed.[147] I'm letting my guilt and frustration get to me. *I'm* the one who barely tried to get to know him all this time. I can't just expect his walls to come crashing down now, just because *I* want them to.

---

147    Sometimes, I wish life were more like an otome game, and I could choose from a list of the right things to say, instead of relying on my brain.

"I'm really sorry," I mutter. "That was cruel."

"No," Marlow says, his shoulders slumping. "You're right. It did fall apart. Which is why I'm uniquely positioned to make sure you don't make the same mistakes as I did. All that matters is, I've got your back."

"Yeah, but *why*?" I press. "That's what I've never understood. Because sometimes it feels like our friendship is really one-sided, for no good reason. I mean, you're helping me with Isaac, you tell me to open up, and yet, I feel like you're afraid to open up to me in the same way. It's just, you know all my secrets and fears and insecurities, so if you're not going to reciprocate, it's going to hurt, because . . ."

*I expect that from Isaac. Not from you.*

Marlow's eyes meet mine, and for a moment, something in them wavers sadly.

I take a calming breath and go on. "The only logical reason I can think of for you keeping everything that happened with Rosie a secret is because you think I'm shallow or vain, that I'd judge you like everyone else, which—I guess in a way, I've established myself as someone who does care about appearances and reputation—"

"That's *not* the reason."

"—or because you're helping me is out of some misplaced guilt over your breakup—"

"Also not the reason."

"Or because, like Isaac seems to think, you're secretly in love with me and the only reason you're helping me is to have an excuse to get close to me."

"That's . . ." Marlow takes a sharp intake of breath. His shoulders shake like he's reached his limit.

"Then why didn't you tell me?" I plead. "I know I haven't made it clear, but the truth is, I *do* want to know more about you, too. So at the very least, what can I do to make you feel more comfortable with me, too? Because I'm sad and I—I don't know what to do."

My stomach's in knots. I've never felt this vulnerable with someone, and it's like I'm hanging by a thread over an alligator pit, and Marlow holds the scissors.[148]

"This has been really bothering you, hasn't it," Marlow mumbles ruefully. "Fine. You're absolutely right. I *am* uncomfortable talking about it, but it's not because of some failing on your part. God, no. It's *me*." He digs through his curls. "I'm scared. That's it. I'm just scared. The reason why I didn't say anything is because it was nice having someone around who didn't look at me like I was pathetic, and maybe selfishly, I just . . ." Marlow's fragile gaze snags mine. "I wanted you to see who I really am. Without the baggage."

I feel my face soften. "What do you mean?"

"You asked me once—why I don't have a Jamaican accent? My accent isn't even that strong, but if my accent ever slipped out, Rosie would tell me she couldn't understand, or her friends would make all these microaggressions, or thinly veiled racist comments. You'd think because Halcyon is a top school, I'd have nothing to worry about. But their racism just comes in fancier vocabulary, is all.

"Except I wanted to fit in, you know? I wanted her to like me, so I *hid* my accent, did whatever I could to make her friends like me."

"You changed yourself," I say softly.

Marlow nods. "I did. Because I thought we were in love. So yeah, I hid my accent. I'd help her with essays when she was tired, get her food

---

148    Sharing your actual feelings, I'm realizing, is a literal nightmare. I don't recommend it.

when she didn't feel like going to the cafeteria, did her laundry. I stopped talking to my own friends and spent all my time with her. But that's the thing about changing yourself for someone: you never truly get to know each other, and then one day, you don't even recognize yourself anymore. Even my parents were getting worried whenever I talked to them about her; it was clear we just weren't good for each other. I was more like her errand boy than her boyfriend.

"So when Rosie broke up with me, when she said she'd never really viewed me as boyfriend material, at first, it was a shock to my system. But then I felt . . . relief. I felt *free*. And when I told her I was good with it, she got upset. I mean, the guy she'd been dating for months didn't seem to even care about breaking up, so I guess I can't fully blame her. So she threw a water bottle at me and called me heartless." He lets out a self-deprecating laugh. "I think she just wanted to get a reaction. But someone must have heard something and assumed the worst, so the rumors just spiraled. That it was a glass bottle, that I'd been drinking, that I'd thrown it. At that point, I'd already stopped drinking, so I don't even know where the hell that rumor came from."

I remember then when Marlow mentioned he used to drink but stopped after his first year. It's like a hundred tiny pieces, a hundred tiny hints, are coming together.

"Campus police even questioned me about it later," he continues. "But even though campus police quickly realized *Rosie* had been the one to throw the bottle, it didn't matter. The rumors were out there, and Rosie obviously wasn't going to go out of her way to correct them. So what could I say? What could I do? People decided to believe what they wanted to believe. I was so sick and tired of it all, I just ended up isolating myself. From everyone. Those days, the only people I had to talk to were my parents or Winston, but of course they're back in Jamaica."

I grit my teeth. My heart aches. More than that, though, I'm *furious*. If Marlow said anything back, it wouldn't look good. But if he says nothing, it doesn't look good, either. So he's right: What could he have done? Who would even believe him?

It's not nearly on the same level, but there's another reason why, besides their obsession with reputation, my family's always pressured themselves to be perfect: because if you're brown and you give any reason for other people to perceive you as a threat, you'd be in danger. Which is why no matter how many times my parents were stopped at the airport, no matter how many times strangers gave us annoyed glares if we even laughed a little too loud in public, my parents could never afford to lose their temper. Being brown meant walking with the weight of a hundred preconceived stereotypes on your shoulders. Keeping a tight rein over our feelings is all we can do.

For Marlow, though—for Black students constantly facing microaggressions and all-out racism on a predominantly white college campus—it's even worse.

Not being able to say how you feel, never being able to show it—it's *unjust*.

"It was selfish, I know, but when I saw you, I—I hoped *we* could be friends," he says. "It's been hard, feeling comfortable with someone again. I wanted to move on and forget everything, but I didn't know how. Then you came along, and at first, when I saw you delivering biryani to Isaac, I felt like I was watching myself making the same mistake with Rosie all over again. But you seemed so *sure* of yourself, so *determined* to fix your relationship with him. And that determination of yours—it's infectious." Marlow gives me a small smile. "You gave me a chance to get my mind out of this rut, to feel helpful to someone on my own terms."

My throat feels painfully dry. "I still wish you'd have told me." Then maybe I could find all his so-called former friends and slap them.

"I'm sorry. I really am." He shifts uncomfortably. "But can you honestly say you would have been my friend if you knew right off the bat? Imagine if on Day One I told you, *Hey, I recently got out of a toxic relationship and I'm still pretty fucked up about it and it's lonely as hell out there, would you be my friend?*"

I hesitate. It's disheartening to admit, but Marlow's probably right; the Anisa of The Past wouldn't even want to be associated with him, out of fear of hurting her relationship with Isaac somehow.[149]

The thought makes me feel a little ashamed.

"But I'm glad we did become friends," Marlow adds softly.

"Why?"

"You're not afraid to fight tooth and nail for the things you want, for the people you care about, and it makes me want to try harder, too. To put myself out there more. And maybe you don't realize it, but you've come such a long way on your own. I really admire you for that."

Something in his voice, affectionate and soft, makes me think about what Isaac had said about Marlow's feelings.

"Well, as long as it's admiration and not a crush," I say, smiling weakly.

"Right." Marlow takes a step toward me. "I guess I *did* say I had a crush on you."

I search his face, but I'm met with this weird intensity that wasn't there before. Something in the air feels like it's shifted. Like there's a crackle

---

149     Do you ever want to fist-fight your past self? Lately, I'm finding I wish I could do that, more and more. Unfortunately, I'm pretty sure that fight would end in a draw. We both have weak arms.

of electricity. I feel my cheeks start to redden, and self-consciously, I clutch my ski boots closer to my chest like a shield.

"But I don't think," he says carefully, "I have a crush on you anymore."

For a moment, my head goes blank.

Because what I feel right now makes no sense.

Because what I feel now is . . . disappointment.

But before I can open my mouth to ask what he means, I hear a voice behind me that makes me nearly jump out of my skin.

"Why are you still here?!" It's Kira, approaching us like a tiny, stomping storm.

"Oh, uh." I laugh nervously. "I just bumped into Marlow, and we got to talking. I was just on my way."

Kira isn't even looking at me. Instead, her eyes are trained on Marlow.

"There is bad timing," she says, exasperated, "and there is *bad* timing, you helpless little man."

Marlow stares back but says nothing.

"Kira, what—?" I start to ask, but she starts pulling me down the hallway.

"You wanted to ski, right? Let's go ski," she says cheerfully, in a way that's so unlike her it sends chills up my spine.

I turn around to throw one last look at Marlow, but he's not looking at me. Instead, his wide gaze is trained to the floor, like he's deep in thought.

But then I notice the way his back seems to be heaving slightly, and he brings his forearm to his face, almost like—

Almost like he's as flustered as I am.

# Chapter 22

## MARCH 2

I ski until my legs feel ready to fall off.

Not by choice, by the way. As soon as Kira decided to drag me off, we practically marched arm in arm to the equipment rental stand, then to the lift, then down the freaking mountain until four p.m. We didn't even stop for lunch.

I rip off my ski goggles and collapse in a heap in the snow near the bottom of the slope, breathing hard. My muscles are burning, but my body feels numb. How is that even possible?

A kid rushes past us on an inflatable tube, screaming gleefully. I'm jealous.

"For a person who works out a lot, you have zero endurance." Kira gracefully slides in next to me and clips out of her snowboard with practiced grace.

"I've decided you're simply not human." I rub at the bridge of my nose.

"You're one to talk. Your hair is somehow still perfect."

I smirk. The secret is hairspray.

"Anyway, what brought this on? I thought you said you were going to hit the hot tub," I ask.

"I was." Kira glances away. "But then . . . stuff happened."

"Stuff happened," I repeat.

I'm suspicious. She very well might have overheard my conversation with Marlow, but I get the sense if I asked, she'd just deny it. I should be grateful she interrupted, though. What the hell was that mood shift at the end there? Even though Marlow was telling me he didn't have a crush on me anymore—something I'd long suspected—there was that familiar, unmistakable warmth in the air that softens everything at its edges and turns your insides into goo. The same way in an otome game, if a guy is about to confess, the screen is filtered with cute little hearts and sparkles.

It was almost as if Marlow was about to confess something more instead.

I nearly laugh out loud. It obviously makes no sense! Even I can't be *that* presumptuous. Clearly, the otome games have been getting to me, making me consider the most ridiculous of scenarios.

But most important, I've gotten the confirmation I needed. Isaac was wrong.

Marlow does not have feelings for me. Case closed.

Better yet, this means there is the possibility that Isaac is *jealous*—an unintended consequence of Marlow being my love coach, and certainly not a bad one. Not that I'm reveling in the thought of Isaac being jealous over me.

At least, not that much.

Still, though. Part of me wishes I got to hear what Marlow had to say. Just out of curiosity.

"All things considered, I do like Marlow," Kira says suddenly.

"Huh?"

"He's a weird kid," she explains. "And he's certainly not perfect. But I get good vibes. Like he actually really cares about you. And I feel like ever since you became friends, you've chilled out a little. Gotten more human. *Even if his sense of timing sucks,*" she mumbles that last part so I don't quite catch it.

"What was that?"

"Nothing." She looks at me. "Anyway, it's about time you start making your own friends instead of waiting on Prince Charming to introduce you to his, in my humble opinion."

"I wasn't wai—" I start. But she's right. I *have* been waiting on Isaac to make a move. My entire first semester of college I spent with my head down, hoping Isaac would call upon me to bring me into his circle, show me around. So Isaac had no idea. I guess I still have a problem with letting Isaac know how I feel.

It reminds me of something Marlow had said, after we'd gone to the SASA meeting. *Isaac has now seen you trying, hard, for him. It's probably the first time you've ever been vulnerable. You actually looked human for once.*

I sigh.

"Well, whatever. Between you and Marlow, I suppose I lucked out."

Kira's face contorts. "Ugh."

But she reaches a hand toward me and helps me to my feet. "You know, I did hear a rumor about him, though."

I stiffen. "What?" It must be about Rosie. His past. Is she worried about his reputation the way Isaac is?

"He doesn't have one, but *two* pairs of yellow Crocs. One of them's a *backup*," she says severely. "Who does that?"

"That does sounds like him," I reply, laughing. And even I can hear the affection in my voice.

Things are still a little awkward between us after our last conversation, but I'm ready to talk to him again. I hate to admit it, but not having him around makes me feel . . . well, *bored*. Life is painfully boring without him.

But first, I need to focus on spending time with Isaac. Now that I feel a little better, I can do that.

It's the whole point of this trip, after all.

Together, Kira and I start shuffling through the snow back to the lodge.

"Did you bring a your own bodywash, by any chance?" I ask. "The ones at these hotels are always cheap and drying."

"Nope." Her eyes glint with amusement. "But I did bring a bar of Irish Spring."

"You're terrible."

Eventually, we reach our room and go our separate ways: Kira, to the café to grab lunch and take her long-awaited soak in the hot tub, and me, to the bathroom.

But it's not until I'm in the shower that it hits me:

Kira isn't in any classes with Marlow. Which means there's no way a rumor like that about him would reach her ears, unless . . .

She looked into him more herself.

The sun's gone down by the time I'm out of the shower and getting ready. Current status: leaning against the table to get a better angle of my face in the mirror, and carefully reapplying my lipstick. I curled my hair a little, too, which probably took longer than I should have. I tried not to think about how much I miss having short hair.

I check my phone again and frown. I sent a couple more texts to Isaac almost half an hour ago, asking where he was and whether we could meet up.

He still hasn't responded.

He and his friends have obviously eaten lunch by now; it's dinnertime.

And it's getting too late to hit the slopes. So where would he have gone?

On one hand, I hope he's having fun. It's probably been a long time since he's been able to leave campus and have a moment to be a normal college kid.

At the same time, the idea of him having fun without me curdles my stomach. It's my own damn fault for wallowing all day over Marlow.

I'm starting to regret not taking Isaac up on his invitation.

I grab my coat and head into the hall. The lobby is my first destination: a huge, round room with arched pinewood ceilings and a stone fireplace. A giant moose head graces the mantel,[150] and there are several wood and leather armchairs, deep enough to sink into, angled by the fire.

The lobby is pretty quiet, though. By now, I suppose most people are grabbing dinner at a nearby restaurant or settling down in their rooms. Unless you're Kira, who, as she announced, does not plan on ever leaving the hot tub. But I recognize Isaac's friend Kasim camped out in one armchairs, playing chess with another friend who I'm assuming is also from the SASA.

I could ask Kasim for help. I'm desperate to find Isaac. But am I *that* desperate?

I dig my teeth into my lip, mulling over whether to approach Kasim. Mom would call me an ullu[151] for dawdling.

"Hey, it's Muffin Girl," comes Kasim's booming voice. "Hey, Muffin Girl!"

I look up in horror. *Muffin Girl?*

---

150      Hopefully fake because that would be absolutely barbaric.

151      Ullu is the Urdu word for owl, which in the West is probably considered a compliment, but in Pakistan, at least, is considered an insult. Pakistan doesn't see a "wise old guardian" when it looks at owls. It sees owls and thinks, "Dang, this bird ate way too much sugar. Idiot."

He waves me over, and I try not to let a groan escape. The decision, lucky me, has been made for me.

Chin held high, I approach.

"I didn't know you were on this trip, too," he says, all cheer. Up close, the boy looks like a bear wearing a human suit. The sleeves of his T-shirt look ready to burst, and he has enough muscle mass to make four other people.

"*Hi.*" I smile politely. "You're Kasim, right?"

"Yeah. You recognize me from the SASA meeting?" He lets out a goofy laugh. "I'm flattered."

"Mm-hmm." I stare at the chessboard. "If you move your rook there, you can take his knight and then it's checkmate," I inform Kasim's friend.

Kasim's friend, who seems to be making a valiant but feeble attempt at a moustache, lights up. "Oh my God."

Back to Kasim, who now stares at the board in dismay.

"Why," he whispers.

*Because you called me Muffin Girl, you bear child.* "I'm actually looking for Isaac, so . . . ?"

"Oh, uh," he regains himself, "he's somewhere with Ellie."

My stomach sinks. "Ah." *They're alone?* "Is he now."

"As usual. The two of them are practically attached at the hip." He grins conspiratorially and hits the guy sitting next to him. "Wouldn't be surprised if they became a thing soon."

"Ah."

*Ah.*

Kasim is mistaken. At least, I *could* reason that, if it weren't for the fact that his friend also seemed to know exactly what he was talking about. Like everyone in SASA knows that Isaac and Ellie are a possibility.

Now that I think about it, Isaac never did say who I was when I showed up to the SASA meeting. Could it be that he didn't tell anyone about us?

"You could try outside," Kasim suggests. "Pretty sure they were headed to the deck."

I nod robotically.

My head's gone blank as I zip up my coat and leave the lodge. I'm hit by a gust of brisk air for just a moment. The sky has a slightly pink haze to it, like it's about to snow.[152]

I'm walking along the path lit by icicle-coated lampposts, casting the lodge in an ethereal orange glow. Someone's salted the sidewalk, and it crunches beneath my feet: the only sound I'm registering.

It's like the Winter Dance all over again. Isaac isn't answering my texts. Because he's with someone else?

I don't think I could handle that again.

The deck is easy to find; it stands out like a dark silhouette against the stars and makes for a perfect view of the night sky. I bury myself deeper in my coat and quietly start climbing the stairs until I hear low voices, the steady crackle of fire.

"I don't think you've relaxed a day in your life," comes Ellie's voice. "Stop looking over your shoulder."

"I can't help it. I keep thinking my parents are going to drag me off. And my mom's built like a linebacker. She literally could."

*They're here.* I'm close to the top step; another step, and I risk being seen.

*Is there a reason why we're hiding?* I can practically hear Marlow's voice at my ear.

---

152    Normally, I love the snow. Winter is my favorite season, after all. But right now, it feels especially gloomy.

No, but—

Ugh, I should say something. I should say something instead of hiding, like a coward.

Ellie laughs. "As controlling as they sound, I don't think your parents are going to come all the way here."

"You don't know them," Isaac responds. "They would. My parents would never let me come out on a ski trip. They'd call it a waste of time. It's *suffocating*."

I find myself agreeing with him. But I'm surprised. I wish I'd known this was how Isaac really felt about his parents. I'm not even their kid and I feel their excruciating pressure of expectation, even more so than with my own parents. But I didn't know it was affecting him this much.

Why wouldn't he tell *me*? The one person who might actually understand?

Ellie lets out a long sigh. "I don't know how you do it."

"What, live like this?" Isaac chuckles, a soft, sad sound that carries on the wind. "I don't think I have a choice. I care about my parents, and I respect them, but if I ever tried to talk to them about what I really want, they'd disown me. It makes me feel . . . two-faced."

The fire lets out a crackle, a hiss. In the momentary silence, the howl of wind resonates through the valley.

"I don't think you're two-faced," Ellie says gently. "You're just doing the best you can."

I peer over the deck finally, and now I see them. For a moment, Isaac says nothing, his eyes searching Ellie's. Like there's some hidden meaning in her words.

And then it happens.

It's like gravity, the way they naturally fall into each other. Their mouths connect in slow motion, and for a moment, I see the glint of metal on Isaac's wrist—the bracelet, catching light from the nearby lamppost.

It's a perfect, almost cinematic kiss, all fireworks and perfect alignment. The kind I'd see in the rom-coms Marlow made me watch.

The kind that's the start of something real.

Seeing Isaac kiss someone else makes me feel like I'm back in fourth grade, when we'd first moved to Pennsylvania. The moment I'd walked into my new classroom, the other students looked me up and down, homed in on my unibrow, my bug eyes hiding behind thick glasses, the gangly awkwardness of a child dressed by a rushed parent. They'd laughed at me. *Why do you look like that?* one girl asked aloud. I didn't understand they were calling me ugly. Not immediately.

But they made me feel like a total fool.

I feel like a fool now.

"Isaac." This time, his name escapes my mouth like a sharp intake of breath.

Isaac and Ellie stop, frozen in time until—

"Shit." Isaac breaks away, his face pale. *"Ani."*

I see it in his face: the horror. The fear of being caught. But not the regret.

I bound down the stairs and fly like I'm the one who's been caught philandering. The ski lodge is huge and I have no idea where I'm going; I just want to get far, far away from him.

I follow the path. The cold beats against my cheeks, and the snowfall dampens all sound, save for the heavy crunch of footfall beneath me and another set of feet farther back. If I ever wanted to compare our athletic prowess, I guess this is one way to do it.

My lungs feel like they've suffering from freezer burn.

*Isaac kissed her. Isaac kissed her.*

We've never even—

I take desperate gulps of air. It never feels like enough.

But I don't stop running, even when I hear a familiar voice calling my name.

I don't stop until someone grabs my arm.

"Anisa?"

I expect to see Isaac, but it's *Marlow* who's somehow found me. His eyes are wide with concern, breath coming in rapid bursts of white clouds.

"What's wrong?" he asks.

I don't even know *what* to say. I couldn't talk even if I wanted to.

Footsteps resound from behind us; Isaac has caught up. His gaze darts nervously between me and Marlow. "Ani."

Marlow stands in front of me, almost protectively. "What did you do?"

"This is between us." Isaac takes a step forward. "Ani. Can we talk? Alone?"

I shake my head. For once in my life, I do not want to be alone with him. And I want Marlow here, *need* him *here*, to listen and see all this so I know it isn't happening inside my head. That this all isn't some stress nightmare I just need to wake from.

Marlow's eyes narrow. "You gonna explain what happened?"

"Ani saw something"—Isaac grits his teeth—"she *saw something* that was a *mistake*. And I don't want her to get the wrong idea."

Anger flares in my chest.

"Wrong *idea*? Pray tell, what *wrong idea* do you think I'm having? Please, enlighten me."

"It was nothing."

"*You kissed Ellie,*" I whisper. Marlow's eyes go wide.

"It was this one time," Isaac argues. "I know you're upset, but please don't make this a bigger deal than it has to be."

"Don't gaslight her," Marlow growls, and I feel a bloom of gratitude in my chest.

Isaac glares back. But then he closes his eyes, checking himself.

"Last week," I continue, "just last week, you said we were *partners*, and now you're kissing Ellie. What am I supposed to think?"

"I know. I know. And I'm sorry."

Except Isaac's *sorry* doesn't even sound fully genuine.

"You know, deep down I knew." I let out a bitter laugh. "I *knew*. But I refused to believe. Is that why you always say you're too busy to spend time with me? Because you're in love with someone else?"

Isaac's jaw twitches. "I never said I was in love, I just—"

"Why didn't you tell me? You said you loved *me*. I thought you wanted to marry—" I swallow. I know I'm grasping at straws; the truth is quite literally right in front of me, but *still*. "Why would you do this to us?"

"Our *parents* want us to get married!" Isaac spits. "The community expects us to get married. But aren't you tired of living for other people, of living on autopilot? Don't you want to be free? Don't you want to follow your own path for *once*?"

Isaac's face is red—from anger or the cold, I can't tell. "You need to wake up, Ani. We're not even formally engaged; we're just *kids* following a script already written for us. All this talk about our future—there's no substance to it. Our parents, and even you—all of you only loved the *idea* of us, the optics of it, the perception of it. And if it weren't for our parents pushing us together, can you really stand there and tell me we'd have any sort of meaningful connection?"

I balk at the sudden onslaught of emotions toward me. Like I'm everything he hates distilled into a single person.

"We don't even know each other," he adds, his voice low. "Not in any way that really matters."

"We *could* have!" I fire back. "You had to have seen how hard I was trying to bridge the gap. You'd have to be willfully ignorant not to! But you never even gave me the *chance*." I take a shaky, wet breath. "You were *never* going to give me that chance, were you?"

His silence is his answer.

I want to scream at him and hurt him the way he hurt me; he deserves it for being so cruel, for treating me like dirt. There's just no excuse for this. But I'm too sad to even think straight. I don't understand it. If Isaac never truly loved me, if he had long ago decided we weren't going to work, why give me false hope for so long?

I'm so disappointed in him: for stringing me along like this, for playing me like a fool. And no offense to Ellie, but I can't believe that Isaac would be the kind of brown guy to pursue another girl, pulling a *Big Sick* on me, instead of trying to work things out with me and our families first. As if he somehow viewed Ellie as an escape from perceived cultural shackles, and me as a mere afterthought.[153] It's unfair. It *hurts*.

More than that, though, I'm disappointed with myself. I wasted so much time caring about what other people thought about me, what Isaac thought—and look what it got me.

There's just a heavy, loaded stillness that makes my bones ache. Then the vibration of someone's phone. Ellie, maybe, trying to reach Isaac. After all, he did just run away from her.

"You don't get to act all innocent," Isaac finally says, shaking, "when

---

153     And why? Why are brown girls *always* an afterthought?

I saw you and Marlow all over each other after the dance."

*Is he—is he talking about the hug? He saw that . . . ?*

"She was crying, you ass!" Marlow shouts. "Because of *you*, might I add. Because we saw *you* with Ellie."

"Or maybe you're just like me." Isaac stares directly into my eyes.

Raw fury pulses through my veins now. In a way, Isaac is right about one thing: I guess I *don't* know him. The person standing in front of me isn't the Isaac I thought I knew. The person standing in front of me is selfish and mean and not someone I'd *ever* want in my life.

Isaac never had to love me. He didn't owe me anything, I know that. But he could have at least been *kind*.

Don't I deserve—?

No. I *know* I deserve better.

"I'm not like you, Isaac," I reply. "Because I would *never* do this to you."

Isaac's phone vibrates again. There's an impasse, but Isaac finally relents; with a groan, he pulls it out from his pocket.

But his eyes widen when he sees the screen.

"Hello?" he answers quickly.

I hear a faint, familiar voice on the other line that I can't quite make out.

"Walaikum assalam, Aunty. Yes, she's here. With me." Isaac glances at me. The fire in his eyes has faded. "We're out on a field trip with a group. In the Poconos."

*Mom . . . ?*

"Okay. I'll let her know."

Isaac puts away his phone.

"Ani. That was your mom. She's been trying to call you. You have to go back home. Your dad's in the hospital."

"What?" It's like the entire world has spun off its axis. I feel dizzy with nausea. Marlow's body tenses beside me.

"What happened?" My voice is weak. "Is he all right?"

I don't even care that Isaac cheated on me right now. That fight is a million miles away.

"I'm not sure," Isaac answers calmly. "All she said was that he's been admitted."

What do I do . . . ? Of all the times to be trapped in the Poconos. And it's snowing.

"I'll drive you," Isaac offers. "We can go now—"

"And trap her in a car for three hours with you? Hell no." Marlow throws Isaac a dirty look. "I'm sure there's a shuttle somewhere, or maybe a train—"

"It's *late*. Public transportation isn't going to be running." Isaac looks at me. "The sooner you get there, the better."

He's right. I can't afford to be picky. And frankly, Dad takes priority.

"I'll be fine," I assure Marlow.

"Okay. If you're sure. Just—call me if you need anything, okay? And don't worry about your stuff. I'll ask Kira. We'll bring it all back to your dorm tomorrow."

"Thank you, Marlow."

He reaches a hand toward me, like he's going to pat my head, but he decides against it. His arm falls limply back to his side.

"Be safe. I'll be thinking of you."

I nod quietly, touched by his words, and follow Isaac to the parking lot.

# Chapter 23
### MARCH 2

It is the longest car ride of the century.

Thankfully, Isaac put on some soft indie music, which doesn't calm me down—nothing would—but it does fill the silence.

For the first hour, Isaac doesn't say a word, and neither do I.

In the second hour, he asks if the temperature is okay. I say yes.[154] He asks if I need to make any trips to a rest stop. I say no.

We descend back into stillness.

But at one point, I start reciting a dua, a short prayer for my dad, that helps me feel like I have at least *some* control because I don't know what else to do. And eventually, I hear Isaac muttering the same dua under his breath, which only adds to the complicated mess inside my chest.

It's amazing how quickly things can change—how when the world deals you a blow, all the invisible tethers that bind you to your people work their magic and bring you together, regardless of history or bad blood.

The world has a funny way of reminding you that there are things much bigger than yourself.

When we arrive at the hospital, Isaac swerves the car to the front entrance.

---

154     Of *course* the temperature is fine. The car he's driving is an Audi A6. A luxury sedan. With heated seats. A college kid driving this nice of a car feels criminal.

"Go," he says, his face grim. "I'll park and meet up with you."

I nod and rush into the hospital so fast that I nearly crash into the sliding doors. I'm immediately hit with the smell of bleach and rubbing alcohol, and the faint metallic tang of medical equipment. The lighting, somehow both pale and eye-achingly bright at the same time, already graces me with a headache, and half the walls are covered in a faded green-and-pink wallpaper that looks better suited for the nineties, the rest an ugly white popcorn texture.

A nurse leads me to my dad's room as I take short, sharp breaths. I'm anxious. Scared, even. But my feet keep moving until I reach the door.

I'm not prepared for what's inside.

Dad is lying on a hospital bed, his eyes closed and his face pale. He's hooked up to a heart monitor, an IV, and some other medical devices I don't recognize. It's only been a couple weeks since I last saw him, but he looks a little thinner. Older.

I swallow the sob threatening to escape. "Dad."

Mom is standing by his bed. She clearly rushed here because she's wearing her old lounge clothes: a tattered brown cardigan and a pair of gray sweatpants with a red stripe down the sides. Her glasses are sliding down her nose. In the corner of the hospital room, Zaina is sitting in a pale-red armchair, still wearing a heavy coat, and it's no wonder. It's cold in here.

"Ani," Mom says tiredly.

"I'm so sorry I didn't see your call." I take a step inside, feeling strangely out of place. Like this is all someone else's life, a scene from a bad movie. "Is he sleeping . . . ?"

"Yes. And Isaac already explained everything. About you being in the Poconos."

Mom's face is grim. If she's mad that I didn't tell her about the ski trip, she doesn't show it.

"What the hell is going on? What's wrong with him?"

Zaina glances at Mom.

"What aren't you telling me?"

Mom hesitates.

"*Mom.*"

"He was diagnosed with colon cancer over a month ago."

Colon cancer . . . ?

I don't know much about it, but from what I've heard, it's one of the worst kinds.

"You've known for over *a month*? And you didn't think to tell me?" I snap.

"You knowing wouldn't change anything," Mom says sharply. "And we didn't want it interfering with your studies. You can't afford to mess anything up if you're going to grad school. Do you really think you would have been able to focus on your studies if we'd told you?"

No. The answer is clear and immediate in my mind. The reality is, how the hell is anyone supposed to focus on anything when someone they care about is dying?

But still, it hurts. Isaac shattering my heart, this diagnosis—it's no longer the threat of my family breaking up. My family, my future, is being *destroyed*. Horrible images run through my head: Dad, wasting away. A funeral. The kind of emptiness that robs you of all feeling.

That hug in the laundry room. *I love you*, Dad had said, and it'd caught me so off guard then. Had he been trying to tell me about this?

"Plus, your dad was starting chemo," Mom continues, sighing. "There were still a lot of unknowns."

Is this why Mom and Dad decided to postpone their divorce? Because Dad was getting chemo?

"So now what?" I ask. "How bad is it? How long?"

"Five years. Inshallah."

"That's—that's *nothing*."

Five years. In five years, Dad could be *gone*.

Dad and I have never been very close, but we never needed to be. He's a good dad. A good person. He doesn't deserve this.

My head whorls painfully. How does this just happen? Was it stress? Was he not eating well? I don't understand. How can something like this just drop completely out of the blue?

It's like someone's dug a hole through my chest. The edges of my view turn white until the room itself disappears. My breathing becomes ragged, and I start to heave for air.

There's a hand on my back.

"Hey," comes Isaac's voice by my ear, but it sounds far away. "Ani. Ani, I think you're having a panic attack. Breathe. You need to breathe."

Guess he found the room okay. *Easier said than done, you jerk*, I want to tell him, but I can't find my voice.

"Ani," Zaina says. I see the faint outline of her face in front of me, Mom standing beside her, face etched with barely restrained panic.

"Slow down. Breathe deeper. You got this. In through your nose, out through your mouth."

*It's okay,* I repeat in my mind. *It's okay.*

I close my eyes and focus on breathing. I've never had a panic attack before, but this is the worst I've ever felt in my entire life. I'm not sure how much time has passed, but when I finally start to regain myself and the room starts coming back to me in bits and pieces, I realize I'm kneeling by Dad's bed, my face burrowed into the blanket at his side. The steady beep of his heart monitor soothes me.

"Do you want me to call a nurse?" Isaac asks when my eyes open again.

I shake my head slowly. "I'm fine now." Relatively speaking. My bones feel like they're still rattling and the floor beneath me still feels like its undulating like waves. But the worst of it is over.

"Oh, Isaac! You were acting like a real doctor," Mom exclaims. "I'm so proud. See, Zaina? This is why you should think about medical school."

Zaina rolls her eyes.

My head starts to clear and I'm feeling better, but something's telling me this is just the beginning of a very long journey. The thought terrifies me.

I have to be strong.

"Sorry, everyone. For worrying you," I say softly.

"Don't apologize, idiot." Zaina's flicks my forehead, muttering. "It's our fault for dropping this on you, anyway."

Poor Zaina; I wonder if she feels guilty for keeping Dad's diagnosis a secret from me. That must have been hard.

"Sit down in a chair and rest, Ani," says Mom with uncharacteristic gentleness. "Your nani should be here soon. I have a few things to take care of at work before I take a leave of absence. . . ." Mom takes a deep inhale. "So Nani will stay at the hospital and look after your dad in the meantime." She looks at Isaac, eyebrows furrowed. "Isaac beta, will you be heading back to your dorm? Visiting hours are almost over anyway, and I'm sure you have a busy schedule."

Isaac shakes his head. "It's okay, Aunty. I can stay. I'd be happy to."

Slowly, I get to my feet. "Actually, I think it's better you go. Isaac's got a *lot* on his plate right now,"[155] I explain. I don't need Isaac hanging

---

155    Is my tone a bit sarcastic? Maybe. But he deserves it.

around, reminding me what I've already lost. "Right, Isaac?"

Isaac says nothing for a beat, then he sighs.

"Right."

"I'll walk him out," I tell Mom.

"Good girl." Mom looks pleased. "Isaac, come visit us again soon, all right? Hopefully in better circumstances."

Isaac smiles weakly.

As soon as we're a safe enough distance to avoid Mom or Zaina finding us, I spin on my heel to face him, long hair whipping around me.

"So? Are you going to continue to make excuses or are we going to talk like actual adults?"

Isaac's expression is an unfamiliar one. He looks conflicted, as if a hundred thoughts were swirling in his mind like dollar bills in a money booth, and he's struggling to catch hold of a single one.

He won't even look at me.

It's almost funny, how quickly things can change. I've practically worshipped him for years and now . . .

Right now, he feels like a stranger.

"I'm sorry," he says finally. "For earlier. For everything. I've gone through a lot of stress lately, and I think the pressure of it all . . ." He shakes his head. "In a way, I think I took it out on you. Maybe for months now. You deserve better."

"Yes. I do." I fold my arms across my chest. "Why didn't you just tell me? If you had just told me—"

*Then maybe I wouldn't feel like such a fool.*

First Isaac, now my parents, to an extent, even Marlow—it feels like *everyone's* been hiding things from me. All the while I've been living my life as if everything were fine, as if everything were going to plan.

"I know." He stares at the floor. "I should have. I think I was conflicted. I wanted both: you and Ellie. Making my parents happy and freedom."

"Well, you can't have both."

"Yeah."

"And it's a dick move to try."

"Yeah."

"So then, let's make it easy for you. You obviously have feelings for Ellie; even I can see that. So pick Ellie."

That gets his attention. He looks at me now, eyes wide.

"I didn't expect you to say that. You'd just—you'd give it up that quickly?"

I glare at him. "It has nothing to do with *giving up*. But I'm not into competition, certainly not like this. You and Ellie clearly have something going. You and I *don't*." I swallow. My throat's dry. "The thing I don't get *is*, if you've known that for a while, why did you keep stringing me along? Stringing our families along?"

"Because you're—" Isaac bites at the inside of his mouth, mulling. "You're everything I *should* want. Logically, we're a perfect match."

His eyes trail back to the floor. "But that's just the thing. I'm tired of people expecting things from me. Of living a preordained life with no free will. And whenever our future came up, it felt like you would just go along with whatever they wanted. I think part of me resented you for playing into our parents' hands. We never felt like a team, you know?"

"That's not—" I start, but then I remember when Marlow had asked why I loved Isaac. How I'd answered that it was because it's *always* been him. That I simply couldn't ever imagine being with anyone else.

"Truth is, I'm not even sure I want to take over my parents' practice anymore. But if I told you . . ." Isaac rubs at his eyebrows, lines etched deep between them. "I don't know. I kept thinking you would be disappointed. You'd realize I'm not perfect at all and maybe even take my mom's side."

"How could you think that . . . ?"

"Because look at you! You don't get it, Ani. You're unapproachable. The moment you decide to do something, you make it happen. Hell, seeing you trip and fall at the SASA meeting was one of the first times I've ever seen you make a mistake. I'm surprised you didn't just tell gravity it was wrong and stop your own fall."

"Me? *Unapproachable*?" I ask. "That just sounds like an excuse. And I'm *far* from perfect. I mean, have you seen the way I trip all over my words around you?"

"I never saw it that way," He smiles weakly. "And maybe it is an excuse, but the reality is, I've never felt like I could let down my walls around you. I suspect you feel the same. I think we've been putting up a front for so long we don't know how to take down our walls around each other. And that's not love. That can *never* be love."

God. The irony of it all.

I let my head fall back; the weight of my long hair feels especially heavy today.

"So you don't want to do medicine anymore, huh," I mutter. "You could have told me. All of it. Any of it."

"Maybe," he answers mournfully.

"And Ellie? You do want to be with her, right?" His parents will practically flay him alive for it. If he truly loves her, sees a future with her, then he'll have to be ready for a long fight.

"If she wants me, too. I have to talk to her first, come clean with everything. But I'd like the chance to figure that out." Isaac gives me a determined look. "I've never been given the chance to consider anything other than what my parents wanted. And I want that chance. Like anyone else."

"Fine." My voice sounds surprisingly calm. "Then it's settled. It's over. Better now than fifteen years into a loveless marriage."

"True." The ball in Isaac's throat bounces up and down. "In that case . . ."

He starts fiddling with something at his wrist, and I hear the click of a clasp being undone.

He hands me back the bracelet I had given him two years ago. A promise that things would never change between us. It sits in his trembling hand like a sad, dead snake.

I take it, carefully stick it into my pocket.

"I'm sorry," he says. "I really am."

"Yeah, well . . ." I shrug. "It's not like I'm in want of other options. I'll have guys lining up to be with me in no time."

Isaac chuckles, then gives me a serious look.

"So are we—are we good?" he asks.

Memories and daydreams of Isaac and me flash through my head like a cruel slideshow. All those times people talked about how wonderful a couple we would be, swooning over a beautiful wedding that would never happen. The texts, the phone calls, the slow, heart-fluttering process of trying to get to know each other. And the thought of us, of our own family—a future I'll never know. It's all painted over with *this* Isaac, who might have loved me, once upon a time—but not enough to stop him from being dishonest, from gaslighting me into believing *I* was the one who was overreacting.

The wounds he inflicted are still too raw. I need time and distance. To be who I want to be, without him.

"No," I reply truthfully. "No. But maybe someday. On my own terms."

Isaac sucks in his lips. "Fair enough."

I watch as he starts to walk away.

But then he stops suddenly, as though he's remembered something.

He turns around. Looks at me.

"Hey, Ani. About Marlow . . ."

My back tenses. "What is it?"

"Nothing. Just . . ." Isaac smiles faintly. "I hope you find your own path. I really do."

**Hey** 9:18 PM

**Hope you got there safely** 9:18 PM

**Text when you get a chance?** 9:18 PM

**Kira and I packed up your stuff, bus is leaving first thing tomorrow** 9:18 PM

**And I just want you to know** 9:20 PM

**No matter what happens** 9:20 PM

**We're here for you** 9:20 PM

**Get some good sleep, Anisa.** 9:22 PM

## TEXTS FROM ELLIE

Hi 11:08 PM

I'm probably the last person you want to hear from right now but I just wanted to let you know Isaac and I talked 11:08 PM

I'm so sorry 11:09 PM

He mentioned he had someone in his life 11:09 PM

Someone his parents were setting him up with 11:09 PM

But I couldn't help it 11:09 PM

Before I knew what was happening, I had fallen for him 11:09 PM

I know it's no excuse. 11:10 PM

But for what it's worth, I'm just really, really sorry we hurt you 11:10 PM

# Chapter 24

## MARCH 15

About two weeks after my talk with Isaac—and once the doctors are certain Dad's bilirubin levels are relatively stable—Dad's discharged from the hospital. Now we're back at home, and on Dad's insistence, we're acting as if nothing happened.

Except for the fact that Nani's here, too, eyes watching Dad like a hawk, waiting for any sign of him in pain. If he even groans a little, she's ready with pain meds and a cup of lemon and ginger tea.[156] I think it's lessened some of the pressure off Mom, who still seems unsure how to take care of him. Maybe she's still wrapping her head around the situation. To be honest, we all are, which is why I decided against taking a leave of absence from school. With everything that's been happening, I need a sense of normalcy, something that hasn't changed. Even with Dad sick, I still have to keep up my grades, after all—no, especially because Dad is sick. And I know if I stay home, I won't be able to focus.

Even Nani's surprised by my decision.[157]

"Are you sure, beti?" she'd asked earlier today, vigorously scrubbing the bottom of our giant pressure cooker. "When does your semester end?"

---

156    Apparently she drove the nurses nuts at the hospital. I'm not surprised.

157    And Nani's not surprised by anything.

I look up from the dining table, where I'm catching up on some reading for my Chaucer class. We're solidly into the month of March; today marks the start of spring break, which means I'll at least have the next week to spend time with family and discuss Dad's future treatment plans. But this isn't exactly how I'd envisioned my first spring break.[158]

"I still have a little less than two months to go before school's over."

"Mm." She sets down the pressure cooker. "So there's still a lot of time left."

Mom steps into the kitchen from downstairs. "At least you'll see Isaac around on campus. It's good that you'll have him for support."

She's carrying a load of laundry; I recognize some of Dad's comfy sweaters on top of the pile.

Thankfully, she was too distracted to notice that I dropped my notebook, the one Marlow gave me, at the sound of Isaac's name.

"Y-yeah . . ." I say softly.

If you're wondering whether I've told her about Isaac, the answer is no. But how am I supposed to tell her that Isaac and I have broken things off? Just a few days ago, I heard her on the phone with her cousins in Pakistan, talking about what my wedding dress color should be. The answer they settled on was maroon, by the way, because it would look good with Isaac's complexion. Not even *my* complexion!

I do feel guilty for not telling Mom. But I *can't*. Especially now, when my future wedding with Isaac seems to be one of the only things that makes her happy. It'd be the first time in years she'd get to see some of her cousins. And with Dad's diagnosis . . .

My only hope now is that she can be reasonable.[159]

---

158    But we'll take little blessings where we can get them, right? Haha . . . ha . . .

159    Pray for me. Send me good luck vibes. Anything, please.

Mom disappears into the laundry room, and I try to focus on some work I have to do for class, but not even ten minutes go by when my phone vibrates, distracting me once again. I almost ignore it, thinking it's another notification from Instagram—I haven't posted all week, and my DMs are getting full from people wondering where I've been—but then I see Marlow's name flashing across my screen. A new text.

**How's everything at home?**

**If you're bored, I'll gift you a new otome**

I crack a smile. After I told him about Dad's diagnosis, Marlow's been texting a lot—mostly just checking in to see how I'm doing. If I don't respond right away, he sends another, simply telling me about his day. It's nice, actually. Getting messages about the mundane helps me not want to scream.

He hasn't even asked me what happened with Isaac. It's like he knows talking about him isn't what I need right now.

Speaking of which, I haven't been able to stop thinking about what Isaac said, either—about Marlow and finding my own path.

Now I wish I'd asked what he meant.

In comes another text from Marlow:

**btw I started playing Rose in the Embers**

**Criminal that there's not an option to slap some of these men because some of them are toxic af**

I laugh softly.

**Play Victor's route. His is actually good**

**Wait no WHY are YOU playing an otome???**

Three dots appear on the screen, then:

**Research.**

**And I'm bored without you here.**

My heart does a funny little flutter, and I set down my phone.

I think . . . I think I miss Marlow. And I still haven't thanked him for sticking up for me against Isaac.

Except I'm also worried about what will happen if I do talk to him. What will he do now that Isaac and I are over? He's texting normally now, but things have felt a little weird between us. Different. Not to mention there was that whole thing with Marlow saying he doesn't have a crush on me anymore. I can't help but wonder what changed.

Not that it really matters, obviously. I'm just, you know, *curious.*

I sigh and slump in my chair. I can't even be certain of my own thoughts anymore.[160]

So instead, I focus on homework, the only thing that makes sense in my life right now.

A while later, Mom has left the house to run some errands, and Nani's gone upstairs for her afternoon nap, leaving me to finally focus on work. Meanwhile, Zaina disappeared into the basement to play some online game called *Cambria* with her friends, which means the house is quiet for once.

---

160     And apparently, it's showing. Nani even informed me that I "really should get dressed" instead of wearing my pajamas all day because it made me look "like a sad person."

282

I've actually finished a solid amount of work when the doorbell rings.

"Zaina, can you get it?" I shout. There's no answer. I take a deep breath, preparing to shout again when I remember Dad's sleeping, so I pry myself out of my chair and trudge to the front door.

A familiar head of curly black hair bops from the other side of the window, and my eyes go wide.

I can't believe what I'm seeing. No, there's *no way.*

Panicking, I quickly pat down my hair, check my face in a nearby mirror, and resign myself to my fate before prying the door a few inches.

Marlow beams the moment his eyes meet mine.

*"How the hell are you here right now?"* I squeak.

Oh God, help me! If Mom finds out he's here, she'll fillet us both. I've never had a friend just drop in on me like this—in a way, I'm kind of touched right now—but having a guy friend randomly show up at my house, *especially* Marlow, will definitely make her think the worst.

Marlow frowns. "Nice to see you, too. I got a ride from my old roommate Charlie who happens to live in this area. Super easy."

That's still a forty-five-minute drive from campus. Would an old roommate really agree to drive him all the way out here?

For a moment, I take Marlow in: his too-light-for-this-weather jacket, his messy curls, the familiar, mischievous twinkle in his eye. I'm sure his shirt says something stupid, but for some reason he's holding a shoebox, blocking my view. It's been thirteen days since I last saw him, but with everything that's happened, it feels like forever.

"No, I mean—I was just thinking about you, and now you're—" *Here.* He's really here, at my house.

He grins. "So you were thinking about me."

"No," I reply quickly. "How do you even know where I live?"

"Zaina told me. Hope that's all right. I probably should have asked you first, but—"

"Since when do you and Zaina *talk*?!"

"Oh yeah, we swapped friend codes and we played games together once or twice. It's fun. She kicked my ass in *Fortnite*, though."

*I'm going to kill Zaina.*

I step outside and close the door behind me. "Look, I'd let you in, but if my mom comes back and sees you here . . ."

"Ah, that's okay. I figured as much." He shrugs. "I don't want to intrude without your parents' permission anyway. I'm like a vampire. They gotta invite me in. It's good to see you, though," he adds.

I bite back a smile. "*That* bored, huh?"

"I meant what I said." He shoves the shoebox in my direction. "Speaking of which—this is for you."

"What's this?" I take it, hesitating.

"A care package. I thought by now you'd know a care package when you see it." Marlow's face breaks into a proud grin. "This one's got thick socks for your dad—I have no idea what kind he likes, but I got one that I think is good for chemo patients—and a knitted hat. There are a couple muffins in there from the Main Line Bakery, too . . . oh, and a heating pad for pain. Thanks for the inspiration, by the way."

I told both Marlow and Kira about Dad, but they have yet to push for details. Kira simply asked if there was anything I needed, and Marlow told me if I wouldn't be able to come back to school, to not worry about our paper and that he'd tell Professor Friedman the situation.

But I can't believe he made a care package for my *dad*.

"Thank you, Marlow," I say, my voice shaking. "This is . . . really sweet."

"It's mostly selfish on my part. I wanted an excuse to check on you."
His eyes bore into mine. I know what he's really asking.

My grip tightens on the box.

"Be honest with me, Anisa. How are you, really?"

I avoid his gaze.[161]

We'll do a quick emotional check-in right now. How do I really feel?
I feel played, for one thing; I feel like I've wasted so much time on
someone who didn't even like me back. Worst of all, I feel abandoned.
I've been following this happy little path to a future with Isaac, only to
turn around and realize Isaac was never with me.

So yeah, everything's wrong now. Somewhere along the way, I must
have messed up and now I'm adrift without an anchor.

"I'm okay," I reply.

"Don't give me that." His voice softens. "Can we talk about what
happened with Isaac?"

"It's over. Simple as that."

"What do you mean, it's—"

"Isaac doesn't want to be with me. Game over. I got a Bad Ending in
my own romance." But no, that isn't right; life isn't an otome game. It is
real and complex and painful beyond imagination.

"Thank you for all your help," I continue, letting out a shaky exhale.
"You know, earlier. But it's officially over, so . . . now I have to face the
fact that it's real: that I committed myself to someone who had one foot
out the door the entire time."

Marlow takes a step forward. "Anisa," he says softly. His eyebrows
draw together, and his usually sunny demeanor crumples, giving way

---

161     It's like he's mastered the art of puppy-dog eyes.

to what I can only call . . .

Anguish. Anguish, for *me*.

Behind my glasses, my eyes start to burn as tears start to well up, threatening to spill.

"Stop thinking that you didn't do enough. *He's* the one who fucked up, not you. Someone not loving you is not your failure; it's theirs." Marlow puts a soothing hand on my shoulder. "And if Isaac didn't see how hard you tried, how simply amazing you are, well—it's his loss."

I huff darkly. "Wish I could believe that. But I couldn't even be myself around him. Why would anyone want to be with someone who doesn't know the first thing about being in a real relationship?"

"No. No, no, no, we're not having that. None of that self-deprecating bullshit. Especially not because of Isaac."

"Is it self-deprecating, though? Or am I just stating facts?" I sniff loudly. Damn it, it feels like no matter how much I wipe, my nose insists on spewing more snot. "How did I not see any of this coming? How am I supposed to trust myself anymore? It's pathetic. Hell, I still don't understand why *you* put up with me. Why you agreed to be my love coach. I mean, look at me, I'm a mess in every sense of the word. I'm—"

Marlow interrupts me by pressing a finger over my mouth, and I feel myself flush.

"I don't think you understand," he says in a low, coarse whisper. "I do not 'put up' with you." His eyes are deep pools of ink, pulling me in, and for a moment, I catch my own wide-eyed reflection in them. "I am here, Anisa, because I *want* to be."

With that, my breath catches in my throat. As I settle into this wordless, warm haze between us, something stirs in my chest.

And then it finally, finally clicks.

I suddenly remember Victor's Happy Ending in *Rose in the Embers*: the final CG where Victor holds the main character's hand while they watch the sun rise, just before kissing her.

Only now, it's Marlow's face, superimposed over Victor.

Oh no.

*No.*

It's not possible. I hate it. Why *now*? God is *mocking* me.

I should have known the moment he walked into my life with those stupid Crocs that he would ruin my life.

*How long? How long have I been in love with Marlow?!* I demand the universe.

I rack my head, trying to remember where it all went wrong. Was it the moment I saw him? Was it when he comforted me after the dance? Was it when he carried me to the nurse's office? Was it all the times I found my eyes, my thoughts, drifting back to him? Or—

The *plan*. Thinking about it now, it makes sense: the plan to win Isaac—Marlow was with me every step of the way. Which means the plan worked but—

For the wrong person.

No. Way. It's unacceptable. And yet, it feels so undeniable, so obvious. But what am I even supposed to do with this information? Isaac and I calling things off is one thing, but being in love with *Marlow*? Yeah, that's exactly what my parents need right now. I can hear Mom's hundreds of objections already. Marlow isn't Muslim, for one thing. It's not like dating's an option, either; in our household, if you're dating, it means you're seriously considering someone for marriage. It's a one-way ticket. This can't happen. Not now. Maybe not ever.

*But I want—*

I want to *scream*. And why does my chest hurt—is love supposed to make your chest *hurt*? I shouldn't have let him get so damn close.

Except . . . I *did*. Of course I did. Because I *wanted* him to be. And maybe Isaac knew all along. In fact, he probably saw in me a reflection of himself. I just didn't know it yet.

The jingle of keys suddenly shakes me from my spiral.

Standing a few feet away from us on the little stone walkway to the house is none other than my mother, her long wool coat billowing gently in the wind, her knuckles white as she clenches the bag of groceries in her hand.

*"What is this?"* Her sharp voice strikes like a whip cutting between us. Her eyes are wide, and she's shaking with fury.

"Mom!" I create some distance between me and Marlow. My head spins so fast, I nearly drop the shoebox. She came back faster than I thought. God, why *now*?

"What is this about Isaac?" she demands. "What do you mean Isaac doesn't want you?"

My face is ablaze. How much did Mom hear?

Marlow jumps into action. "Asalaamu alaikum,[162] Mrs. Shirani." He gives her a placating smile. "I'm Marlow. We met briefly, at the cafeteria? I'm sorry to drop by like this so suddenly."

And just like at the cafeteria, she completely ignores him.

"Anisa, what is going on?" she asks again. *"What did you do?"*

It's too late, and I'm tired of biting back my feelings. So I decide to come clean.

---

162    I'm startled and impressed by his pretty decent pronunciation—clearly, he wasn't lying about enjoying learning about other religions—which I would have commented on if I wasn't wishing I could disappear off the face of the planet right about now.

"Isaac and I had a fight, and we decided . . ." My throat tightens painfully. "We decided it would be better if we didn't get married to each other."

Mom stares back, her shoulders heaving under her coat.

"No," she says after a beat, "*absolutely* not. I don't care *what* happened between you two; you can't throw away everything we have worked for. Everything is in line for you to have the perfect life. Everyone in our community thinks you and Isaac are getting married. You are supposed to be together." Her words come fast and shrill. "And Isaac's family has *status*. If you break things off, what then? You think you can humiliate them like this? How will you get married to any respectable boy after this?"

I shrink back at the sheer blaze of her fury. I fully expected her to be disappointed, even mad, but I didn't expect her to act like *this*. So downright cruel. Does she have to rub it in my face?

I already know.

"Do you have to act like it's the end of the world?" I fire back. "I'm still young. Marriage isn't even important right—"

"If you don't get married, I can't support you for the rest of my life. What happens when I die, too?"

"I'll have a job after I graduate," I say, indignant. "And then grad school like I always planned. I can always live alone and support myself. It's not the *fifties*." I don't know how my mom always expects me to get into the best schools but still somehow doesn't understand that I can make my own income. As much as I want a happily-ever-after—and God, I do—I shouldn't *need* a man.[163]

---

163     Sometimes, I'm certain my mom has made such good progress—and she has. But I guess old habits die hard.

"No," she says, shaking her head, "That isn't enough. I need you to get *married*. And you won't find better than Isaac."

I inhale sharply. Why does she have to say it like that . . . ?

"With all due respect, Mrs. Shirani," comes Marlow's gentle tone, "I don't think it's fair to put that kind of pressure on Anisa. And it was a decision made by both her and Isaac. What about what they want?"

Mom's head swivels, her attention now on Marlow. "You. Stay out of this," she says sharply, then glares at me. "Did you not tell him you were engaged to Isaac?"

"We were never formally *engaged*, why do you keep—" I clench my fists at my side. "Isaac and I aren't happening. Please accept that."

Mom stares back in disbelief, her nostrils flaring. "I knew this would happen. I *knew*. It's your fault for spending so much time with this boy." She gestures at Marlow like he's nothing more than a nuisance. A fly to be slapped away.

Marlow steps toward her. "Mrs. Shirani, please, that's not true—"

"Leave! You've done enough damage!"

"Ammi, please!" I finally scream. I haven't called her that since I was little.

There's tense silence. Mom says nothing; just breathes, her air coming in rapid clouds.

"We're going inside," she says finally, gesturing to the door. "Now."

Without waiting for my response, she strides past me with all the force of a storm and stands sentry by the doorway, waiting.

Marlow and I exchange furtive looks.

"Say the word and I'll be here. Anytime," he says comfortingly. A promise. A vow.

I nod. I don't want him to go, but this is my fight.

I take a deep, consolidating breath and follow Mom inside the house. She slams the door behind me, before leading me to the living room. I'm not even sure I can feel my legs. I've never been more terrified in my life.

I sit on a plush green armchair while Mom remains standing, and as I lean forward, my long hair is like a protective curtain around my face. From downstairs, I can hear the faint sound of Zaina playing her video game, and from the family room, the loud ticking of the clock hanging over the wall where we've hung my parents' favorite family photos.

I have a death grip on the shoebox in my lap as I wait.

"What is that?" Mom asks. "Did he give that to you?" She takes a step toward me, but I move the box behind me.

"It's *mine*!" I snap. I'm surprised by the anger, the protectiveness in my voice.

"It's—it's mine. Please."

Mom clicks her tongue.

"I need you to go apologize to Isaac," she says quietly, though somehow, it feels like she's still yelling. "You need to *fix* this."

Funny. I'd said the same thing to my parents only a couple months ago. Except here, there's nothing to fix. Isaac cheated on *me*. And now my mom is acting like *I'm* the one who's ruined everything. I'm tempted to tell her, but then the question of who he cheated on me with will come up, a question that could reach Aunty Lubna. And maybe Isaac deserves it, in a way, but I can't do him dirty like that. I won't tell on him and Ellie.

So instead, I say: "Isaac and I realized we want very different things. It's that simple."

"I don't understand." Mom starts pacing. "Why *now*, Ani? Why did you have to drop this on us now? Your dad and I have enough to worry about. Do you really need to stress your dad out more?"

Something in me breaks. Bringing up Dad now—it's a low blow, and I have had enough.

"Why? Why are you acting like this?" My shoulders tremble as I stare down Mom. "Just tell me. It's not like I had control over this. Why is it so important to you that I marry Isaac?"

Mom stops pacing. Looks at me with red-rimmed eyes.

And I realize she's crying.

"Because," she says brokenly, "I want to give you what I didn't have. A happy, stable marriage. I love your dad, but it's been hard. For both of us. And now . . ." She closes her eyes tight. "I just want you to have a good partner. To have a life where you are pushed to be greater than yourself. To always have opportunities. And I want to make sure you always have people to care for you, because I—I don't know what's going to *happen to us.*"

My head goes blank. This was not the answer I expected.

She sinks into the couch across from me, her shoulders quaking. "Your dad and I need to see you married, to get that peace of mind. I can't—" Her voice cracks. "It wasn't supposed to happen like this. Not like *this.*"

I sit down beside her. "Mom . . . ?"

"I'm not even sure he'll make it to five years." She holds her head in her hands. I don't think I've ever seen her cry, but she cries hard now, rattling sobs that undulate through her body like waves.

"What are we going to *do,* Anisa?"

Oh.

Understanding hits me so suddenly, I swear I physically recoil. Because I get it now. I get it all now.

Mom is just . . . a person. A very scared person, flawed sometimes, and capable of mistakes like anyone else—even when she means to do what's right. And the reason she's acting like this? I don't even think it has anything to do with Isaac, not really.

In a way, she's like me. Trying to process a horrible piece of news and trying, *trying* to help stop her world from falling apart, and she's *terrified*. Because even though Mom and Dad disagree on so many things, they've been together for so long. Years of deciding whether to stay married no longer matters because now, a decision has been forced upon them. Now she'd have to continue repairing a relationship with a dying spouse until one day, she'd be alone: alone and guilty. Alone and with an avalanche of different emotions.

So of course she wants me to get married as soon as I graduate. We've never been close, and with Dad gone, our whole family dynamic could change. She just wants some peace of mind. Even if she is going about it all wrong.

Emotion bubbles up my throat, burning my eyes as I rub her back.

And I shove my feelings about Marlow deep down in my chest, where my brain can't find them. Some things are just more important.

"We're going to be okay," I tell her. "You don't have to worry, not on your own. I'm going to be here for you and Dad, until the end, inshallah. Whatever happens, we'll get through it. Together."

Mom's mouth parts in surprise before she takes my hand and squeezes it. For a moment, I marvel at how hers looks so like mine.

But from the corner of my eye, I catch Zaina, peeking over a nearby wall, a somber expression on her face.

SUMRA

**ANI** 12:23 PM

**What is this we're hearing about you and Isaac???** 12:23 PM

**Everyone's talking about ittt** 12:23 PM

**Are you okay?** 12:23 PM

NADIA

**ALSO if it doesn't work for you two, what hope is there for the rest of us?!?!?** 12:24 PM

**(But we are very worried about you so please respond)** 12:24 PM

SUMRA

**Obviously we don't know the situation but just a heads-up that Aunty Lubna apparently knows** 12:25 PM

NADIA

**We love you!!** 12:25 PM

# Chapter 25

## MARCH 25

Spring break's over, which means I'm back on campus.

And when Tuesday comes around, I stride into my Race & Ethnicity classroom, head held high. Today, I've opted for black ankle boots, a long mulberry skirt paired with a ribbed button-up blouse, and finally, a faux sheepskin bomber jacket (given to me for free from an upcycle clothing company) to top it all off. The moment I posted a selfie this morning, I was flooded by comments on my Instagram. *You're back! Where have you been? Looking fab as always. We would like to hire you as our new brand ambassador. . . .*

Unfortunately for me, as soon as I spot Marlow, all my earlier confidence deflates. He's busy talking to a Halcyon student sitting beside him—the one who always wore a red hoodie and glared at him whenever he walked in. But they both seem more relaxed, and Marlow's smile is . . . even more disarming than usual.

My stomach lurches when I replay what happened the last time I saw him, but I quickly regain my nerve. In any case, I'm glad he's starting to feel more comfortable talking to the people he'd usually ignore, like the stuff with Rosie isn't holding him back the way it used to.

Things really are changing.

Marlow's jaw falls open as he notices me taking a seat behind him.

"You're *here*." He looks me up and down as if he's checking to see I'm real.

"Why wouldn't I be?" I ask, smiling. "Our paper's due today, after all." I know everyone's expecting me to take the rest of the semester off, but I don't like leaving things half done.

Marlow's eyebrows furrow, but before he can respond, Professor Friedman walks in and immediately calls everyone up to turn in their papers. Marlow and I stand together.

"Turn it in together?" he asks, waving his printed copy.

I nod.

We walk side my side, my hand on one side of the paper, and his on the other—and we both hand it in to Professor Friedman.

I walk back to my desk, only now realizing the bittersweet enormity of this moment. The paper is over. The paper we've been working on together for the past two months is done. And so is my relationship with Isaac.

The bonds that connect Marlow and I—they're all fraying.

I can feel Marlow glancing my way, like he wants to say something. But I look straight ahead.

When class ends, I grab my bag and flee the humanities building, surprised when I'm hit by beams of gentle sunlight. It's getting warmer, which means spring's just about here. I just have to get through the rest of the semester, and—

Marlow calls out to me, jogging to catch up.

I stop. Debate running away.[164]

*Anisa!* you must be thinking. *Don't be dramatic! Just talk to the poor kid!*

---

164     But Marlow has far longer legs than I, and I don't like to lose.

To which I say, *I don't want to! I'm embarrassed!* Look, I know I should be used to Marlow catching me in all my worst moments by now, but him seeing me get torn down by my mom feels far more personal than anything else. It makes me feel vulnerable, *naked*—to which, if I admitted it out loud, Marlow would quip with some stupid joke.

But I also don't want him near me. Because if he's nearby, I get these weird thoughts in my head, thoughts I should not be having when my dad is sick and my mom is barely holding on. It's hard enough not to think about him when he's *not* close by. Silly things, too, like: How would Marlow and my dad get along? What do Zaina and Marlow talk about? Would Mom make Marlow some chicken karahi of his own?

Clearly my head isn't on straight. I need to get these fantasies out of my head. I need to focus on what's important.

"I was almost expecting you not to show up," Marlow says, half smiling.

I fold my arms across my chest. "Why? Now, more than ever, I should be going to school."

His smile wanes. "Yeah, of course, but—"

"You trying to get rid of me? Don't worry, the semester will be over before you know it." And then it'll be easier to avoid Marlow for good and these ridiculous feelings will fade away.

"No, that's not . . ." He sighs. "I'm sorry. I don't know. It's just—"

Marlow's interrupted with shouts and laughter coming from the quad.

I freeze at the sight.

It's the Holi festival, and the quad has erupted in a symphony of vivid color. There's a DJ beneath a tree, blasting a familiar dancey Bollywood song, and seemingly a hundred students, dancing and squealing as colorful powder explodes around them in clouds of orange and blue and red and yellow. Other students on the fringes—some I recognize from the

SASA—offer bowls of powder for passersby to take from, luring them into the celebration.

My heart swells at the sight. It's beautiful. It looks so *fun*.

I catch a familiar face in the crowd: Isaac, his body already covered in colorful powder, with no sign of the original color of his clothes. I can see a flash of white teeth. He's smiling. Laughing.

He looks so happy.

Ellie is nearby, aiming another shot of powder his way. She manages to get a shot in from behind, a cloud of green bursting off his back.

So many conflicting emotions roil in my gut. But I'm surprised by the one that's loudest of all:

I'm almost kind of happy for him. Almost. Of course, I'd be lying if I said I wasn't still disappointed by him, or I didn't also resent him a little. He hurt me, badly. But maybe it's because I've grown up with him—because maybe, in a way, I'm finally starting to understand him: Isaac, the *person*, flawed and foolish and trying to find his own happiness. I can't fully hate him. Hate is exhausting, after all, and I've got better things to do.

But that's weird, isn't it? Seeing Isaac happy with someone else should still hurt. It hasn't even been a month since we broke things off.

Why doesn't it hurt?

"You okay?" Marlow looks at me, worried.

I bite back a smile. There's another burst of color nearby, this time a cheerful pink, so close I can feel it on my skin.

I don't know what comes over me, but I feel this itch in my hands, this urge I can't ignore. Before I can even understand what's happening, I stride across the quad, heading straight for the Holi festival, boots digging into the soft ground beneath me.

For Isaac.

"Whoa." Marlow follows me close behind. "Wait, wait, wait. Hey. Let's think this through. I know you're mad at Isaac, understandably, but maybe let's not act on our emotions in front of a crowd—"

I'm like a woman possessed. I don't listen. Instead, I grab a handful of red powder from an open container splayed on one of the tables.

"Anisa, wait."

I stop in front of Isaac. His laughter dies as he notices me, and his whole body stiffens.

"Ani . . . ?"

I smile. "Close your eyes."

"What?"

One thing you should know about me is that I have *very* good aim. Perhaps it was those weekends spent in high school, putting in the extra time to get better at various sports. Or maybe it's simply sheer determination.

But as soon as Isaac's eyes close, I throw a ball of powder that lands perfectly in the center of Isaac's face, exploding upon impact.

As the literal dust settles, Isaac blinks his eyes open again in a state of complete shock.

I'm completely undone. I double over, laughing. It's a completely unfiltered laugh, loud and ugly. "Oh my God. You should see your *face*."

"How *could*—*why*—why would you—?" he sputters, clearly at a loss for words in a way so delightfully unlike him.

He coughs, spitting out some excess red powder. Then his eyes meet mine and for a moment, there's this moment of unspoken understanding. He lets out the quietest huff of a laugh. At least, I think he does. I can't tell with all the powder on his face.

I've never seen him look more ridiculous, more imperfect.

He looks like a normal kid.

Close by, I hear the familiar sound of bright, cheerful laughter joining in. It's Ellie.

"Incredible. That was *incredible*." She can barely choke out the words. I think she's *crying*. She tries to high-five me but half misses.

"*Et tu*, Ellie?" Isaac whines uncharacteristically, wiping beneath his eyes with his index fingers. "This is a charity event, you monsters."

I laugh even harder. Harder than I should. It's fun seeing Isaac like this. But it feels like something inside me has suddenly been unchained for the first time and I feel good. Relieved.

"My turn!" says Ellie, throwing a ball of yellow powder. She hits him square in the neck with a splat.

Isaac wails a pitiful, "*Why?!*"

"I'll throw in an extra hit for you," Ellie tells me with a wink before running off to chase him. The two disappear back into the crowd.

Satisfied, I wipe my hands off. A bit of red powder has gotten on my new jacket, but I don't even care.

I take a deep breath and bounce back, light as a feather, to Marlow, who apparently opted to stay back and watch.

I beam at him, strangely proud. "I needed that."

Marlow stares at me, bewildered.

But then the biggest, most tender smile I've ever seen breaks across his face; he drapes an arm around my shoulders and rubs at my head, messing up my hair.

"You did good," he says against the top of my head. "You did good."

I go completely still in his grasp. His body is warm against mine, and I never really noticed it before, but he smells kind of nice: the faint smell of salt mixed with something lemony, almost sweet. Oh hell, it almost smells like *Irish Spring*. Since when does Irish Spring smell good?[165]

I feel the rush of heat rising up my neck to my cheeks.

I tear myself away. "Um."

"What is it?"

"Nothing." I smile stiffly. I just want to suddenly get away. Far away from here.

"Did you want me to take a picture of you for your Instagram?" He gestures behind us. "I bet it'd look really good with Holi in the backgr—"

"No! No. It's fine. Anyway, I should, uh. I should go."

"Wait." Marlow grabs me by the wrist, his touch featherlight. He gives me pained look, like he's battling a hundred different thoughts at once and trying to settle on the right words.

Then he sighs.

"You never told me. How—how did everything turn out with your mom?"

The way he looks at me so earnestly, his big, dark eyes like warm pools—it makes me not self-conscious, the way Isaac's stare once did. But I feel embarrassed. It makes my chest ache.

I yank my wrist back easily. "We talked. Things are fine. She's letting me off the hook with Isaac, for now."

Albeit reluctantly, but still: I think Mom's reflecting on things, too. In her own way. At least, I hope.

"Is she forcing you to finish the semester?" he asks. "Because I really don't think it'd be a bad idea to slow down, spend time with your family, especially now."

*"No."* I'm starting to get annoyed by his questioning. "Anyway, can

---

165    No wonder he and Kira got along.

301

you just stop? I've already made my decision to finish the semester. You don't need to be nosy."

"I'm not being nosy. I'm trying to make sure you're actually taking care of yourself. For once."

"That's none of your business." I start walking back to the bus stop. "Our paper is over, anyway. Isaac and I are over. So why are you still hovering over me?"

Marlow follows. "Do you not want me around?"

I spin to face him. "I didn't say that, I just . . ." Of *course* I want him around. That's the terrifying thing. In fact, I can't imagine not having him around anymore. I've grown to rely on him; if I'm drowning, I know he'd be the first to swim out to help me. But that's the *problem*. The more I rely on him, the more I find myself wondering what will happen when he inevitably leaves. And after everything that's happened, after the pure chaos that's been my life, it only makes sense he would.

"I still don't *get it*," I mutter. "Why do you even care so much? Have you not gotten enough sordid details of my personal life?"

His face falls a little, hurt. "I didn't realize there was a limit."

"Well, maybe there is. Especially since now, more than ever, I need to be focusing on school and making sure I don't do anything to stress out my parents anymore. But if you keep asking me these questions and—and hovering around . . ."

It *confuses* me.

"I don't even know what we are," I continue. "We're not partners for the paper anymore, obviously. You're not my love coach anymore because, I don't know if you noticed, but *that* ship has sailed. So what are we to each other? Why are you still here? Are we friends? But that doesn't feel right, either. So what am I supposed to think, especially when you're always so nice to me in a time when my mind's a mess about everything as it is? You said you don't even have a crush on me anymore, so what—"

"I love you," Marlow blurts, like it's all one word.

It's like my heart stops. No, *time* stops. And all I hear is his breathing.

"I love you," he repeats again. "I hoped my little crush would go away eventually, but instead it just evolved, and if I'm being completely honest, sometimes I wish it didn't. Because I know . . . I know you'll never feel the same way about me. And that's truly fine, it's—on one hand, yeah, it sucked, having to bury these growing feelings while being your love coach, but the reality is, not being your friend, not seeing you and talking to you, would have sucked so much more."

When I don't respond, he swallows and goes on. "This isn't meant to be some dramatic confession, but more to say I made a choice. That my head and my heart were in agreement to be your friend because it made *sense*. And I just want to make sure you're making the right choices for yourself, too. That whatever you choose to do going forward makes sense to you."

My cheeks are ablaze. He loves me. A crush is one thing, but Marlow *loves* me . . . ?

It takes a few breaths, but my mouth finally starts to work.

"You're lying. There's no way."

His gaze is hot against my face. "Why is it so hard to believe?"

"Because—" I bite my lip. "You just *can't*." I can't explain it. It's simply an irrefutable fact in my head. But more than that, I don't want to entertain the idea of him and I. I don't want to hope for more. Not now.

"No, the reason why you don't believe it," says Marlow, "is because you can't fathom the idea of ever being valued for you, *all* of you. You should be *cherished* and settle for no less. That guy"—he gestures back at the quad—"has made you feel not good enough for so long that you don't even see how fucking amazing you are. You're clueless. And yet you could probably do anything you wanted. If your parents asked you to bend the world to your will—God, you'd probably find a way to do it. And somehow, you still don't have a clue. But I see it. I wish you did, too."

I feel my stomach unwind. It feels like everything in my body has suddenly come undone and now I'm floating.

I don't even know what to say. What are you supposed to do when the person you love actually loves you back? When they see you in a way you could only wish to be seen?

Marlow's patient, heated stare meets mine, and for the first time in my life, I'm struck by want. Wanting this. Wanting us. Wanting to try. A plunge into the unknown that's frightening, yes, and exhilarating, too. With Marlow, I feel safe.

But . . .

The timing of it is all wrong. This isn't how it's supposed to go. Not now, not when Isaac and I have only recently broken things off, when things are still so uncertain. There's no way my mom could handle the news. I've already disappointed my parents enough.

No matter how I look at it, there's not a single good reason for this to happen. Even if I do want it.

"I can't—"

"Anisa," interrupts Marlow, putting a hand up. "You don't have to say anything. You can toss that confession right in the garbage if you want. I'll be—" He exhales. "Nothing will change between us, so please don't feel bad. My intention isn't to add more on your plate, I just . . ." He smiles. "I just wanted to tell you why. And now you know. I'm sorry."

My eyes start to burn. It'd almost be easier if he'd been mad at me. Rosie's an idiot for ever hurting him.

I'm an idiot, too.

"I gotta go," I breathe.

Something cracks behind his beautiful brown eyes. And just like that, the spell between us is broken.

"Okay," Marlow says gently, the smile never leaving his face. "But don't forget. I'll always be here. As your love coach, or anything else."

I look away.

This time, I flee and I don't look back.

# Chapter 26

I guess you could say I end up listening to Marlow, because the next day, I go to the academic adviser center to tell my dean about Dad's diagnosis.

It's a headache, but after an hour-long conversation, I decide to stay enrolled but not live on campus anymore. Luckily, my professors are all understanding about me not being able to attend class in person—mostly because it's late in the semester, anyway—and they all agree to send recordings of their lectures so I can follow along. There won't be any negative effect on my academic scholarship, either. I just have to make sure I do well on my finals.

Maybe it's a cowardly way to put distance between me and Marlow. I know I can't avoid him forever. But I don't think I have the strength to face him right now. In fact, I think it'll be refreshingly quiet not having to hear his incessant worrying or ridiculous jokes, or see his silly meme T-shirts.

The strangest part about me taking a leave, though, is Mom's silence. I was certain she'd try to talk me out of it, but ever since our little heart-to-heart the other day, she hasn't really said a word about anything. I've decided to take it as a good thing, mostly out of necessity; if I have to deal with another *bad* thing on top of everything else, it will become my villain origin story, and yes, that is a threat.

"Should I put this here?" Kira interrupts my thoughts.

She's holding my floor-length mirror, the one I used to take my selfies throughout the semester, over a cardboard box I've labeled FOR HOME—BEDROOM.

"You can keep it, if you want."

She shakes her head before setting it gently in the box. "No need."

I go back to packing my toiletries I've brought in from the bathroom—my various shampoos and body washes, my loofah, my shower tote. I'm hoping to finish moving out of the dorm by this evening so I can be back home for the weekend. Kira's been helping me.

"So. Prince Charming," she says as she starts clearing through my half of our shared bookshelf. "You guys broke up."

I shove my toothbrush in a little pink travel case.

"Yeah." I told her as soon as I'd gotten back to campus, but she never brought it up again. I think in her own way, she's trying to give me time to wrap my head around everything.

"I'm sorry. That's a lot, on top of everything else," Kira comments, forehead rumpled.

"Yep."

"Can I just say something?"

I look at her.

"Good riddance."

I blink. "What?"

Kira sits at the windowsill. "Listen, I'm just saying he had as much personality as the color gray. So he's smart, has a bright future. Whatever. He's boring as *hell*. You can do better."

I'm floored. I had no idea she felt that way. I mean, I knew she always got a little . . . stiff whenever Isaac was around, but I figured that was just Kira and strangers. "Why didn't you tell me that *sooner*?"

"Because you adored the guy. Would you have listened?"

I pout. "Probably not."

"Glad you see it now, though."

I sigh.

Geez. Isaac was my dream guy for so long and Kira didn't even like him. Who else was holding out on me?

"Anyway, I—" she hesitates. "I know shit sucks, and it certainly doesn't help that you're also dealing with a breakup. But one day, you're going to look back and Isaac will just be a tiny blip on the timeline of life. And you'll be too busy doing your own thing."

I smile faintly. "Yeah. That's the hope."

"How are you feeling otherwise?"

"I'm all ri—" I start, but then I bite my lip. "Could be better. But I'll get there."

"You're thinking of taking summer classes, too, right?"

I nod. "Trying to graduate a semester early, if I can swing it." It'll hopefully give me more time to spend with Dad.

"You going to miss me for the rest of the semester?" I ask, knowing full well Kira's answer.

"Definitely not. Now I'll have the room to myself. I can't get you out of here fast enough."

"Ha *ha*." I violently begin folding my face towels.

"But hopefully next year you'll get your own room, too." The corners of Kira's mouth curl ever so slightly. "Then maybe you won't have to worry about waking up early to tweeze your chin hair and do your makeup."

I drop the towel in my hand and spin to face her, horrified. *"You knew about that?"*

I feel *humiliated. How?* How long has she known? I could have sworn she was fast asleep every time. I even used a silent alarm to make sure I didn't wake her. The dorm is old—like 1890s old—and the floors creak a little, but I'm *very* quiet, damn it.

Oh God. Was it not enough that she knew about my love of romance novels?

First Marlow, now Kira. You might as well alert the press at this point.

"Sorry, Ani, you're not that slick," says Kira. "And since we're being honest here, for what it's worth, I like both looks. With and without the makeup. There's something charming about the glasses." She pauses. "By the way, if you ever want to borrow my epilator for your upper lip hair—"

"Shut up, shut up, shut *up.*"

Kira's smirk deepens. But her voice lowers as she says, "But whoever made you feel, you know, gross in the past should *pay.* Even if that means you."

I'm startled by the sudden kindness, the protectiveness in her tone.

As usual, Kira makes me feel like I'm the only one making a big deal out of it. It's reassuring, in a way that is so typically her.

I smile and return to my towel folding. I'm already almost done packing.

I try not to think about the lonely days to come.

"Oh, right," I remember, "you should check your email."

"Huh?" Kira tilts her head in question before crossing the room to sit at her laptop.

She opens her school email, and from the corner of my eye, I can see her clicking on different emails until:

"No. Fucking. Way."

"I thought you might like it. It's just a screenshot for now, but yes, I won the LØVE LIFE EP. You should be getting it in the mail in a couple days."

Her mouth falls open. *"You beat XOLOVE47823?"*

I smile and shrug. Finally, my Instagram came in handy. There is, I have learned, a lot of overlap between the fashion industry and K-Pop enthusiasts. I just sent out a couple DMs to people I knew who could find other channels to grab the EP, and boom, the rest is history.

Kira's hand is shaking over her touchpad. "I didn't ask you to—"

"Yeah, well. I did. Think of it as a goodbye present."

Her ears go pink. My heart swells, strangely satisfied.

"I'll miss you," I tell her. It just pops out of my mouth before I give myself the time to chicken out. Kira's never been one for open affection, and hell, I'm not either, so I feel shy admitting it aloud.

But I feel compelled to say it.

I've never really had a best friend before. I'm not even sure what it means. But Kira—I think she's it.

Kira stares back, then looks away, deep in thought.

Carefully, I place the towels in my suitcase. The sound of me zipping it closed feels louder than usual.

"If you don't keep in touch," Kira says finally, softly, "I'll kill you. My parents' house is only an hour away, so it'd be easy."

My gaze lifts. "To keep in touch or to kill me?"

"Both."

I laugh.


The next two months go by like flecks of sand in an hourglass, and before I know it, finals are upon me.

My Chaucer final essay was more draining than I expected, especially since I had to pop allergy medication like candy as part of my longstanding battle with spring, so when Dad finds me hanging half off the couch in the living room, staring into space, it's no wonder he looks worried.

"Why does my beautiful daughter look so sad today?"

He's wearing a cute, oversized knit sweater and baggy sweatpants, and there are some new gray flecks of hair by his ears that weren't there before.

He's also wearing the socks that Marlow got for him. I didn't tell him it was Marlow, of course—though I know I should, eventually. But it's strange. When I handed over the care package, Dad asked if it was from Isaac. When I answered it was "from a new friend," he didn't press.

*I hope to meet them*, he said.

"Beautiful?" I sit up. "Even when I do this?" I stick out my tongue and pull at my eyelids so my irises disappear. I'm wearing my ancient pink Adidas track jacket and my broken Coke-bottle glasses, so it probably looks especially absurd. I think finals have broken me.

Dad smiles warmly. "Yes. Some might say startlingly beautiful. But beautiful nonetheless."

"Startlingly, huh."

He helps himself to some daal and rice in the fridge that Nani made specifically for him and sets himself down on the table. He had chemo yesterday, so it's encouraging to see him keep up his appetite. Most chemo patients have a hard time, I've learned.

Dad getting chemo. What a surreal thought. But I guess . . . this is our life now.

The reality of it chafes at my already-weakened heart.

"And finals are going well, even though you haven't been able to attend class in person?" Dad asks, taking a spoonful of daal.

"Oh, definitely." I smile reassuringly. "I miss being in a classroom, but finals have been all right. I'm lucky."

"Good." He puts the spoon to his mouth, chews thoughtfully. "I know your mom will appreciate you being here. Not that she'd say it out loud."

"Yeah?" I pull my knees to my chest. I find it hard to believe, but I hope so. Even if Dad will live for another few years, God willing, I want to believe staying at home now is the right answer, at least until Mom starts settling into this new normal. I don't know what else to do.

Slowly, Dad sets down his spoon.

"We've put a lot of pressure on you, haven't we." He stares into his bowl like he's personally wronged it somehow.

"You wouldn't put that kind of pressure on me if you thought I couldn't meet your standards," I reply. "And you guys want the best for me." That's what Mom said the other day, at least.

"Yes, that's true. But I'm worried for you."

I squint. "Worried for me? Why?"

"Life is short, Ani. Life is very short."

There's a long pause as I try to wrap my head around the weight of his words. He must be going through so much on his own. And yet he's worried about me. I wonder if that's why he randomly hugged me that one time. Because he knew he was dying and he was frightened. For himself. For us.

"You are focused on school, and that's good," he continues. "But you also have to allow yourself to find what brings you joy, and bring that joy to others. Don't lose sight of that. Because all of this"—he gestures vaguely around us—"means nothing. You can't take it with you in the afterlife. So you may as well spend this life being happy."

Dad has changed since his diagnosis. He's always been gentle, but it's like in the face of this horrible thing he's dealing with, he's also glimpsed at some kind of big *secret* that's given him wisdom beyond measure.

It's heartbreaking. But also powerful.

More important, I think it's helped him with Mom. They seem to be talking more, spending more time together.

Now *I* want to hug him.

"Are you happy, beta?" he asks.

I smile even though my chest hurts.

"Of course, Dad." How could I say anything else? How could I tell him that now I'm up the river without a paddle, that my future is completely up in the air and I don't even trust myself anymore? That's the problem with feeling the need to be perfect all the time, in all aspects of my life—with being used to perfection. Failure feels *catastrophic*. Failure isn't supposed to be an option. And even if deep down, I know that Isaac and I aren't good for each other after all, my brain still tries to convince me I've failed somehow.

But worst of all, despite everything, I already miss Marlow when I don't even have the right?

"I'm just tired of finals." I add, "You better finish every bite."

He chuckles. "You sound like your nani." He takes another spoonful of daal.

"Oh God, please don't say that."

I wait for Dad to finish before I take away his plate. After Dad goes upstairs, I go to settle back on the couch when there's a loud knock at the door.

Marlow?

I bound toward the front door, throw it open—

Aunty Lubna is staring back at me, her face more pinched than usual, in a long white fur coat that screams Meryl Streep in *The Devil Wears*

*Prada*. She looks amazing. But terrifying.

She doesn't wait for me to let her inside.

"Where is your mom?" she asks.

I think she's been at our place once, for Mom's one-time attempt at an aunty book club, but she glances around the parlor now, taking it in with narrowed hazel eyes. Her upper lip curls a little when her appraising stare lands on the wallpaper Mom chose for the hallway. Mom was so proud of that wallpaper.

Then she looks at me, and I realize I'm still in my tracksuit and broken glasses, both of which I'm pretty sure are stained and smudged.

I shrink back. Is it too late to convince her I have a twin sister? But then I remember: her opinion doesn't really matter now, does it? I've spent so long being afraid of her, trying to get on her good side, that suddenly not having to anymore feels both strange and . . . freeing.

"I see," she says stiffly. "Is that how you dress at home?"

I laugh weakly, tugging at a strand of my hair. "Yes, Aunty. Just when I'm home."

"I shouldn't be surprised. Girls these days can do anything with makeup."

My face flushes as I struggle to find the words to say. But Aunty Lubna just clicks her tongue impatiently.

"If your mom isn't here, then I'll just say my piece. My son has informed me that you have broken things off. Is this correct?"

So Aunty Lubna found out. Did Isaac tell her? But then, why is she confronting *me*? Why not talk to *him*?

I steel myself.

"I know it's disappointing to hear, but yes. We've gotten to know each other a little better, and we realized"—I take a breath—"we're not a good fit after all."

Her nostrils flare a little.

"Mm. My son has also informed me that he no longer wants to study medicine. Do you have any idea why?"

"N-no, but . . . that's great." I'm glad he finally told her.

"That's great," she repeats flatly. "*No*. Isaac is my only son. We have standards. Certain expectations. We have invested a lot in his education under the assumption that he would take over our practice."

"I understand that. But I also think he should be allowed to pursue whatever he wants."

"I thought you might say that." Her hazel eyes narrow. "Unfortunately, he doesn't have the luxury. And when I expressed this to Isaac, he stopped returning my calls. When I went to his campus, he threatened to run away, talked about joining the Peace Corps instead of going to medical school. And you don't know anything about this?"

*Isaac.*

"Where is he?" I ask, worried. "Is he still on campus?"

"Of course. He's not welcome at home for the moment."

She probably threatened to disown him. Isaac must be suffocating. But since she can't get to *him*—

She's come for me.

"I'd appreciate an answer," Aunty Lubna presses. "Did you know anything about—"

"I *didn't*."

"Really?" She folds he arms across her chest. "Because I'm starting to wonder if perhaps you might have encouraged this behavior."

315

I—what? Aunty thinks I did this? She gives me a lot more credit than I deserve.

"No! Of course not."

Mom emerges from the hallway, summoned by the noise. "Ani?" Her eyes go wide. "Lubna? What are you doing here?"

"Ah, so your mom is here. Good. Then maybe you can explain to both of us why Isaac would do this. Because all I know is that it wasn't until you came along that he started acting out, especially this past year, when you started at Marion. Who knows what you two have been doing, talking about."

"Unfortunately, Aunty, I don't have that kind of influence over Isaac. And even if I did, I wouldn't want to discourage him."

"Wouldn't want to—?" Aunty Lubna scoffs. "You know, I thought pushing you two together would be a good idea because it would keep him responsible and focused on his future. I didn't want him to have to worry about finding a girl. And you were at least a good girl from a good family. A known quantity." She looks me up and down again. "At least I *thought*."

My teeth clench. No. I realize it now. She just liked me for her son because she thought I'd be easy to control. It's like the world has been one giant game of rock, paper, scissors, and now I'm starting to see all the patterns, the secrets—the things I couldn't see before. I wonder what changed. When *I* changed.

I wonder if Marlow and Kira would be proud.

My mom takes a step toward us. "Lubna, what are you talking ab—"

"I don't care *what* you two decided," Aunty Lubna goes on, ignoring Mom. "I need you to talk to him and convince him to stop this foolishness!"

"I'm not going to do that," I answer, my voice low. "And I certainly don't have to."

"Then did you also know that he is seeing someone? Some white girl from some nobody family?"

I don't like her talking about Ellie like that. And now I'm getting mad. "I know you envisioned someone different for your son, but instead of putting *Ellie* down, talk to *your* son. And maybe realize that constantly dictating every single aspect of his life means you risk pushing him away."

It's not like I care to defend Isaac and his life choices—the same ones that hurt me. But it doesn't change the fact that Aunty Lubna is wrong here, especially to demand anything of me.

I can see it on her face; she realizes she's not getting anywhere. And she doesn't like it.

"From what I've heard, Isaac isn't the only one making a huge mistake," she hisses.

The blood drains from my cheeks.

She looks at my mom, smug. "Do you know, Sabina? That your daughter has been seen running around with a non-Muslim *kala* boy?"

She says it like it's an ugly word, like I'm supposed to be ashamed. I always knew Aunty Lubna was old-fashioned, but *this*? God, no wonder Isaac felt so suffocated.

She's horrible. *Horrible.*

"What is your *problem*?" My shoulders quake. "Aunty, do you not hear yourself? You're being racist. Racist! That's *completely* unacceptable. You do *not* get to say shit like that."

"You're cursing now?" Aunty Lubna puts a hand on her chest in feigned indignation. "Maybe it's better this way, then. Maybe it's good you and Isaac are no longer together. If this is how you really dress, if this is how you talk to your betters, then who knows what else you're hiding? I should have known. I always *knew* there was something wrong with y—"

"HOW *DARE* YOU TALK TO MY DAUGHTER LIKE THAT?!"

Mom is now standing between me and Aunty Lubna, hackles raised like she's about to attack—and the sneer that was once on Aunty Lubna's face has been replaced by a look of utter shock.

"Mom . . . ?"

Mom looks *furious*, and even though she's shorter than Aunty Lubna by nearly a foot, the glare in her eyes has melted the woman in place. She looks like she could challenge the sun to a fight and win.

"Don't you ever come into my house again, you vile woman!" Mom rumbles. "You should be *ashamed* for treating our children this way!"

Aunty Lubna's breath comes in short, shallow bursts until she regains herself again.

"The entire community will know what kind of family you really are," she says shakily. "They will all know that you are nothing but a cheap, ugly, pathetic family pretending to be something they're not, and you will be friendless and alone."

"Good," comes Nani's solemn voice from the stairwell. "The Prophet, sallallahu alayhi wa sallam, says we must carefully consider the company we keep." She walks to the front door and opens it. "Please leave, Lubna. Allah Hafiz."

Aunty Lubna doesn't move. Neither does Nani. It's a silent battle of wits.

Finally, Lubna lets out a strangled noise before half stomping out the door.

Nani closes it.

Quiet descends upon our little house. My bones are aching, but I finally let out a long, much-needed breath.

I still can't believe it. Did Mom just stick up for me?

Mom turns to me. "I know I have some nerve. It's hypocritical for me to say anything when I've done the same thing to you, perpetuated the same—" She sighs, shakes her head. "But maybe that's why I needed to say something. Seeing Lubna like that—it was like seeing a mirror."

I laugh tiredly. "You're not like that."

"I was getting close. Pushing you to be with Isaac—saying such awful things about that other boy—"

"Marlow. His name is Marlow."

Mom nods. "Yes. And I see it now. I wanted to give you the life I never had, but what's the point if I'm going to destroy our relationship in the process? I don't want us to become like . . ."

*Like Lubna and Isaac.*

"I don't want that, either," I tell her. "I want us to be closer. Especially now. But I think sometimes I felt like . . . you wouldn't love me if I didn't follow your wishes."

So I've been afraid. Afraid of opening up, afraid of being myself.

I thought it wasn't so bad, having the road map for my life already set for me, but maybe I was lying to myself the entire time. I knew I didn't have a choice, so I never considered anything else. Living every day on autopilot, just like my parents wanted.

"Oh, Anisa. I'm so sorry," Mom says, her eyes watery pools. "For pushing you, for making you feel like you had to be perfect by our standards or else we wouldn't love you. But that isn't true. It was *never* true. At the end of the day, we just want you to be happy."

It's like something in me shatters.

I hug my mom tightly. I can't remember the last time I did. "Thanks, Mom."

Mom hugs me back for a long, long time.

"And about Marlow . . ."

"Hmm?"

Mom holds my shoulders, looks me in the eye.

"Do you really like him?"

"What?" I panic, my eyes darting away. Where did this come from?

"Because I think he really cares for you. *Values* you. Even I could tell." She chuckles. "He had the nerve to stick up to me, after all."

"Who?" asks Nani.

I tug at a strand of my hair, saying nothing. Marlow. I wonder what he's doing now. We haven't talked in weeks.

"Don't worry about it, Ammi," Mom answers before looking at me again. "He's at least in STEM, right?"

"Um, well, he's really interested in psychology and therapy."

"What about his religion? Is he Muslim?"

"No, but he's taken classes; he's read about Islam." I give my mom's hand a squeeze. "I understand what you're trying to say, and yes, I'd like to be with a Muslim guy; you know it's what I always wanted. And it'd be nice if sometime down the road, that's what Marlow wanted, too. But I'm not ready for that conversation right now, and it'd be wrong to pressure anyone into anything, especially when he and I . . ."

I don't even know if Marlow still feels the same way. It's not like he's said anything about . . . wanting to *pursue* anything definitively.

I take a breath. "For now, Mom, I just want us—all of us—to *breathe*."

Mom opens her mouth to say something. Closes it. Then she looks at me pleadingly. "Will you still go to law school, at least?"

"I might not do business law," I answer carefully, thinking out loud, "but I still want to do law. But I might also explore doing more with makeup and fashion. Maybe learn more about personal styling. On the side, at least."

The future, after all, is full of possibilities now, and I'm not going to limit myself anymore.

"Oh, thank God." Mom hugs me again. "As long as I can say you're a lawyer, I'll be happy."

I settle in her arms.

Yes, this is how it should be. I should just focus on family. I should just focus on *this*.

Right?

"Challo," calls Nani, waving us back up the stairs. "I need to recite ruqyah, cleanse ourselves of the evil eye that woman brought. But we should watch a movie. Spend time together."

Mom snorts and separates from me. "Good idea. I could use a distraction. Ani?"

So could I. Thinking about Marlow brings up this ache in my chest I've been trying to ignore.

"Coming!" I say cheerfully before following Mom and Nani upstairs. I may as well be flying.

But as soon as I'm in the hallway, I'm yanked, violently, into Zaina's room.

# Chapter 27

The door slams behind me.

I haven't been in Zaina's room in a while, but unsurprisingly, it's like a whirlwind swept through it. Compared to my room, it's all dark wood—at least a quarter of it covered by laundry, and I can't tell if it's clean or dirty—with flares of dark red on the curtains and sheets. Her laptop is open on her unmade bed with messages from Discord popping up on her screen with cheerful little beeps.

Zaina leans against a wall, an annoyed expression on her face. She must have heard everything.

"Hi," she says, her smile not reaching her eyes.

"Hi . . . ?"

"What is wrong with you?"

I adjust my glasses on my face. "I'm assuming you're only saying that because you're shocked by how selfless and amazing I am?"

"Uh-huh. Sure. I guess you did just beat the final boss."

"Boss of what?"

She rolls her eyes. "Never mind."

"Okay, so is there a reason why you've decided to bully me right now?" I ask. "I want to watch a movie—"

"Mom basically just gave you permission to be with Marlow. Or at least, the closest thing to permission you're ever going to get. And you two actually like each other." She scoffs. "But you want to keep playing at being Miss Perfect? You and I both know that's not true, you freaking slob."

"I am not a slo—"

"Freak."

"Stop saying—"

"Moron who plays porn games when they think no one's watching."

"Did Marlow tell you that? Was it Kira?!"

Zaina simply shrugs while I silently promise to strangle Marlow the next time I see him.

*The next time I see him.* Though at this rate, I'm not sure when that'll be.

There's that uneasy pinch in my chest again.

"Look, I get wanting to be alone for a bit. To focus on us." Zaina's eyes go downcast. "And knowing you, you're worried about going after some other guy so soon after Isaac."

I push my glasses up the bridge of my nose. "Well, yeah. I should spend some time on my own for a while, don't you think?"

"Should, should, should. Who cares about the 'should'? All that matters is what you *want* to do. And having Marlow around, especially now, wouldn't be such a bad thing. He keeps you honest. He's a good guy. And he's head-over-heels for you. You know he asked me for book recommendations to learn more about Islam? This guy's clearly in it for the long haul, God help him."

My heart shoots to my throat. "Wait, wha—?"

"And did you know when he came to drop off that care package for Dad, he took a bus? He walked *three miles* to get to our house."

I blink, confused. Marlow told me he got a ride from his old roommate.

He took a freaking bus? There isn't even a bus stop anywhere nearby.

All that for a five-minute visit?

"And let's be real, your options are pretty limited, you being a freak and all." Zaina smirks. "At least Marlow's actually 3D."

"But what about Dad?" I reason. "Is now really the time to—"

"What do you *want*?" she repeats. "Because right now it sounds like you're looking for excuses, and if I know you—which unfortunately I do—you're going to pick the wrong choice, like it's one of your stupid otome games. So think of this as me helping you. Again."

My eyes start to fill. Maybe Zaina's right.[166] I guess I've only ever had one path, so I don't know anything else. Maybe part of me is afraid of these feelings. I've never truly *wanted* anyone before, not out of a sense of obligation or the desire for a perfect Barbie Dreamhouse life, but out of—

Well, *love*.

"And if it makes you feel any better, at least one of us approves of him, so . . ." Zaina looks away for a moment before her face contorts in horror. "Oh hell no, please don't cry. You're *hideous* when you cry."

"*Zaina*," I whine. "When did you get so *thoughtful*?"

"Well, I certainly didn't learn from you." She points to her door. "Now get out. Isn't there a set deadline when everyone's supposed to have moved out of the dorms?"

Crap. I'll have to drive. I haven't showered yet, I'm still in my tracksuit, my glasses. What day is it, even? I pull out my phone from my pocket. Most people would have already turned in their finals. Marlow lives in Jamaica—what if he's already left campus? He could be on a plane

---

166     Minus the part about otome games; I've gotten a little better since that first night I had to call her for help during Victor's route. *God.*

right now. No. I need to talk to Marlow face-to-face. I *need* to talk to him before he leaves!

I'll tell Mom, grab the car, and—

*"Go!"* Zaina jerks me out of her room.

She doesn't have to tell me twice.

About an hour later, I'm at Halcyon. It's sunny; the cherry blossoms have blossomed, enveloping the campus in gorgeous pink clouds. But I don't have time to admire them. I didn't even have time to shower, to get ready.

Why didn't I see it sooner?

Marlow has always been the calm in the storm, the familiar face in the crowd, the voice of reason in the dark. He's far from perfect, of course, but then again, if these past few months have taught me anything, it's that so am I. That's exactly the point. Because perfect is boring. And life has been anything but boring since Marlow came into mine. Maybe that's why I instantly had a visceral dislike of him the moment he walked into our Race & Ethnicity classroom. My body knew. My heart *knew.*

It made room for Marlow the moment I'd seen him.

But if I can't tell him, and Marlow leaves for Jamaica? What if he hates me?

I've called him a dozen times, but there's been no word, so I break into a run. Campus is more chaotic than usual; everyone's busy moving out of their dorms. I don't care that I'm getting weird stares as I dart through small herds of other students, carrying boxes and bags full of their things. I don't even care that people can see me in my week-old tracksuit and broken glasses, my wild, unbrushed hair splayed around me like a living Jackson Pollock painting.

I don't have time to waste.

I remember where Marlow's dorm is but I'm not a Halcyon student, so I can't get in. And since it's the last day to move out, dorms have already mostly emptied. It takes me a while before I find another student who looks me up and down, then shrugs, probably chalking my ugly tracksuit, nervous sweat, and blotchy cheeks to the aftermath of finals.

"Can you let me into Franklin?" I ask breathlessly.

"Wh—?"

"It's that dorm, I think?" I point halfway across campus. "I'm a Marion student. I can't get in, but—"

"Sorry." She shakes her head. "I don't have my keycard on me."

*Crap.*

"Thanks anyway," I say, already running in a different direction.

I whip out my phone and start typing out another text to Marlow:

**For the love of God, answer me. Are you on campus?**

*What if—and hear me out before you say anything—what if I acted as your love coach?*

I keep running, cursing that my tracksuit isn't better ventilated, only stopping to ask any other students I find if they know a Marlow Greene and have seen him anywhere. But of course, either they have no idea who I'm even talking about, or they do—some people had the nerve to give me a wary look—but didn't know where he could be.

Eventually, I reach the familiar Hadley Hall, the math and science building. I'm distracted by my glasses, which keep rolling down my nose like it's a damn Slip 'N Slide when I accidentally shoulder-check someone.

I stumble backward, landing butt-first on the grass.

"Ow, damn that hurt!" I whine. "Sorry—"

"Ani . . . ?"

I look up.

It's Isaac.

He must be moving out of the dorms, too; I hadn't even thought about that. He's holding a giant duffel bag over his shoulder, and beside him is Ellie, her fairy-like face crumpled in concern.

Isaac stares back at me with wide eyes, and he keeps blinking, like he's trying to clear his vision of the bizarre mirage in front of him.

Oh. Except the mirage is *me*, in all my true glory. And now Isaac knows what I really look like.

"Are you okay?" Ellie asks, and reaches out a hand.

I grab it and let her pull me back to my feet.

"I'm fine. Just in a hurry," I answer. I'm surprised by how calm I feel about this situation. In another world, in another time, this would be the definition of humiliating: Isaac is right in front of me, with the new love of his life, and they've both just seen everything I've been trying to hide about myself since we were kids. I can't even remember if I've taken off the pimple patch that was on my forehead.

And yet, it feels so freeing not to care anymore.

The lump in Isaac's throat moves up and down. "Wow. You look. Uh, different."

"Yeah. It's a thing I do sometimes," I say, waving a hand dismissively. "Anyway, have you seen Marlow?"

"Marlow?" Isaac blinks again. "Uh, no? No. Sorry."

"Can we help?" Ellie offers.

"Yes, actually." I'm back in business mode. "He's not answering my texts, but he could still be in the dorm or something. Any chance you could let me in?"

Ellie shakes her head sadly. "We just dropped off our dorm keys. I don't think we can get back in."

"But if we see him around, we'll let him know you're looking for him," Isaac adds. He seems to have finally recovered. "You could try the student center. Maybe they'll let you in the dorm?"

"It's worth a shot," I reply, and start running again.

"Hey," Isaac calls.

When I stop and swivel to see him, he gives me a meaningful nod.

"Good luck," he says.

His words stir me with a slurry of emotions. For some reason, it feels like a goodbye. Like a chapter finally closing.

I beam.

"Thanks!"

I sprint to the student center in the middle of campus and follow the signs to the main office, sweaty and breathless. Thankfully, there's a secretary still there at the desk.

"Can you let me into a dorm?" I heave.

The secretary—a younger guy who probably just graduated himself—raises a brow. "Are you a student? Did you lose your keycard?"

I consider lying, but I toss the thought clean out of my head. Damn me and my moral compass!

"I'm a Marion student. But my friend lives in Franklin, and I need to talk to him—please?"

The secretary stares at me dubiously.

"I'm not a stalker or anything! Wait, that's probably what a stalker *would* say. . . ." I run my hand through my hair, frustrated.

*I think you're more flustered now than when I caught you playing that otome game.* I swear I can hear Marlow's voice in my head, teasing me.

"Yeah, no, sorry, I really can't just let—"

"I can help," someone says in a throaty, languid voice.

Kasim appears behind me, holding a cardboard box full of textbooks in his beefy arms like it weighs five pounds.

"Which dorm? I'll take you."[167]

The secretary gives us a disapproving look but doesn't oppose.

"Thank you!" I follow Kasim close behind. "I'm heading to Franklin."

"Cool, that's on my way. I'm Kasim. You are . . . ?"

"Anisa. You know me! We've met, like, twice now! Come on, I don't look *that* different, do I?"

A beat passes.

"Wait, *Anisa*?" He stares, still walking. "Damn, finals hit you *hard*."[168]

Ugh.

"Yeah, you could say that," I reply, pouting. I'll forgive the rude remark, but only because he's helping me.

He leads me to a stone building at the back of campus, and with a swift swipe of his student ID, we're in.

"You good?" he asks.

My chest flutters nervously.

"This works." I give him a small wave. "Thanks, Kasim."

"No sweat. Get some rest; you look like you need it," he throws over his shoulder.

I double-step up the staircase until I'm in Marlow's hall. It feels like it was just the other day that Marlow led me through here.

---

167    I've never been happier to see a desi bro in my life.

168    Nothing is more humbling than when you don't wear makeup for a day and everyone around you asks if you're sick. Though I think Zaina just says it to tick me off.

I wipe my face with my sleeve, take a deep breath. And then I knock on Marlow's door.

"Marlow?"

No response.

I bite my lip. And I try the handle. Slowly, the door opens, and it swings with a muffled squeak on its hinges.

But the room is empty, save for a bare wooden desk and slightly lopsided bedframe by the window, and the faint smell of the lemons of Irish Spring.

My stomach sinks.

I was too late. Just my luck. It feels like a cruel joke.

What's the point of the world making you realize exactly what it is that you want in life when it's already out of your grasp? I know Dad said everything happens for a reason, but what reason could there possibly be for this? It's not fair that people can just walk into your life with the potential to change everything, with no sign, no warning. They just do, in barely perceptible increments, and if you don't realize it in time, they slip through your fingers.

Hell, I'm not even sure Marlow changed anything. Maybe all he did was make me feel more . . . me. But that was enough. That was more than enough.

I sink to the floor.

Serves me right, I guess. I took Marlow for granted for so long. Got so used to him always being there that I assumed he'd always be there.

But still.

*Say the word and I'll be here. Anytime.*

You *jerk*. You weren't supposed to leave yet! You said you'd always be here and then you go back to Jamaica? Or was that just some metaphorical bullshit?

Fueled by frustration, I stand, even as my legs wobble beneath me. Stupid Marlow. Stupid, stupid Marlow!!!!

But then I catch it: through the single window in Marlow's dorm room, among the throngs of people moving off campus, is a familiar shock of yellow on the campus quad, like the most hideous beacon that ever existed. I couldn't miss it if I tried.

Crocs. It's someone wearing yellow Crocs.

I bolt outside.

"MARLOW!!" I scream at the top of my lungs. It feels like dozens of heads swivel to stare at me. But if there's one big thing I've taken from all those rom-coms Marlow had me watch, it's that love—true love—means to suffer a loss of dignity, and worst of all, not even care.

I see his back now, the familiar dark brown neck, those black curls.

I dart across the quad. "MARLOW!!!"

Finally, Marlow stops and swivels. His face lights up with surprise. For a moment, it looks like he almost drops the plastic storage bin he is carrying.

"Crocs!" I'm gasping for air, choking on my own laughter. I can't believe it. Those horrible Crocs have saved me. "Your freaking *Crocs!*"

Marlow gives me a small, cautious smile. "You didn't come all this way to insult my Crocs, did you?" he asks.

He's wearing a white T-shirt and black Adidas sweatpants, and the baseball cap on his head is pushing his loose curls so they peek out from the sides and frame his deep, dark brown eyes. I may look a little messier than usual, but Marlow looks good. Cute.

More important, though, all the anxieties and stress and droning on in my head and heart—it all settles at the sight of him.

"I've been texting and calling for the past *hour*," I interrupt. "Where the hell have you been?"

"Oh." Marlow sets down the storage bin and slaps at his pockets, but they're empty. "Crap, sorry. I left my phone in my bag."

"I thought I'd missed you. You're flying home soon, right?"

"Yeah, something like that." He takes a step toward me. "You all right?"

"I'm good. I'm good. I just, uh—" I put a hand on my chest, and I exhale another torrent of breath. I didn't realize how dry my throat was. "I just need to catch my breath."

Marlow chuckles, and the warm sound makes my spine tingle. "You do look a little flustered and sweaty. Though to be fair, you do kind of look like that most times I see you."

*"Shush."*

I hide my smile and run a hand through my slightly damp hair. Though the Halcyon campus is alive with the sounds of other students, talking and laughing, the occasional honk of a car horn, the chirping of birds, there's a comfortable silence that settles between us. For a second, I just bask in the peace of it. It's been so long since I've felt peace.

Marlow shifts on his feet. He almost looks . . . nervous.

"Sorry, it just, it's been a while," he says gently. "It's good to see you. Especially like this."

"I had to rush here," I tell him. "I needed to talk to you, no matter what."

Marlow's face turns serious. He waits for me to speak.

"I feel like these past few months, I've changed, you know? I feel surer of myself and less worried about what other people think of me. I feel like I don't have to pretend anymore. And I like it. And I have you to thank."

Marlow shakes his head. "No. You have *nothing* to thank me for."

"I do, though. And I have to say it, before you go." I steel myself and look directly in his eyes. "*Thank you.* For being my friend. For helping me figure things out with Isaac. For sticking up for me. For the love coaching. For *everything.*"

Something in Marlow's eyes wavers, and he looks away.

"I thought I might not hear from you again. After everything that happened. I thought maybe you wouldn't want to see me anymore. I felt maybe I deserved it."

"I'm sorry I made you feel that way. It's not true— Why would you think—?"

"I mean, at first, I only wanted to help you with Isaac because I understood what it feels like to care about someone who doesn't feel the same way. I saw a lot of my situation in yours." I remember Marlow saying something similar from the very beginning: how he wanted to help because he knew how it felt to be alone. "I convinced myself that if I helped you—I don't know. I could prove to myself I'd gotten better. It was all for purely selfish reasons, really."

Marlow finally meets my gaze again, and this time, my heart clenches.

"But then being with you was fun. It was *really fun.* I loved learning about you, all the sides you kept trying to hide. Your brutal honesty, your stubbornness. Your clumsiness. Your weirdness."

"*Hey—*"

"The point is, it just feels like I should be thanking you." He shrugs. "I'm not even sure you really needed the love coaching, anyway. Isaac was the one being a jerk."

"True. But I learned a lot. Still learning. And you helped." I hold his hand. "I've decided from now on, I'm going to be less hard on myself.

Give myself time and space and patience."

"Good. You deserve that." He gives my hand a little squeeze. "Which is why I want you to know that I'll wait, too. I'll be your friend, stay close by, for as long as you want. Whatever you need going forward, you have it."

"I do. Want you close, I mean. If that's okay." I push my glasses up my nose, feeling a little embarrassed. "But maybe not just as a friend."

Marlow's body goes still as he stares at me, eyes wide.

"Wait. Are you sure? You're not just—you want...?"

"Yes. I want to be with you," I respond, with a clarity I didn't know I could have. "I love you, Marlow. I love you, and I know we haven't known each other for all that long, and I know it's a bit sudden; it's only a couple months since Isaac and I broke things off. But I know how I feel. And if you still feel the same way as you did before, if you still want"—I gesture at myself, laughing softly—"all *this*, then . . ."

"I want all of you, Anisa," he interrupts, earnest and desperate and impossibly sweet. "For as long as you'll let me."

He takes another step toward me, and it's then that I finally notice how small the distance is between us. How the rest of campus moves around us in vague blurs of color, how time flows, oblivious that the entire world as I know it feels changed.

"O-oh," I mutter. My cheeks burn.

I'd imagined big, dramatic romance confessions, like the ones in my books and otome games, a hundred times. They didn't look like this. Not in the middle of Halcyon's quad. Not with me in a tracksuit. Certainly not with a guy in Crocs.

But this—this is love, isn't it? This is safety. This is everything.

For so long I'd focused on this perfect life with Isaac, that I completely lost sight of who I am. Who I could be. I lost sight of how many wonderful people surround me, the wonderful things I have in my life. I have no idea what the future will bring anymore. I don't know exactly what I want to do with my life yet. But at the very least, right now, I know who I want to spend it with.

The rest will follow. I know it will.

I smile.

"So was that some cheesy pick-up line you wrote as part of your love coaching techniques?" I ask.

"Absolutely," Marlow nods, all dimples. "And now you too can learn how to seduce anyone with Marlow's Love Coaching Class, all for the low price of $99.99 per month."

I laugh. "I'll pass."

My God. What a waste it would have been to live by the standards of other people for the rest of my life. I could have missed out on *this*.

I bridge the gap and throw my arms around Marlow, there in the middle of the campus quad.

"I wish you didn't have to go," I say, burying my face into his shoulder.

Marlow squeezes back. "I'll see you soon."

After a moment of indulging in his warmth, that familiar Irish Spring smell, I pull away.

"But when you get back, can I buy you some new shoes?" I ask.[169]

This time, Marlow laughs.

---

169    Jokingly, of course. I think I'd be almost sad if Marlow switched out his Crocs. I guess they've grown on me a little.

# Epilogue
## JUNE 3

I have a bob now.

It happened a few days after I finally told Marlow how I feel. I was in the bathroom, brushing my teeth, and when my reflection looked back at me, it felt like she was crying out to me. Like she needed something.

A change.

So I watched a YouTube tutorial on how to cut your own hair, and pulled out the scissors.

At first, Mom was mortified when I emerged from the bathroom, but I've learned to style it properly and I think my new haircut's finally grown on her.[170] The Mom of old wouldn't have been so forgiving, but she's changed, too. Mom and Dad have even started going to couples therapy, to help them navigate what's ahead. It seems to be working; Mom certainly seems to be more chipper these days. like there's a weight off her shoulders. And Dad's been going out of his way to spend more time with her. I'm proud of them.[171]

---

170    Pun intended.

171    I've started seeing a therapist, too! She's a really nice hijabi Muslim lady who gets all the cultural nuances and listens to me prattle on and somehow manages to see everything I don't. I think it's making me understand and even like myself a little more. 10/10, highly recommend.

As for Dad's and Zaina's reactions to my hair, Dad said I looked nice either way, and Zaina said she didn't notice much of a difference. Typical. Instagram loved it, so there's that, at least.

Maybe it's cliché, chopping your hair after a big breakup and big life overhauls, but I've always been one for dramatics.[172] Another extra bonus? Summer classes have started, and short hair, I've learned, is great in this heat.

I walk through the hall. I love the feeling of starting a new class, and not just because it gives me an excuse to buy a new notebook. It feels like a new beginning. A fresh start.

Today, I've opted to wear a black tank with a linen button down, and black trousers. The all-black look makes my lavender eyeshadow pop; I've been playing around with bolder, fun colors lately. My short hair swishes satisfyingly around my neck as I strut with my every step until I reach the door.

I clear my throat and stride into the classroom: International Film History, inspired in part by Marlow making me watch all those rom-coms.

As usual, I'm early, so there's only a small smattering of students in the lecture hall, which means *I* get my pick of the best seats. The most important thing about a lecture hall is being in the middle, so you don't have to crane your neck, but also being far enough in the back that there's not too much focus on you, all while still being close enough to get a clear view of the board. Common sense? Maybe. But it makes all the difference.

But as I'm shimmying my way down the row, I realize there's an interloper, slumped in my perfect seat.

---

172    It also feels like a silent fuck you to Aunty Lubna, which is a great extra bonus.

Only, he looks familiar.

I'm greeted with a dimpled smile. A head of familiar black curls. Gentle brown eyes with a mischievous twinkle.

*Marlow.*

How? *How??*

My brain goes a mile a minute as I rack my brain. Why is Marlow on campus during the summer? Is he taking summer classes, too? And why is he in *mine?*

None of it makes any sense. We've been texting a little since he'd supposedly left for Jamaica, but I've been really busy.[173] I never even got around to telling him I was taking summer classes. The only other people who knew, besides my parents, were Zaina and Kira. Did one of them tell him? Was it pure luck?

"You're almost late," he says. "For you, I mean. Not for normal people. You're early as hell for normal people."

Marlow's here. He's really here.

My chest whirs with happiness.

*"What are you doing here?"* I demand.

"Ya know, it's funny—I've never taken summer classes before." Marlow shrugs. "Kira did say there was a high chance you'd take this class. Glad she was right."

Kira. Of course. I swear, somewhere in the distance, I can hear her cackling.

"What about home? What about Jamaica?" My voice comes out like a squeak. "I thought you were *gone.*"

---

173     Besides driving Dad to his chemo appointments and prepping for these summer classes, I've been making more fashion and makeup content for Instagram, focusing mostly on South Asian beauty. It's honestly been so much fun.

"Oh no. My parents decided they'd try backpacking across Europe for the summer for their big thirtieth anniversary, so even if I went home, I'd be alone. So I kind of told my parents about you—they want to meet you, by the way—and we decided it made more sense for me to stay here, live in summer housing on campus. Then after you and I, uh, talked last time, I thought it'd be more fun to surprise you."

*So he's been here the* whole time?[174] Dizzy, I hold on to a chair for balance.

"Crap." Marlow stands. "Talk to me. Are you mad? Was this a mistake?"

"No, of course not, but—*why?*" I manage to ask. "Really, why would you stay *here*, on campus?"

"Isn't it obvious? I wanted to stay close by," Marlow answers, his smile fading a little. "I figured I can't do anything if I'm an ocean away. Just in case, you know?"

I let out an exasperated laugh. "So you stayed, what, in case I need another love coach?"

"Always," he replies.

My chest feels all buttery-warm. I can't believe he'd done all this, just for me. Behind us, more students begin filing into the classroom. Class starts in five minutes, but right now it feels like we're in our own little world.

"You're ridiculous," I say. "You know how sad I was? I really thought I wasn't going to see you all summer."

"Yeah, but you have to admit, being surprised like this is so much more fun." Marlow grins.

I can't deny that. Something tells me this won't be the last time, either.

---

174    I'm sorry, did I hear that right? His parents know about me? Wow. It's serious. We're serious. Wow. Wow!!

I'd have the rest of my life to be surprised by him.

"Oh, if you want me to move seats, I can," Marlow offers suddenly. "Knowing you, you want the middle, right? Or if you're mad and don't want *anything* to do with me—I'll sit somewhere else. It'll be like I'm not even here. I'll be like a ghost. A sexy ghost, but a ghost nonetheless."

"Is that a joke?" I point to his shirt. "Because your shirt has a little ghost on it who's saying *Don't ghost me*?"

Marlow looks down at his shirt. "Oh! Ayyy, I forgot I was wearing this one."

He laughs. It's a beautiful sound, and even as other students start piling into the lecture hall, it's the only thing I hear.

"Weirdo," I say softly. I can't believe I thought I'd get good love advice from this kid.

"Your haircut looks awesome, by the way." His gaze is affectionate. "Change looks great on you."

"I know," I say automatically, and sit beside him. My body feels like it's floating.

I lean toward Marlow's face. "I would like to kiss you now," I tell him.

His eyes go wide. "Wait, really? Wha—Anisa—"

Before I can talk myself out of it, I press my lips against his. It's soft, tentative. Slow-moving and patient. I can feel his heartbeat through his skin, or maybe it's mine.

Reluctantly, we break apart, and for a moment, we rest our foreheads together.

"People can see us, you know," Marlow whispers.

I smirk. "Is that really something to care about right now . . . ?"

But then that warm, fuzzy mind-numbing cloud is lifted, replaced, instead, by utter panic.

I pull away. "Wait. Crap. I'm sorry, did you not want to?"

Oh God, forgive me for I have sinned! I've been playing way too many otome games and clearly it's rotted my brain. I don't know what came over me. I'll swear off otome for the rest of my life!!!

"I'm *so* sorry, Marlow. I shouldn't have just kissed you without—"

Marlow's lips gently, chastely graze my forehead, silencing the tempest of panic whirling in my brain.

"It's okay," he says, so tenderly I think my heart might burst right then and there.

"It'll *always* be okay."

# Acknowledgments

There's something oddly satisfying about the number three. It's a number that represents balance; for some, it carries religious and spiritual meaning. In China, three is considered a lucky number because it sounds like the Cantonese word for "life." In the study of numerology, three is considered a number symbolic of optimism, of vibrance.

*If You're Not the One* is, *technically*, my third book. And I began writing this book having convinced myself that this would be my very last one. I'd given up on my career, and this book was my farewell. At least I'd written three. Three was a respectable number. Three books and I'd be done.

Which is why, when the book began to take shape, I was surprised by how much love and *optimism* there was bouncing off the pages. Anisa is heartbroken for much of the story, yes, but despite all odds, she refuses to give up on what she wants. And in some strange, inexplicable way, the energy of this fictional character was infectious. It took a while to get there—this book was delayed, twice—but I found myself desperate to see these characters find their unambiguously happy ending. In short, I fell in love with Anisa and Marlow. And in loving them, I learned to love writing again.

So first and foremost, I strangely feel compelled to thank Anisa and Marlow. Thanks, you two.

I must also thank my editor, Jennifer Ung, whose brilliance and dedication and understanding quite literally brought me to tears. If it wasn't for her, I might have done something silly and drastic, like change my name and move to a swamp and never write again. I'm so blessed and grateful to have her in my corner. Thank you, Jen. I adore you.

Thank you to the incredible team at Quill Tree/HarperCollins: Rosemary Brosnan, Jon Howard, Jill Amack, Sean Cavanagh, Liate Stehlik, Audrey Diestelkamp, Patty Rosati, Kerry Moynagh, Tom Pombo, and Laura Raps.

Thank you to my agent, Hannah Bowman, and the team at Liza Dawson Associates. I'm so lucky to have the best agency in the industry (and no, I'm not biased!).

I feel SO lucky to have been blessed with Fatimah Azzahra's absolutely perfect cover art (a second time)! I truly cannot stop staring at it! And to Erin Fitzsimmons and David Curtis for their beautiful work on the design—thank you for your breathtaking work.

I owe so much to my friends and family: my beautiful sisters, Farheen and Hiba; Madiha; Humda; Sana and Ayla; Hassan and Emily; RK, Jeremy, Josh, Linden, Pablo, Jeanne, and the rest of the gang at Odyssey; Gina Chen; Karuna Riazi; Emma Mills; Eric Smith. So much love to Shaan, Alina, and Nadia, always.

To all the readers who've supported me and sent sweet messages these past few years, including Ramishah, Jawayriya, Nihaarika, Azanta, Lili, and Humnah: you are truly a source of light for me. Thank you.

Thank you to Cara, the source of so much laughter in my life. The moment I saw you, I knew you'd be my best friend (and the person I'd harass the most about the importance of staying hydrated). I wouldn't have it any other way.

And, of course, to Stephen: Marlow's goodness came from you. Thank you for being my inspiration, and more important, for being the one who'd held my hand through it all. I love you.

Alhumdulillah, alhumdulillah, alhumdulillah.